Airabeth

The Sacred Seven Series, Volume 1

JoJo Bee

Published by Writer Strong, 2026.

Published by Writer Strong 2026

Cover design by its_torie33

This novel is entirely a work of fiction. The names, characters and incidents portrayed in it are the work of the author's imagination. Any resemblance to actual persons, living or dead, events or localities is entirely coincidental.
Second Edition, March 2026
ISBN (Paperback) 978-1-0693320-0-4
ISBN (Hardcover) 978-1-0693320-2-8
ISBN (ebook) 978-1-0693320-1-1

<u>*Dedication*</u>
For my brother and best buddy, Josh.
Your tender heart and warrior's spirit inspired the premise of this book.
Without you, the core of this story would be lost.
Thank you for always being there to support me, and for igniting the main theme of this book:
The power of siblingship.
I would go to Airabeth for you in a heartbeat.
And I would win to save you.

Chapter One

Listen to me. This isn't right. You have a choice. Don't be reckless. *Listen to me.* Stop this madness. Walk away. This isn't you. *Listen to me.* Why are you doing this? Where is this coming from? No, stop! Stand down—

I don't.

Instead, I drag my bowstring back, hand hot over the handle, as I aim the arrow between the young girl's eyes. Her limbs are small and useless in their fight against me, practically twins to the sticks on the ground, but I don't ease up on her. Not even as she begs.

"I ask of you, please, show mercy!" Tears glisten down her cheeks in perfect lines, tracking through the dirt on her flushed, smooth skin. I might've felt bad for her if I weren't so desperate, but now's not the time to get soft.

You're doing the right thing. This is necessary. She deserves this.

I didn't come into the forest looking for trouble, but trouble found me, and it came in the form of an ignorant girl trying to fight me for the deer *I* killed.

My spine still aches from where she attacked, but unfortunately for her, the element of surprise was her only advantage. The girl can't throw a punch if her mother's life depended on it. Worse, she can't take one, either.

For a moment I wonder who raised her, who allowed her to become so weak and incompetent.

Needless to say, our scuffle didn't last long.

Three minutes ago, she meant nothing to me — just another random face in a place where it's best to go unnoticed — but now she's grabbed my attention, and that's not a good spot to be in.

I dig the tip of my arrow into the flawless, unblemished skin between her brows, delighting in the trickle of blood I draw. "You were stupid to go after what's mine," I say, my nerves unusually calm, despite the circumstances. "Who told you it was smart to try and steal someone else's kill?"

I jut my head toward the dead deer, my arrow protruding from its throat.

A perfect shot.

"Take it," she says, chest heaving beneath the knee I pin her with. "It's yours, I don't want it anymore." Her amber eyes widen to the size of moons, my finger teetering to the edge of the bowstring. Deciding. "I shouldn't have brought you trouble, I — I'm sorry."

Her voice breaks over the woeful apology, doing little to provoke pity from me.

"You don't want to do this," she whispers. "This is what they want, can't you see? Don't let them take away your control —"

Kill her now, you'll be doing her a favor. The words slice through my thoughts, as cold and sudden as death. *If you don't do it, someone else will, but you're not like the others. You won't draw out her demise and make her hurt. You like to finish things quickly.*

"They're trying to manipulate you!" the girl says, frantic. Her eyes bulge as they beg me to listen, to understand. "Block out their influence. Silence them! Show them you're in—"

"Shut up," I snarl, and press my arrow deep into her forehead, creating a cut the length of a thumbnail. Her skin turns bloodless under the weight, almost sickly, as if she's suddenly gone ill. "If you continue to shout like a damn barbarian, you'll attract something much crueler and deadlier than me."

At the mere mention of Soul Eaters, the girl's heart pounds harder under my kneecap, her terror spiking with my own.

This deep into the forest, our only hope of avoiding the unearthly creatures depends on how hungry and miserable they are. With us being miles away from civilization, we must be close to Soul Eater territory, making us the perfect human meal they've been waiting for.

Since the vicious creatures struggle to survive outside of nature, we don't see them stalking through our towns and villages, but they've managed to turn our forests into their homeland.

It's a risk to hunt this far away from Tempus — one we've been desperate enough to take — but I'm not leaving this sky's forsaken place until I catch something.

You're running out of time. Hurry. Decide.

I consider my options, debating on whether I should leave the girl here and trust she won't come after me, or finish her off.

A heartbeat passes.

I have to kill her. I need that deer, and the only way to get it is to eliminate the threat. My family won't last the week without food, and we've seen too many people die from starvation to know it isn't pleasant.

"Please, don't let them make your choice for you."

I look down at the girl. A mistake, I realize, when an ugly pang slices through my gut, similar to regret.

"Don't let them rule over you. Distinguish your voice from theirs. Focus on *your* thoughts, and nothing else."

My thoughts.

At the girl's words, a darkness lifts, freeing me from a shadow I didn't sense was there. I gasp, the fog in my head clearing, and slam back into my consciousness, abrupt and painful.

Fear grips my heart in its fist, clenching tighter and tighter, as I glance down at my hands, at the stranger pinned beneath me.

I can't remember how I got here. Why I'm doing this.

Where's Elisha?

I distantly remember my twin brother telling me he went south in search of quarry, but I haven't seen him in a while. I hope he's all right. The whole point of him joining me on my hunt was to stay together, not split apart.

I lean back, prepared to run and pretend this never happened, but an odd pressure builds in my head, freezing me to the spot.

For a moment I'm paralyzed, a crawling sensation rippling through my veins.

It makes me wonder if something is rummaging around in my head, seeing and taking what it wants, but I don't run away from it. Instead, I hunt it down, digging deep into my mind to find the culprit, the presence that I sense is there.

I search blindly in the dark, an unpleasant tingling traveling over my scalp, when a narrow path of light catches my attention, beckoning me forward. I follow the trail, my blood cooling, when I notice the door to my thoughts is open for the taking.

I frown at the sight.

I never unbolt the lock. I can't afford to. So why is it —?

And then it hits me.

The Masters' strongholds.

They're here. They've found a way inside my head.

You must keep your thoughts sacred. My father's words come to me in a memory, transporting me back to a time when I was happy, and he was alive. *The Masters will do anything to exploit you and get inside your head, but you must never let them steal your independent thinking. They will use strongholds to speak against you, it's their only way of control. The strongholds will cause you to think a specific way — the Masters' way — and cage you to the lies they want you to believe as truth. The longer you stay trapped by their deceit, the easier it becomes for them to manipulate your thoughts, corrupting your mind until it's no longer your own. You never want to reach the point of no return, Nadia, because once you do, you submit yourself to them, becoming a Soulless, a follower of the Masters' hateful reign.*

The memory ends almost as quickly as it came, but the Masters' strongholds don't cease, their voices tempting my hands to do violent, unspeakable things. I sink back on my heels, wanting to leave this moment and forget I was here, but my body rebels at the submission.

It's okay if you kill, the strongholds say, rising and falling in a multitude of voices, ranging from young to old, neither male nor female, but something in between. *You're doing this for your family. That doesn't make you a murderer, it makes you a hero, so do it. End her!*

I shake my head, refusing to accept the lie they present as truth.

I need to let her go. This isn't right. I should leave —

If you let her walk, you'll lose a lot more than the deer.

The words tingle in my fingers, urging me to release the arrow into her brain.

I clutch my bow tighter, hands shaking from the effort it takes to keep from firing.

This isn't me. These ideas, these thoughts . . . they aren't mine. They're the Masters'.

This is how they work, slow and meticulous, their attacks subtle, nearly undetectable.

I drop my aim.

What are you doing? You pick up that bow right now! This is *who you are!*

I grit my teeth against the war brewing inside my head, unable to think above anything other than the two roaring words:

Kill her.

Come on, the Masters murmur. *Act now. This is right. Trust us.*

No, I won't end her life.

Yes, do it.

No, I can't.

Yes, you can.

"No, I can't."

I say the words out loud to believe them, and the moment they release into the air, my mental guard flashes up, an impenetrable wall. Layer by layer, I start to create my barrier — my psychological shield — and imagine a barricade standing between me and the Masters, blocking them from my mind.

It takes longer than I'd like before I'm able to shove them out completely, but once I do, I fall to the side, my limbs heavy with exhaustion. I scoot away from the girl and bury my face in my palms, shaken from the mind control I didn't know I was under.

"Mine," I whisper the word under my breath, chanting it like a prayer. "My mind is mine, and mine alone." I return to myself slowly, as if waking from a terrible dream. "Mine, mine, mine, mine, mine, mine, not the Masters.'"

Or, the Sacred Seven's, I should say, since that's how they like to be addressed.

Sickness. Cruelty. Warfare. Addiction. Doubt. Fear. Obedience. These are the names of the Masters who rule over our world, and although most of us haven't seen them in person, their spirits are a constant presence in our lives.

As each of their titles suggest, every Master is responsible for planting a destructive thought in our mind — torturing us until we surrender ourselves to them — so they can steal our souls and use them for power.

By taking away our independent thinking, the Masters drain the color from our vitality, then use its energy to enhance their strongholds, increasing their strength.

My parents used to tell me life wasn't always this wretched, but when the Masters engaged and defeated the Emperors — our initial and righteous leaders — in war, our world took a turn for the worse.

No one knows where the Emperors went after their loss, but rumors claim they live in some unearthly kingdom, where no human could dream of reaching.

I try not to be mad at them — it's not their fault the Masters are lunatics — but they left us to fend for ourselves, standing by as the Sacred Seven take us out, one by one.

I've survived nineteen years without being ruined by my enemies, but soon enough, they'll come for me. And if today wasn't a sign of that, I don't want to see it when it comes.

I return my attention to the girl, and when I meet her gaze, the only thing I can think to say is, "It's yours." I gesture to the deer, an apology for what I put her through. It takes some gentle convincing to assure I mean no harm, but eventually she listens, escaping with the quarry I caught and my family deserves.

Never mind that.

I did the right thing by giving it away, and I don't regret not taking it.

Besides, I've already caught one deer today. I'm positive I can catch another.

I WAS WRONG.

Hours have passed since I last saw the girl, and I have nothing but blistered feet, and an aching back to show for it. There's food in these woods, I know that, but I'm getting slow and tired, my hunting skills suffering under the cruel hand of exhaustion.

My shot is off, my agility is lacking, and my instincts are not at the standard I hold them to. The only thing aching more than my pride is my hungry belly, and although I'm determined to find something edible, night is creeping in.

My chest constricts at the danger that comes with it, a sensible part of me warning I should find Elisha and start for home. The last thing I want is for me and my twin to get lost and become prey to something much bigger and hungrier than us, but I can't leave without getting what I came for.

It's my job to put food on the table, and if I can't do that, what use am I to my family?

I was against my brother joining me on today's hunt, but he insisted it would be more productive if both of us went looking for food. He promised he'd stay close to my side and wouldn't veer off. I promised the hunt would be short and I'd catch something quickly.

I guess that makes us both liars.

I continue on, the humming of crickets growing louder the deeper I creep into the woodland. Besides a sweet, earthy fragrance, yesterday's rain has left behind a slippery terrain swollen with mud. A nightmare for being quiet.

Every step is a concentrated effort, a balancing act, to prevent my boots from sloshing. At some point I give up, opting to remain still and let my prey come to me.

I close my eyes to heighten my hearing, waiting for a hiss of movement.

Minutes pass, and then I hear it.

The rustling of leaves. The careful footsteps of a predator.

I draw my bow on instinct, eyes whirling to the trees behind me. I follow the outline of a shadow and take a hesitant step toward it, sweat dripping down my back, my forehead. The weight of the opportunity bears down on me like a brick, whispering how I can't afford to lose another animal.

I hardly advance three steps before an unseen force — large and menacing — jumps through the bushes, attacking me from the side.

I don't have time to gasp or shout as it tackles me to the ground, forcing the air from my lungs.

I'm already rolling to my feet, a terrible pain bursting through my head.

What the bleeding hell was that?

I squint through the darkness, spinning to find the thing that's ambushed me, then immediately wish I hadn't. As the details of my attacker's face come into view, I recognize what he is. What he wants. How he thinks.

He's a vulture of a man, a creature that shouldn't belong to this world, or the next.

Sky's, I hope he'll show me decency. I hope he'll let me go.

But deep in the bones of my shivering spine, I know he'll make me hurt.

Chapter Two

"And what do we have here?" the stranger asks, eyes wide with an excitement that knots my stomach. "It's a little late to be out here all alone, don't you think?" He closes in on me, his footsteps quick and powerful, not wasting any time.

Even in the dark, it's impossible to miss the enormity of him, his forearms bulging. So different from mine. Although his shredded clothes hang off him in rags, there's no denying the power sculpted beneath.

One good hit. That's all he needs, and that'll be the end of me.

"You're a Flame," he says, his words twisting with a sick pleasure. "How precious. How lucky." He smiles, eyes dark with violent intent. Gooseflesh erupts on my skin, urging me to move, to *run*. I may not be as fast as him, but I'd rather risk my life in a footrace than subject myself to whatever plan is in his mind.

"Did you hear what I said?" he asks. "I know what you are, how you think." He advances swiftly, eager in his hunt, but it's not his cruelty that has my body trembling. It's the word he used, the one I hoped he wouldn't utter out loud.

Flame.

That's what he called me.

My heart beats in my throat at the mention of my Soul Status, and although it's a title that could get me killed, I try not to react to it. We're alone. No one knows we're out here, but more than that, no one heard what he said.

For now, the scale still tips in my favor.

I won't be able to deceive him outright — he's a Soulless, trained and ordered to sniff out people like me — but if I can make him second-guess my Status, even for a moment, escape is possible.

"Isn't it funny how fate has brought us together?" he asks, the black pits of his eyes swallowing the moonlight. "I felt a strange urge to come to this part of the forest, and I almost resisted, but now . . ." He scans me from head to toe, freezing my blood. "I'm sure glad I didn't."

He reaches into his back pocket and retrieves a blade, its sharpness stark with the promise of pain.

"The Masters will reward me greatly when I turn you over to Airabeth," he says, hand tightening around the weapon. "Imagine all the riches they'll give me when I gift them a Flame. And a pretty one at that."

I might've been indifferent to his statement if he hadn't mentioned Airabeth — the Masters' homeland — but he did, and now that's all I can think about. That place is a nightmare for people like me, and if I'm lucky enough to survive this day, I won't have to go there.

For the first time in my hunting career, I understand the fear of the animals. The entrapment they must feel. I'm being hunted. Chased. Degraded. When the Soulless looks at me, he sees nothing but a sack of meat and a good payday. Though how can I expect him to see anything more? The Soulless live under the law of the Sacred Seven, so if the Masters regard Flames as cattle, so do they.

Panic swallows me at the thought, devouring every ounce of courage I thought I had.

The Masters like to categorize us, labeling humans as either Flame or Soulless to determine whether we resist their mind control or give in to it. Our power lies in our resistance, in the ability to notice when the Masters are interfering with our thoughts — a skill they're trying to eliminate.

I've heard enough stories to know how the Masters test and torture the Flames they capture, doing everything they can to break down their minds and turn their souls dark, converting them into compliant, unfeeling Soulless.

"Tell you what, Flame." He tilts his head to the side, red hair sweeping into his eyes. "I'll give you a ten-second head start before I rip your heart out."

A bubble of fear expands in my chest, growing larger and larger with every breath.

Even so, I stand my ground, refusing to run and turn my back on him. Playing defense will only put me at a disadvantage, and nobody ever survived a fight by being a coward. As tempting as his offer may be, I'm not going anywhere.

He is only human, after all – no different from me – and he will bleed. I just have to be quicker, smarter, better than him.

I shift my bow into position, moving quickly so the Soulless won't catch my intent, but he's already charging for me, reacting faster than I anticipated. I sidestep out of reach, ducking as he swings high for my throat, the blade whizzing past.

Fumbling for my bow, I try to fit an arrow against the string, but I lose my grip, giving the Soulless an advantage. Defenseless, I am tackled to the ground and he smashes my face into the dirt, breaking my nose. A metallic taste fills my mouth a moment later, but I rely on adrenaline and jump to my feet, the pain forgotten.

I raise my bow for a second time, confident in my aim. My arrow buries itself in his thigh, stopping him mid-sprint.

Red seeps from the wound, but it doesn't slow him down for long.

He screams, rushing forward with a newfound determination.

I consider bolting in the opposite direction, but when he raises his dagger, I reconsider.

Running won't do me any good if he throws the blade in my back.

I reset my bow and launch another arrow, trusting my reflexes will be faster than his. Luckily, my boldness is rewarded and I hit him in the knee, taking him to the ground with a screeching wail.

The Soulless squirms in the dirt, trying to stand, but he's wounded and helpless, no longer a threat.

Still, I go for his dagger. I'm not taking any chances.

The handle is hot and clammy in my hand.

I bring it to my belt to sheath it when he snatches my wrist, rising like a ghost from its grave. I fall back, trying to pry myself away from him, but he's too strong, too close.

"I was going to go easy on you, girl," he says, lifting his chin, then spits in my eye. "But you've made things interesting. If you'd come with me, I wouldn't have to break your wrist, but you're asking to be punished, and I have no problem delivering."

And with that, he cocks my wrist to the side, forcing it to bend at an unnatural angle.

I cry out and tears spring to my eyes, obscuring my vision. I react on impulse, my attention straying to the arrow in the Soulless' thigh, blood oozing around the shaft, less than a hand's length away from me. The gruesome display does little to stop me— I grab it and yank it out with all my strength, tearing through bone and muscle.

The Soulless gasps, his mouth gaping as he falls to his knees, letting me go. I clench my wrist, the skin red and already bruising.

I step away from him, somewhat troubled by what I've done, as he wraps his hands around the gash, trying to stop the bleeding.

"You think yourself cute, don't you?" he snarls, eyes blazing. "Think you're smarter than everyone else because you're a Flame? You're the runt of society, sweetheart, and in order to make us strong again, we must remove the weak. Sooner or later, you're going to get caught, and whether that's by me or someone else, I don't care. Flames are dying every day. Although you've survived longer than most, you aren't the exception. Soulless rule the earth now, and if you're not with us, we have ways of changing your mind."

My heart sinks at the poisoned words, at the truth and cruelty within them.

The Soulless are outnumbering us more and more each day, and as the Sacred Seven grow in power, Flames — the only people who still believe in the Emperors and their rule — are becoming extinct.

My older brother says the Sacred Seven torture us because they get off on the power, the manipulation, that comes with invading our minds. I think they torture us because we're the only people standing between them and world domination.

Despite the Masters' efforts, Flames reject the strongholds path to wickedness, focusing on nursing the virtues the Emperors have planted into our souls. Since we are the only people who believe in the Emperors, the Masters target us, striving to eliminate every Flame until there is no one left to follow the Emperors, erasing their legacy from earth.

At the rate the Sacred Seven are working, we're coming to a point where humans don't have a mind to even think about the Emperors, let alone follow them. Soon enough, the Masters will become the only leaders humans know to exist, and the legend of the Emperors will be just that — a legend. If the Sacred Seven manage to turn every Flame into a Soulless, the truth of our history will disappear, erasing the Emperor's legacy and entire belief system.

"Don't you . . . get it," the Soulless says, straining to speak through the pain racking his body. "I'm not . . . leaving . . . until you're . . . trapped in . . . Airabeth." He manages to stand, taking a few wobbly steps toward me.

I kick him once in the stomach, pushing him back into the open path.

"You think you're safe . . . once I'm gone?" he asks, falling to his knees once again. "You're never safe, girl! They're gonna find you, they always do. And when they come, they'll —"

A blood-stopping screech blasts from somewhere across the forest, drowning out the Soulless in all his outrage.

I whirl, muscles tensing, and try to make sense of that horrendous noise and where it came from. Whatever creature has decided to join us is distinctive, unearthly, and if it's as near as I suspect, it must be —

A flash of movement catches out of the corner of my eye, racing toward the Soulless in a blur of brown and gray. I open my mouth to warn him, but it's no use. The animal — no, the *Soul Eater* — already has its razor-sharp fangs in his jugular, clamping down like a vise.

The man shrieks, but the cries don't last, his throat exploding in a shower of blood and tissue.

I can't move. Can't think. Can't breathe.

I stick my fist into my mouth to keep quiet and force my legs to take me behind a tree, moving on instinct. I squat behind the trunk of a large spruce and peek around to see if the Soul Eater has spotted me. It hasn't. The damn thing is still occupied with the Soulless, grabbing his head and tearing it from his body.

The ripping of meat and marrow sounds in my skull, making me sick. But worse than the strength of the ghastly beast is its freakish appearance. With its bear-like body and wolfish face, the creature has the build of a carnivore, but the agility of a feline — a complete monster of the Masters' creation.

The Sacred Seven must've had fun designing this beast. They're constantly varying the Soul Eaters' appearance, leaving us to wonder what the next vile fiend will look like. Sometimes it's as simple as a Soul Eater materializing as human, but oftentimes, they're crafted from nightmares, similar to this one.

I clamp down on my tongue when the creature angles its head in my direction, searching for a scent.

It's caught my smell.

I tremble at the realization, anticipating the worst, when the Soul Eater picks up the Soulless' beheaded corpse and makes off through the bushes, not once looking my way.

I remain still. Silent. Somewhat stunned.

The thing can't be gone. It must have seen me. It must be coming back. But as the seconds turn into minutes, I start to believe in the impossible. The creature didn't sense me, didn't know I was here, but how?

The Sacred Seven have programmed the Soul Eaters — their *pets* — to hunt and eat the souls of Flames, so why did it go after a Soulless — its ally — when it should've gone for me, an enemy?

"Nadia?"

I spin at the sound of my name and reach for an arrow, looking for the person who's called to me. When I find him, I blink, positive I'm hallucinating. I take a step closer, afraid to speak for the chance it isn't him.

I decide to risk it. "Elisha?"

Chapter Three

"Where the bleeding hell have you been?" I gnaw on the inside of my cheek until it hurts, preventing myself from shouting at my brother for his prolonged absence.

"Are you all right?" Elisha whispers, hurrying down the path to meet me, rather clumsy in his haste. He stares at me through sapphire eyes — an alarming reflection of my own — and gestures to my crooked nose. The blood dripping from it. "Nadia, what happened to you? I heard screams and came as quick as I could."

His eyebrows draw in, concern crinkling the lines in his forehead, aging him by a handful of years. He tries to hide the shake in his hands, particularly the one clutching the dagger I gave him. Just in case.

"Go home," I say, gesturing to the path behind us. "I'll catch up once I've caught something for us to eat." Although part of me expects him to disagree and drag me home with him, Elisha remains silent, saying nothing.

We both know I'm not the weakest link in our chain. There's a reason why he usually stays home and cooks our meals while I go out and catch them, opting for the bloodier side of the equation.

Although soft and kind and wickedly intelligent, Elisha is filled with words and poems and blind expectations, encompassing every trait that makes us vulnerable to the Masters' capture. He's everything I fear to be, which makes him easy to love, but difficult to understand.

I don't know how much time has passed since we started this hunt, but we must be at least seven miles from Tempus, our village, which puts us half a mile short of the line separating Tempus from Bronzebury — a village swarming with Soulless. The closer a Flame gets to Bronzebury, the easier it is for Soulless to sniff us out and turn us over to Airabeth, where no Flame ever keeps their soul.

Normally, a fact like that wouldn't scare the wits out of me, but that's because I usually hunt alone. With Elisha by my side, I can't take risks or act on a whim — I refuse to gamble with his safety — but I've already put him in danger by venturing this close to Bronzebury.

I curse myself for not keeping a better track of our surroundings. I let my run in with the girl distract me — a careless mistake — and left us standing miles away from Tempus, jeopardizing our safety.

"I'm sorry," my brother says finally, stepping closer. "I shouldn't have left you out here alone. I thought I could catch something on my own and save you the trouble. What happened?" he asks again, pointing to my injuries. "What were those screams?" Sweat clings to his face from forehead to jaw, his mouth pinched, as if holding back the urge to vomit.

I try not to feel guilty about his unsettling appearance. This is the farthest he's traveled to come looking for me, and he's exerted himself more than he's used to, so he is bound to feel unwell. Every inch of him is dangerously thin, despite his attempt to hide it, which I'm sure contributes to his queasiness.

No matter how many layers of clothing he wears, there's no masking the protrusion of his wrist bones or the hollow of his cheeks. Even his skin droops at unnatural angles, dangling off his skeleton like a hangnail gone awry.

"Your hair," I say, attempting to divert from the worry in my chest. "I need to cut it. It's getting too long." I pick up one of the brown scraggly locks, so similar to mine, its length passing his shoulder.

Although poverty has taken a lot from us, it hasn't robbed him of his charm. I've lost count of how many times a young maiden has *accidentally* bumped into him, or *accidentally* dropped their bag in an attempt to catch his eye.

Unfortunately for my brother, financial instability seems to be a dealbreaker for most, so none of his connections ever go any-where. I bet if we weren't so filthy poor, he'd be married by now, with a family of his own.

It breaks my heart he can't have the life he deserves, but what are we to do? The Masters have taken everything from us, leaving no one, not even the Soulless, with the resources needed to survive.

"Nadia." Elisha uses a tone I'm not used to, reminding me of our father. "Don't give me that look," he says, but I roll my eyes any-way, not needing to be chastised by someone ten minutes younger than me. "Whatever it is, we'll deal with it, but I can't help you un-less you tell me what's going on."

I huff out a breath and rest my head against a tree trunk, de-feated. Even if I wanted to lie to him, he'd know. One of the perks of being twins. So instead of trying to deceive him, I direct my own question at him.

"It's past curfew," I say. A better conversation than talking about my run-in with the Soulless. "You should go home and clean up."

Judging by the lack of daylight, it's been hours since we last saw each other, and by the looks of it, he's run out of food and drink. I'd offer him some of my own, but my canteen ran out two miles back, and I didn't bother bringing anything to eat. I didn't want the extra weight slowing me down.

"I'm not leaving you out here," Elisha says, his concern morph-ing into mild irritation, a mood he usually reserves for our older brother, Sasha. "What do you expect me to do? Stay home like a coward while you wander out here alone, hurt and suffering?"

"What about when we get home?" I shoot back, though I'm not sure why I'm getting upset. I should be glad I have someone who cares whether I live or die, but I'm tired and edgy, and I can't take care of us both in a place like this. "Sasha will chop your head off if he finds out you came here with me."

Elisha waves his hand through the air, as if he can't be bothered to think about our older brother and his temper. "He doesn't know."

"Only because he took an extra shift tonight."

"So? He doesn't know," he repeats. "I thought you'd be happy about that."

"And Diana?" I ask. "She'll rat you out if she isn't in a good state of mind."

"Diana is the last person I'm thinking about right now."

I glare at him. He knows our sister wouldn't be put off so easily.

Ever since our parents' capture, Diana hasn't been the same in mind or spirit. She's become erratic, unstable in her moods. What-ever money our family manages to save, she squanders on alcohol, which turns her cold and unfeeling, difficult to trust. One day, she's quiet and kind — a glimmer of her old self — and the next she scolds me, hating that I resemble our dead mother.

I never truly understood that. I might've looked like Mom when I was young, but not anymore. Where my mother was soft and satiated, I'm hard and angular, lacking the curves and swells of those who are better off. She had the most beautiful hair, too. Dark and curly, always well-kept. Aside from the caramel tint, my locks are nothing like hers, the ends straggly and dull, uneven where I gave myself a haircut.

It's an insult to my mother, thinking we look anything alike.

"Do you ever feel cheated?" I ask, the words tumbling out of me, a river of confession I didn't plan on releasing. Perhaps it's exhaustion or hunger that's made my tongue loose. "We haven't had a day in ten years where we haven't had to fight," I say, "and ever since Mom and Dad died, the pressure to survive just keeps mounting and mounting. I can't help but feel like we've been conned out of the lives we deserve. We were kids when it happened, Elisha. Our childhood was taken from us, and those are years we're never getting back. Hasn't that ever made you feel bitter?"

Elisha watches me for a moment, considering a response I've never challenged him to make before. He tucks a strand of thick hair behind his ear, weighing his next words. "I see where you're coming from," he says, and though his eyes are the color of mine, they have Father's understanding and Mother's kindness. Two qualities that didn't pass down to me. "But there is a war to be won, and fighting is a natural result of that," he goes on. "Sure, things are hard, but we're capable of handling hard things."

The stars in his gaze flicker, awakening a fire I need to put out. Flames are the only humans with a mind to dream, and although ambitions themselves don't pose any harm, acting on them does.

I want my family to have hopes and goals and visions for a better future, but Elisha tends to get lost in the fantasy. He's so full of optimism and desire, but if he lets his guard slip in public, he'd be dragged to Airabeth.

"Don't you want that, Nadia?" he asks, his voice rising with enthusiasm, making what I'm about to say much more difficult. "Don't you want to fight for something important? Don't you want to work toward a goal, knowing your life is serving a purpose?"

And because I love him, I lie to keep him safe from his dreams. Something he would never do to me.

"No," I say, my voice strong, despite the guilt infecting my conscience. "I just want to be happy. Dreaming is for fools, and if you had half a brain, you'd know that. People like us don't get happy endings, so stop trying to write one when the Masters are holding the pen."

Just then, the trees jostle behind me, covering Elisha's reply. I raise a finger to my lips when he turns to me, his face pale. "Stay quiet." I mouth the words, careful not to make a sound.

My twin's eyes widen to the point of madness, the whites around his irises glowing, when he looks past my shoulder, staring at something behind me. "What is it?" I mouth, my spine rigid.

"Look," he responds simply.

My blood freezes as I become aware of the presence lurking behind me, but instead of recoiling from it, I turn, afraid I'll miss my chance at saving us if I don't. I nearly choke when I spot a doe, large and beautiful, striding down the path. She stands less than seven paces away, close enough to catch.

When I glance at Elisha, the desperation on his face turns wild. He places a hand on his stomach, no doubt imagining what it'll be like to have a full belly again.

I think of all the nights he's gone to bed hungry, his stomach growling in the dark, loud enough to wake me.

With that memory in mind, I steel my nerves and reach for an arrow from my quiver, seizing a moment I might not get again. But my hand comes away empty, and my heart drops. I must've used all my arrows on the Soulless. I chew back the hysteria clawing up my throat, forcing myself to stay calm.

Think, Nadia. Think.

I look back to the majestic creature, and as she ambles toward the bushes, I notice the limp in her back leg. She's hurt. She'll try to run if we charge, but if we're quick enough, we could catch her.

Elisha must have the realization the same moment I do, because he's already stalking toward her, his knees bent and ready to pounce.

I place a hand on his forearm. "How are we going to do it?" I say the words so quietly they could be mistaken for the wind.

"I'll hold her down," he responds, his words no more than a breath of air. "You do the rest."

I flinch from him, ready to protest, but he's stronger than I am, so he has to be the one to hold her down. I'm not sure I have it in me to do the rest.

My eyes sting at the reality of what I must do, but through it all I remember the promise I made to my siblings after our parents died. I would keep them safe. I would fight for us, keep us alive, no matter the costs.

I meant those words at ten years old. I still mean them now, nine years later. And it's on that promise I stifle my humanity, suck back my tears, and snap the doe's quivering neck.

Chapter Four

Night is thick by the time we exit the forest, our limbs trembling under the weight of the doe, her body lying awkwardly in our hands. It's been hours since Elisha pinned down the hind and I snapped her neck, but the shadow of her spirit still hovers close, probing for sympathy that doesn't come.

I wish I had the decency to feel sorrow for what I've done, but I take comfort in knowing my family won't go hungry tonight. I don't regret what I did, not even as the doe's pleading whines echoed through my core, begging for mercy.

It's been miles since I've felt my fingers, my forearms shaking under the weight of the doe's underbelly, almost too heavy to carry. Even with Elisha bearing the front half of her body, my knees buckle, struggling to uphold the back end of her carcass.

Sweat leaks through the thin fabric of my clothes, turning my shirt wet and sticky, but I try not to complain about it. Instead, I let my mind wander, my thoughts settling on memories I'd rather forget, but use as a distraction.

It's in moments like these, afraid and exhausted, that I miss my parents the most. Although it's been years since that fatal night, their presence is etched into Tempus, trailing my every move. Everywhere I go, I'm reminded of them, and although I told my siblings I want nothing more than to leave the trauma of their deaths behind, relocating is out of the question.

With Tempus being close to the village of Bronzebury, moving would draw suspicion from our community. Only Flames yearn to get away from the Soulless and devastation they cause, and since we pretend to be our enemies in town, our sudden departure would raise the type of alarm we're trying to avoid.

I pine for the day when I can take off my mask, trading my role of the villain for the Flame I am. Over the years, my family has learned that the smartest way to keep Soulless off your trail is to imitate them, even if you have to sacrifice your pride to do it. Act like the enemy and you won't be treated like one. That's the philosophy we live by, no matter how difficult it gets.

In a world like ours, it's impossible to know who can and can't be trusted, so it's best to keep to yourself and push everyone away. On rare occasions, a Soulless can be spotted by the lack of light in their eyes, but for the most part, there's no telling who's with me or against. For now, I'll carry on being lonely, making friends with the sins I commit and the animals I kill. At least with them, I know I won't be betrayed.

"Emperors, give me strength." I struggle to adjust my hold on the doe, nearly losing my grip entirely. Thanks to my brother's six-foot frame, we have to pause every few minutes to correct our hold, the height discrepancy causing imbalance. But as time slips by — the night turning into morning — we limit our breaks.

When I first started venturing into the woods, Sasha gave me two rules to follow: don't hunt near Bronzebury and be home by dinner. His rules were simple enough. But simple also means easy to ignore. And feeding my family was worth ignoring his rules.

"Nadia."

I'm surprised to hear him speak. He hasn't said a word since we killed the doe, but once the meat is cooked and his stomach isn't growling, he'll forget all about it.

"What is it?" I say, too tired to summon anything more. When he doesn't respond right away, I glance over, his face drawn and plastered with sweat. "Hey, are you feeling alrigh—?"

"Fine," he interrupts. "I'm fine." His eyes droop as they stare into the black night ahead of us, his lips discernibly chattering, almost blue.

I'm about to tell him we should pause for a break, but he stumbles over his feet, the weight of the doe slipping. We both stop, fighting against the uneven balance. I bend my legs to equal the load, but I'm not strong enough to hold this position for long.

"C'mon, Elisha, tilt her toward me."

"I can't," he pants, his arms weakening around the doe. "My stomach —"

My brother drops to the ground, his grip on the animal gone.

Every muscle in my body gives out under the full mass of the hind, and I crash to the ground, taking her with me. The top half of her body falls on my legs, pinning me to the earth.

It takes every ounce of determination I have to push her off, scrambling to my brother.

"Elisha?" I rush to his side, a trickle of red dripping from both his nostrils. "Elisha? Elisha!" I tap the side of his face, urging him to open his eyes, but nothing happens.

A visible shiver starts to rack his body, but his skin is hot to the touch—a worrisome combination. I remove my jacket and wrap it around his shoulders to keep him warm.

I lift his shirt up to check for injuries, maybe a tick bite or some strange rash, but nothing is there. Just smooth, shockingly pale skin.

I can't see or figure out what's wrong with him, and that's the worst kind of illness to deal with because—

The Master of Sickness.

The name comes to me abruptly as I connect him to our situation.

I've heard stories about his power—stories that would keep even demons up at night. Its basic fact that when Sickness bombards a human's mind with diseased thoughts, the brain starts to produce the physical symptoms of that ailment, believing that they're truly ill. If left with Sickness's influence for long, the mind will begin to think the body is genuinely diseased.

If Sickness has his grip on my brother's mind, I need to get him home before the strongholds grow and take his life.

I rise to my feet and shuffle behind him, ready to lift him to my chest.

But. . . the doe.

There is no chance I can carry both.

It's a cruel mockery to have to leave our hard-earned dinner behind, but as long as no one else stumbles by and takes it as their own, I can come back for it later. Elisha is the priority.

An opportunity like this will not come again. The words tingle at the base of my skull, enticing in a soft, sweet timbre. *Leave him. Elisha would want you to take the doe. Feed your siblings. Fulfill your promise.*

I almost laugh at the Masters' impeccable timing.

Elisha is my brother. Sasha and Diana will understand.

The voice inside me presses on, louder this time. *The rest of your siblings will die if they don't eat. Elisha knew the risk in coming out here, he knew the consequences. It's his fault for putting you in this situation. You should leave him. Take the doe and go!*

"My mind is mine. My mind is mine. My mind is mine," I mumble the words aloud to separate my thoughts from the Sacred Seven's, knowing I'd never consider abandoning my brother.

In one single pull, I take hold of Elisha, dragging him backward.

You're making a mistake. You'll kill your siblings if you take him with you. Do you love him more than the others? Does his life mean more to you than theirs?

It takes less than ten steps before fatigue kicks in, but I can't stop. I have to get Elisha home—I'll carry him on my back if I have to—because if we don't get him the help he needs before the strongholds become irreversible . . .

Well, I have no interest in wearing my brother's blood tonight.

Chapter Five

6,542.

    6,543.

6,544.

6,545 . . .

I count my steps to forget my legs pleading for a break and do my best to remain upright.

Although my energy is gone and burnout has settled in, my priority lies unconscious in my arms, reminding me that no amount of suffering can deter me from getting my brother home.

Elisha hasn't stopped slurring unintelligible words since he lost consciousness, but it's not the mumbling that sends my heart into a fit of panic. It's the convulsions, the sporadic flailing of his limbs, that put me on edge.

The strongholds are tightening, getting worse by the second, and there's nothing I can do to stop them. I put an end to all the dark scenarios floating through my head and try not to think about how terribly this night could end.

I glance up to see how much farther I have to travel, and when the familiar hill leading to home rises before me, my determination melts into a puddle of despair. I barely have the strength to make it up that incline when I'm healthy, let alone carrying Elisha.

You won't make it. Unease blazes through me like wildfire, spreading faster than I can control. *The distance is too far, you can't do this alone. Elisha is going to die, and it'll be your fault. You'll never make it. Never make it. Never —*

I take a step toward the hill.

I used to love the idea of our house sitting on the west side of the market square, entirely secluded from the rest of the village, but now, struggling and battling alone, I wish I had some neighbors to help me out.

I understand why we chose privacy over community—staying alive is more important than making friends—however, that doesn't seem so logical now.

By the time I reach the top of the hill, my calves are cramping, screaming for relief. I can see my house from here, barely ten meters from where I stand.

I fight against the shuddering in my legs and take another step, when a crippling spasm shoots down my spine, immobilizing me from the waist down. I clench my teeth to conceal a scream, forcing myself to stay upright.

My body doesn't listen.

I crash to the ground, dragging Elisha down with me. For a moment all I can do is lie there, until I look over and see my twin sprawled out beside me, his cheek pressed against the gravel. Unmoving.

Just rest for a second, my exhaustion speaks, reveling in idleness.

Elisha has lasted this long. A few extra moments aren't going to hurt him.

The thought tempts me into stillness, encouraging me to take a longer rest, but I refuse.

We can't stop now. Not when we're so close to home.

I prop myself up on my elbows and prepare to stand, fearing the agony that'll surge up my back in return, when the door to home opens.

A mix of dread and relief flows through me when I see Sasha run toward me. Even from this distance, I catch the rage in his eyes.

I'm sure he'll yell and forbid me from going into the woods ever again.

Deep down, I know that'll only last until we need our next batch of food.

He sees Elisha lying beside me, pale and barely breathing. "Have you both gone mad?"

"Grab him," I say, and jerk my head toward Elisha. "The Master of Sickness . . . I'm not sure how, but . . ."

My words are a jumble of undeveloped thoughts, but I don't need to finish them for Sasha to understand. He wraps a sturdy hand around my elbow to help me stand, but I shake him off, needing a moment to collect myself, to make sure my back isn't going to spasm again.

"Why were you gone for so long?" Sasha asks calmly, yet displeased.

I look down, embarrassed to meet his eyes.

Even so, I notice how his shirt hangs looser than it did a week ago, nearly drowning him, despite his tall frame.

He's losing weight. We all are.

"It's fine, I was just—"

He raises his hand. "If you're going to make up an excuse, it better be a good one."

I glance up at him and meet his frown, his pale blue eyes glazed and distant. A reflection of our mother's. "None of this would've happened if you hunted alone, like you were supposed to." The words are flat, the insinuation behind them like a blade to my heart.

"You're blaming Elisha's sickness on me?" I flash him a glare. "I didn't tell him to come with me. He offered. I was so far into the forest, I didn't think he'd follow."

"I told you not to hunt near Bronzebury," Sasha whispers, and looks over his shoulder, as if expecting someone to materialize there. He rubs a hand over his buzzed scalp. "Why would you go there? Why? I told you nothing, not even food, was worth that risk. There are other ways to get what we need, and you don't have to go near Bronzebury to do it."

Though he says the words softly, I don't miss the subtle jab behind them. A reminder of the last time I wasn't able to nab a kill.

Sasha's way of things has saved us from a week's worth of hunger on multiple occasions, but he never tells me what he trades or bargains to get what we need.

I don't ask, either.

Whatever he does outside of working for Milo to make sure we eat isn't worth repeating. But that's why I risk traveling so close to Bronzebury. I need to keep him from doing things he isn't proud of. Otherwise, what use am I to him? To my family?

"What happened to your face?" Sasha asks, eyes scanning over my injuries.

He gently grabs my chin between his fingers to assess the scratches, the broken nose.

A familiar darkness settles over him.

"Did someone find you?" he murmurs, his mouth barely moving. "Was it a Soulless? Does anybody know—"

"No," I say, and twist my head out of his reach. Not a total lie, considering the Soulless who attacked me is dead, but he doesn't need to know the details. "Can we discuss this later, please? Elisha needs help, and I can't carry him on my own."

Blood drains from Sasha's face at the mention of our brother, his eyes cloudy and downcast. He scoops Elisha into his arms, carrying him like he would a small child, and hurries toward the house.

"Come inside," he mutters to me without looking back.

I follow behind as he retreats to the house, rather used to the image of him leaving.

Sasha and I rarely see each other anymore, and if we do, it's only for a brief moment. Our dynamic never used to be so hostile, but when circumstances change, people tend to change with them.

He asks about my hunts. I ask him about work. And that's where our conversations end.

Now that I think about it, the last real discussion we had was about a week ago, when he told me about his new job. Well, new-ish job. He's been working for someone named Milo for about four months now, and although I've never seen or met the guy, he's done decent things for my family. It's enough to make me appreciate his help, but he hasn't earned the entirety of my trust by any means.

Considering Milo's the one who recruited my brother—no doubt detecting a morality in him that's difficult to find—I have to believe Sasha is making the right decision by putting his faith in a man I don't know. It's a choice that affects not only our family, but the totality of the Flames existence.

In the hopes of inspiring retaliation against the Masters, Sasha and Milo are working together to build an army of Flames, doing everything they can to restore our peace and give people freedom.

Every week, Milo gives Sasha a list of potential Flames, and it's my brother's job to go out and confront them, convince them to take a stand against the Sacred Seven. Their goal is to bring a few thousand Flames together—enough to build an army—and if they can manage that, we have a greater chance of fending off the Masters' strongholds.

"He's really burning up." The fear in Sasha's voice cuts through my thoughts, drawing me back to reality. "Can you get the door?" He struggles to adjust Elisha in his arms, so I jog around him to pop open the latch, ushering him inside.

I lag behind to give him some room, wondering if there'll ever be a day where we aren't entering this house, but a different one.

Heat. Food. Beds. It'd be nice to live in a place that had all that.

To put it lightly, our home is more of a hovel; a building with deteriorating walls, a cramped kitchen, one bedroom, and one bathroom that's too small to serve our family of four. I try to be grateful for it. Some people don't even have that. But life isn't meant to be endured, it's meant to be enjoyed, and I don't want to spend the rest of my life merely surviving.

I walk inside and prop my old, chipped bow behind the door, distantly hating that it's the only form of hunting gear I own. Decades ago, the Masters banned our modernized weapons, leaving us with nothing but antique and outdated equipment to use on our hunts. For years, the Masters have reveled in our struggle to kill our own food, ensuring nothing – not even our dinner – comes easy to us.

"Empty handed again, I see," my sister grumbles from the dining room, her dark hair strategically braided over both shoulders to hide the protrusion of her collarbones. She dresses in nothing but an oversized sweatshirt that falls below the knee — quite modest for a woman of her taste — and reveals a pair of legs that are far too boney.

She leans a slender hip against the wall, scowling.

My brothers think I'm paranoid when I tell them she can't be trusted, but deep down, we know that's a lie.

Call me petty, childish, but I'll never understand how my brothers forgave her betrayal so easily. It happened years ago, I know that, but all our problems started with her, and with the way things are going, they'll probably end there, too.

Sasha says she did it because she wasn't thinking clearly, stating she was intoxicated or experimenting with some illegal toxin at the ripe age of twelve. I don't care if the substances made her act strangely. There's no undoing what she did. Even now, I want nothing more than to scream in her face, to ask her why, why, why?

Why did you do it? Why did you turn them in? Why did you kill our parents?

Chapter Six

Whenever I think of them, I'm reminded of the night they were taken.

I was ten years old and crouched under the dining table, hiding like a coward, while my brothers rushed toward the Soulless smashing through our living room window. It was an act I should've joined them in, an act I should've gladly endured, but I didn't – couldn't – think to intervene, frozen in my fear. I shrank away, afraid for my own well-being, and let my brothers deal with the madness. The violence. We were outmatched, outnumbered.

The sight was wild, unhinged, even in memory, and I can still hear Father's screams and the shattering of Mother's bones.

Before that night, I never knew what a tendon looked like, and I wasn't particularly interested in finding out, but when one of the Soulless grabbed hold of Mother's elbow, twisting it like he was wringing out a mop, I learned about the fragility of human bones.

That was the first time I ever saw the underbelly of human flesh, and it was a horror I hope to never see again. Even still, the dreadfulness of Mother's mutilated arm didn't hold a candle to the flare in Father's eyes, his gaze hard enough to shatter the world and universe beyond.

I always knew he loved her but to what degree, I didn't understand. I only learned the depths of his devotion the night she was taken away from him.

He tried to catch her before it was too late, but one of the remaining Soulless grabbed him, overpowering our family in authority and strength.

I was completely bewildered by the fear in Father's eyes as he turned to look back at us, desperate for one final glance.

Even in my youth, I knew that once the Soulless dragged my parents from our house, there would be no one to tuck me in at night or hug me in the morning. I wouldn't have a father to walk me down the aisle when I got married, or a mother to give me advice on how to raise my first-born child.

Don't be afraid, be strong for each other, and never lose sight of your beliefs. It's the only thing the Masters want to take away from you. Don't give it to them.

Those were my father's last words to us, and I couldn't muster the courage to say anything back.

Instead, I closed my eyes when the Soulless hauled him off, my mother's screams echoing down the halls long after they were gone. It was Sasha who crawled under the table to get me, his hand grazing my shoulder, soft and tentative, trembling like never before.

I didn't leave that spot for a long time, and neither did he. We sat there for hours, not saying a word. I don't know how much time passed before I finally opened my eyes to look up at him, but when I did, a shame I'd never known rushed through me, drowning me in a tide.

Marred with the Soullesses' rage, Sasha bore a split lip and bruised cheekbone, his skin purpling. Elisha, who stood by the door and stared at the knob like it would magically open and reveal our parents, had similar injuries.

I can't recall a time where I hated having such clean, untouched skin like I did in that moment. It was a sign of my cowardice. My gutlessness. I didn't fight. Didn't try to keep our family together.

Sasha did his best to console me, assuring me that they would be just fine, and I believed him. I had to, if I wanted to keep myself afloat, but now that I'm older, I know better than to fall for such fallacies. People don't go to Airabeth to endure– they are taken to do hard labor until they're worked to death, or worse, until they lose their minds to the Masters. There are no survivors.

To this day I don't know what's worse: my lack of courage, or the fact that I wasn't the only one who left that day without scars. Throughout the whole ordeal, Diana supported our mother and father's capture. She just stood there, nodding every so often when a Soulless asked her a question, confirming our parents' Soul Status as Flames.

She's the one who turned them in, after all. She's the reason they went to Airabeth and died, treated worse than butchered cattle. According to Diana, her motivation behind the act was made out of paranoia rather than a sound mind — a side effect of the new liquor she was experimenting with. The ale she drank was stronger than she could handle, making her rash and disillusioned. My sister claimed she was having bad visions — visions that promised suffering and death to her and our siblings, if she didn't turn our parents over to Airabeth.

"We're safe now," she whispered, speaking through sobs as I screamed at her, overcome by her betrayal. "I made the sacrifice, just like the vision said. I did it to save us, Nadia. It's what Mom and Dad would've wanted. We're free now. The Soulless will never suspect our Status after tonight."

She was right about that.

Since a Flame cannot be sensed until they turn thirteen, we weren't forced to endure the same torturous end as our parents. It's one of the only times our youth has come in handy, exempting us from Flame suspicion. More than that, Flames aren't known to turn each other in, especially ones that are family. Diana's action spoke for all of us, her disloyalty making us all look more Soulless than Flame.

For months, even years after Diana's betrayal, my brothers and I wanted nothing more than to stay cooped up in our house, detesting the world we lived in. But in order to stay alive, we had to maintain a certain image: pretending to be Soulless, despising the Emperors and those who followed them.

We walked around town like nothing happened, like our parents' deaths didn't affect us, while the truth ate us alive.

The facade was difficult to maintain back then. It's easier now, given our worsening circumstances. Starving, cold, lonely and afraid, we're reaching a point where pretending to be Soulless is becoming more of a reality than an act.

I'm no longer a child, and my skin isn't clean, and I've stifled that little girl who cowers when things get scary or difficult.

Perhaps that's why I'm not offended when my sister sneers in my direction, cursing the dirt clinging to my boots. A symbol of hard work, casting aside the weakest version of myself. "We all know you look like a dog, but do you have to smell like one, too?" Diana leans away from the wall, sniffing at the filth covering my clothes. Seems like today is one of her bad days, her mood proportional to the amount of hard liquor she's been downing. "Looks like you decided to roll around with the pigs instead of catching one. Have those beasts finally accepted you as one of their own?"

She closes the distance between us, her emaciated legs shaking despite the summer heat. I resist the impulse to back away as she flicks a piece of mud off my shoulder, smirking at the ruin of my face.

On the far side of the room, Sasha lays Elisha down on the carpet, then bolts to the kitchen in search of a remedy.

Diana's attention flashes to Elisha for a too-brief moment, her face flat. Uncaring. "What happened to him?" she asks, feet planted to the floor without concern.

"He fell ill," I say, not bothering to elaborate.

"Well, I can see that," she says, turning back to me, her upper lip curling into a grimace. If I didn't know any better, I'd think she just saw a rat eating its own feces, rather than our ailing brother. She can hardly seem to stand us, but we tolerate her because she's family and that's what family does, right? We stay, no matter how unpleasant our interactions may be, and they've always been unpleasant. All our lives, Diana and I have argued and been at each other's throats for reasons I can't remember, but without Mother's hand to pull us apart, we've only gotten worse.

When I was little, I used to hear girls tell their friends, "You're the sister I never had," but I've never seen the appeal in having a sister.

Sasha barrels back into the room with a vial in his hand, fingers wrestling with the cap, ripping it free.

"Why don't you get over there and help him," I tell her, unable to muster the energy to do it myself. "I'll be out in a minute."

I don't wait to see if she listens. I hobble to the kitchen, desperate to wash some of this dirt off my face. Now that I'm home, the adrenaline from the forest is gone, and the pain from my nose is starting to set in.

I go to the sink, eager to take care of the injury, when the mess of the kitchen stops me short. I barely make it past the threshold as I take in the empty bottles of liquor scattered on the floor and counters. Some flasks are upright. Others are tipped over, staining the hardwood. The floor is sticky where the alcohol spilled and dried, making a mess I'll have to clean up.

My blood heats, the beginnings of a headache pulsing behind my temples.

The costs of all this liquor, the wasted money, the foul effect it has on her mood . . .

I walk back into the foyer, rage swelling with every step.

"You can't keep doing this." I stalk over to where Diana lounges at the small table in the corner of the living room, playing with a loose string on her sleeve. Sasha kneels beside Elisha on the couch, gently spooning medicine into his mouth. "We can barely afford to eat." I walk around the table to meet her eyes.

Diana keeps her gaze low, refusing to engage.

"Where did you get the alcohol from?" I nudge her shoulder to get a reaction.

She spits out a low, hateful laugh. "Where do you think?"

My blood pressure soars.

"Is he here?" I ask, unable to keep the snap from my tone. I look down the hallway out of habit, half expecting her horrible boyfriend to come waltzing out of the bedroom.

"Nooooooooo," she drawls, meeting my eyes at last. "But he will be. He's coming over for dinner. And I'd prefer you start calling him by his name. Phoenix isn't some animal, you know."

"He's a brute," I say.

"*You're* the brute."

"Knock it off. Both of you." Sasha's voice is loud enough to rumble the floor, but I barely hear him over the nonsense spewing from Diana's mouth.

"You're just bitter that I have something you never will," she's saying, voice raised, words black with venom.

"And what is that?" I ask.

Her eyebrows lift high on her forehead. "A *man*."

"You think Phoenix is a man?" I try not to balk at the statement. "You think you have a relationship I want? Something I crave?"

"Every woman craves affection."

I almost laugh. "A real man wouldn't treat you like an abused dog. Phoenix plays with your head; he only likes you when you're drunk."

She bares her teeth, eyes flashing. "Phoenix loves me, and we're gonna get married someday. He told me so." She smiles, hands clasped in her lap, the anger in her face shifting into something calm, almost happy.

"You don't see the way he is in the Market," I say. *Because you're never there.* "He flirts with everything that moves. *He'll take home any girl stupid enough to throw herself at him.* "He has no respect for his mother." *I saw him hit her once.* "And I've never seen him speak to his sisters without yelling." He called one a whore, the other a swine. "What makes you think he'll treat you any differently?" I hold her stare, not even blinking as I wait for her response.

Diana's nostrils flare. Although she's only two years older than me, her face is leathery and worn, run down by stress and contempt, the thieves of her youth. She traces a finger on the armrest of her chair, mouth tightening into a thin line. "And I thought you'd be smarter than our parents," she says, her voice low. "They got what they deserved in the end. If you're not careful, you'll be no different. I suggest you don't test me, *sister*, or you'll get what's coming to you."

The last sentence barely leaves her mouth before she rises from the table and storms to the front door, slamming it shut behind her, escaping to the village square. I don't realize I'm walking to the door too until I pause in front of it, my fists balled by my sides, caught between staying and pursuing her.

"She isn't worth the headache," Sasha says, as if that's reason enough to stay. "After all the trouble this night has brought you, there's no use in running off and bringing more."

I turn to him, but he isn't staring at me, he's focusing on Elisha.

"She's said worse to me," he adds, sitting back on his heels, waiting for the medicine to take effect. "She doesn't mean it, she's just angry."

And although I appreciate his words, they're an empty attempt to comfort. Mood doesn't give Diana the right to treat our family like scum. We share the same blood, but hers runs cold.

"Is there anything you need me to do?" I ask, chewing my thumbnail to the nub.

Sasha sits back on his heels to survey our brother, sighing deeply through his nose. "He's going to be fine," he says. "Just give him some time." He looks up at me, scanning the filth covering my face and clothes. "You should get cleaned up. Get some rest."

I cross my arms, refusing to leave Elisha alone in this state.

"He'll be fine," Sasha repeats, jutting his head down the hall toward the bedroom. *Everyone's* bedroom. "Go. Rest. You've had a long day." When I don't make a move to leave, he stands, nudging me forward. "I'll let you know when he wakes up. I promise."

Accepting that Elisha is in good hands, I stop resisting and leave him to recover.

I start for our bedroom, which is really just the storage chamber stuffed with a few sleeping pallets, but at least there's a furry blanket to sleep on and a door that locks.

Sasha doesn't say anything as I pass, but I tell my feet to walk slow, to not carry me too quickly. The last thing I want is for him to ask if I'm all right, and considering we don't have these conversations anymore, I fear my reaction.

I put on the mask of someone unbothered, refusing to let myself crumble in his company, and proceed with a confidence I don't naturally feel.

Only when I reach the bedroom and bolt the door behind me do I fall to my knees and allow myself to cry.

Chapter Seven

"Where are you going?" I ask, catching Sasha leaving. Again.

I sit up from the couch, head groggy from sleep, and rise to meet him at the door. He sighs and turns to me slowly, as if it pains him to be caught sneaking out. Hours have passed since I returned home from my hunt, but after Sasha finished giving Elisha his medicine, he moved my twin to our bedroom, leaving me to nap on the couch.

I'm not usually a heavy sleeper — I'm used to being on alert — so if Sasha thinks he can slide past me without my detection, he's got another thing coming.

My brother doesn't spare me a glance as he shrugs on his tunic, the sleeves frayed and oversized, tailored for the fed body he used to have.

"I'm going to see Milo." He bends down to tie his laces, grimacing as he stands upright. Sasha outgrew his shoes three years ago. It's been months since I've seen him go without socks, and I can only imagine it's to hide the permanent damage his cramped, wilting boots have done to his toes.

"Elisha's fever has gone down," he tells me and goes straight for the door, a slight limp accompanying the movement. He motions toward the bedroom where Elisha now sleeps, his snores calm and gentle, steady as a metronome. "The antidote should wear off in a few hours, so it shouldn't be long before he wakes up."

My heart lifts. "So, the medicine is working, yeah?"

When Sasha nods, relief flows through me.

"Milo's lucky, then," I say, imagining all the ways I would've tortured him if something had gone wrong. "He's already putting you in danger with your ridiculous job, but to outwardly give us a vial and claim it removes strongholds when it doesn't—"

"But it does," Sasha says, a new fire lighting his eyes, startling me. "You should be thanking him. Without that vial, Elisha would be dead, so it's best you be a bit more appreciative about it."

I'm taken aback by his tone, his sudden shift in mood.

I wasn't happy when Milo gave Sasha a bottle of medicine as his previous payment, I'll own up to that, but I don't understand why I'm being faulted for it. With how hard my brother works, it seems ridiculous for Milo to barter medicine in exchange for this month's services, especially when it remains to be untested and unproven.

I don't know the science behind the antidote, but Sasha promised it calms the mind and encourages meditative thinking, making it easier to block the Sacred Seven's influence. With the Master of Sickness killing Elisha from the inside out, the medicine should slow down his brain activity and allow him to overcome the strongholds, freeing him from their clutches.

"I'll ask Milo if he can spare enough food to help get us through the week," Sasha says, not meeting my eye. "Will you be all right until I get back?"

I nod, wishing I had the nerve to tell him to not leave me alone. Only problem is, I'm not exactly the sentimental type, and to be honest, neither is he, so I don't say a word about it.

Instead, I ask, "What if I went to see Milo?" When my brother doesn't respond, I continue, "I failed my task and came home empty handed today. It's only fair that I take on the responsibility of getting us food."

Besides, I think it's finally time I meet Milo myself and see what he's really about.

"Stay here and get cleaned up," Sasha counters, jaw set with a determination an earthquake couldn't shake. "I'm sorry," he adds, his body shifting in front of the door, as if fearing I'll run past him and sprint right through it. "But Milo has a new list for me, and this is my job. I can't afford to lose it."

Emperors above, another list?

"Already?" I ask, and when my brother doesn't correct me, disappointment pierces my chest. Another one of his three-day absences. He'll run around Tempus, a village of over two thousand, for the next seventy-two hours and investigate those Milo believes to be Flames.

I don't like his job, I've told him that before, but my opinion has no sway over him.

"Oh, but before I go. . ." Sasha disappears into the kitchen, returning a moment later with a medium-sized box in hand.

At the sight of my raised eyebrows, he elaborates. "I did a favor for Milo a while back. I asked for this in return. Sorry it took so long."

I stare down at the package, guilt prickling my stomach. "Sasha, you know we can't afford to —"

"I didn't get you anything for your birthday," he says. "Consider it a late gift."

He nudges me with a shoulder, insisting I take it.

It's been a while since I've gotten a real gift, so I'd be lying if I said I wasn't excited.

Perhaps that's why I accept the box, my hand shaking as I slide back the lid, peering inside.

My heart stops when I realize what he's gotten me.

"Have you lost your mind?" My words are a breath of strange, jubilant wonder.

"You haven't read anything new in a while, and I knew you needed some fresh material."

I look at Sasha, his eyes shining with a light that I feel. "I thought it might bring you some joy. Emperors know it's gone slim these past few months."

Disbelief halts my response, my mind caught between question and gratitude.

It's been almost nine years since the Sacred Seven banned the Emperors' book shops from the mortal lands, eliminating every tale filled with love and hope, leaving us with nothing but horror stories centered around submission, brutality and violence. Up until now, I didn't think any of the books that remind us of the Emperors and what they stand for remained. In the eyes of the Masters, reading and learning about anything outside of the Sacred Seven's beliefs is a crime, a surefire sign that one is a Flame, a rebellion that's punishable by death.

"How?" I ask, and turn the book over in my hands, reveling in its weight.

"Milo is a clever man," Sasha answers. "He knows someone, who knows someone, who can find what you want."

"But what did you have to trade to get this? You worked hard to get us goods, and you exchanged it all for this, I..."

"Can't you just say 'thank you' and accept it?" He puts his hands on my shoulders, then pulls me into a hug. "You deserve to be happy, Nadia, and I hope this can give you that." He lets out a ragged breath. Tears spring to my eyes. "Even if it is only for a moment."

"Thank you," I say, and hold my breath as we break apart, my throat thick with appreciation. "But this better not be some parting gift, because if it is, I'll kill you, so you better be careful out there."

He flashes a crooked smile and starts for the door. "I'll be fine," he says, and although he acts calm, sounds calm, *looks* calm, none of it provides any comfort.

He hasn't shown an ounce of fear since our parents were taken, and I sometimes worry the trauma of our past has turned him numb to all the things that are supposed to make us feel most alive.

"How are you not afraid?" I ask, genuinely curious. "With everything you do, how can you not be scared about what could happen out there?"

"I am scared," he admits, and the honesty surprises me. "But faith and fear cannot coexist in our hearts, and since we can only pick one, I choose to embrace the side that's going to serve me best. I don't know if Milo's plan will work, but we won't know until we try. Besides. . ." He smiles, opening the door. "Giving up isn't in our blood. Try to remember that, okay?" He steps outside. "It's a secret no one knows about us." He winks to lighten the mood, but I stay rooted in place, saying nothing. The door closes behind him and I let him leave, not bothering to say aloud what we both already know:

Our secrets will only get us killed.

Chapter Eight

My feet scream in defiance as I limp down the tiny hallway toward the bathroom. Blood leaks from the popped blisters running along my heels and toes, the skin raw and swollen.

I make it to the bathroom out of sheer determination and sit on the edge of the tub, my body throbbing. Although I want nothing more than to lie down and sleep, I begin the slow, torturous removal of my clothes in preparation for a bath.

I don't look at the bruises blooming across my ribcage—a bitter reminder of my evening with the Soulless—and turn on the faucet below the small, cracked mirror anchored on the wall. I try not to stare at my reflection as I re-set my crooked nose, yelping as I do it. This is the third time in the last handful of years I've had to push the bone back into place, and it doesn't get easier or any less painful.

Click. Knock. Thump. Thump. Thump.

I turn the faucet off, startled by the sound of the front door opening, and turn my attention to the hallway. I hear the scuffle of footsteps in the foyer, followed by a rummaging that comes from the kitchen, the dishware rattling.

I stand up, expecting to see Sasha running around the house, having forgotten something. But when I peek my head into the living room, he is nowhere to be found.

I rub my eyes, chest suddenly tight.

Thump. Thump. Thump.

I take cover in the dimness of the hallway, my heart rate spiking as the footsteps come closer.

Thump. Thump. Thump.

Louder.

Thump. Thump. Thump. Thump.

Quicker.

Those footsteps don't belong to Sasha, I'm sure of it. While his strides are soft and sneaky, these are clunky and awkward, and I'm not sure what to make of that.

I consider calling out, to make sure I'm not overreacting, but if Sasha *was* home, he would've announced himself by now.

Grab the toilet lid, my instincts roar.

I run back into the bathroom and throw on my tunic and pants, hands trembling as I grab my weapon of choice. The porcelain is cold and smooth in my hands, its weight strangely comforting.

Stay hidden. Wait until the intruder leaves.

I consider obeying the small, but visceral, part of me that considers nothing other than my best interests, but I'm not the only person in this house. Elisha is sleeping less than five feet away. There's no way I can carry him out of here, especially in the state I'm in. And since we can't run or hide, I'm left with one other option I have no choice but to take.

I can't hear anything above the violent pounding of my heart as I charge into the foyer, ready to confront the intruder, when I slam into something—someone—made of steel.

I bounce back, vision spinning, and bring the toilet lid down blindly.

I hear the grunt of a male, the swoosh of movement as he dodges my attack, cursing colorfully.

"Nadia, stop, it's me!"

My blood runs cold at the guttural voice.

I step back, weapon raised.

His deep brown eyes are the first thing I see, followed by the long, straight lines of his nose, and the delicate curve of his mouth, which tilts into a terrible smirk.

My stomach writhes with disgust.

"Phoenix," I breathe, and lower the lid, my hands aching from gripping it. "What are you doing here? How did you get in?"

My sister's boyfriend holds up his right hand to reveal a silver key—a key neither I nor my brothers decided to give him.

I can't believe Diana gave him a spare.

"Didn't mean to scare you," he says, and raises his arms in mock surrender, the game between us already starting.

I prop the toilet lid against the wall, my arms too tired to hold it. "Diana isn't here, so you can leave." I don't bother trying to sound polite, but Phoenix watches me, his hands thrust deep into his pants pockets, making himself comfortable.

He leans against the wall, legs crossing at the ankles. A silent sign he isn't going anywhere.

"I can wait until she gets back," he answers, and dips his bald head to the side, a snake dressed in human skin.

I gesture to the door as a quiet dismissal. "That might be a while."

He laughs, the dark rumble piercing my stomach. "Better watch that tone of yours," he says, and although his voice is kind, I don't like the cold shift in his eyes. "We're about to be family, so you best learn to play nice."

He takes a step toward me. I take one step back, my back hitting the wall.

"We'll never be family," I say, and shove past him to create some much-needed distance. But the moment I lay a hand on his shoulder, he snatches my arm, pulling me to him.

I wince as my feet drag across the floor, the open blisters stinging upon contact.

"What happened to them?" he says, glancing down at my swollen ankles. His eyes are glassy, and there's a chilling stillness in the way he watches me. "Looks painful. I could help with that if you'd like." He leans into me, his face so close to mine, I see the freckles on his nose. Smell the reek of liquor on his breath.

I twist my head away from him.

"I don't want you seeing my sister anymore," I blurt, surprised by my own boldness. The idea of Diana marrying Phoenix delighted me a few months ago, so I'm not sure when my desire to see her leave changed. In theory, Phoenix would take her away from us, removing her from our lives for good, and that would be a mercy.

But now that I've had time to think about it, the flaws in my fantasy have emerged. Diana can be a menace, of course, and although she tends to make most of our lives harder, I cling to the hope that she'll get better. If she runs off with Phoenix, she'll lose herself in him, sinking deeper and deeper into his dark orbit of abuse. No matter how wretched she may be, Diana is still my sister, and I'm not going to lose her to this dishonorable man.

Phoenix surveys me carefully, forehead wrinkling in confusion.

I force myself to hold his stare, to not back down from him.

"And why is that?" he asks, his mouth dipping to the hollow of my ear. "Jealous?"

I grimace and press myself harder into the wall, wishing I could disappear into it. "You think too highly of yourself," I say, but the insult doesn't quite land like I want it to. My voice shakes, betraying my facade.

With Sasha gone and Elisha unconscious, being alone with Phoenix is starting to scare me.

"It looks an awful lot like you're flirting with me," he says, and rubs a hand over his jaw, smirking suggestively. "With all this bickering, I'd say we have a little thing forming between us." He leans into me again, his chest flush with mine. A sense of disgust I've never experienced before washes over me.

"What are you doing?" I ask as innocently as I can, not wanting to provoke him. Phoenix is drunk and reckless, and having nothing to defend myself with, I don't want this conversation escalating beyond what I can handle.

"How did you get that nasty cut on your forehead?" he asks, and traces a light finger over the mark, disregarding my question. "A Soulless, perhaps?"

I pale at the scarily accurate guess, my heart pounding in my ears, making me dizzy.

"Did someone find you out?" He smiles, baring a few too many teeth. "Is that how you got hurt, trying to fight them off? Don't worry," he whispers, "I won't tell. I find *this* to be much more enjoyable."

He grinds up against me, trapping us to the wall.

"What is the matter with you?" I hiss, and try to push away from him, abandoning my plan to play docile. If I don't do something, he'll have me easily. I have to fight, even if that means risking my life.

"Stop playing games," Phoenix murmurs, and grabs my wrists, pressing them to the wall above my head. I try to pull my arms down to break his grip, but Emperors above, he's strong. Much stronger than most of the men in our village. I suddenly remember that Diana told me he's a blacksmith, which would explain his strength and stature.

"Why don't you like me?" he whispers, a somber note entering his voice.

I always knew Phoenix was cruel, but this is savage even for him. We're alone. No one knows he's here, and even if I scream, no one will hear me.

"Let go of me, Phoenix."

"Oh, come on," he groans, brushing his mouth against mine. "We're just having a little bit of fu—"

I drive my knee up, aiming for his groin, but my range of motion is limited. I hardly have room to get my foot off the ground, let alone hit my mark, and by that time, Phoenix catches my intention.

He grunts and stomps on my foot, the heel of his boot digging deeper and deeper into my toes.

I start to scream, but his hand clamps over my mouth, muffling the sound.

"If we are going to trust each other," he says, panting over every word, "we must put a stop to these schoolyard antics."

I almost laugh at that, but before I have a chance to say something truly regretful, he backs away, letting me go.

I sag to the ground and rest my head against the wall, savoring air that isn't contaminated by Phoenix's breath.

Get up. Run. Leave.

The words repeat themselves in my head, urging me to escape. But when Phoenix makes an abrupt turn toward the kitchen—only a few meters short of the bedroom down the hall—staying becomes my only option.

Up until now, he hasn't figured out that Elisha is sleeping less than a handful of feet away. Even if Phoenix decides to hurt me in a different fashion, it's crucial I keep it that way.

I force myself to stand, to follow Phoenix and ensure he doesn't do anything stupid, when I hear him rummaging through the drawers, the cutlery clanging.

Hobbling to the kitchen's entryway, I ask him what he's looking for, but he doesn't respond, doesn't even blink. His silence is hollow but focused, completely void of the lethargic energy I've grown used to. He walks past the fridge, going straight for the row of drawers. He pulls open the second one, digging through it.

"What are you doing?" I ask, taking a cautious step forward. Phoenix is known to make unannounced visits now and again, but he's never stuck around the house long enough to know where we keep our things. This doesn't stop him from moving around the kitchen with surety, looking for something in particular.

"Phoenix." I say his name with force, wanting him to leave. "I think it's time for you to go, okay?" I approach him slowly, afraid to excite him. "Phoenix," I say again, trying to get him to look at me. He doesn't, head down, fingers buried in the drawer. Cutlery rattles, his hand stopping for a brief moment.

My heart lurches when he snatches a knife from the drawer, the blade shining in the morning light draping through the window. He lifts the sharp edge to his throat, his arm moving almost robotically.

"Phoenix, stop!" I lunge to knock the knife from his hand.

I'm too late.

The blade is already slicing across his neck, producing a thick line of blood that spills over his fingers, dropping him to his knees.

I step back, hands over my mouth in silent horror.

What do I do? What do I do? What do I do? What do I do?

What do I do?

Nothing.

I do nothing except stand there, watching him bleed out. I wish I had the heart to scream, or cry, or shout for help, but I don't do any of those things. Instead, I'm numb. Every breath is tight. Too tight. I can't breathe.

Phoenix is clutching at his neck, trying to stop the bleeding, before I unfreeze and stumble to the sink to empty my stomach. I throw up white liquid, expelling everything but my lungs, until I'm left gagging uncontrollably.

This can't be happening.

But it *is* happening, and for a brief moment, everything is still. Quiet. Terrifyingly eerie. Phoenix's blood is pooling around my bare feet, between my toes.

I need to get out of here.

Without looking down at him, I tiptoe around Phoenix's body and rush to the living room.

On my way to the door, I try to think of a plan, but nothing seems logical. I look back at Phoenix. He's no longer trying to stop the bleeding, his hand limp by his side, covered in red. I squint to see if I can find the rise and fall of his chest, but there's no movement.

Dead.

He's dead.

I can't deal with this alone. I don't know what to do.

I need to find Sasha.

I make it to the door, hand shaking on the knob, when a crawling sensation inches up my spine, forcing me to pause. Paranoia takes over, making me feel watched.

I turn slowly, positive my nerves are playing with my imagination.

They aren't.

There's a man standing in the middle of my living room, soundless and unmoving. A complete animal of a man, he takes up the entirety of the space, making my house look three times smaller. Strands of long silver hair escape the edges of his mahogany hood, the rest of his face hidden in shadow, overly discreet.

Emperors above, who the bleeding hell is that?

I stop, snatching the candle holder from the table in my hands, poised to strike. I stare at the hooded stranger, not knowing what to make of the dark hood shadowing the top half of his face.

He tilts his head to the side—a wolf assessing its kill—and takes a slow step forward. "Nervous, Nadia?"

I recoil at the sound of my name, at the fact that he knows it.

We can't have courage without being afraid. I remember my father's words and lean into them, needing his strength now more than ever.

"If you're going to kill me," I say, my voice hardly audible over my heart's wild pounding, "at least have the decency to show your face."

I regret the words as soon as I say them, fearing his reaction. Based on the sheer size of him alone, he could smother me with a single hand.

"Indeed," the stranger says, his voice so deep, I have trouble understanding him, "I could."

I freeze.

Did I say my thought out loud?

"It must be your lucky day," he says, and throws back his hood to reveal himself to me. "Because I'm not here to see you."

My blood stops dead at the sight of him.

I've never seen this man before in my life, I'm sure of that, but I'm smart enough to know an enemy when I see one. Especially when that enemy waves a large, transcendent hand through the air, eyes glimmering with power as he says, "You certainly don't know how to welcome a Master into your home, do you?" He clicks his tongue and surveys the room, grimacing at the scarcity he finds. "Now, where's your eldest brother?"

Chapter Nine

I stifle a cry and push myself against the wall, squeezing the candle holder like it's a sword instead of a basic household item.

Emperors above. A Master —

"Don't be afraid," he says, his voice richer than the red gemstone rings adorning every finger. "I'm just here to speak with Sasha, and then I'll be gone. Now, where is he?" He repeats his question, something dark and chilling entering his tone. It doesn't take a genius to see he isn't the type of man who likes to repeat himself.

He drifts forward without a sound, his cloak billowing behind him. Though the majority of his figure stays hidden beneath the overcoat, the strength in his shoulders is obvious, the muscular expanse of his back too large to conceal. But more disturbing than his size is the ancient power trapped behind his face—a face that hardly looks older than mine, despite the millennia he's spent on this earth.

"Are you a mute, Nadia?" he asks, addressing me casually. "Your name is Nadia, correct? Nadia McBride?"

And while I stare straight into those crushing green eyes, I miss everything he says.

This is the man who killed my parents, the man who took everything away from me and masses of others alike. He's captured millions of souls, tarnished everything that was once decent and kind about the human mind, and is slowly bringing our world to its knees.

I don't know what's harder to comprehend: the fact that he's managed to take over the majority of our lands, or knowing there are six others who did it with him.

There's so much I want to say, so much I want to do to avenge the lives he's ruined, but I'm a mouse under his paw, trapped and helpless.

"How did you get in here?" I ask, my voice quiet, but firm.

I glance down the hall, looking for the toilet lid I left behind.

The Master lets out a low laugh, jutting his head toward the front door. "You should really keep your doors locked, sweetheart. It's a wild world we live in. You wouldn't want just anyone sauntering in here, unwelcome and unannounced now, would you?" He winks, the fullness of his eyebrows lifting in amusement. "I think a 'thank you' is in order, by the way," he adds, hands clasping behind his back, showcasing the strength of his chest.

I glare at him, my heart pounding so fiercely I have trouble thinking. "I don't—"

"You should be grateful I went out of my way to take care of that . . . that . . . what did you call him?" His lips curl with amusement. "That brute."

I don't dare look to the kitchen—to the spot Phoenix lies—and try to make sense of the last several minutes. Then it hits me.

"Y-you killed him," I say, more statement than question. "You put a-a-a—"

Yes, I put a stronghold in his mind, why is that so surprising to you? I press myself harder into the wall as the Master's voice breaks through my barrier, invading my thoughts. *I was merely playing a game to test how strong his shield was, but considering the outcome, I can only conclude that he's as weak as they come.*

"You killed him," I whisper again, his strongholds humming at the base of my neck, pushing for a way in.

"Phoenix killed himself," the Master says, smoothing the material of his tunic. "And to be fair, when I sensed a male presence in your home, I thought it was Sasha." He shrugs, glancing at Phoenix. "But alas, even the best make mistakes."

I nearly drop to my knees at the thought of Sasha being here — of him being the one laying on the ground, surrounded by a pool of his own blood in place of Phoenix.

"Besides, Phoenix had a choice," the Master says, walking closer to me, the scent of sandalwood—of *him*—overwhelming the room. "Humans always have a choice, but when given the option of right or wrong, you people always choose wrong. You were all born to be evil, so why suppress your darkest urges? Why keep fighting the war when the war can't be won?"

War.

And then it hits me, the type of stronghold he specializes in.

"The Master of Warfare," I say.

He bows at the hips, twirling a dazzling hand through the air. "In the flesh, sweetheart."

"What do you want?" I snap, though I'm sure playing brave isn't going to earn me anything more than a slap to the face.

Warfare gives me a flat stare, his arms crossing behind his back. "I've been informed by a trustworthy Soulless that Sasha has been trying to build an army of Flames to form a resistance against the Sacred Seven. Is that correct?"

I straighten my spine, using all the strength I have not to crumble under the weight of his words.

In response to my silence, he continues, "Evidently, during one of your brother's little escapades, he mistook a Soulless for a Flame and revealed his plan to one of my spies, so I'm simply here to collect my debt for the treason Sasha has committed."

I'm going to kill Milo. If I make it out of this day alive, I am going to hunt him down and torture him for giving Sasha a list with a

Soulless' name on it. Was it intentional or a mistake for him to lead Sasha to a Soulless disguised as a Flame? After months of working together, what reason would Milo have to turn on my brother?

I blink and reveal nothing, my breathing steady as I say, "I don't know what my brother does in his spare time, but I can assure you, he isn't a traitor."

"You think me a fool, girl?" Warfare's eyes blaze with the same hatred I hold for him. "Your brother has been caught, so stop with the charade. You better start cooperating because if you don't, I'll stop being so nice and drag you to Airabeth to . . ."

He trails off, gaze drifting to the dining room table, a muscle twitching in his jaw.

I follow his stare, my pulse quickening as I realize what's grabbed his interest.

The banned book.

"How did you get that?" Warfare asks, striding toward Sasha's gift to me. He runs a delicate finger over the cover, and then his arm darts out like a viper as he knocks it to the floor, denting the spine.

"I bought it," I say, the lie coming easy. I'll say anything, even if it means marking myself as a Flame, to get Warfare's attention off Sasha and on me. "At the market. A vendor sold it to me for cheap."

"You don't seem like the law-breaking type," he says, eyes snapping to mine.

I swallow hard and Warfare catches it, sensing my nervousness.

"Is it so hard to believe that I'm capable of finding and getting what I want?" I ask, dragging out my story as best I can. The Master can't find out Sasha gave me the book.

"You want to know what I believe?" he answers, pointing a stern finger in my direction. "I believe that you—"

A click sounds at the door as someone turns a key in the lock, cutting him off.

"Nadia, good news!" Sasha's voice is muffled from behind the front door, and at this moment, it's the worst sound I could hear.

"I got us some pork," he says, "and potatoes, and bread rolls. And you won't believe what—"

My brother stops mid-sentence when he steps into the foyer, his deep-set eyes drifting to the candle holder clenched in my hands. His mouth quirks up, approaching a laugh. But when he sees the widening of my stare, the trembling in my limbs, his smile fades, melting into a frown as he looks behind me, eyes locking on the Master of Warfare.

Slowly, he sets the bag of groceries on the floor.

I want to scream at him.

Why didn't he stay with Milo? Why is he here? He's never home this soon after their meetings.

Warfare's eyes shift between Sasha and I, a peculiar light sparking his gaze.

"Well," the Master says, his smile so sharp, it could cut out a heart, "it appears things have gotten a little more interesting."

Chapter Ten

"Nadia, get over here." Though Sasha is calling to me in a grave voice, he doesn't look away from Warfare, his eyes brimming with a challenge that defies all logic. My mother used to say that provoking a Master is a lot like approaching a shark with a bucket of blood, but since our capture is imminent, it seems fighting is the only way we're going to get out of this.

Gone are the days of living safely and acting methodically, because going to Airabeth is no longer a hypothetical event, but a truth we must face. If my parents' demise taught me anything, it's that freedom isn't given, it's defended, and if we don't fight for ours, our enemies will take it away before we even realize it's missing.

"Nadia." Sasha repeats my name, his urgency prompting me to move.

Legs aching, feet burning, I shuffle to his side, my heart racing at the sight of his pallid face.

He grabs my hand then, squeezing until it's painful.

He starts nudging me toward the door and I shove back, resisting him.

Run, his expression seems to say, eyes darting to the exit. *Now is your chance. Go!* I shake my head and pry my wrist from his hold, willing him to understand.

We're going to find a way out of this. We're not splitting up.

"How sweet," the Master says, circling about the room like he owns it, far too comfortable in our space. "You two trying to protect one another from a fate you can't escape is really quite adorable."

My heart thrashes as his stare travels between Sasha and I, his finger wagging between us as he takes a long, cat-like step forward. "You two look so similar. Practically twins."

At the mention of twins, I glance to the door Elisha sleeps behind, praying the medicine will keep him sedated until this is over. If Warfare finds out he's here, there's no saying what I'll do to ensure his safety, and judging by the flare in Sasha's eyes, he's thinking the same.

"No need to fret," Warfare says, softening his gaze in mock sympathy. "I don't care about the boy in the other room. I'm not here for him." His gaze travels between Sasha and I, suggesting that we're the Flames he's interested in burning out.

"What will it take," Sasha asks, "for you to spare my sister's soul?" He angles his body in front of mine, implying a sacrifice I didn't agree to, and glowers at the Master.

"So precious, the two of you are." The Master's lips peel back into a saccharine smile, revealing every one of his pronounced teeth. "Usually when I come to take families, siblings are quick to throw each other into the streets, if only to protect themselves. This. . . is quite refreshing."

Warfare gives me a wink, his eyes glazed with a passion that makes my skin crawl.

Sasha watches him intently, no doubt preparing to throw himself in front of me should the Master attack. "So, you came here to punish us, is that it?"

The Master raises a sharp brow, looking as surprised as I feel to hear my brother speak such indignant words. "No," he says, crossing his wrists behind his back. "Just you."

Sasha stares at him for a tense moment, nostrils flaring. "I don't bow down to you," he says, spitting at the space between us and the Master, before taking a step—a stupid, unexplainably foolish step—toward him.

What the bleeding hell is he doing?!

"Is that so?" Warfare asks sharply, running a hand over his mouth. "It'd be in your best interest not to enrage me, young man."

"You are not my god," my brother answers, face reddening to the point of concern. "I don't bow to you. My soul rests in the path of light, and I follow the way of the Emperors, our true leaders. Not you."

Warfare angles his head, a smile forming. "Wouldn't expect anything less from a Flame. You're all brainwashed by Emperors who don't even exist, and because of that, you believe in a philosophy that will only leave you starved, poor, and unfulfilled. I, on the other hand, only have your best interest at heart. The Sacred Seven protect you from daydreaming about unrealistic things, and we keep you grounded in reality. The mortal world isn't a happy place, so it's time you stop trying to change it into something it can never be."

"The Emperors are the reason we still have coloring to our souls, but you're too stubborn to admit it. Without them, we'd be nothing but callous, unfeeling beasts like yourself. Because of them, we fight for what's right," Sasha spits back. "We chase after what we want, and we fight for our destiny. We do everything we can to become the people we're supposed to be, and we do it all despite the criticism and fear. You can do whatever you want to me, but I won't let you control my life. I'd rather die than surrender myself to you."

I pinch my brother's side to get his attention, and he finally looks at me, an apology in his eyes.

It's not enough to cover what he's done.

The position he's put us in.

With such hatred reserved for the Emperors, the Masters can't bear the idea of our righteous leaders, let alone a conversation about them. According to song and legend, the hostility between the two groups wasn't always shared, yet it's hard to remember a time where they used to settle disputes with their voices, instead of swords.

"If I have to hear one more word about those parasites," Warfare growls, wintry eyes hardening, "I will slice open your throat, and paint pictures with your blood."

I stiffen at his words, certain they are a promise.

"You don't strike me as the artistic type," Sasha says, seemingly unfazed by the threat. "But if you're feeling creative, by all means, give it a try." He extends his neck to the Master, offering himself like a lamb to the slaughter.

I pull him back, cursing his foolishness.

Centuries before the war between them started, the Masters and Emperors used to govern the human lands together, taking equal responsibility for the health and conditioning of the mortal spirit. Side by side, they led humanity to fruitfulness by sowing their divine power into our souls, giving us the strength and knowledge needed to survive.

Even so, after decades of trying to construct an ideal world, humans still had one thing that couldn't be controlled– free will.

Despite the guidance of our rulers, mortals were still vulnerable to deceit, impulse, gluttony, selfishness, and pride, falling victim to the traps the Masters and Emperors warned us against.

Do you hear your brother's stupidity? Warfare asks, his voice booming inside my mind, shattering my mental shield. *He only puts you in danger by speaking nonsense. Clearly, he has no care for your life.*

"Sasha," I whisper, but he doesn't hear me.

The Master of Warfare coils his strongholds around my thoughts, his voice tightening, building into a crescendo. *He should be punished for such foolishness, don't you agree?*

"Sasha," I repeat more loudly, and this time, he turns. "He's in my head. He's —"

You should kill him. Killing him is the only option. You'd be doing him a favor, really. He has no future. Not like you. You are better than him. You have more purpose.

I drop the candle holder and fall to my knees, my fingers aching with the urge to snatch Phoenix's knife from the kitchen.

Kill him. Do it. You have to. It's the only way out of this.

I dig my hands into the carpet, preventing them from drifting to places they shouldn't.

Imagine how good it would feel to slice through flesh and bone. Perhaps killing will bring you the release you've been needing.

I lean against the wall for support, needing to stay here, in this world, instead of the everlasting darkness Warfare pulls me into. I'm falling, falling, falling into madness, a shadow, slipping into oblivion.

I turn to my brother for help, then realize he's no longer standing by my side.

He's walking toward the Master, his face blank.

I shrink back against the wall — half aware, half caught in Warfare's strongholds.

What is he doing?

I force myself to watch through blurry eyes as the Master puts something in Sasha's hand. A moment later, light reflects from my brother's fingers.

It's only when he stalks over to me, do I realize what he has.

A blade.

No!

He's going to end you. The words caress the edges of my mind, pushing for a way inside my heart. I squeeze my eyes shut, trying but failing to keep my shield up. *You better kill him first, or else you'll die.*

"Here." I glance up and see the Master hovering above me, offering a dagger from his scabbard. "Take it."

My hand buzzes with a disturbing want, the greed for bloodshed consuming every nerve. "Please," I mumble, hardly recognizing the plea in my voice. "Stop." But I know it's a pointless ask.

The Masters have come to resent us, loathe us, for not accepting their influence centuries ago. Unlike the Emperors, they stopped encouraging us to fight off wicked thoughts, but rather, started inciting them, going as far as to plant cynical ideas into the mortal mind themselves, aiming to control us. Ruin us.

Mercy is not a gift the Masters are willing to give, and the Emperors learned this the hard way when they fought against the Sacred Seven's treachery, starting a war neither side was prepared for. Due to conflicting beliefs, the Emperors and Masters could no longer coexist on earth, so they fought for the throne, agreeing that whoever lost, would return home to their unearthly kingdom.

After the Masters victory, they gave themselves new titles, new names, to form the Sacred Seven we've come to fear.

Murder is good, the voice inside me whispers. *The taste of power is infectious. This is what you want, what you* need, *to feel something again. To feel alive!*

Drunk on the Master's strongholds, I take the dagger, though I don't remember telling myself to do so. I rise to my feet, the hilt of the weapon cold against my palm.

"Excellent," the Master purrs, his eyes twinkling with delight. "Now, gut each other. Last one standing wins back their mind." Although his order echoes plainly throughout the room, I hardly hear it above the blood rushing to my head, descending into darkness.

Sasha flips his blade end over end, his expression calm. Cold. Unfeeling. It's the only warning I get before he lunges for my throat.

Chapter Eleven

I barely duck fast enough to avoid Sasha's blade, the sharp edge missing my neck by less than an inch. My mind tells me to push forward and strike back, acting on impulse, but my heart forbids me, yearning to surrender.

Submit, don't engage. Submit, don't engage. Submit, don't engage.

I chant the words over in my head, my body shaking with the effort it takes to keep from attacking. The Master's dagger rests heavy in my hand, the hilt almost too large to hold, and though I don't drop it completely, I don't raise it, either. Refusing to initiate.

Stab him. No. *Stab him.* No. *Stab him.* No. *Stab him —*

I can't do this. Even with the Master's strongholds screaming at me, I won't kill Sasha. *Think of it as hunting,* Warfare calls in my mind, his voice low and hideous, filling every corner. *Killing shouldn't be a problem for you, given that you do it every day. Please, don't tell me your heart has suddenly gone soft.*

I chew the inside of my cheek, thoughts dizzy with indecision.

Put the blade down.

My spirit beats the order into my bones, going against every terrible desire the Master tries to plant there.

Put the blade down. Put the blade down. Put the bla —

If you decline participation, Warfare chides, sensing my intuition, *I'll take your soul as well as your brother's, right here, right now.* He tightens his grip on my mind for emphasis, invisible nails digging in, taking me captive.

Maybe if I pretend to concede, to oblige him, it will suffice. He came here for a show, he's made that clear enough, and if I don't give one, there's no chance Sasha will walk away from this alive, least of all with his soul intact.

"If you don't fight at your full capacity," the Master drawls out loud, drawing my eyes to him, "I'll tell Sasha to gut himself, then force you to clean up the mess." My spine locks at the threat. At the image of mopping up my brother's entrails. "Now stop delaying so I can crown a victor."

His words are like venom in my veins.

If I refuse his command, Sasha dies. If I comply, my brother has a chance at living, but only if he beats me.

Tears slide down my cheeks.

They don't match the searing anger bursting through my blood.

Warfare has given me an impossible task, so really, there's only one thing I can do to give Sasha a chance at survival–fight with everything I am and hope he's good enough to defeat me.

Or in this case, kill me.

It'll be worth it, though, losing my life to him. My father used to say the most honorable victories are conceived through great sacrifice, never selfishness.

I take comfort in those words now, especially as I raise my blade and thrust it toward Sasha's neck, striking to kill. The dagger practically lunges from my hand as it nicks the base of his throat, drawing a thin line of blood that frightens the breath from my lungs.

He stumbles back, surprise flaring through livid eyes as he touches the open wound.

I lower my blade to give him a chance to regain composure, but the Master is in my head, coaxing me forward.

What good is inflicting pain if you don't take advantage? he asks. *You're being passive, sweetheart. Shall I remind you what happens to those who disobey orders?* He digs his strongholds into my mind until something pops, a strange and dreadful dizziness overtaking me.

I gasp and fall to my knees, momentarily blinded by a searing, burning pain rolling through my head. The sensation only lasts a few seconds, but by the time I recover, Sasha is already charging me like an untamed beast.

Fear brings me to my feet, and I sidestep him just in time, missing his tackle. I whirl to defend his following strike, but my brother is fast. He snatches my hand so quickly I barely see it. He twists my wrist, nearly snapping it, and I'm forced to drop my dagger.

I kick the back of his knee to get away from him, and he buckles, crumpling to the floor with a groan.

This is your chance to finish him. Don't waste it!

I push Sasha onto his back and pin him down with my forearm, knuckles raised and prepared for blood.

You did your best, the strongholds speak. *You were better. The strong survive. The weak perish. That's life. You gave him a chance, and he failed. What more could you have done?*

I bring my fist down into his jaw without mercy, but then Sasha looks at me with large, consuming eyes and I see a strange conflict lingering within them.

I hesitate.

Even under Warfare's control, his gaze is kind. Familiar. A part of him is still in there, fighting against the strongholds provoking him to kill me.

Bash your knuckles into his skull. End this misery for him. For you.

The words tingle in my hands, urging me to do things my heart knows are wrong.

I'm still staring at Sasha, conflicted and confused, when he raises the hilt of his dagger and slams it into my shoulder. I stagger back and swallow a scream, looking down to find my collarbone red and angry from the force of the dagger's hilt.

The initial pain of my injury is delayed, replaced by shock, but it doesn't stop my eyes from watering, my lips from quivering.

Do you see what you're letting him do? Warfare roars in my head, trading my thoughts with his own. *He has no mercy for you. No care. Why show compassion to a man who's trying to murder you? What happened to self-preservation?*

My immediate instinct is to barrel into Sasha, to stab him in the stomach and slice the blade up his sternum, but I'm stopped by an odd sound.

A sound, I realize, that shouts from within.

You're stronger than this, stronger than Warfare. I start as the new voice — *my* voice — breaks through the Master's strongholds, powerful in its call. Don't give in. The battle is in your mind, not with your brother. Focus your thoughts. Stop this.

And I do.

Slowly, parts of my mental shield begin to flash up, brick by brick, layer by layer, and though the wall isn't big enough to block Warfare's influence entirely, it's enough.

I shuffle to the side and press my back against the wall, cradling my arm to my chest, relieving pressure off my crooked collarbone. Sasha leaps into an offensive position and speeds toward me.

I cringe away from him and throw my good hand up to protect my face. "Sasha, please, stop!" I shout, but he grabs me around the waist, sending my shoulder into a fit of agony. He doesn't seem bothered as I hit the ground, screaming in pain. He grapples for my wrists and pins them above my head, gaining the upper hand.

Nausea turns my stomach as he brings his blade to my chest, preparing to end me. "Sasha, STOP! I'M YOUR SISTER!"

Despite my plea, I brace myself for impact.

But when it doesn't come, I open my eyes to find the dagger hovering idly above my heart.

I stare at my brother, chest heaving. I watch as he searches my face, waiting for him to speak.

"Nadia." His mouth moves oddly around my name, eyes burning with the panic of a wounded animal. I nod once, my hand shaking as I slowly pry the dagger from his hand. The pressure in my chest eases as he willingly lets me go, the blade no longer pressed against me.

Sasha slumps back on his heels to give me space.

I sit up, wincing.

He turns to me, eyes flashing between my ruined collarbone and the weapon I've taken from him. An unnatural darkness flickers across his gaze, skin paling at the realization of what he's done.

I place my hand on his arm and start to tell him it's not his fault — none of this is — but he's already rising to his feet, glaring at Warfare.

The Master angles his head in answer, a twinkle of surprise lighting his eyes. *How did you do it?* his expression seems to say. *How did you block me?*

I take great joy in his perplexity, but like all good things, it doesn't last. That ancient fury is back within seconds. Unlike me, Sasha doesn't seem put off by it.

In fact, he takes a step toward the Master, a familiar recklessness shining in his eyes.

"Sasha, don't!" I yell, but my warning comes too late. He's already running for the Master, nearly reaching him before Warfare cocks his head to the side, halting Sasha in his tracks.

My heart drops to my stomach when the Master narrows his eyes, no doubt planting another stronghold in Sasha's mind.

A quiet groan slips from my brother, his neck glistening with sweat as he glances between me and the Master.

I go to him, remembering to tuck his dagger into my back pocket. Just in case. I have no idea what the Master is whispering inside his head, but if it's anything like before, I can expect Sasha to start swinging soon.

"You have to fight it," I tell him, shifting to his side. "Listen to my voice. Focus on me and nothing else."

His gaze darts to mine, but the sharpness within it freezes me to the spot.

What has the Master done? Without his mind fully intact, my brother is a stranger.

If he kills me, what will happen to him? Our family? He'll never recover from taking my life. He's too good for it. And once Warfare is finished messing with his head, who knows what kind of permanent stain that'll leave?

Emperors above, I wish I taught Elisha how to hunt, or at least bargain in the market. Who will get the food, the clothes, if Sasha becomes incapacitated and I am dead? Sky's, why did I shield my twin from the ugly parts of the world? I should've been preparing him, training him for a moment like this. A moment when Sasha and I might not be around to provide.

As the youngest of the four of us, we never thought to share our responsibilities with Elisha, but perhaps that's the problem. We babied him too much, and instead of readying him for the world, we let him live in naivety.

"Nadia," my brother whispers, his voice a river of lethal calm. "You have to kill me. Please. Before I do something to hurt you further." He fists his hands in the hem of his shirt, resisting the urge to reach for me.

But even as his eyes darken to black pits, I risk a step closer, positive I've misheard.

"Nadia," he growls. "He's got his grip on me. I can't hold it off much longer." The veins in the column of his neck bulge, turning him red.

"W-what are you saying?" I ask, my eyes stinging with tears. "You can fight this, it's possible, you just have to—"

"You don't . . . understand," he pants, worrying me. "He's not going to let us both . . . walk free. He wants me . . . not . . . you."

I look at Warfare, my heart seething with rage. "You said if we don't fight with everything we have, you'll take our souls without question." I point to Sasha. "Aren't you going to tell him to fight me? To take my life?"

The Master bites his knuckles with devilish satisfaction, his mouth tilting into a merciless slash of white. "I must admit, I did not expect this turn, but seeing that this alternative is much more entertaining, I'll allow it."

His smile grows at my fury, and I consider bolting across the room to strangle him, but Sasha is cupping the back of my neck, bringing my ear to his mouth.

"I don't have much time," he says, his voice unusually hoarse, "so I need you to listen." The veins in his forehead bulge, straining against Warfare's strongholds. "You have to find the rest of the Flames . . . on the list. You're the only person I trust, and I know you're capable of doing . . . what I ask." Before I have time to refuse or ask questions, he rushes on. "The Masters will try to stop you. They'll attack your mind and try to suppress your independent thinking to make you . . . predictable. But you . . . can't conform. Don't let them steal . . . your dream of finding . . . a better life."

"Sasha, I—"

"Grow your mental shield — keep it strong. Remember, the Sacred Seven will always try to scare you away from the things you want most. But you can't run from them. You must chase them with everything you have."

I glower at him, my dread turning into stark irritation. "What gives you the right to make a decision I didn't agree to?" I ask, jabbing his side. "Stop talking like you aren't going to be here anymore. We will get out of this—"

"He won't stop until I'm dead, don't you get that?" Sasha's eyes blaze with an anger I've never seen before. "And you shouldn't be the one . . . to get rid of me."

He reaches out a quick hand, his palm a blur as it clamps down on my injured shoulder, clenching the dislocated bone. I fall back, a quivering scream exploding up my throat, and knock into the side table. I grip the edge to keep upright, my vision blurry with stars, dazed by agony.

My face grows hot with betrayal, and it only festers when Sasha reaches for the dagger in my back pocket. I pivot to block the blade from view, but he sidesteps me, his arm too long for the distance I try to create.

The weapon is in his hand a moment later, the hilt clenched between unrelenting fingers.

My heart beats hard in my throat, and I raise my hands in surrender, approaching him like I would a frightened animal. "What are you planning to do, Sasha? Take your own life?" My voice breaks over the thought of him doing such a thing. "Just give me the dagger. We can figure out a way to—"

I don't finish the sentence.

I'm already lunging for him, pushing him to the ground, before he does something stupid. I scramble for the blade, but he pushes his free hand against my chest. I elbow him in the side to gain some leverage, but he doesn't budge.

The pain of my collarbone is finite compared to the pain of losing him, so I ignore the screaming ache, fighting like I'm uninjured. We wrestle for the weapon, both of us grunting and panting, until I finally get my hands around the hilt.

"You're being selfish," I say through gritted teeth. "We need you. You can't . . . do this." My hands shake against my brother's overwhelming strength, and even as I kick him in the ribs, he doesn't falter.

"You are the one . . . who's always been meant . . . to achieve the things . . . I never could," Sasha gasps, face purpling with strain. He flips the blade over in our hands, the point aimed at his neck. "This was my destiny. You must . . . fulfill yours. Fight . . . for your dream. Don't be afraid."

Sweat drips from my hairline and into my eyes, my collarbone screaming as I work to wrench the dagger away.

An abrupt sob breaks past my lips when the blade skims Sasha's throat.

I'm losing my grip.

"Please," I breathe, my hands slipping on the handle. "Stop." I lean all my weight away from him.

It's not enough to redirect the dagger.

"Our souls will see each other again someday," Sasha whispers, his eyes glistening with a pain that pierces my heart. "I love you."

I scream as he tugs the dagger down, the blade angling toward his throat. "No! Sasha, PLEASE DON'T!"

Chapter Twelve

The blood. It's everywhere. Running where it doesn't belong. One moment it's all inside of him, painting his veins, organs and cells, living where it's supposed to, and then it's painting his neck, chest, and shirt, the floor, my lap, my hands.

It doesn't mean anything, though. It *can't* mean anything, because he isn't gone.

He can't be.

The human body contains liters and liters of blood, so he must have more in him, and if he doesn't, I can lend him some of mine. I don't know if it's possible, but maybe if I can find a medic to help me, I can donate whatever he needs — a lung, a kidney, my heart, anything, as long as he lives.

"Sasha," I whisper his name and shake him by the shoulders, the world tipping beneath me when he doesn't respond. "Sasha." I tap his cheek and poke his side, urging him to open his eyes. I need him to look at me. "Sasha!" I shake him again and place my ear to his chest, waiting for a heartbeat.

It doesn't come.

It takes a long while before I realize it never will, but I can't accept that reality, not without trying to change it.

With shaking hands, I start scooping blood back into his throat, into the gaping slash. I press hard to stop the bleeding, willing life back into him, but the blood won't stop leaking.

"Please," I mumble to no one in particular. Perhaps to whatever Emperors care to listen. "Fix this. I'll do anything. I won't hurt another animal. I won't steal from the market. I won't fight with my sister. I'll love more and hate less . . ."

I make every promise I can think of, but no one comes for me. No one answers my call.

"Where are you? Why aren't you helping me?" I whisper the words, praying to the Emperors like I've never prayed before, pleading like a beggar. "Why are you letting this happen? Why aren't you saving him?"

I wait for a response, not sure if I'll hear the answer in my spirit, or feel a shift in the air, but I get neither.

Only a terrible silence shadows my soul.

I'm running out of options, out of time, and I can't mend Sasha on my own, not without some supernatural hand. The blood won't stop flowing, the wound won't clot, and it's been minutes since he's opened his eyes. Since his heart stopped beating—

He's dead, Nadia.

My heart lurches at the words, rejecting the idea.

Dead. Dead. Dead. Dead. He's dead.

You did this. This is all your fault. YOUR FAULT! "My fault," I whisper.

"The smell, it's quite fascinating, isn't it?" Warfare sneaks up behind me, a ghost in human form, and places a hand on my good shoulder, squeezing. "It amazes me how little time we have before a corpse begins to stink."

I shrug off his touch, his words somehow muffled, as if covered by a hand.

How did this happen? Why couldn't I stop it? How can I fix this?

"I suppose congratulations are in order," he goes on, but all I hear are the cluster of words Sasha said to me, not knowing they would be his last.

You have to find the Flames on the list . . . You're the only person I trust . . .

He won't stop until one of us is dead . . . Don't be afraid . . . I love you . . .

I close my eyes and claw my head.

No. No. No. No. He wasn't supposed to die, not this soon, this young, this way.

"You did this," I whisper to Warfare, the words so quiet I'm not sure if I say them out loud or in my head. "I would've gone to Airabeth with you. I would've done whatever you asked, if only you spared his life."

The Master chuckles, but the sound can't be mistaken for one of amusement. "You are in no position to bargain with me," he trills, "though I do find it humorous that you think you are."

I rise to my feet and face him, wincing from the abrupt movement, the tendons pulling in my shoulder.

"And just so we're clear," he adds, rushing on before I can say my piece, "I didn't kill your brother. How could I, when I didn't lay a finger on him?"

"You're playing ignorant, right?" I take a tentative step toward him, his idiocy churning my fear into anger. "You may not have physically touched him, but—"

"But the Sacred Seven's strongholds only speak truths, girl, and those truths made your brother take his own life." He stalks toward me, closing the distance in less than three strides. "It's not my fault humans are so weak and insecure. The Sacred Seven only heighten the temptations already inside you, and since you're all either driven by power, coin, sex, or the desire to be loved, it's quite easy to find the weak spots."

He pauses, frowning at a slight wrinkle on his shirt. He takes the time to smooth it out before continuing. "I only tell people what they already know, and most of the time, the truth is too hard to bear, so humans give up. They quit. And the moment they do, their souls become mine."

"You won't touch my brother's soul," I say, but as soon as the words leave my mouth, I feel like a fool.

Sasha is gone. His spirit lost. The damage done. The Masters already have his essence in their arsenal. That information alone is enough to make my stomach roll.

My spine stiffens as Warfare sidesteps me, making a beeline for my brother. "Well, well, well, what do we have here?" He gestures to something I can't see, the enormity of him blocking my view.

But judging by the spryness in his steps and the wild light in his eyes, the finding must excite him, which terrifies me.

I don't look at my big brother's face as the Master approaches him, nabbing something from his front pocket. I stand on my tip-toes to see what he's found, and when he turns to show me, my heart turns sick with dread.

Milo's list.

Warfare unfolds the paper like it's a birthday card, his joy un-tamable as he starts reading off the names, tongue dancing around each syllable. "Scarlett, Teresa, Darin, Hamilton, Violet, Layla, Carson . . ."

I stop listening after that, a graveyard silence settling in my ears.

My head spins as he lists off the identities of possible Flames — possible *allies* — who Milo was recruiting to fight in the resistance.

A dark laugh is the Master's only response. "This is simply gor-geous, isn't it? I'm most excited to pay each of these Flames a visit after this." He rips the list to shreds and drops the bits on Sasha's body, where they with his blood. "Is this the only list your brother had?"

Had.

Past tense.

The reality of the situation refuses to set in.

"Yes," I mumble, my tongue heavy in my mouth, numb with disbelief.

"You have one chance to tell me the truth," Warfare says slowly, "or I'm going to pay your other two siblings a visit."

I waver at the mention of my family. Of the siblings I didn't tell him I have.

He's bluffing. He must be bluffing, how does he know —?

"Do you think I'm stupid, girl?" Warfare grins, rejoicing in successfully catching me off guard. "I know more about you and your family than you think."

And that scares me more than I care to let on.

"It's the only list," I say, telling the truth. "Sasha always carries the lists with him."

Warfare clicks his tongue, as if deciding my fate. "Who else was working with Sasha on these lists?"

"I don't know," I lie, wanting to protect Milo's identity. If I'm going to finish the work Sasha started, he needs to stay alive. He's the brains behind the mission, the leader and creator of it all. Without him, a resistance group doesn't exist, and the Flames need something to be a part of. Something to hope for.

Warfare turns his head to the side, assessing, as he stretches his strongholds toward me, hunting for lies. My body inevitably locks up at the invasion, but I empty my mind, hiding Milo in the farthest corner of my thoughts.

Warfare's search starts off small, his presence hardly noticeable as he ambles through my head, not bothering to be discreet. A faint buzzing sensation travels from the crown of my scalp to the bottom of my spine, growing stronger the longer the exploration goes on.

I remain still, my face slackening in an attempt to hide my panic.

Seconds pass before the tension starts to intensify, the pressure tightening to the point of crying out, of begging for mercy. I grit my teeth to distract from the ache, but I'm losing ground, the pain too severe to hold off.

I'm slipping, slipping, slipping into an agony that could kill me, and just when I think I can't take any more of it, Warfare backs off, the discomfort gone.

"Although your Flame essence is clear," he says, "I told you I came here for your brother, and I will uphold my promise. With him out of the picture, my mission is complete."

He walks over to Sasha's corpse and picks it up, flinging it over his shoulder like a sack of potatoes.

"Where are you taking him?" I ask, hating that Warfare is touching my brother's body and carrying it away from me. "What use is he to you?"

The Master adjusts Sasha on his shoulder, turning his back on me. "My private business has nothing to do with you girl. Be glad of it."

"So that's it?" I ask, desperate to keep Sasha here, with me, where I can give him a proper burial. "You know I'm a Flame," I say. "Why aren't you taking me to Airabeth? I'm nothing but a threat to you in Tempus."

Warfare pivots to face me, mouth twisting to the side in con-sideration. "I'm sure what's happened here today is enough to turn your soul dark, and if this visit has taught you anything, it's that no good can come from being a Flame. And who knows? Maybe I'll come back to pay you a visit." He waggles his eyebrows playfully. "Besides, if I take you to Airabeth now, there will be no one here to clean up Phoenix's body."

He turns his back on me again, but this time, I let him go. "Have fun taking care of the mess."

Chapter Thirteen

It's been three days since I buried Phoenix in the backyard, but the smell of his blood still clings to me. My fingers hurt from the number of times I've scrubbed them in hot water, unable to rid myself of the metallic scent that sticks beneath my nail beds, making me sick.

I can already feel Sasha's absence in the air, our house hollow and empty — no longer a home without him in it. Over the past few days, I've barely left the house, and I feel like I've forgotten something, like I'm leaving a vital piece behind, when really, it's him I'm moving forward without.

Elisha woke up yesterday morning with nothing more than a slight headache and foggy memory of the moments leading up to his unconscious state, and for that, I'm grateful. It's allowed me to delay filling him in on the harder, crueler hours he missed, but I can't avoid his questions forever.

Where is Sasha? How long has he been out? What happened to you? Why are you crying?

Even Diana has been showing signs of concern, suggesting that the remnants of her drunken episode have worn off. I capitalize on her wherewithal and sit her down at the dinner table beside Elisha, preparing myself for the conversation to come.

There isn't going to be an appropriate moment to tell them everything that's happened, so I might as well do it now and get it over with.

By the time I finish relaying all that's occurred these past few days, I swallow the lump in my throat, struggling to meet my siblings' eyes. Diana cries loudly beside me, her shoulders shaking with the intensity of her sobs, nearly screaming from the pain this news has brought her. Elisha stares at his hands clasped on the table, eyebrows crinkled as he processes in that quiet, careful way of his.

We sit like this for a while, none of us willing to break the suffocating silence that hangs heavy in the air.

"And then what?" It's Elisha who speaks first, his eyes downcast and focused as he picks at a callus on his palm, breaking the skin. "Warfare just left? He killed Sasha, then left without saying anything else?"

I nod once. "Pretty much, yes."

Diana wipes her nose with the back of her sleeve, her face red and wet with tears. "Is he coming back?" she sniffles, her voice thick with an emotion I've never heard from her before. "He knows where we live now. How do we know he isn't going to come back?"

"I don't know," I answer honestly.

"We need to move," she says, hands shaking in her lap.

"Where would we go?" Elisha counters. "We have no money."

"We'll figure something out," she says. "We can't stay here."

"I'm going to the Market," I say, rising from my chair on unstable legs, suddenly needing to be anywhere but here. "I'll bargain for some food to get us through the week." The groceries Sasha brought home for us are almost gone. "I'll be back in a few hours."

Before my siblings have a chance to protest, I'm out the door, stalking into the afternoon heat. I bask in the sun beating on my face, the sweat dripping down my back, as I trudge down the cobblestone path.

I wanted to apologize to my siblings. I wanted to tell them I'm sorry for failing Sasha. Our family. But when the moment came to voice the words, I choked.

I can't stand to be in that house anymore. I can't stand to be in the kitchen or the living room where Phoenix and Sasha bled out. More than that, I can't stand to look at Elisha and Diana's somber faces, each of us knowing our lives are never going to be the same from this moment on.

The truth in that is difficult to accept, so I push it aside and focus on the task at hand– getting us food.

It usually doesn't take me long to get to the Market — it's less than a kilometer away from our house — but today, it takes me over thirty minutes. It's like my feet are stuck in the past, afraid to move forward and acknowledge that Sasha is dead and never coming back.

"Are you all right, girl?"

I turn to a voice that belongs to an older woman, her hair long and gray, eyes crinkled at the edges. She gestures to her face, and it's only when I wipe away my silent tears do I realize I've been crying.

"Yes," I whisper, wiping hastily at my eyes. "Thank you."

I disappear into the hustle of the Market, trying to forget the memory of the blood leaking from Sasha's throat, and keep my eyes on the path ahead. Anger boils in my chest at the sight of the Masters' flags scattered throughout the Market, every shop and food stand displaying the gold insignia of a crown surrounded by black flame. A reminder that no one keeps the color of their soul.

Eager to escape the busy streets, I duck into the nearest butcher shop and pray the clerk is in a friendly mood. The moment I step through the threshold, I notice the few dozen cow, pig, and duck carcasses hanging from the racks behind the front counter, filling the shop with the fresh scent of iron. A large freezer packed with beef, chicken, and rabbit sits on the far side of the room, surrounded by a horde of customers.

One glance around, and I already know I'm surrounded by more Soulless than Flame, but I can't find the nerve to be bothered by it. I walk up to the counter without hesitation and address the clerk — a dainty woman who can't be older than thirty — and ask for a deal on some packaged chicken.

"Sorry, kid, but if you have nothing to barter with, I can't trade you any meat," she says, refusing to budge at my pleading stare.

"I *will* have something to barter," I say weakly. Desperately. "When I make my next catch, you can have all the furs. Enough to pay for a week's worth of food."

"And when will your next catch be?" she asks.

"Tomorrow," I say. "Most likely." If I'm successful.

"Most likely doesn't cut it, kid. I need you to be sure. I'm not in the business of charity." She gestures to the next customer in line, but I step in front of them to block their advance.

I take a deep breath to control the flush in my cheeks and loosen the clench in my jaw. Losing my temper will only make her turn me away. "I understand your position," I say calmly. "But —"

Her eyes turn cold, almost deadly, as her face slackens, completely void of all emotion. I wait for her to say something, to blink or force me out of her shop, but she doesn't. Instead, she walks to the exit, the rest of the customers following, leaving me dumbstruck and alone.

It's only when everyone is gone that I understand the reasoning behind their departure.

The Master of Warfare enters the shop like a spirit, his presence cold and sudden, sending shivers down my spine.

"I changed my mind," he says by way of greeting. "I thought killing Sasha would be enough to ruin you, but your mind was strong enough to consistently block my strongholds, and I didn't give that the attention it deserves."

I swallow hard, trying not to show the fear I feel. "I think you have too much faith in me," I say, then realize that's the wrong response.

He advances on me again, my knees knocking in answer.

I glance to the door. If I sprint to it, will he catch me?

"I'm surprised a Soulless didn't detect your Flame Status sooner and turn you in, if I'm being honest." He circles the shop, assessing me from head to toe. "I don't know how you've made it this long without getting caught, but I suppose since you've stuffed yourself in this quaint little town, it'd be hard for anyone to find you. I'm not going to lie, I'm a little impressed."

I don't say anything, unsure how he expects me to respond.

"When I speak to you, I demand a reply," he says, eyes sharp and missing nothing. "Unless, of course, there's a reason you've gone so tongue-tied." He gestures to himself and gives a small turn. "Perhaps it's my beauty that keeps you in awe."

I clear my throat, nails digging into my palms.

"You're clearly overestimating my abilities," I respond honestly, "which is nothing but a waste of your time and mine."

He grins, showing his teeth. "Now, that's where you're wrong, sweetheart. You're just the type of Flame I've been looking for. It's been a while since I've come across someone like you. Your strength fascinates me." He quirks his head to the side, looking more animal than man. "And that's why breaking you will give me the greatest pleasure. It'll prove that no one, not even the strong, can best the Sacred Seven."

My heart plummets at the implication. "So, you've come to take me to Airabeth?" There's no use in talking around this. Masters don't track down Flames to simply exchange pleasantries.

Warfare clasps his hands in front of him and twirls his thumbs end over end. "I think you'd be much happier serving in my estate than staying here," he says, gesturing around the shop, "huddled away in this disastrous town you call a home. And I have such exciting plans for you."

I swallow my dread.

He stretches his power toward me, the pressure of a stronghold building in my mind, squeezing like a vise. "How do you do it?" he asks, genuinely curious. "Who trained you to flash up your shield on command?"

I bare my teeth, jaw aching with the strain. "Why the interest?"

He doesn't give me an answer, instead asking, "Do your other siblings have the same abilities?"

I draw back, trying to escape his words as if they had teeth. "Please," I say, more of a confession than a plea. "What can I do to make you spare their lives?"

He smiles. "I don't want Elisha and Diana," he says. "I only want you."

I try not to flinch when he says their names. "You said that about Sasha," I deflect. "And yet here you are."

"Yes, but you and Sasha are. . . well, were. . . the strongest of your family. Without you two to take care of them, Elisha and Diana will wither away and lose their souls to us eventually. That's all we're after. We don't want to kill humans and depopulate the world for sport. We are simply removing those who refuse to follow the Sacred Seven's rule. People who influence others to reject our rule need to be removed because without the influencers, such as yourself, there will be no one left to keep the Flame traditions alive." He gestures to the door behind him. "So, shall we go?"

"Is this how you take all Flames?" I ask, scanning the room for a weapon. Surely there has to be a knife laying around here somewhere. We're in a butcher shop, for sky's sake. "You're not even going to give me a chance to fight for my freedom?"

Warfare grabs his chest in mock offense. "I'm hurt that you think so little of me. The Sacred Seven *have* evolved over the years, and we've learned that taking Flames to Airabeth without further investigation was a waste of time. Simply put, we've started offering the Tests to learn how to break down the strongest Flames we can find. We give everyone a chance to fight for their freedom, but most are too afraid to accept the challenge, so they simply welcome their fate and stay in Airabeth willingly."

I wring my hands together, unsure of when they got so sweaty. "What sort of challenge are Flames too afraid to accept?" I ask.

He answers with a serpentine smile, voice tipped with cruel pleasure as he says, "You won't like the answer."

"Tell me," I demand, a strange boldness pumping through my veins. If there's any chance that I'll be able to escape Airabeth and return to my family, I have to take it.

He rocks back on his heels — the first sign of restlessness I've seen. "There are a series of Tests," he says, eyes alight with an eagerness that concerns me, "and if you win, we let you leave Airabeth without resistance. But if you lose, you stay and work for us until you realize we are your true gods and submit to us, soul and all."

A flicker of hope kindles in my chest. "What kind of Tests?" I ask, greedy for the specifics. "What do these Tests entail?" I've never been particularly smart, but if passing some Tests will grant my freedom, I'll do anything to win.

"Sharing that information would be like giving away fish to a beggar," Warfare says. "Last time I checked, you aren't a beggar, are you, sweetheart? The information I *can* share with you is that there will be seven Tests in total. Each one will be designed by a Master using their unique set of skills. Over the course of several weeks, your mind will be tested, and we'll be able to determine how bright your soul truly shines. If you are strong enough to get through the seven Tests in Airabeth, we'll let you go and never pursue you again. I must warn you, most Flames die in these Tests before they even get a chance to fail them, so I suggest you think this decision through."

I bite so hard on the inside of my cheek it bleeds. "And my family?"

"What about your family?" he asks.

"If I win, what will happen to my family?"

He rolls his eyes. "If you win, your family will be free, too. It comes with the deal, should you find yourself victorious."

"And the Flames on the list?"

The Master raises an eyebrow, undoubtedly intrigued. "Brave one, aren't you, bargaining with me like this?" He drags his tongue along his front teeth, debating. "All right, why not? Just to make things interesting, if you win, the Flames on the list will be safe from persecution too. That's how confident I am you won't win, Flame."

How delightful.

"And if I lose?" I ask. It's only fair to know both outcomes, right?

His answering smirk is quiet but all-knowing, a terrible slash of darkness and humor. *You lose, and you live the rest of your life in Airabeth.* He speaks the information to my mind, sending a shard of ice through my blood. *Your family and the Flames on the list will also join us in my lands, living to serve and provide whatever I ask.*

I think of Sasha, wondering what he would do.

Don't do this, I imagine him saying. *There's another way. This isn't smart. We can't gamble our lives away. We'll figure something out.*

But he isn't here to tell me what to do, and if it were my life on the line, he would take the Tests. He would shake the Master's hand and agree to the terms, because that's his way, and he wouldn't complain about it. He would fight for us. He would fight for our freedom and give us a chance at living a life away from the Sacred Seven's influence.

"So?" The Master pins his stare on me, the interest in his gaze more palpable than ever. "Are you going to fight for your independence and risk the Tests, or are you going to skip the humiliation and work in my land?" He presents a smile so cruel even the Soul-less would flee from it, but that's not what I think about when I look at him. I think about winning. About how beautiful it would be to force him to grant my family freedom.

"I'll take the Tests," I say, caught up in the magnificence of this fantasy. "But how can I trust that you're telling the truth? How do I know the Tests aren't rigged, or that you won't kill me outright or revoke the offer and make me serve in Airabeth once we get there?"

Warfare shrugs, waving a large hand through the air. "What choice do you have, other than to trust that what I say is true?"

None.

I have no choice. I will either submit myself and my family to a life of slavery in Airabeth or take the biggest risk of my life and fight for our independence from the Sacred Seven's reign.

The decision is easy.

"What will happen to my siblings while I take my Tests in Airabeth?" I ask, concerned for their safety. "They'll know something is wrong when I don't come home."

"As soon as we cross into Airabeth, the memory of you and Sasha will no longer live in your siblings' minds," the Master says, the words coming easily. I distantly wonder how many times he's said these words to other Flames in my position. "It's a standard precaution," he rushes on, "in order to prevent your siblings from interfering or doing something stupid on your behalf."

I bite my lip, fighting a rising panic.

"I will plant a stronghold inside their heads so they won't know who you are,"

Warfare says, "but once your Tests are over, win or lose, their memories will be restored to normal. Until then, their lives will resume as usual."

Warfare moves his hand closer to mine, waiting for me to take it. To meet him halfway. "So, do we have an understanding?"

I don't know if it's my human ignorance or blind faith that gives me the confidence to move, but I step forward and grasp his palm, his skin unnaturally hot against mine.

The Master shakes my hand once, twice, three times, before pulling me close, his mouth brushing the shell of my ear as he whispers, "Welcome to the den, sweetheart."

Chapter Fourteen

"Here, put this on." Warfare tosses me a red handkerchief as we leave the Market, his mouth quirking as he tells me to wrap it around my eyes and give up my sight. "I can't have you knowing the path from here to Airabeth," he says, and gestures down the road. "Unless you prefer I pluck your eyes out."

I want to assure him the blindfold isn't necessary — I could never memorize the directions from here to Airabeth in one go — but I do as he says, my shoulder aching from where Sasha smashed it, and tie the cloth around my head.

My eyes may be obscured behind this handkerchief, but they aren't blind to the Master's cruelty, and the evidence of that plays out in my head.

There's no forgetting, no *forgiving*, how the Masters ruined my family and the happiness we had, or how every joyful memory has been tainted and framed by death.

Now, when I think of my mother, I no longer remember her laugh, I hear her cries. Now, when I think of my father, I no longer remember his kindness, I see his sorrow. Now, when I think of Sasha, I no longer remember his stories, I recall his feral face, his dagger aiming for my throat.

Misery and hardship stain the edges of every picture I see my family in, and while I tell myself to shut it out, to stop ruminating on the somber parts of our history, they're all I see.

The Masters pulled the worst out of us all, and now that one of them is standing by my side, I realize what an active role they've played in our lives, causing nothing but chaos and suffering.

I go to remove the blindfold, desperate to escape this darkness in search of light, but Warfare's hand snatches my wrist. "I wouldn't," he says, and then he's pulling me behind him, nearly yanking my shoulder out of its socket. My collarbone yelps, still tender from Sasha's attack. I stumble behind the Master, his strides too long, too quick for me to keep up.

I don't know how I'm going to make it through the next few hours, let alone days, without some form of medical attention, but if our deal is going to strike true, Warfare is obligated to help me once we get to Airabeth. Is he not?

If I'm hurt, I won't have a fair chance at passing the Tests. And his experiment will be rigged, his results inconclusive. It won't be a fair deal. But does he even care about what's fair and what's not? Does he have any semblance of mercy beating within that wretched heart of his?

Even as I think the words, my chest constricts, a black shade looming over me.

My skin prickles where the Master's fingers touch, and though I want nothing more than to push him away, I have no idea where we are, where we're going, and I can't risk getting lost or running into a Soulless. The Flames and my siblings are tied to my deal as much as I am, their fates dependent upon my ability to pass or fail these Tests. I can't let them down.

"This way," Warfare says, making an abrupt turn to the left. He shifts slightly as he retrieves something from his pocket—a set of keys, I realize, as they rattle against each other, jingling faintly. I hear the slight *click* of a lock as he turns the key and opens a door, pulling me inside.

"Watch your step," the Master says, and I almost trip over my feet as we descend a flight of stairs, travelling down, down, down into something unknown. I try to make sense of my surroundings, but based on the slight chill in the air and the echo of our footsteps, we are no longer above ground, but below. Perhaps in a tunnel of some sorts?

Once we reach the bottom of the stairs, Warfare guides me forward, a strange hum vibrating beneath my feet. "Over here," he says, and guides me onto an undisclosed platform, my head dizzy with fear. "Sit there," he instructs, and pushes me down on a soft cushioned bench, taking position beside me.

I try not to grimace at the way his shoulder brushes against mine, uncomfortably close, and focus on calming my breaths.

Moments later, the whir of an engine blares out, followed by the rumbling of wheels on tracks, strangely specific.

A train.

Are we on a train?

No, that's impossible. We don't have trains in Tempus. We don't have trains anywhere, the Masters removed them. The only transportation available to the mortal lands are our own two foot, if we're lucky.

I open my mouth to voice my thoughts, then think better of it. Warfare isn't going to answer my questions, and I'd rather make it to Airabeth in one piece, than inspire him to pluck out one of my eyes. Or worse.

For now, I stay silent and endure Warfare's presence, yearning for the moment I can escape his touch.

THERE'S A TERRIBLE throb in my head. An ache in my legs. I don't know how long it's been since we stopped being transported and started walking again, but when Warfare finally orders me to stop, I'm overcome with the urge to sit and rest my body, wavering with exhaustion.

"Take off your blindfold," he says, and I immediately rip off the handkerchief, not needing to be told again. My eyes blur as they adjust to the light, blinking rapidly against the blinding sun.

Strange, considering we left my village mid-afternoon.

With how long we've been travelling, I expected the moon to be out — the heat gone and replaced with evening's chill — but the sun sits high and eastward, signaling early morning.

Have we really been hiking for an entire day?

"Time is different here," Warfare says, guessing my thoughts. "The hours are opposite of Tempus's, so I hope you can stomach it."

I open my mouth, not sure what sort of retort is about to come, when the rustling of leaves comes from my right. I turn to the noise and spot a family of rabbits hopping down the cobblestone path, their fur so white they could be mistaken for clumps of newly fallen snow.

My mouth falls open at the glorious sight, the glorious weight, of the well-nourished creatures. It takes me a moment to register the abundance, to not shout in wonder and scare them away.

Catching edible animals is hard enough as it is, but to find fat, respectable ones such as these is nearly impossible. A miracle by most huntsmen's standards.

I reach behind me on instinct, ready to retrieve an arrow, but my hand comes away empty. Weaponless. A reminder that I'm not in Tempus anymore.

I watch as the parade of rabbits hops down the path, the display of life indicating I'm in a world far from my own. I need to start preparing for the worst.

Airabeth's forest — that's where the Master has taken me — and although I'm not one to marvel over nature, this surpasses any woodland I've ever been in. Even in imagination, I could never conjure the vibrant red oaks and weeping willows that spread before me now, each one weaving out and around the path like an intricate braid, almost too perfect to behold.

Birds of various species chirp and twitter overhead, their feathers shimmering gold, red, and blue. Surrounding the open trail, the ground sprouts summer grass so green, I'm afraid to step on it, especially with the beds of tulips and lilies scattered throughout, giving color to the land.

I resist the urge to inhale deeply, the delicate scent of earth and fresh air an ecstasy for my nose. Intoxicatingly beautiful.

"Why did we stop here?" I ask Warfare, half-expecting us to have arrived at some dungeon, or torture chamber designed for my ruining.

"Welcome to your first Test," the Master says, but the casual tone of his voice doesn't match the impact of his words, so I'm sure I've misheard him. "The Test of Fear." He spreads his arms wide, eyes smoldering with a sadism I've only seen in nightmares.

"I hope you're not too tired from our walk," he says, eyes scanning my form, detecting the fatigue. "Though with all that hunting you do, I'm sure your endurance is strong, so this should be easy for you."

I stiffen at the shift in his tone, his statement landing like a stone in my gut.

"Test?" I croak out, my mouth dry. "But we just got here, I don't—"

"We didn't agree on a timeline, did we?" The Master raises a defiant brow, almost mocking in its playfulness, and waves a hand between us. "You will do what I say, when I say it. That was the deal, sweetheart."

Before I can wrap my head around the fact that this is it, that I will be performing my first Test right *now*, Warfare says, "Listen carefully, because I'm only going to say this once." And judging by the stern look in his gaze, I don't doubt him. "Within these woods lives an Amphista, which is a lethal tarantula. It is said to be one of the oldest creatures in all of Airabeth, and can cause death with a single bite."

My head spins, unable to focus on anything but the terror of this moment. Spider? I'll be fighting a spider? The Master of Fear would force me to face one of my biggest fears. It makes sense in a sick, twisted sort of way.

No. No, I'm not ready. I haven't slept or eaten in hours, and my collarbone is still injured from where Sasha smashed it, impairing my movement.

"Your task is to hunt and kill the tarantula," Warfare says, seemingly unaware of the emotional turmoil raging inside me, "and I will provide the weapons to help you do so."

"Weapons?" I ask, wondering what kind of defensive tool he could be hiding in those too-tight pants of his. "What weapons—"

The Master snaps his fingers, and a quiver full of arrows and a bow appear — just *appear* — in his right hand, as if they've always been there. He looks so comfortable holding the weapon I wonder if he knows how to use it.

"The tips of the arrows are laced with poison," he explains, and I tell myself to focus, to listen, despite the ringing in my ears. "They will stun the Amphista, if you manage to hit it, so this should give you enough time to kill the creature before it kills you. Everything you need for the Test lies within this very weapon, so for your sake, don't lose it. Before sunset, I expect you to be at the Sacred Seven's manor with the tarantula's eyes in hand." He smiles gravely, bringing a chill to my skin. "I'd also like you to bring back a small piece of the Amphista's brains, should you make it that far into the Test. You know what will happen if you fail to fulfill the expectations required."

My shoulders rise to my ears, the reality of my situation unavoidable.

This is it. This is really happening. By sunset, I will either be on the path to save my family or ruin them.

The Master places the weapons on the dirt before me, then turns without another word. I eye him cautiously, wondering where exactly he plans to go, when he travels back the way we came, most likely to whatever thing transported us here.

With shaking legs, I bend down to pick up the bow and quiver, fingers trembling as I grasp the fine wood, fearing the worst.

But as soon as I nock an arrow to the string, I steady, the action familiar and intimate, reminding me of home. I close my eyes in silent prayer, adrenaline dulling the pain in my collarbone.

I need to be stronger, faster, smarter than I've ever been in any chase. Unlike my normal hunts, there will be no second chances, no shot at redemption if I make a mistake, so if I plan on winning, I need to be ready from the get-go.

There is no room for error.

Chapter Fifteen

I keep my steps light on the dirt path, the rocks smooth and even beneath my boots. Even the animals — squirrels, frogs, and rabbits alike — move soundlessly across the land, invisible to the ear.

The Amphista won't sense me coming, but I won't sense it either, and I have yet to decide if that works in my favor. With the barest of sounds to indicate any hint of life, these grounds are perfect for a hunter, but a nightmare for prey. I haven't figured out which of the two apply to me, though I'm sure I'll find out quicker than I like.

I rest my bow in the crook of my arm and examine the woods, head pounding with an adrenaline that makes me see double. It's been over ten minutes since Warfare left me behind, and I haven't moved.

I come up with a handful of excuses as to why waiting out the Amphista is the smart thing to do, when really, I'm too gutless to hunt it down.

I'm wasting time. I need to keep moving. Find it and get this over with.

But what happens when I *do* find the Amphista? What happens when it attacks?

Don't scare yourself out of your mission. Sasha's words carry on the back of the wind, his voice crafted out of my own sorrow and guilt, providing more torment than comfort. *Go and accomplish what needs to be done. Fear is temporary. Regret is forever. You decide what to live with.*

I think of my brother's strength, his bravery, and try to use it as my own.

I wish he was here to deflate the doubts swelling in my chest. I wish he was here to tell me everything will work out like I want it to. Some small part of me still believes that he will appear. That somehow, he'll emerge from the bushes, and we'll go home, and everything will return to the way it was.

Hours ago, I would've done anything to get my family out of Tempus.

Now, I'd do anything to go back — to keep things the way they were.

You can't escape. There's no way out. You failed your brother. You'll fail the others. Your past dictates your future, don't you know?

I grind my teeth and clench my hands, the Masters' strongholds coming at me.

"Stop," I whisper under my breath. "You can do this. You are in control. You are stronger than the Sacred Seven."

You think yourself smart? You think you've made a noble decision by coming to Airabeth? You're a coward, and cowards get rewarded with death and nothing else.

Maybe this is a bad idea. Maybe I've overestimated my abilities, and this deal is a trap to kill me and everyone I care about. Who says Warfare will stay true to his word? What if I end up winning the Tests, and he takes our souls anyway?

Am I a fool to trust a handshake, a verbal agreement?

For sky's sake, he didn't even give me time to truly mourn the death of my brother before throwing me into this bloody trial.

How am I supposed to focus when I can still smell Sasha's blood on my hands?

Stop it, I tell myself. Stop letting your mind run away from you. Take a deep breath. Center your thoughts. It's the only way you're going to—

A loud, devastating whine slices through my thoughts.

My legs lock up, tightening to the point of pain, and grow weak beneath me.

A cardinal part of my mind screams for me to *run, run, run*, but I clench my bow to keep still, preparing to fire.

I train my gaze on the path ahead, too scared to blink or breathe.

I curse inwardly as the anticipation mounts, the silence becoming too much to bear. I almost yell just to break it, but then the creature's enormous shadow comes into view, angling across the bend of the trees. My mouth screws shut at the sight, tightening into a thin line.

This is my chance. I have to face it. I can't run.

My knees buckle. Hot tears prick my eyes. I quietly pray for the thing to stop, to turn around, to not come closer. There must be another way to defeat it, but the Amphista is done waiting, and so am I.

That is, until it decides to reveal itself to me.

The Amphista is a creature from hell, and though I've never been to the underworld myself, these are the demons I imagine must live there.

With one head protruding from the front and the other at the back end of its large, circular body, the Amphista is two beasts contained in one body — a complete monster of a creation. Towering over me, the tarantula's eight legs are as high as my eyes, their ghastly tips ending in several sharp talons, perfect for shredding out throats. The creature breathes evenly through a two-dotted nose, a pair of dark yellow tusks protruding from either side, extending longer than my forearm.

The Amphista watches me through a multitude of green eyes –eight on each head– and blinks with animalistic curiosity, seemingly fascinated by my presence. Besides the brown fur and black dots covering its skin, there isn't much to the tarantula's exterior, which is concerning, given its age.

From what little information Warfare told me, I was hoping this thing would show signs of deterioration or weakness, but there are no graying gums or wrinkled flesh to be found, not even around its eyes. If anything, age seems to have only made the creature stronger, its body rippling with muscle and agility.

I wonder how many people have tried, and failed, to escape this thing. I wonder if anyone's gotten close.

"A human," one of the heads croons, its voice a wet sound of energy and chaos. "And a Flame at that. Are you lost, little one?"

"I don't know if we should call her bold, or a complete imbecile for venturing out here," chirps the other head, equally as vile. "What do you think, brother?" It tilts its head, eyes large and all consuming. Siblings. That's what they are. "Didn't anyone tell you that Airabeth's forest is no place for a Flame?"

The brothers share a laugh that exposes razor-sharp teeth. Perfect for killing.

My stomach rolls at the thought of them sinking into my neck, slicing through my jugular.

"So why are you here, girl?"

I crush my grip on the bow, knees knocking, heart pounding.

Kill it. Shoot it. Do something! But it's like my fingers are invisibly bound. I can't bring myself to fire an arrow. To run. To do anything, let alone reply to the tarantula's question.

But when a horrible hiss — a warning — shoots from both of its wet, ebony maws, I'm shocked into answering. "I came here on command," I whisper, my words no louder than an infant's breath.

Be brave, Nadia. You're doing this for your family, your people.

As soon as I have the thought, a voice — much louder and stronger than mine — takes over. *You're not going to pass this Test,* it sneers, deeper and harsher than Warfare's. *You're weak, and deep down, you've always known it. You run when things get hard. You cry when you don't get your way. Such frailty doesn't last here. You're as good as dead, girl. Dead. Dead. DEAD!*

The Amphista narrows its eyes and stalks closer, taunting me.

"You say you come here on command," the creature says, somewhat intrigued. "What does this so-called *command* entail?" Two heartbeats pass by, and when I don't respond, the Amphista snarls, "Answer us, human, or we'll rip out your throat!"

The tarantula's gaze widens the longer it stares at me, and for a sickening moment, I think it's going to follow through on its threat and swallow me whole.

"Pretty eyes," the right head comments, batting its multitude of eyelashes. "So blue, so brilliant."

"Indeed," the left one agrees, inching that much closer. "You see, girl, we've been looking for a new set of eyes, since our current pairs have grown weak with age. Can't you tell?"

The Amphista dips low and leans in, its faces now level with mine. From this proximity, its qualities become distinct, and I notice things I couldn't before — not when it was standing at its full height.

Now that it's close, I take in the creature's eyes, mouth, and bulbous nose, my heart plummeting as I realize none of the features are of arachnid descent, but of human origin.

How—?

"That's right, child," the heads sing in harmony. "Whatever part of a human we eat, we gain on ourselves. And we'd love to have such ocean-blue eyes, wouldn't we, brother?"

The heads exchange a look that brings gooseflesh to my skin.

They want my eyes. I need theirs. How poetic.

"Now, answer my question, you mute," the creature says. "Why. Did. You. Come. Here?" The Amphista is growing impatient, but I can't let it bully me into submission. As soon as I give them control, it's over. I need to challenge them, to keep them distracted.

"I'm here to kill you," I admit, and though my voice sounds weak, I feel strong, somehow ready. I want this nightmare over with.

The Amphista howls a bone-splintering laugh, and for the first time since I've met it, the tarantula's attention isn't on me.

Now. Do it now, while they aren't looking!

I nock an arrow against my bowstring, suddenly wishing I'd counted how many shots I have to fire. Judging by the weight of my pack, I'm guessing between fifteen and twenty, but will that be enough to kill a century-old spider?

I let my first arrow fly, knowing there's only one way to find out.

Chapter Sixteen

The Amphista doesn't notice my shot until it's too late.

Blood rains from its abdomen in a river of black, my arrow protruding from a spot below its sternum. The creature's shriek fills the forest, the sound so violent and feral it rattles the trees, obliterates my eardrums.

I don't stop to see if Warfare was right about the arrow's ability to stun the tarantula.

I'm already racing down a path that could easily lead to a dead end, or worse. I try not to think about what possible horrors might be waiting at the end of the trail and push my legs into an all-out sprint.

With every pump of my arms, my ruined shoulder explodes with pain, the muscle tearing further and further from the bone. I don't know how I'm going to win this Test with such a gruesome injury, but if I have to use my feet to fire another arrow, I will.

Surviving is my only option.

The tarantula's scream grows louder and angrier as it realizes what I've done, roaring a sound I've never heard any animal make. I swerve to the right, sprinting for the waist-high grass, and hope to lose the Amphista amongst the sea of green. I quickly learn the tall weeds only slow me down, the thick stems catching against my calves and ankles.

I make a sharp left to get back on the path, already panting.

Coward. Coward. Coward. Coward. Coward! You're doing it again. You're running away because you're scared. Scared and pathetic. A spineless maggot!

How am I going to get out of this?

Warfare said the arrows were supposed to stun the creature, or at least slow it down, but the tarantula isn't weakening.

I reach a fork in the path and take the right side, bolting to a large willow tree a few meters ahead. A wild, frustrated wail erupts from the creature, but I don't know if it's because I caught it off guard, or because it knows I'm delaying my inevitable demise.

I don't dare look back to see how close it is and duck beneath the willow's long, drooping branches. I have less than a second to string my bow and hit the tarantula before it charges by, so when I see a flash of brown rush into the clearing, I fire blindly, hitting its backside.

The creature howls, and I join in its misery — my collarbone popping in three different places as the bow recoils into my shoulder. I shove my knuckles into my mouth to stifle a scream, doing my best to swallow the dread of it all.

I don't look down to see the extent of the injury, but if the white sparks staining my vision are any indication, I assume the muscle is dislocated. Even so, I don't have time to think about it. I just string another arrow with my non-injured arm and launch it in the general direction of the Amphista.

I anxiously wait for the tarantula's crushing scream to signify I've hit it, but nothing comes. Three shots go by, and on the third, I finally connect, the spider shouting its disapproval. Peeking through a break in the leaves, I see the creature wildly convulse, its legs twisting and contorting in a terrible dance. My stomach roils at the horrific sight, but the surge of nausea only intensifies when the tarantula rights itself again.

Nothing is working. The arrows aren't enough. The beast isn't coming down.

I don't have the luxury of despairing over Warfare's lie about the arrows because the tarantula is already whirling toward me.

My bones burn with panic as I retreat to the path.

What am I going to do? What am I going to do? What am I going to do?

The Amphista is a raging presence behind me, its teeth gnashing and snapping at my heels. I don't think about the repercussions of glancing back to see how many centimeters separate us. I just do it, fear and curiosity getting the best of me.

The tarantula is right on my heels, one of its mouths inches from swallowing me whole.

I urge my legs to run faster. Harder. But my lungs are tired, and every breath is a hot, searing flame in my throat.

The Amphista shouts again, but it's not the roar of fury that has my bones trembling. It's the thousands of black widows that come pouring from the tarantula's mouth, racing toward me in a sea of tiny bodies.

I nearly choke on my heart as it hammers in my chest, the spiders surrounding my feet within seconds, climbing up my feet. Legs. Waist. Chest. Neck. I scream and try to kick the little vermin away, but there's too many of them and I'm running out of speed.

I'm slowing down.

My energy is draining.

I'm not going to make it.

"We were going to be gentle with you," says one of the heads, its mouth foaming with venom. "But now, we'll take our time. I think we'll go for your eyes first. Or maybe last. It's important you witness everything we do to you."

My knees ache as I push myself around a bend in the path, going straight for the stream of water a few feet ahead. The frantic, basic instinct to survive propels me forward, but it doesn't give me the vigor I need to outrun the Amphista.

I slap at my face to kill the smaller spiders crawling up my chin and cheeks, some of them escaping into the collar of my shirt, itching their way across my skin. I curse as they start to climb around my eyes, obscuring my vision.

The tarantula is closing in on me, its breath hot against my neck.

Don't look back. Don't look back. Don't look back.

The hiss at the nape of my neck is my only warning before one of the creature's predatory legs wraps around my torso, thrusting me high into the air.

I have little time to react, or even scream, when the Amphista brings its faces to mine, eyes corrupt and hungry. Ready for the kill.

"Such a pity," the tarantula fumes, its breath ragged and foul against my cheek, "that you thought you could kill us with that pathetic bow." The Amphista opens its mouths wide, welcoming the black widows back inside — a silent signal to retreat. I watch in horror as the thousands of spiders scurry up the tarantula's body and back into their home, seemingly finished with their purpose.

I shiver at the absence of the black widows creeping across my skin, thankful they're gone, but fearing the inevitability of what's to come.

"It's insulting, really," the creature says, "to assume you could defeat us with such a tiny piece of wood."

I squeeze my weapon harder in response, and the Amphista catches the action, chuckling faintly.

It's my only notice before it reaches out to pluck the bow from my hand, using its sharp, menacing claws to snatch it away. I reach forward in protest, but it's too late. The Amphista bares its fangs and snaps the handle in half, destroying my only source of protection.

The Amphista draws me closer to one of its dreadful faces, its mouth open and cavernous. I look around the forest in distress, as if expecting someone to burst through the trees and save me, but no one is coming. No one knows I'm here.

A frustrated sob bubbles in my chest, and I get the terrible feeling that this is it, this is how I'm going to die. But then a dark, orange liquid starts oozing from the Amphista's abdomen — my arrow still lodged there — and a spark of promise flares, an idea emerging.

The wound is close enough for me to kick, and if I do it quickly, I might have a chance at catching the tarantula off guard. It's a basic plan, but it's the only one I've got, so I take it.

I drive my leg back as far as it'll go and thrust my foot forward. The creature screeches as the tip of my boot punctures the wound, inflicting more damage.

Immediately, the tarantula's grip slackens, and I find myself plunging from the air, the earth surging toward me in a blur of green and brown.

Bleeding hell, I didn't think this part through.

My shoulder yelps the moment I smack the ground, but the need to survive pushes me forward.

I get to my feet, searching wildly for a branch or a rock to defend myself with. But one look at the Amphista tells me I won't be needing protection anymore.

The creature stumbles, its wounds spraying black-orange fluid, and sways to the side, losing consciousness. For a moment, I can't believe what I'm seeing. Can't believe that Warfare was right, the arrows *are* laced with some fatal poison.

The Amphista's body slumps, its strength diminishing.

Before I know it, I'm running off the path, the tarantula's body collapsing to the ground right where I stood. The impact of the fall rocks the earth, rattling my bones. A low, tired moan is the last thing I hear before the creature goes entirely still, its body unmoving.

I stand there, both hands braced on my aching knees, and try to regulate my breathing. It takes minutes before I realize the creature isn't going to rise. It takes longer to grasp that it's because of me. That I'm the one who killed it.

But the lowering sun is a cruel reminder that my mission is far from over, and I don't have time to marvel over what I've done.

The air is growing cooler, the daylight diminishing by the second.

I drop to my knees and get to work.

The Amphista eyes aren't going to uproot themselves.

Chapter Seventeen

My skin is wet with the tarantula's blood, every inch of me splashed with the foul liquid and bits of flesh. I don't have a knife, so I settle for the rough edge of my bow and use it like a saw, shaving back and forth, back and forth, over the Amphista's large, furry faces.

I hold my breath as blood bubbles around my hands, splattering all the way up to my elbows, creating gloves of black. I gag at the sight, my nostrils burning at the sour stench of ichor. I hide my nose in the hem of my shirt to escape the odor, but the nausea doesn't subside. I'm unable to stop the rush of vomit as it climbs up my throat, splattering all over the ground and cuffs of my jacket.

I wipe my mouth with the back of my hand, then get back to work.

The sky is darkening. My hours are running out.

I can't stay here much longer.

Come on. Come on. Come on. Come on. Come on! How long is this going to take?

Finally, after what seems like days of cutting, stabbing, and ripping, I manage to remove every eye from the Amphista's sockets. I can't remember if Warfare instructed me to bring back all sixteen, but I'm not taking any chances.

I sit back on my heels and tuck the eyes into my jacket pocket, breathing heavily.

Thirty seconds.

That's how much time I give myself before I dig my hands into the ruin of the Amphista's faces and scoop out their innards. I hold my breath as I pull out chunks of black sludge and sinew, staining my forearms with gunk. Grimacing, I plunge my hands deeper and reach for the Amphista's brains, tugging at the slimy, solid mass. The organs are heavier than expected, but I manage to yank them free, cursing as I do.

I use the rough edge of my bow to hack at the brains, shaving a small piece off either one. With shaking hands, I place the fatty tissue in my pants pocket, nearly fainting at the carnage I've created.

Almost over. This dreadful Test is almost over, and although I don't want to see Warfare again, I'd rather be stuck in his manor, than stuck out here, trapped in this unknown and unpredictable land.

Yet, as soon as I start to weave through the forest, a question tears through my mind, stopping me cold in my tracks: Where is the Sacred Seven's manor?

I have no direction. No map. No compass.

Which way did I come from? Which way is east? Airabeth's territory is located on the eastside, is it not? Or is it west?

I can't remember.

I circle the woodland to look for an obvious exit or clearing, but the longer I stare at the trees, the more everything starts to look the same.

Fear pushes its way inside my mind, but I shove it away, refusing to let it take root. I can't lose my head about this.

There must be something around here that'll tell me where to go.

I begin to search the forest, not entirely sure what I'm looking for, and dig behind trees and bushes, flowers and logs, hoping to find something important. I even push clumps of dirt off the path to check for any hidden messages, but nothing is there. Nothing is useful.

Now I'm starting to lose my wits.

Seconds of searching turn into minutes, and minutes turn into half an hour, and half an hour of searching is an eternity for me.

I quicken my steps and hunt through the woodland more diligently, but with my panic on high, I start to forget which spots I've checked.

I run a hand through my damp hair to collect myself, afraid of what could happen if I don't, and reflect on what Warfare told me before the Test.

Everything you need to be successful lies within this very weapon, so for your sake, I suggest you don't lose it.

I take off my quiver and empty the remaining arrows, finding nothing. I reach a hesitant hand inside the bag, my breath catching when something rough scratches against my fingers. I go to grasp the strange texture, but nothing tangible meets me at the bottom.

I frown and yank my hand back.

The quiver is empty.

But there has to be something here, there *has* to be, because if there isn't . . .

I peer inside the bag a second time, and pull out the inner fabric, thinking maybe there's an answer hiding beneath—

My heart flips when I see symbols etched into the base of the leather — so small and faint, but there, nonetheless.

I bring the bag close to my face, squinting to make out the lettering.

After a moment of careful reading, I put the sentences together, realizing they're not symbols, but directions.

Directions that must lead to the Sacred Seven's manor.

GO TO THE NORTHERN trees. Left at the valley of oaks. Right at the stream of water. Left at the gardens. Straight to the open field . . .

I recite the directions as I run up a hill made of balms and daisies, the scent of vanilla and clove mixing with the Amphista's foul remnants permeating through my pockets. It's been less than fifteen minutes since I left the forest, and my legs are already aching, pushing me into a panic.

The sky, already a dark, velvety blue, warns of the dwindling time and imminent failure, yet I keep moving, refusing to let today's work go to waste. I've made it this far, so to give up now would be pointless. And I can't fail the people I've promised to protect.

If my navigation skills are correct, the Sacred Seven's house should be on the other side of this mound.

My thighs seize against the hill's incline, back aching with every step. Though the weight of the Amphista's remains slow me down, I pump my arms as best I can, ignoring the grating pang in my muscles.

When I finally reach the peak of the hill, I'm too tired to sob with relief, so I scan the horizon for the Masters' dwelling, sensitive to the passing time.

I'm not entirely sure what I expected to see, but as I take in the manor — no, *palace* — sitting off in the distance, my curiosity spikes. Orchestral music plays out over the land, the mixture of strings and percussion overpowering the chirping birds overhead. A large patio with various couches and tables sits to the side of the manor, but it's empty, eerily silent. Even the gardens are calm. Still. Quiet. Not a worker in sight.

The silence gives me no ounce of comfort.

The tranquility is ghostly, almost staged, as if masking the true horrors creeping along these grounds.

Even so, I sprint across them, not having the luxury of time, and make for the front door. I take inventory as I go, marking all the exits, gates, passageways and doors, not knowing when, or if, the information will come in handy.

I try my best to memorize the layout of the estate, but after ten seconds of studying, I give up. The land stretches so far, so wide, I can hardly tell where one side ends and the other begins. I nearly lose my sense of direction amongst the vast expanse, the lawn extending all the way out to the distant forest surrounding the property, covering acres upon acres of land.

I suppose the sizable amount of space is needed, not only to support the thousands of Flames the Masters capture every year, but to fit the household itself. The seven-story palace is like something pulled out of a fairytale, and even then, this place is bigger than any royal castle I've seen in fiction or painting. Ivory balconies embellished with gold extend from every level, unfolding far into the distance, like outstretched wings. Smooth columns of tan and white uphold the slanted roof, their platforms engraved with lions and ancient designs.

Windows line the front of the house in rows of three, and although the openness should be a comfort, it isn't. There is no privacy here, no chance of hiding from the Masters' prying eyes. With the way the land is laid out, the Sacred Seven can spot anyone who tries to run away from the discomforts of the manor, leaving no room for escape.

I hurry down the stone path leading to the entrance, weaving in and out of the garden maze, getting lost within it. I take every right turn I come across, and eventually, the exit comes into view, revealing the front porch.

I leap up the marble steps two at a time, nearly tripping over my feet, and lunge for the entrance. I stop short of grabbing the handle when I hear a faint noise rise above the music, coming from my left. I turn to it, thinking I've imagined the sound, but it comes again. Louder this time.

I take a step closer, looking far into the distance, when I identify the noise.

A scream. No — a plea, coming from somewhere below me.

I look down, nearly missing the latched door embedded into the grass, blending in seamlessly with the ground. My heart sinks when I spot the lock, large and ancient, impossible to pry open.

The scream comes again, distinctly human, and I wonder if that's why the Masters play music over the land — to block out the cries from the people they throw down there.

Not now. I can't deal with this now, I need to find Warfare. I'm already behind.

I hope I'm not too late.

MY FEAR RISES INTO full-blown terror as I push through the double set of glass doors. Sweat flows freely down my face as I enter the main foyer, my jacket collar hot around my neck.

The moment I pass through the threshold, my muscles tighten.

A den of lions. That's what I've stepped into.

Every instinct screams at me to turn around, to forget about the deal, and return to Tempus. I tell myself there are other ways to protect my family and the list of Flames, but really, it's an excuse to justify my cowardice.

I've already made my decision. There's no bowing out.

The inside of the Sacred Seven's palace is even more exquisite, but unlike the silence that greeted me at the doors, the foyer is teeming with people — with servants — hustling this way and that. The housekeepers disappear and reappear with trays of food, wine, and decadent desserts, each of them hard at work. Not one person notices my presence, or it appears that way, but perhaps that's a small mercy.

I shouldn't be standing here in the open, staring at these Flames and Soulless, who have been captured, lured, and bribed into coming here.

Drip. Drip. Drip.

The blood from the Amphista's remains leak through my jacket and onto the gray marble floor, sparking the attention of a few passing servants. Some of them pause to look at me, but their eyes are glazed. Others leer, glaring with a wrath only a Soulless can have. Few display alarm, although those who do must be newcomers like myself. They aren't yet accustomed to seeing a girl sprayed in black blood.

Drip. Drip. Drip.

I do a quick survey of the house, searching for signs of Warfare, but find none.

This manor is massive. A maze of riches. It could easily take me hours, even days, to scout every room and corridor.

I have minutes, possibly seconds, before I fail this Test. I need to find him now.

I approach the first servant girl I see and step in her path, not bothering to introduce myself or explain my presence. "Where is the Master of Warfare?" I ask, and she flinches. Her eyebrows draw in, eyes widening, when she takes in my face, the blood, the Amphista's heads.

I swallow hard and try again. "Please." I soften my voice. "I need to find him, you must understand."

The stranger stares at me blankly, not even blinking to acknowledge my words. For a gut-wrenching moment, I think she's going to ignore me and walk away, but she doesn't.

Instead, she points down a long corridor to my left. "He's having dinner with the others." She speaks so quietly I almost miss what she says.

"It's the second last door on the right-hand side. Can't miss it."

I don't have time to give my thanks.

I take off in the direction she advised, hoping she knows what she's talking about, and sprint down the wood-paneled hallway. By the time I reach the end of it, I'm out of breath, tired and aching.

I don't bother preparing myself before I enter the dining room, I just do it, knowing this is the first of many meetings Warfare and I are bound to have.

Even so, that doesn't ready me for what hides behind the double set of wooden doors.

Others.

The servant girl said Warfare was having dinner with the 'others', but I didn't stop to consider what that meant.

I wish I had, though.

I wish I would've put the pieces of her warning together, and realized I wouldn't only be interrupting Warfare's dinner, but his friends' as well.

The Sacred Seven. They're here. All of them.

Chapter Eighteen

At first glance, they don't look as intimidating as I imagined — just a group of friends enjoying each other's company over some food and drinks. If it weren't for the slight buzz of power wafting through the air, I wouldn't think anything horrific or strange about them, but that doesn't last.

I can't forget who they are.

As soon as the door behind me slams shut, I want nothing more than to cover my eyes and shield myself from view. Sharp jaws, smirking mouths, downturned eyebrows, all of them snap in my direction, turning me sick with fear.

It's a struggle to keep my legs from giving out — to keep my chin high and proud — with so many ruthless glares settling on me.

"Nadia." Warfare watches me from the head of the table, a golden goblet hanging between his fingers, casual as ever. He takes a sip and watches me over the rim, never once breaking eye contact. "Are you just going to stand there?" His gaze flicks to my bloodied pockets, giving no other reaction to my being here. "Or are you going to bring me my present?"

Every eye in the room slides to me, and it feels like I'm being pummeled by a wave, drowning under the intensity of their stares. There's too much power, too much testosterone, pocketed in one room, and I don't know why I thought I could defend myself against it.

Bleeding hell, I should've left this house when I had the chance.

Warfare lets out an impatient growl and gestures me forward.

I approach the table, shuddering at the hateful gleam shining in his eyes.

The Sacred Seven's faces blur together as I pass, and even with the soft glow of the chandelier lighting the space, tendrils of darkness haunt the room, deflecting any light trying to enter.

Aside from their blazers differing in color and pattern, the Masters are freakishly similar in appearance and build — tall, lean, imperious with power — and look more like siblings than acquaintances. Even their eyes, cunning and dark, are identical in their lack of depth and emotion.

Gooseflesh erupts on the back of my neck as I detect their strongholds, prodding but unmistakable, knocking against the door to my mind, searching for a way in. I build up my shield as best I can, but against their combined strength, my defense is useless.

All they have to do is apply a little more pressure to the nape of my skull, and my mind will be demolished.

Surprisingly enough, they hold off, deciding to play with me rather than take my soul outright. Perhaps it would be easier to beg for death and get it over with, but deep inside, I know that's my fear talking. I won't abandon my duty and the deal I made, and I certainly won't give the Masters the pleasure of defeating me, no matter the cost.

When I reach the head of the table, I retrieve the Amphista's remains from my pocket and drop them at Warfare's feet, blood leaking all over the fine granite floors, ruining the salt and pepper pattern. The tarantula's eyeballs scatter across the ground like roaches, rolling this way and that.

The Sacred Seven curse at the abominable sight, the smell — unable to look away.

I can't seem to turn away either, only I'm not gazing at the tarantula.

I'm gazing at the glorious mounds of food, just waiting to be inhaled.

My stomach grumbles at the magnificent display of chicken, bread, potatoes, rice, corn, asparagus, brownies, red velvet cake . . .

I don't think I've seen this much salvation in my entire life, let alone all in one spot.

The wafting spices practically speak to me, preying on my mal-nourishment.

I can't help but water at the mouth, imagining how good it all must taste—

"Did you cut out your tongue when I wasn't looking?" Warfare snaps a finger in front of my face, and I jump, his brutal eyes brimming with impatience. It's a challenge not to whimper under that predatory gleam, but I hold my own. "Did you hear what I said?"

I don't know how to respond. I wasn't listening.

I shake my head slowly, unable to form a worthy excuse. "No, I'm sorry, I—" Warfare shoots to his feet so fast that his chair topples over, the crash echoing in the otherwise silent room. I grip the edge of the table to propel myself away from him, terrified to be on the receiving end of his wrath.

I vaguely register the other Masters' protests, but no one is brave enough to physically intervene — not that I expect them to.

Warfare anchors a fist behind his head, preparing to strike. I have a heartbeat to block him, to beg him to stop, before he knocks me out cold.

"Warfare, control yourself!"

A deep, commanding voice rings from the other side of the table, preventing the punch from reaching me.

I turn, my heart a drum in my chest, and find a silver-eyed Master staring at us, his hands splayed on the armrests of his chair, ready to stand. "What are you thinking?" the Master snarls at Warfare. "You can't—"

"I know," Warfare says calmly, fist pausing inches from my cheek. Perfectly calculated. "I would never be so rude as to hurt our guest on her first night." He winks at his friend, shoulders loose, entirely in control. "We're just having a little fun."

I suck in a tight breath as he cranks back a large hand — the one he almost hit me with — and runs it through his silver-blue hair, amused by my retreat.

He glances at me briefly, an easy smile on his mouth. "No need to be so on edge, sweetheart. We were just playing a game of reaction. Isn't that, right?" He turns back to the table, righting his chair.

I nod once to avoid further conflict, and thankfully, that's the end of it. Everyone carries on with their eating, and Warfare takes his seat once again, forgetting my existence. No one pays me any heed or gives me any orders, and if I wanted to leave now, I probably could, but the risk isn't worth it.

I'm not sure why I do it, but as the Sacred Seven resume their indulgence, my eyes drift back to him; the Master who spoke against Warfare. I don't let my eyes linger on the horrific scar slashing from the tip of his eyebrow to the corner of his mouth, but since his face is otherwise untouched, it's difficult to overlook.

Perhaps that's why he wears an eccentric pinstriped jacket trimmed with white, the color distracting from the damage done to his near-perfect chestnut skin. And although his hair, as black and bland as his heart, cuts close to his head like Sasha's, he reminds me nothing of him.

How could he when he is the Master of Fear?

I don't know why his title comes to mind so easily, but it does. I can see it in the cruel lines of his eyes. Feel it in the terrible panic that eats at my heart when I look at him. He makes me nervous, more so than the others do, and that alone speaks volumes.

Fear straightens in his seat then, smiling with intrigue, and gives me a wink no one notices, sensing my discovery.

I bare my teeth and almost congratulate him for creating such a brutal first Test, but Warfare's voice fills the room, cutting me off.

"Kneel," he says to me, and swirls his wine once, twice, three times, before downing his glass.

I fight the urge to roll my eyes, refusing to kneel for someone who isn't my god. I'd much rather bark like a dog than bow before him and the men who destroyed my family. My life.

One moment, I'm upright; the next, Warfare is grabbing my shoulder and pushing me to the ground, my nose touching the floor in prostrate position. I wince at the impact, my knees groaning against the tile.

"Congratulations," Warfare announces, his voice sounding anything but celebratory. "You have done everything I've asked of you. I declare your first Test victorious. The date for your second Test will be one week from today, so I suggest enjoy your time off while you have it."

I refuse to look up at him as he speaks, but perhaps that works against me when he shifts in his seat and I don't see it. It all happens so fast, it takes me a moment to register his palm slamming straight into my dislocated collarbone, popping it back in place.

I gasp, unable to scream or cry from the mind-altering pain. Fortunately, the hurt doesn't last beyond a few seconds, but those seconds feel like an eternity. I peek down at my shoulder once the suffering subsides, relieved to find the bone no longer dangling crookedly.

When I glance up at Warfare, he's smiling like a fiend, waiting for an expression of gratitude I'm not going to give. I'm not sure why he mended my injury, or what his angle is, but I have no doubt I'll be paying for it later. The Masters never give anything for free.

"Any bitch with a brain can pass the first Test."

The room goes silent at the bold declaration, an uncomfortable twinge hanging in the air. I keep my eyes pinned to the floor, terrified to meet the face behind that gnarled, twisted voice.

"When a Master speaks to you," Warfare says, grabbing my wrist and yanking me to my feet, "you respond with respect."

He grabs a fistful of my hair and pulls it back, forcing me to look up.

My blood stops dead in my veins as I regard a Master with yellow eyes, the whites surrounding his pupils nowhere to be found. With his blond, straggly hair and graying skin, he's by far the least attractive of the group — a stain amongst the Sacred Seven's glamor.

If I couldn't already tell by the purple-blue veins that pulse and protrude on the surface of his skin, the black gunk he spits into his cup makes his title strikingly obvious.

The Master of Sickness.

The man who almost killed my twin in Tempus's forest.

He smirks, as if remembering the incident, and spits again into his glass.

I ball my hands to prevent myself from choking him, from crawling across the table and slicing through every single one of those hideous veins.

In a way, he's the one who started all of this. If he hadn't interfered with Elisha's health, we could've brought home the deer, and Sasha wouldn't have left to see Milo.

If we brought home the deer, my sister would've been in a good mood, and we could've avoided that terrible fight.

If we brought home the deer, all of us would've been home when Warfare arrived, and we could've had a different outcome.

"You like what you see?" Sickness leans back in his chair and locks his hands behind his head. A powerful movement despite its nonchalance. "I bet a human whore like you would enjoy my company." He smiles at his words, watching me with a hunger so beastly I feel like a lamb. "I've never screwed a Flame as pretty as you before. Bet it'd be fun."

I tremble, my face flaring with heat, and instinctively search for the nearest exit, wishing I could escape. "As if you'd ever get my permission," I say shakily, unsure how else to respond.

Sickness clicks his tongue against his teeth, lifting a fair brow. "I don't need your permission, Bunny." He says it so calmly, so assuredly, I know he isn't messing around. If there ever comes a time where he corners me, alone and vulnerable, he won't hesitate to attack.

A weapon.

I need to have a weapon on me at all times, not only to use against the Masters, but the servants as well. Soulless roam the halls, seeking a Flame to devour, and while the Flames themselves aren't likely to cause any trouble, they'll do anything to protect themselves.

I should know. I'm one of them.

"Please, Nadia, join us for dinner." Warfare waves a hand over the food, welcoming me over, as if I have any interest in being closer to him. "This is the only time you'll be welcomed to eat our food," he says sharply, "so I suggest you enjoy it while you can." When I don't respond, he adds, "You will not leave this room until my friends get acquainted with you. It's something we like to do for every Flame who chooses to participate in the Tests. So, you can either stand there for the next hour and not eat until tomorrow, or you can sit down and enjoy the last decent meal you'll ever eat. Your choice."

I shake my head, refusing to let his threat cloud my judgment.

I'm outnumbered. Outsmarted. I'd be a fool to sit with them. This isn't a meal, it's an interrogation. They'll mess with my mind and exploit my weaknesses, but they won't do it outright, that'd be too obvious. They'll do it slowly, gradually, until I can't separate their thoughts from mine, accepting their strongholds as truth.

But I'm also starving.

How can I expect to think clearly if I don't nourish my body? Sit. Eat. Leave. Win. Simple as that. I need to be ready for my second Test, and risking an episode of fainting isn't going to help that.

The Masters watch me closely, like new meat ready to be devoured, and I suspect Warfare has already briefed them of our deal. Not surprising, considering the bargain involves all of us.

I wonder which Test will be the hardest. Who will be the Master to break me? Who will deliver a challenge so complex, I'll have no choice but to concede and sentence my family to death?

"Sit. *Now*," Warfare orders, a commanding growl in every word.

Beast. He's definitely a beast.

"There isn't enough room," I manage to say, and it's true. Even if I were to sit with them, there are no empty seats.

Warfare snaps his fingers and a red cushioned chair bursts through the doors on a phantom wind, summoned by some power I've never seen before. "Cruelty," Warfare says, and looks to the Master sitting to his left. "Slide down and make some room."

The Master — Cruelty — glares at me for a moment, undoubtedly irritated to have to move for my benefit. He doesn't so much as glance in my direction as I shuffle to the open chair, but he doesn't bother hiding his grumble of disapproval either.

I ignore him, forcing my face a mask of boredom as I gaze at the food, unable to bring myself to feast without shame.

What would Sasha think about this? Eating with our enemies?

"Don't be shy," Warfare says, propping his chin on a hand. "You're our guest, and we treat our guests quite well, don't we gentlemen?" The others nod, chewing loudly as they monitor my movements. "It's time to put some meat on those bones. We don't want you blowing over at the first gust of wind, now, do we?"

I pinch my lips into a thin line, tongue burning with a retort.

It's not a choice to look this way — to be so thin from starvation that my bones jut and protrude, looking more dead than alive.

It's been ten years since I've gone to bed with a stomach full of food, but it's been longer for others, I've seen it firsthand. There are thousands of struggling families who are even worse off than mine, and it's not from lack of brains or work ethic, I'm sure of that.

Over the past fifteen years, the Masters have been slowly robbing our lands of farming fields and job opportunities, leaving us hungry and without pay. Whatever occupations the Sacred Seven *do* allow us to have, they give first choice to the Soulless, and leave us with the sloppy, underpaid seconds. If Flames don't die at the Masters' hands, we die from starvation, and at the rate we're going, it's only a matter of time before our kind goes extinct.

"Go ahead, Bunny." Sickness stabs his fork into a slab of chicken and waves it in front of my face, tempting me. "Eat your heart out, we won't judge. It'll do you some good to fatten up a bit." He tosses the hunk of meat into his mouth, speaking around it. "Who knows, perhaps if you gain some weight, your chest won't be as flat as your back."

The other Masters snort their agreement, laughing between sips of wine.

I inch lower in my seat, wondering why I thought sitting at this table was a decent idea. I didn't expect the Masters to treat me with dignity or respect, but I also didn't think I'd be the target of every joke and insult.

Shame burns a path through my blood as they continue to ridicule me, pointing out every flaw and insecurity I'm well aware of. Thankfully, the hectoring doesn't last beyond a few minutes and they change the subject to politics, seemingly bored of my presence.

It's a small mercy, being ignored by them.

It even gives me the courage to reach for their food, unable to deprive myself any longer.

Cruelty brands a hard look into the side of my head as I scoop various meats and vegetables onto my plate, watching me intently. I ready myself to snatch the knife from my placemat should he decide to pounce, not putting it past him to attack when I'm most vulnerable.

I dig into my meal like an untamed beast, afraid the Master will reach out and take away my plate for sport, but he doesn't. After awhile, I sense his attention shift back to the others, so I keep my eyes down. The last thing I want to do is spark any excitement from him or his friends, especially when I haven't finished my meal.

It's only when my stomach is full and ready to burst that I risk a glance back at him, surprised at the details I find.

If I thought Warfare was a warrior chiseled with power, Cruelty is a god bred for battle, his physique sculpted from centuries of discipline and training. Not only does his black jacket etched with gold bring out the natural tan of his skin, but it also enhances the cut of his body, every inch of him bristling with brawn.

Although I haven't glimpsed the dazzling blue of his eyes since I sat down, I don't need to stare straight into them to notice the alertness they possess, or the savagery they hold. The only thing darker than his intentions is the short, black tint of his hair — a perfect reflection of the callous, unfeeling heart beating within him.

"Looks like the human has taken a liking to you, Cruelty."

I scan the table for the Master belonging to the honeyed voice, and when I find him, I resist a shiver of disgust. At first glance, he doesn't look anything out of the ordinary. Smooth skin. Strong jaw. Downturned eyes. Sharp nose. Light, wispy hair. With every tilt of his head, however, I find that his features shift, transitioning between young Master and ancient goblin, green flesh and all.

I shake my head, my mind doubting what I'm seeing.

Slowly, I take a sip of my wine, finding it easier to identify the Master based on that fact alone. If my instincts ring true, I'm looking at the Master of Doubt, given this little trick of his.

"She can't seem to take her eyes off you," Doubt continues, gesturing between Cruelty and I, waggling his eyebrows. "Perhaps she'd like to become your plaything." A wicked smile splits his face, followed by the others' howling laughter.

Heat climbs up my neck, and for once, I'm grateful the Amphista's blood covers my skin, hiding my mortification.

"All right, all right," Warfare chuckles, "it's time we discuss more serious things." And just like that he turns to me, the light in his eyes sizzling out. "Even though you were brought here on a deal, you must do housework and provide assistance like the rest of the Flames." I sit up straighter in my chair, preparing for his next words.

"What sort of work do you expect me to do?" I ask, not sure if I truly want an answer.

"Usual maintenance and housekeeping chores. Nothing you can't handle, I'm sure." Warfare winks and raises his glass, expecting me to clink mine against it.

I ignore him and shove my plate to the side, ready to leave.

Manners be cursed, it's been almost an hour since I got here, and I think we can all agree I've overspent my time, even if it was worth my while. I gained quite a bit of leverage during this little soirée, and whether or not the Masters know it, I'm not sure.

Warfare fixed my shoulder. I ate and fueled my body. I uncovered all the Masters' titles — including the two who didn't bother acknowledging me — and cataloged their attributes to memory.

The Master of Addiction, for instance, has a face like autumn, with red hair and smokey eyes, looking more like nature than man. Beside him, the Master of Obedience sits tall with a sleeve of tattoos running down his neck and forearms, his expression impassive, as if bored with this entire ordeal.

Out of all the men in the room, I like these two most. They haven't uttered a single word to me since I arrived, and for that, I'm grateful. I wonder how long their silence will last, with my second Test only a week away. It's only a matter of time before they start rummaging through my head, poking in places they don't belong.

"You will be staying in the Flames Quarter for the duration of your stay," Warfare says, rising from his seat. "Tuesday will be here shortly to escort you to your room. She'll explain the tasks expected from you, and—"

Rap. Rap. Rap.

Three knocks sound from the other side of the dining room door, soft and hesitant. Seconds later, a young woman — tall and slender with hair like midnight — appears.

Tuesday, I assume.

And based on the approval flashing across Warfare's face, she's right on time.

Chapter Nineteen

When Tuesday enters the light of the dining room, I have to hold my breath to keep from gasping. Scars, too many for me to count, course down the sides of her cheeks and neck, leaving only her forehead unmarred. Some of the cuts, still raw and red, leak a clear, pus-like fluid, which suggests the harm must be recent.

Some sick, twisted part of me wants to know how it happened.

It takes about three seconds before I realize those gashes are nothing but child's play compared to the damage done to her left hand. Both her middle and pinky finger have been shaved down to the knuckle, leaving a pink, uneven sore.

"Tuesday will show you to your room and further explain your duties," Warfare says, pushing me toward the stranger. "You better get to it before I lose my patience and tire of your presence." He looks to Tuesday at that, and she dips into a low curtsey, her umber skin bloodless under the chandelier's light.

She nods in agreement, her golden eyes piercing even in their fright.

Don't tell the other workers your name, Warfare speaks to my mind, his words slipping through the crack in my shield. *Names don't mean anything here. If someone asks, you go by Sunday. Every servant has been named after a week or month of the year. Whichever one you are given, that is the only time you are permitted to leave the house. Unless, of course, a Master orders you otherwise.*

Warfare's grin turns savage as he spots my pale expression.

Oh, don't look so surprised, sweetheart.

One day of sunshine a week. One day of freedom. I can't believe I had the nerve to complain about hunting in Tempus — about being in nature for the majority of the day — when here, inside this sky's-forsaken manor, I have nothing but artificial light and muted air.

Prisoners of Airabeth would kill to have what I had. *I* would kill to have what I had, now that I know the alternative. I used to dread my life in the village, but after glimpsing the life I'll have here, my home was like a fairytale.

At least there, I could go outside and do as I pleased. At least there, I had my family.

Warfare crosses his arms and leans a hip against the table, a twitch of a smile shading his mouth. *You're one of the lucky ones*, he says, and even in my head, the glee in his tone is clear. *Imagine the others, who only get to see the light of day for one month of the year. Consider it my gift to you for passing your first Test.*

A hot flame of anger burns a trail through my chest.

Thanks to dinner, my strength is already returning, and along with it, a burst of wild abandon. I'm stronger, faster, than when Warfare forced me out of Tempus. I could fight back. I could flee and get away with it. I could—

"Did I stutter, why are you both still here?" Warfare grabs the girl's arm, as well as my own, and ushers us to the door. He isn't gentle as he drags us along, and as soon as he releases us, I reach for the door's handle, Tuesday right at my heels.

We're halfway into the hallway when Sickness calls. "Is *this* what our relationship has come to?"

Tuesday visibly stiffens as we turn to look at him, and I don't blame her for it. The venom in the Master's voice makes *my* throat close up, and I'm not the one being addressed.

"You come in here without so much as a glance in my direction, and you expect me not to notice?" Sickness turns his nose up and settles back into his chair, eyes glowing with power and animalistic rage. "Are you aiming to avoid me, my dear? Have you forgotten our vows so easily?"

Tuesday opens her mouth to respond, but he waves her off. "You'll pay for your disobedience later tonight," he says, and Tuesday's eyes dim discernibly.

Against my own volition, I start thinking about what her impending consequence might be, if her scarred face and botched hand are any indication . . .

Tuesday turns on her heel and walks down the hallway, so I follow her out, storing my morbid thoughts for another time.

"ARE YOU OKAY?"

I don't look at Tuesday as I ask the question, but ever since Sickness threatened her, her shoulders haven't dropped from her ears.

She doesn't respond to my question right away, and although her silence is expected, it's only natural to console her. Or at least to *act* like I care, which I'm not sure I do. If I never see her beyond today, I won't be bothered by it.

"I'm fine," she answers at last, her voice a low, feminine purr. She doesn't meet my eyes as she speaks, and it's a relief.

I can see why Sickness likes her, though. She's naturally beautiful in an understated way, and although her black dress falls below the knee, I can tell she's all legs. Her hair, long and curly, is tied back in a singular braid, drawing attention to the sharp angles of her face, displaying her scars.

"This way," she says, and motions me down a dark paneled corridor lined with abstract murals. "This is the back entrance to the kitchen. It's better if no one sees you covered in . . ." She pauses, mulling over her words. "Mud." Her gaze sweeps over me quickly, as if looking at my bloodied form is physically painful, before setting her focus straight ahead.

That's when I catch the glimmer in her eyes, the boldness behind her golden irises.

Flame. Her Soul Status is easy to identify. She's definitely a Flame and not a Soulless, but how, after all that's happened to her? How has she managed to keep her soul, her mind, after all the brutality she's had to endure?

"How long have you been here?" I ask, surprised by my own directness. But I need to know the truth. I need to know if surviving Airabeth is possible.

Tuesday smirks. "Long enough to know that the black covering your skin isn't mud. I won't ask about it, as long as you don't ask about my scars," Tuesday says, her fingers drifting to her disfigured face, as if remembering what happened to it. Remorse blooms in my stomach, but I nod nonetheless, agreeing to keep our intrusive questions to ourselves.

When I first entered the manor, I didn't have time to survey my surroundings, but now, as we weave in and out of every hall, I take notice.

An elaborate double staircase with an onyx railing is in the middle of the main floor, leading to each of the seven levels and outdoor balconies. Indoor pools and water fountains sit in pockets of the eastern wing, the chlorine scent a sharp tang in the air. Velvet curtains frame the wall-to-wall windows, leaving no room for privacy. Everyone can see what I'm doing, and I can see them, too. Eyes are everywhere, prying and waiting for someone to attack or lose their soul to the Masters, always on guard.

It's a fact I take into consideration as we enter the kitchen.

The room is broad and bright, but empty of servants, and has a series of glass-door refrigerators lining the back wall, the shelves stacked with food. A group of gas stoves circle the middle of the room, while leftovers from dinner sit in one of the many sinks facing the rear entrance. Water leaks from a hole in the roof, and the bucket below it overflows with yesterday's rain, leaving a muddy puddle for the Flames to clean.

Compared to the rest of the house, the kitchen isn't anything special, but it's better than the one I grew up with.

"The showers are over there," Tuesday says, pointing to a door that must hide the bathroom. "You should freshen up and get some sleep. Busy day tomorrow."

Sleep?

I know Tuesday is trying to be kind, but the idea of sleep makes my scalp itch.

With this constant panic spinning through my head, I don't think calming myself enough to rest is a possibility, but I force a smile all the same.

She doesn't return the sentiment.

Instead, she turns on her heel and leaves without so much as a goodbye.

I'm not sure why I'm offended by it. I just met her. We aren't friends.

Chapter Twenty

Night is thick when I jolt from sleep.

My hand instinctively reaches for the left side of the mattress for the candlestick I keep by my side, but it isn't there. Strange, considering I never move it. I roll to my right and feel for my siblings, anticipating the itch of Elisha's hair, or the smokey scent of Diana's clothes.

I sit up in the dark and listen for Sasha's footsteps, suspecting he's in the kitchen, wandering about. He can't be asleep, he's never asleep — he's too tense for that — yet if he's awake, why can't I hear him—

And then it hits me, the reality of where I am, and where I'm not.

Airabeth, not Tempus. Alone, not accompanied. Captured, not free.

The memories of the past few days come running in like a guest uninvited. I push my damp hair away from my face and recall the last several hours, despising all that it holds, and the weight it's left behind.

The Flames Quarter. That's where I am — where Tuesday took me after I showered.

I'm surprised I fell asleep here. I didn't think I would, given the confines of the layout. Dozens of servant beds lay side by side in rows, separated by nothing but a rod and sheer white sheet. The lack of privacy is off-putting, of course, but I don't have a choice in where I sleep or who I split my quarters with. Although I've grown used to sharing a room with my siblings, none of them talked in their sleep or woke up shrieking from night terrors, like people do here.

Apparently, Airabeth has a way of messing with the mind, even in rest.

Before I left Tempus, I rarely had dreams about death, blood, and slaughter, but last night, they were filled with it all, taunting me even in unconsciousness. The nightmares started with the Amphista's gnashing teeth ripping out my intestines, and ended with my blood mingling with Sasha's, his throat severed from ear to ear.

I rub the crust from my eyes, hoping that if I do it hard enough, the images will fade.

"Good. You're up."

The whispered words sober me, and I leap from my cot, spotting Tuesday at the foot of my bed. It's dim in the Flames Quarter, almost black, so when I peel back the curtain blocking my area from hers, I barely register the outline of her mattress.

Despite the unnatural hour, her sheets are already made, the pillow fluffed and inviting.

"You look different," she murmurs, careful not to wake the others. "Without all that dirt on you, I almost didn't recognize your face."

"What are you doing here?" I ask, my throat raw and dry from stifling my sobs all night.

I slowly move to the head of my cot and put the length of the mattress between us, increasing our distance. It's not that I'm intimidated by Tuesday, I'm not, but I don't know her well enough to be comfortable with her invading my personal space.

"Put this on," she says, and lays a dress similar to hers on the cot.

I turn the uniform over in my hands and inspect the material, hating how wonderful it feels in my hands. The fabric is thick and soft to the touch, the seams tight and without holes, easy to stretch.

Judging by the look of it, it might actually fit me, and that alone is a luxury I haven't had in years.

"We've been called for a job," Tuesday explains as she turns to leave, her voice drifting toward the exit. "Get ready. Quick. We don't want to face the Masters' wrath if we're late."

"A job?" I repeat hoarsely. "What do they want at this hour? And it's not Sunday. I'm not allowed to leave the house—"

"I know," she interrupts, flashing me a dark look over her shoulder. "Today is Tuesday, and I've been called for yard duty. The Sacred Seven want you to help me."

"But I thought—"

"Don't ask questions," she says, and her urgency is strong enough to get my feet moving. "Just do as they ask. Unless, of course, you wish to live the rest of your life without a hand."

WHEN WE MEET WARFARE and Sickness on the front porch, the sun is but a tease on the horizon. Despite the early hour, the heat is oppressive — far worse than any Tempus summer — and I worry I won't be able to endure it, unfit for the conditions. I'm not built to survive Airabeth's environment, or the monsters dwelling within it, but as the two Masters lead us toward our task, I know I must follow, fearing the consequence.

Warfare and Sickness say nothing to us as they stroll ahead, murmuring too softly for me to hear. Tuesday and I lag behind.

I seize our moment of solitude and lean into her. "Do you know why we've been summoned?" I ask.

She shakes her head. "No. I don't," but the heaviness in her eyes states otherwise.

"Where are the other Masters?" I whisper. "Don't they like to hang around together?"

"The Masters do as they please," Tuesday says, her voice barely audible above the slight wind. "Two Masters are always present on Airabeth grounds to keep the land in order, while the others go off to do whatever they need to. I'm not entirely sure what their schedules consist of, but believe me when I say, we don't want to know what the Masters do when they aren't here."

Tuesday goes quiet then, suggesting this topic of discussion is over, so I don't ask about it again. Instead, I address the faint screams echoing across the field, reminding me of that strange latch I found on the ground when I first arrived yesterday.

"That's the punishment box," Tuesday explains, rubbing her arms to ward off a chill that's not coming from the air. "The Masters put servants down there if they fall short of their duties, underperform, or simply do something that pisses them off."

"You ever been down there?" I ask, whispering so the Masters don't hear me.

"A few times," Tuesday says, meeting my gaze. "Everyone goes in the box at some point. It's inevitable. The Masters usually keep servants down there for three days before they send a Soulless to retrieve them. It's not a pleasant experience, but you will survive it, should you have the right will and determination."

I don't respond, terrified of the direction this conversation is heading, and remain quiet for the rest of the walk.

By the time we stop in the middle of the expansive yard, I'm already gasping and sweating. Other than Tuesday and I, the field is empty of servants.

If it weren't for the Masters' faces tarnishing my view, the scenery might've been charming.

"Ladies," Warfare says, his eyes snapping to us with an impossible amount of disdain, "you can start your assignment by picking those up." He points to a pair of shovels lying in the grass.

Tuesday raises a slim brow, showing the confusion I feel.

"There's a dead animal over there," he explains, jutting his head to the right. "We want you to bury it. When you're done, come back to the house so I can assign *you*," he looks to Tuesday, "your next task. Sunday, you will go back to kitchen duty."

I nod, still unsure as to why he wants me to help with this particular assignment. I've hardly been in Airabeth a day, and I'm sure there are other servants who are far more equipped for the job, but I don't complain about it.

Being outside in the sweltering heat is far better than suffering in that abhorrent manor, no matter how large it is. I even prefer the smell of the dead animal — sharp and rancid — over the astringent scent of the Flames Quarter, too clean for comfort.

Having said that, I'm not immune to horrid stenches, so I stuff my nose into the hem of my dress. Warfare catches my movement and reaches out to pull the material down, forcing me to inhale the odor.

"Get to work," he says roughly, his hand lingering on my neckline, peeking down my dress. He breathes deeply before pulling away, eyes sparking with a hunger I've only seen in animals. "I don't want that thing smelling up the entire yard."

And with that, he turns on his heel to leave, expecting Sickness to follow, but he doesn't.

With a glass cup clenched in his hand — the contents filled with black spit and something green — the Master approaches us with polished savagery, too graceful to be harmless. "Try not to get too dirty," he says to Tuesday, his smile unnervingly aloof. "I'd prefer you save all your nastiness for tonight, my dearest." He dips his head to the side, eyes wild as he flicks his tongue against her cheek.

Tuesday stands still throughout it all, silent tears pooling in her eyes.

I step forward, prepared to do whatever it takes to stop this torment, when her stern gaze snaps to mine, a warning flashing between blinks of fear. *Don't intervene*, her expression says. *Please, don't challenge him.*

And perhaps if we were in Tempus, I would've listened, but I've seen that look of desperation before, and I'm tired of watching it go on. If I were Tuesday, I'd want someone to help me, and in Airabeth, the choice between stepping in or stepping aside could cost someone their life.

"If you don't mind," I say quickly, drawing Sickness's hateful eyes to me, "we have a job to finish." I level a flat stare at him, hoping my mask of carelessness is convincing enough to make him leave.

He gives me a weak smile, his mouth dripping with whatever gunk he spits into his cup, and croons, "Of course, little Bunny. Enjoy your day of sunshine. For all we know, it could be your last."

Reluctantly, he steps away from Tuesday, and the trembling in her shoulders ceases, her chest heaving with a quiet sigh. She looks up at him, feigning a smile so brilliant, even I am convinced of her love for him, but Sickness isn't swayed.

He snatches her wrist and twists her toward him, a spark of rage in his eyes. "Aren't you going to give me a kiss goodbye?" he asks, and turns his head to the side, giving her access to his cheek.

Tuesday stares at him a moment too long before standing on tiptoes to give him a quick, emotionless peck. He must sense her aversion, because he returns the sentiment with a rough kiss to her mouth.

"I'll see you after dinner, my fiancée, where I shall meet you in my room." The Master shakes with restraint as he pulls away, visibly hating that he can't have more — *do* more — with her. "You haven't forgotten where it is, have you?"

I'm too rattled to hear Tuesday's response.

Fiancée?

That's what he's holding over her, her hand in matrimony?

Sickness lifts a brow, his smile terrible enough to bring the world to its knees. He winks at me as he passes and descends the hill back to the manor, bidding Tuesday farewell.

She nods and waves back.

Once Sickness is out of earshot, the tears in her eyes fall.

"Emperors above, are you all right?" I ask, cautious of my tone as we walk toward the dead animal. I don't want Tuesday to think I'm pitying her, because I'm not, but I'm also not heartless enough to ignore the fact that she's upset.

"You don't have to keep asking me that, you know." She shoots me a sideways glance, and when I meet it, I expect it to be full of scorn and reproach, but it's not. Instead, she grins, the scars on her face deepening. "Don't feel sorry for me, okay?"

I'm about to tell her that I don't, but she rushes on, not giving me the chance.

"Feel sorry for those who have no vision, no hope or joy for the future. I still have dreams for my life, but those who don't are the ones who are truly suffering."

I stare at her for a moment, trying to gauge if she's telling the truth or putting on a show. For argument's sake, I go with the first, hoping that if she can keep her soul after all she's endured, perhaps I can too.

"I'm sorry about Sickness," I say, and the look Tuesday gives me shows she doesn't want to talk about him.

She responds nonetheless. "I could say the same to you, about Warfare."

My heart beats a little too hard at her words, thinking she knows about my Tests and the deal I made. Then again, she was with me in the dining room, so she saw the way Warfare looked at me. How he made a show of pining for my attention, lusting in a way Sickness does with her.

"Does he force you to do things?" I ask, cracking my knuckles against my palm. "Like, does he ever make you spend the night with him, or . . ."

Tuesday shakes her head, understanding my concern. "No, never. Sickness vows to keep me clean and unmarked until our marriage is official. He says our wedding night will be more special that way." She puts her head down, fiddling with her dress. "I'm safe. For now."

She keeps her stare forward, seemingly done with discussing the topic at hand, so I change it.

"Are you afraid?" I ask. Perhaps a predictable question, but I'm curious about the answer. Tuesday is a Flame, I'm nearly positive about that, but whatever response she gives might be a clue as to how much color her soul has left — if any at all.

She looks toward the tree line, as if imagining what it'd be like to risk her life in the wild rather than stay here, imprisoned with demons far worse than Soul Eaters.

"Yes," she confesses, still staring off into the distance. "I don't want to lose who I am and forget what I stand for. But if I don't marry that goon, he promised to make my family suffer, and you do what you have to do to protect the ones you love."

Her eyes flash to mine then, as if sensing I know how she feels. "Do you think you made the right decision?" she asks, and based on the crease between her brows, her question confuses her just as much as it does me. "About coming here, I mean. I don't know what circumstances brought you here, and I know better than to ask, but you must have had your reasons. Sometimes I wonder if my family and I would've been better off running for the rest of our lives, but then I think that's not really a life at all, so what's the point?" She shakes her head. "I don't know. I always go back and forth with what I should've done."

"You made the decision you thought was best," I say, believing in that more than I'd like. "And deciding is better than making no decision at all. If you don't choose, the Masters choose for you, and if your choice is a mistake, at least you go down on your own merits."

Tuesday's mouth twitches at that, as if ready to smile, or say something back. But her attention is already shifting from me to the task ahead, and the moment she sees the thing we're supposed to bury, her jaw drops. "Emperors above," she gasps, covering her mouth with a hand. "What in the sky's name is that?"

For a heartbeat I think she's overreacting — dead carcasses are nothing new to me, and there's nothing to fear from the dead — but as soon as I glimpse the animal slumped in the grass, I realize it isn't an animal at all.

It's a human.

A spoiled, raw, and mutilated corpse. Just lying there. Rotting minute by minute. Surrounded by flies.

I take a hesitant step closer, the smell so unbearable I have to hold my breath.

I lean in to get a better look, to make sure my eyes aren't playing tricks on me and find that they aren't — I'm seeing just fine. The bile in my stomach turns to tar when the details begin to take form through the rot, showing signs of a young man.

My heart drops to the soles of my feet as I make out the cuff of a brown jacket, the glaze of slate eyes, the slash across a slim throat—

I don't dare utter his name out loud. I don't dare to even *think* it.

But the longer I stare at the corpse, the more I'm convinced that those are his eyes, and that is his jacket, and the cut on his throat — right over his Adam's apple — is exactly where his life bled from him . . .

Sasha. My Sasha.

Grief nearly drops me to my knees, stealing my strength and everything I am.

Even so, I manage to remain upright, forcing myself to see the world through glazed eyes instead of clear ones.

Now is not the time for a public breakdown.

If Tuesday discovers my connection to Sasha, she'll be one step closer to exposing my Tests, and my deal with the Masters will no longer stand. I have no other choice than to mask my misery and steel my heart, but how can I hide the burn in my eyes when the tears won't stop coming? How can I hide the quiver in my lips when all they want to do is scream?

My big brother. Dead. Spoiling. Unrecognizable.

The air is heavy between us. "You know him?" Tuesday asks.

"No," I say, and pitch my voice low to prevent it from shaking. "You?"

All I can do is stare at him, shock stealing my ability to move, to turn away.

Tuesday shakes her head and props a hand on her hip, digging her shovel into the dirt.

"Well," she sighs, bending her knees to lift the soil, "let's hurry and get this over with. I think the poor bastard has suffered enough."

I don't say anything as I copy her movements, wondering how she'd react if she knew that the *poor bastard* she's referring to, is — *was* — my brother.

Chapter Twenty-One

I'm standing in front of a sink, hands raw from hours of scrubbing silverware, when I feel an abrupt tap on my shoulder. I suck in a breath, fingers clenching a knife beneath the dirty dish water, preparing to swing.

Although I have yet to be attacked by a Soulless, I've been waiting for it to happen. Since the kitchen is currently empty of workers, now would be the opportunity to strike. This afternoon, most of the servants are either on break or delivering the Masters' lunch, so the Quarter is a ghost town. A perfect target zone for hunters looking for game.

"A word, Miss Sunday."

The voice that addresses me is deep and smooth, and although I've only heard it in my head, I know who it belongs to.

I glance over my shoulder, fingers tingling around the knife, and glimpse a striking pair of diamond eyes, ever-changing in their emotion.

Blood rushes to my cheeks at the sight of him and I tremble in my effort to not strangle his long, muscled neck. It's been almost one week since I last saw Cruelty, and standing in his presence only reminds me of our previous encounter, which has easily become one of the worst days of my life.

Although my mind still reels from digging Sasha's grave, the idea of binding his spirit to Airabeth has become a far worse torture than the burial itself. With his soul forever caged in this land, he'll never be free of the Masters' torment, and if my big brother —

the most selfless person imaginable — can't find the rest or peace he deserves, none of us will.

It's a thought that turns my stomach to sludge.

I brace a hand on the lip of the sink, savoring its coolness, and try to calm the sickness racing up my gullet, threatening to spill over and stain the cutlery I just washed.

"Are you ill?" Cruelty asks, his body angling away from me, as if fearing I'll vomit all over him.

Now that I think about it, puking on his fine clothes might be the best thing that's happened to me all week.

"I need to speak with you," he says, eyes snapping to the exit door. "In private." And although he doesn't raise his voice, the tone isn't kind. "You've been summoned to do work in another part of the house," he elaborates, and when I don't respond, he moves closer, bringing a chill to my skin.

"I think it'd be wise if you don't pick a fight about this," he says lowly. I have to crane my neck back to peer up at him. "I'd hate to make a scene, wouldn't you?"

My first instinct is to refuse his order, but obeying instructions is part of my deal. I leave when I'm asked. I work when I'm told. Anything less will result in disaster.

I don't say anything as I untie my apron and hang it on the clothes rack, waiting for him to lead the way. He grabs my elbow as we walk, guiding me through the house like I'm being difficult, though I follow easily behind him.

It's only when we turn down a dark hallway, quiet and empty, that he decides to let me go. "You look terrible," he says, and as his eyes sweep over me, there's no mirth behind them. No hint at some greater evil delighting in my misery. "Did you get any sleep?"

I keep my eyes cast down on the carpet. I'm in no mood to learn his antics.

The burial for your brother, Cruelty says, his words echoing in my mind, impossible to dismiss. *It needed to happen. We needed to ensure you'd keep your deal a secret, even under the most stressful of circumstances. You didn't tell Tuesday about your brother, or your arrangement with Warfare, so your family lives to see another day. You should be happy about that.*

I scoff. *Happy.* I've nearly forgotten the meaning of the word.

"Go to hell," is all I say, and though I mean it, my words lack the punch I intended them to have.

Still, I manage to get a reaction out of him, his voice low and bitter as he says, "Take a look around, Flame." He gestures down the hall, toward the darkness beyond us. "Looks like I'm already there."

And if it weren't for the exhaustion obscuring my judgment, I might've thought he was kidding, but his mouth is slack, and his gaze is clear. How could a Master ever despise being in Airabeth, surrounded by his fellow Masters, at the peak of his power?

"We're here," he says, and whatever displeasure I thought I saw is gone, replaced by a callousness I've come to expect.

My heart kicks into overdrive when we halt in front of a large wooden door, the paneling carved from the richest dark spruce I've ever seen.

Cruelty curls a hand around the rusted latch, gesturing for me to enter.

I don't move an inch, unwilling to turn my back on him.

If you don't move now, I'll force you inside. My scalp prickles as his voice fills my head, giving me no choice but to oblige or risk being controlled by him.

I stalk forward silently, greeted by darkness, and prop a hand against the wall, using it as a guide.

I sense the Master at my heels, preventing me from turning back.

It doesn't take long before an array of voices, cackling and rough, come from ahead, not far in the distance. I follow the sound, a crack of light appearing a handful of steps away, welcoming me forward. I step into the opening, blinded by the aggressive glare.

I shield my face to limit the brightness, and slowly, the room starts to take form, revealing the small horror I've stepped into.

Ancient. Beautiful. Terrifying.

Those are the words that come to mind, as I take in the coliseum's concrete walls and matching ceiling, the room uncharacteristically bare in the overhanging lights. I suppose it would be difficult to fill a dungeon such as this, considering its depth and size. The diameter of the floor alone must fill a quarter of the property.

I spin around and study the layout, guessing that whoever created it decided to model it after an arena, which puts me on edge. Red dirt on the ground. Hundreds of seats above the main floor, perfect for an audience.

I don't have time to finish my inspection.

I'm on my knees before I know it, Cruelty's hand shoving me to the ground, sending flares of pain through my spine.

I grit my teeth to keep from grimacing, and glance up to see seven thrones, each differing in color and design, perched atop a dais. The Sacred Seven regard me from that dais, relaxing in their thrones. Imperious as ever.

I lower my head to hide my emotion, a mix of fear and anger, when Warfare breaks the silence. "Look at me." His command is calm but authoritative, leaving no room for refusal.

I stare at my bare knees, taking a moment to collect myself.

How long has it been since my first Test? Five days? Six? Why haven't I been keeping track?

A snarl from Cruelty rumbles behind me, and it's my only warning before he grabs a fistful of my hair and yanks it back, forcing my eyes to the Masters.

"Was that so hard?" Warfare hisses, teeth flashing in the light. He sinks deeper into his chair, legs spread wider than his shoulders, comfortable.

"Welcome to your second Test," he announces, and waves a hand about the dungeon. "The Test of Warfare, designed by yours truly." If I didn't know any better, I'd think he wanted me to pass my first Test just so I could suffer through this one.

Cruelty lets go of my hair and pushes me to the ground, abandoning me for his throne on the dais. He kicks a generous amount of sand into my face as he passes, laughing as I wipe the grit from my eyes and mouth.

"Listen here, sweetheart, because my next words are going to be useful to you." It's hard to concentrate on Warfare's voice as I blink dirt from my stinging eyes, but I manage to pay attention. The future of my family's lives depends on it, I remind myself once again. "Find the key buried in the sand, climb the hill, unlock the chains before The Fryer burns the boy to death, and you win. Ready? Good."

I blink. "Wait, what? I don't understand!"

I rise to my feet and raise my hands in protest, but Warfare ignores me and snaps his fingers, the ground shuddering in response.

A humming sensation shoots from the bottom of my toes to the top of my skull, throwing me off balance. The rumbling — violent and ceaseless — grows and grows, shaking the entire chamber, until a mountain of sand ascends from the ground, sprouting up, up, up toward the high arching ceiling.

I open my mouth in mute horror, unsure if I'm going to scream or vomit — perhaps both.

"I-I don't understand what you expect me to do!" I shout above the chaos, looking to the Masters for an explanation.

Sickness smiles and points to the peak of the hulking mountain, leaning forward in his seat. "Take another look, Bunny."

His gaze travels up, and I follow it, my heart beating so fast I think I'm going to pass out. I bend my head back and squint against the light, unable to see anything beyond the glare.

Then I hear him.

"Help me, please! Hurry!"

A young boy is bound to a platform on top of the mountain, body thrashing against the chains that hold him down.

My limbs tremble at the hysteric cry — at the fact somehow, some way, an innocent sits on the peak of the sand hill, stuck and without aid.

Curse the Sacred Seven! Curse their diabolical ways!

"He's a Flame," Sickness says, joy oozing from every word. "Barely thirteen years old. And if you don't find that key in time. . ."

Attached to the ceiling above him is a large red, burning light, merely inches from the boy—

A horn sounds and The Fryer flashes on, slowly burning the child's small, helpless body.

It will roast him to death. If I don't find the key and unlock his chains, the light will *burn* him, and he'll die, and it'll all be my fault.

"If you save the boy before he goes up in smoke, you win," Warfare says, explaining the Test in more detail. "The Fryer will turn off and on in rising increments until he dies, or . . . you can press this." He flips open a hidden compartment in the armrest of his throne, revealing a blue button the size of my palm. "If you press this button, you automatically win, and the Test will be over."

Too easy. That proposition is too easy, there must be a catch —

"But in return for your decision," he explains, "the light will descend and kill the boy. A life for a life, if you will."

And there it is.

My ultimatum.

The war between doing what's right to save a child I don't even know, or doing what's wrong to save the only people I love.

I stare at the Masters, my feet backing away from them as if I have anywhere else to go.

"You can press it at whatever point you'd like," Warfare says, his fingers caressing the base of the button. "The choice, as always, is yours."

I shake my head, desperately wishing I could refuse to participate in this sick, twisted game. "Oh, and one more thing," the Master chimes in, gesturing to the audience seats, "the crowd can intervene and participate whenever they like."

For a moment I think he's yanking my tail — there's no one here but us — but then the entrance doors to the stands push open, and I realize Warfare isn't messing around.

Reluctantly, as if being pushed by a phantom hand, servants begin to file in, filling up a portion of the stands. They enter through the balcony doors, twelve rows high, and it doesn't take a genius to see something is off with them.

Even from here, I make out the hollowness of their eyes, the tightness in their movements.

All Soulless. All soldiers of the Masters' hateful reign.

"Participate?" I repeat. "What do you mean, participate? Participate how?"

And as if my Test couldn't be any more ridiculous, the audience reaches under their seats.

I nearly cry out when I see what they have:

Crossbows.

Bleeding hell, they're going to shoot me.

"Oh, I'm going to enjoy this." Sickness leans back against his throne, and the others snicker around him. "Let the Flame burn."

Chapter Twenty-Two

I run three steps before I drop to my knees and search for the key, digging furiously in the sand.

Come on, come on, come on! Where is it?

"Please, *hurry*!"

I snap my head up just in time to see the boy twist against his chains, his limbs so small and frail. My throat closes up in panic.

Look away! Stop staring at him. Focus on your task, you fool!

I turn back to the sand, searching with a madness I hope will reward me, though I'm not holding out hope. The sand is too layered, so thick I can't tell if I'm grabbing the key or empty clumps.

Emperors above, how am I supposed to find a small scrap of metal in this expanse of sand?

I filter the sand between my fingers, making sure nothing solid hides within it, but I quickly learn that fastidiousness slows me down. I don't have time to be this thorough.

Panicked tears sting my eyes, and no matter how many times I tell myself to be calm, the fear wins out, amplifying every touch and sound.

From my right, I hear the Masters whisper to each other in a frenzy, laughing as they wager on how long it'll take for me to find the key.

"Ten minutes tops—"

"No way, I say fifteen—"

"Not a chance, she won't even *find* the key before the light burns him to death, that I can guarantee—"

An abrupt horn echoes off the walls, rattling the dungeon.

I don't look up to watch The Fryer flash on, eliciting horrific screams from the boy.

I leave my spot near the entrance and start scouring the outskirts of the arena, hoping the key is within this vicinity.

You're running out of time, a voice within me calls, turning my blood to ice. *The Flame is as good as dead. Dead! His soul will be gone, and he'll live in Airabeth for the rest of his life. Sound familiar? You couldn't save Sasha. What makes you think you can save the Flame?*

I close my eyes to shut out the image of my brother's rotten, lifeless corpse.

This won't be like last time. I won't let it be like last time.

The Fryer flashes off, giving the boy a reprieve.

I'm still combing through the sand, my hands slick with sweat and hopelessness, when a cluster of shadows emerges out of the corner of my eye — gray and wistful, but undeniably real.

This way. Come this way, child, they speak, their formless shapes surging toward me. I tell myself not to look at them, to just keep digging, digging, digging, but they're too close to ignore, my skin itching in their presence.

Press the button, and all of this will be over, they say, their voices ancient and howling, filled with centuries of wisdom. *You couldn't save your brother, little girl, but you can save the others. All it takes is one gentle press. . .*

My hands cramp beneath the sand, my bones locking as the shadows wrap around me, crippling my limbs. I use all my strength to pry myself free, to keep searching for the key, but my fingers won't move, as if caught by some unexplainable force.

It's right there, child, move toward it. Press the button, and all this pain will end.

I ignore them, but the shadows roam closer, snaking themselves around my wrists and forearms, traveling all the way up my shoulders. They start twisting tighter around my hands, splaying my fingers wide.

A bone pops in my thumb, and I scream, choking on the sound.

I fall forward on my elbows, begging the phantoms to stop this sick game, but my pleas fall on deaf ears. They use their sorcery to bend my fingers in directions they should never go, snapping them in two.

Another scream bursts from my throat as my hands go numb. I go into shock as my forearms begin to curve forward on their own accord — twisting, snapping, shattering below the elbow. . .

"What are you doing?!"

The young Flame bellows from the mountain, his hysteria so fervent it drags me from my daze — from the horror done to my crooked, misshapen limbs — which I realize aren't misshapen at all.

I glance down at my forearms, noting they're perfectly intact, and tug my palms from the sand, my fingers moving freely and without struggle.

No pain, no resistance.

What the bleeding hell is going on?

I turn back to the shadows, but they're no longer there, the chamber as empty as it was when I first arrived. My knees buckle at the thought of the hallucination, at the stronghold the Master of Warfare must've put in my mind.

"Keep digging!" the boy yells, and when I look up the mountain, I spot the top half of his head peering over the edge, only his eyes visible.

"Don't worry," I shout to him, my mind slow to recover from the shadows' delusion. "I'm coming. I just need to find the—"

An unexpected pain blasts through my arm and knocks me to the side, replacing my words with curses. The Sacred Seven cheer and laugh at my suffering, Sickness being the rowdiest of them all.

My heart drops like a stone when I inspect the injury to my bicep, the muscle bleeding from the arrow bolt lodged clean through it. I look to the audience to seek the servant who struck me. I find him instantly — a tall, plump man with a sagging belly and blank eyes, aiming his bow at my head.

I call him out, using language my mother would shun me for, but he doesn't react. Instead, he averts his gaze to reload his weapon.

I'm already running around the mountain, using it as a shield, before he can fire.

Blocked from the audience's view, I take the opportunity to yank the bolt from my arm, whimpering as the sharp edge breaks through sinew, causing blood to spurt. The only good thing about these bolts is that they don't seem to hit as deep as traditional hunting arrows, sticking just beneath the skin. Not exactly a mercy, but I'll take whatever leniency the Masters provide.

I sag against the mountain and breathe through the pain, thinking up a plan.

The arena is massive, overwhelming.

It could take hours to find the key, and with the servants shooting me down whenever they want, I don't know if I'm capable of —

I stop my negative train of thought.

I have to keep trying, this can't be the end for us.

I run back around the mountain, not caring if I get hit by a bolt, until one launches into my upper thigh and brings me to my knees.

I try to stand to shake out the pain, but my legs refuse to hold my weight.

I glance to the stands to tell my attacker to piss off, but when I see who's pointing their bow at me, it's a face I recognize.

Tuesday's weapon is raised to eye level, her scarred fingers strong and certain over the string.

I don't have time to blink before she releases it.

No, Tuesday, stop!

I squeeze my eyes shut and brace for impact, but when the hurt doesn't come, I peek through my lids to find the bolt buried at my feet.

Three steps short of hitting me.

Missed.

She missed, and I thank the sky's for averting her target, leaving me unharmed.

Tuesday looks hard into my face, her features unmoving, like she's never seen me before. But instead of gazing through detached eyes like the Soulless, there's an awareness to her, a liveliness that surprises me.

And then, the unthinkable happens.

Her mouth twitches — a shade of a smile — before it returns to that straight, emotionless line.

"Oh, come on, you can do better than that, honey! *Do as I taught you*!" Sickness roars from his spot on the dais, his face feral as he leans forward in his throne.

Tuesday missed me on purpose, I'm sure of it. But why, when Sickness is less than ten feet away from her? Why is she protecting me, only to risk getting caught?

I don't have time to question her motives. Not as she glances past the Sacred Seven, toward the corner of the room.

Is that where the key is? I want to ask her. But how could she know such a thing?

She flicks her eyes to the corner again — the only assurance I need — and gives me the smallest nod humanly possible.

I sprint to the spot, my breath a flame in my throat as I fall to the ground, digging where Tuesday told me to. I find nothing at first — nothing but handfuls of sand and despair.

This is the end. I failed. We're not going to make it. We're not —

Something solid and cold knocks against my fingers, breathing hope back into my lungs.

Too good to be real. This is too good to be real. It must be a trick. But even if that's true, I withdraw my hand and open my palm, heart catching when I see a silver key resting atop it, the metal sparkling under the light.

Holy hell, I can't believe it!

"Shoot her!" the Master of Sickness screams, but I'm already running before any of the servants have time to hit me. I place the key inside the pocket of my dress, my thighs aching as I sprint toward the mountain.

"Hang on," I yell up to the boy, the Fryer on once again, causing steam to rise from his body. "I'm coming! I'm — *oof*."

More bolts, too many for me to count, come pouring down on me in a river of silver, their heads nailing me in my sides and upper back, blood gushing from the wounds. I drop to all fours and crawl around the mountain, wondering how I'm going to get up it without—

Another bolt connects with the outer part of my knee, and I go lightheaded, my thoughts blanking. I rip out the metal tip to limit the pain and almost lose myself completely, my vision blackening at the edges.

I sit up and am about to toss the bolt to the side when I glimpse my blood dripping down the wood. I squint uncertainly at the sight, watching as my blood shifts in color, alternating between red and purple, then back again — a shimmering mirage of sparkling fluid.

I lift the bolt to get a better look, positive I'm hallucinating again.

But when I reach out to smear the strange liquid on my fingertips, it stays put, proving its existence. How are these bolts turning my blood a different color? I rack my brain, searching for answers that aren't there. How, when the material is made out of nothing more than metal and wood?

As soon as I think the questions, a solution comes.

The Masters must've laced the bolts with power, like they did for my first Test. Without the ammunition Warfare provided, I never would've been able to defeat the Amphista, and although the Tests are hard, they're designed to be passable.

There must be a way to get up the mountain, but it's my job to find it, and looking at the bolts now, I think I have. I have no clue how the Masters expect me to use them, or if my ridiculous idea is going to work, but I have to try. It's the only thing I can do.

I stab the bolt's tip into the mountain, and to my disbelief, the sand clings around it, cementing into place. I pull down on the hilt to check its strength, and when it doesn't budge, I spear a second one beside it, creating a foot support.

Repeating the action five feet above, I construct hand grips as well — planning to use the bolts as makeshift climbing holds.

My breath is an erratic mess of panting and whispered prayers as I step onto the first two bolts, beginning my scale up the mountain. As a child, I was never labeled as adventurous or daring — those titles belonged to my brothers — but now I wish I had been. Perhaps if I climbed more trees, or jumped across rooftops, I'd be less afraid of heights or the prospect of falling.

With all of the bolts lodged in my flesh, I have plenty of material to make new handholds and footholds as I go, but that doesn't mean I won't bleed out by the time I reach the end. I scream whenever I have to remove a bolt from my body, but each cry means I'm one step closer to the Flame, so I try to revel in it.

My arms tremble so much I can scarcely keep my grip on the hilts, and for one terrible moment, I doubt my ability to make it to the top. I'm injured. Weak. Bleeding out. If I lose my grasp on one of these bolts, the boy under the Fryer won't be the only one dying in this chamber today.

"You're running out of time," Warfare shouts, but beneath his warning, I detect a sliver of worry.

I must be close to the top.

I dare a look overhead, doing the very thing I told myself *not* to do when I first started this ascent, and find I'm a foot away from the mountain's crest. I reach for it, my fingers aching as they grip the platform's ledge.

Breathing hard, I yank myself over the lip and roll onto my back. I can hardly suck down air fast enough, but one look at the burning, blubbering boy has me moving again.

Bleeding hell, it's hotter than hell up here. I hold back my cries as I see the hot, bubbling welts on the boy's skin. His eyes are so red, they look like they're bleeding.

I fumble the key from my dress pocket and turn to the Flame's chains, cursing when I see what I'm up against.

Three dozen locks tie him to the metal slab, and only one will release the boy from captivity.

How in the sky's name am I supposed to know which lock that is?

Try. You have to keep trying.

With little time to spare, I start jamming the key into every outlet, my hands shaking. "I'm going to get you out. Don't worry." I try to keep the boy calm, but when I glance into his brown eyes, a wave of terror shines through.

My hands move quickly over the locks, but after hammering the key into multiple outlets, I start to panic, forgetting which ones I've checked, and the ones I haven't.

There are too many possibilities. Too many fears. Not enough time. The back of my neck begins to bleed under the searing light, my entire backside erupting in welts. I'm going to melt away on this mountain with a child I promised to free.

I start to feel dizzy, my hands swelling under the unbearable heat, when three bolts, one after another, land in the dirt at my feet, side by side. I look up through the glare of the light and find Tuesday with her bow aimed in my direction, pointing down at the three arrows.

Three arrows.

Three.

Is she trying to tell me the third lock will free the boy?

My rationalization doesn't seem sound, but I'm hurting, desperate, afraid. I'll take advice from anything, even my own fantasies, if it gives me a chance at passing this Test.

One. Two. Three. . .

I continue down the locks, and when I land on the third one, I insert the key and turn it to the left.

This is my last chance. This has to be it. It has to.

I suck in a breath when the lock doesn't resist, clicking open. The chains fall loose around the boy. I let out a short, delirious laugh at the small miracle, marveling at the improbability of it all.

It worked.

The Fryer blares hotter above me, burning the skin off my back, and I reach a hand toward the Flame, untangling his limbs from the rusting chains. He swears as the light melts the skin off his face, but I'm too busy trying to free him to inspect the extent of the damage.

Will he be blind after this Test? Will he ever look the same? Will his injuries be repairable?

My arms ache as I pull the Flame to me, momentum sending us both falling back and away from the platform, mere inches from tumbling off the mountain's edge. We both sit up, and for a moment, the only sounds that fill the air are our loud, ragged breaths.

And then, quicker than I can follow, The Fryer turns off, darkening the arena.

I close my eyes and try to gain some semblance of calm, my heart pounding so hard my ears ring.

Bleeding hell. We did it. It's over. We're alive.

The mountain rumbles, sinking slowly beneath us, until it returns to ground level, the tightness in my chest loosening once I'm back on solid footing. I turn to the Flame, wanting to know if he's all right, but he's already stumbling for the exit, no doubt rushing to find someone to help repair his horrific wounds.

The Masters let him go, and I'm thankful for it.

My entire body quivers as the Masters descend from the dais, their faces drawn and unreadable. "You're expected to be in the kitchen by five tomorrow morning" is all Warfare says, turning for the exit.

I open my mouth to say something, perhaps a clever retort, but my mind is full of fog. I can't think beyond the beating in my ears, or the incessant urge to cry, despite my victory. My back throbs, the skin between my shoulder blades melting, fusing to my dress.

I got lucky today, and luck like that won't come again, especially as my trials get harder.

Emperors above, I'm such a bloody fool.

A fool for taking the Tests.

A fool for believing I could win.

A fool for thinking I could beat the odds and save my family.

Chapter Twenty-Three

That night, I couldn't sleep. I can't sit, can't stand, can't lie down. Every position is painful, every breath like a knife to my lungs. I tell myself this discomfort is temporary, that the hurt won't last forever, but deep down, I fear I won't make it through to morning.

My wounds from The Fryer and arrows are getting serious, becoming more and more infected as the hours drag on. I was so exhausted after my Test, I didn't bother cleaning them, thinking they'd heal on their own.

I reposition myself on the rock-hard cot and stifle a groan, but Emperors above, if this level of agony keeps up, sleep is never going to find me. I have to do something about this. I have to find a way to get some rest, or I won't survive till morning.

I roll out of bed and tiptoe into the Flames' kitchen.

The other workers won't be up for a few hours yet, and while the privacy is welcomed, the quiet leaves space for all my fears to come creeping in, spoiling my headspace. Normally, distractions from my usual thoughts are appreciated, but the possibility of losing a limb to gangrene isn't the diversion I had in mind.

Warfare made sure that if I passed his test, it wouldn't be without consequence. Now, as I walk to the medicine cabinet at an agonizing pace, I'm not sure my victory was a victory at all.

Perhaps this torment, this anticipation for more pain, is far worse than if I lose the Tests outright. I can barely move, barely breathe without screaming, and it's only going to get worse. I'm sure of it.

How am I supposed to recover by my third Test? I hide my face in my hands, wishing for an answer. How am I going to make it through the next hour? How am I supposed to endure this pain for five more trials?

"You look like death warmed over."

If I weren't so dull from fever, I might've startled at Tuesday's presence, but I'm in too much pain. Besides, I'm getting used to her sneaking up on me.

"I came to see how you're doing," she says, her face half hidden in darkness. "I heard you rustling throughout the night. Couldn't sleep?"

Despite my ginger steps, the wounds in my side pull as I meet her by the window, the only source of light this time of night. "I didn't know anyone else was up," I say, my voice weaker than I'd like it to be, though I don't think she notices.

I lean a shoulder against the wall for support, grateful for its coolness.

"It's hard not to be awakened by all that self-loathing of yours," Tuesday says, cracking a smile. I don't return the sentiment. Every ounce of my energy is being used to stay standing, and anything more will result in fainting. "Your cuts, how are they doing?" she presses, the air between us thickening.

"Fine," I say, though it's getting harder to keep my eyes open. "Just restless, is all."

Tuesday makes a sound in the back of her throat, a sort of disapproving *tsk*, before leaving to grab two chairs from the kitchen closet. She gives me a hard look, one I imagine a mother would give her troublesome child, and gestures for me to sit.

"Infection will set in if you don't take care of those gashes and burns," she says, gathering medical supplies from a corner cabinet.

What I don't tell her is that infection already *has* set in, because I don't need her telling me what I already know. I have a good chance of going into septic shock, and without medical intervention, I could die on this very floor.

Tuesday sits in the chair across from me — her hands quick and efficient despite the damage done to them — and spreads a roll of gauze, scissors, thread, a needle, and rubbing alcohol on the counter beside us.

"Why are you doing this?" I ask, then blush at my shamelessness.

It's been a while since I've confronted anyone who isn't blood related, but given that Tuesday has seen more of me than anyone else in Airabeth, I like to think she's become more than an acquaintance.

"Is it so hard to believe I want to help you out of the goodness of my heart?" she asks, her mouth splitting into a fake, saccharine smile. She lifts a dark brow, as if hinting at a joke, but I don't get the punchline.

She sighs when I don't reciprocate her amusement, folding her arms across her chest. The scars on her face become more vivid as she leans forward in her chair, drawing closer to the light.

"You seem determined. More so than most," she whispers, but since we're alone, her voice is strikingly loud. "I don't want to see that light crushed because of a few fixable wounds. I don't want the Masters to win. And judging by how much they despise you, I think you have something they want. Why wouldn't I help someone who fights for the same things I do? We both want the same thing. We both want to get out of here alive, with our souls. It'll be easier if we do it together."

I have an instinct to look over my shoulder, to make sure a Master or Soulless isn't spying on us, but the urgency in Tuesday's eyes keeps me still.

And perhaps it's the fire in her gaze, the determination in her voice, that makes me do the very thing I told myself I wouldn't when we first met:

I trust her.

AN HOUR PASSES, AND Tuesday's hands are still at work.

She threads my wounds one at a time, scolding me for squirming away from her touch, though it's difficult to stay seated. More often than not, it feels like she's doing more damage than repair, each pass of the needle and thread biting through my skin.

I tell myself not to whine and grumble, despite my urge to. For a while, the self-talk works, distracting me from the pain. But as Tuesday nurses my wounds one by one, we eventually reach the injuries on my back, which are the worst of the lot. She presses a cold compress to the burns, covering them with some sort of jelly, before layering each one with bandages.

When I ask her how they look, she doesn't tell me, but I know my flesh is raw, red, and seeping. I cower through most of the sewing, then look to Tuesday's own scars as a reminder of what true pain must feel like. She's endured much worse, for much longer than I have, and she hasn't once complained about it. Not ever.

It makes me want to do the same.

"Thanks for doing this," I say, and even though I mean it, the words come out lame. Besides my family, no one has gone out of their way to look out for me, so I don't know how to express gratitude to someone outside of my kin.

Sasha used to say friends were a liability — a burden we couldn't trust — and I always believed him, agreeing with his philosophy. It's no secret Soulless are known to befriend Flames only to turn them over to Airabeth, so we didn't bother meeting new people. We had each other. That was enough.

And yet, with Tuesday . . .

If she wanted me gone, she would've let me die at my second Test. She wouldn't have told me where the key was, and she certainly wouldn't be helping me now. Perhaps Sasha was wrong about letting people in. Not everyone we meet is out to harm us, and even if they are, there *are* people worth suffering for. We just have to find them.

Tuesday doesn't flinch as she sews a slash on my shoulder, her gaze filling with an emotion I can't decipher. She pours alcohol onto a gray cloth and brings it to the open cut.

I jump away from her as soon as it hits my flesh, the sting so harsh, it makes me hiss.

She pulls me back to finish the job, removing dirt from the infected wound.

"How did you do it?" I pant, watching as she bandages the marble-sized hole. "At my Test. You knew where the key was and which lock would free the boy. How?"

She doesn't look at me as she speaks, concentrating on stitching up my wound. "Being with Sickness does have its advantages, girl." She turns her head to look over a shoulder — a habit I understand all too well — before turning back to me, her mouth barely moving as she speaks. "A few days ago, I heard him talking with Warfare while I pretended to be asleep in the next room. I wasn't going to tell you about it, so don't go thinking I help Flames freely, especially those stupid enough to take the Tests." She smiles softly. "But watching you fight in that arena, running like you actually had a chance at winning . . ." She releases a long breath. "What can I say? You inspired me." She shakes her head, looking over her shoulder again. "We shouldn't waste our breath talking about these things. If Sickness figures out what I did for you, he'll —"

Our discussion is broken by a creak at the door.

Tuesday's hands pause mid-stitch. I stop breathing, afraid to make any noise.

We stare wide eyed at the kitchen entrance, watching as a dark silhouette steps through the threshold, filling the doorway.

"For sky's sake, D!" Tuesday whispers, her words clipped with an anger that makes the intruder balk. "You scared the bloody hell out of me!"

"My apologies," he answers, his voice warm and nurturing, uncommonly kind. "I didn't know you were in here. And with company, no less." The stranger, fair-skinned and beautiful, gives Tuesday a clever grin that brings a blush to her cheeks.

I've never seen this man — D, Tuesday called him — around the kitchen before, though I suppose his muscular stature has a better use than cooking and cleaning. He must work in the yard or do some sort of manual labor. He has the calloused hands to show for it.

He uses those very hands to reach for Tuesday, then pauses, shoving them in his pant pockets. He turns to me after, as if remembering my presence, but averts his gaze. For a moment, I'm embarrassed — am I truly that unsightly? — before realizing my uniform is on the floor.

My face burns, and I wrap my arms around myself, cursing the burns on my back. If it weren't for these ridiculous injuries, I wouldn't have been forced to undress so Tuesday could repair them, but alas, I've been stripped to my underclothes.

"Sunday, this is December. December, Sunday." Tuesday introduces us and returns her attention to my shoulder, the tension in the room mounting as she deliberately avoids D's gaze.

"It's a pleasure," December says, and extends a hand in my direction. I take it, his palm enveloping mine as he adds, "I prefer if you call me, D, though." He doesn't explain why, and I don't ask. The fact that he averts his gaze from my exposed flesh shows he isn't a sleaze, and for now, that's enough. I don't need to know anything more about him, even though I'm tempted.

December. He has a month's name. He only gets to go outside for one month out of the year. I wonder what he's done, what his mind is like, to receive so little from the Masters.

Once the last of my wounds are fully bandaged, I throw on my dress and thank Tuesday for helping me. After I'm clothed, she tells D he can turn back around. When he does, his shoulders stiffen, as if struck by the golden eyes staring back at him.

Tuesday sucks in a breath herself, her fingers twitching as she hunts for something to say.

They stand like this for a while, just staring and longing and completely enthralled with one another.

It takes me three seconds too long before I realize I should leave and give them some privacy. They clearly want to be alone, and while I don't know their history, it'd take an earthworm not to see they're romantically connected.

"I'm going to take a walk," I say, and hurry to the exit door. "It was nice meeting you," I say to D, and he returns the sentiment, not taking his eyes off Tuesday.

A smile tugs at the corner of my mouth but fades just as quickly.

I'm happy for Tuesday, I really am. She deserves to be cared for, to be loved beyond imagination. But what about Sickness? How does she plan on marrying Sickness if her heart already belongs to someone else?

THE HALLS ARE RELATIVELY quiet as I wander through the house, traveling aimlessly to distract from the pain of my stitches. Every so often, I come across other servants walking about, displaying the same stress and exhaustion I feel, struggling to find rest. We don't look at each other as we pass, not wanting to break the silence of the corridor.

With every corner I turn, I can't help but ball my hands into fists, expecting a Master to emerge from the shadows, but they never do. The tightness in my limbs pulls at my stitches, so at some point I relax a little, needing the relief.

Although my wounds are clean and bandaged, moving is an effort. I should be in bed, seeking at least an hour's sleep before the sun comes up, but my mind is buzzing, itching with restless thoughts.

It's too dark to fully see where I'm going, but I don't dare switch on a light. Drawing attention to myself is the last thing I want, especially after what I've heard this past week. Each night, the Flames Quarter fills with screams of the innocent, drawn out by Soulless who torment those who have yet to surrender to the Masters, pushing them into despair.

Every time I hear it, I sob into my pillow. Every time I hear it, I don't intervene.

When did I become such a coward?

"Ow, careful!"

I slam a hand to my chest, my heart beating so hard, I almost miss where the voice comes from — to the left of the main foyer.

"It bleeding hurts!" the voice pleas, growing louder the closer I come to it.

"You're going to be fine," says a second voice, clearer and deeper than the first. "One more, then we're done, okay?"

I follow the sound, circling down a hallway lit by candles. I stop at a door standing ajar, the glow from within pooling onto the floor, illuminating my bare, blistered feet. I tilt my head to see through the crack, the swells of conversation flowing over me.

I might've thought the whispered chatter to be lighthearted — joyful, even — if I hadn't stepped closer to see who it belongs to.

I inhale a sharp breath, pulling a stitch near my stomach. I grunt and press down on the bandage to keep blood from spilling out, but it's too late. My dress darkens, red leaking through the fabric.

I turn to run, needing to get out of here before someone sees me. I hesitate when shadows shift along the floor, approaching.

Caught! They've seen me, leave, go! No. Wait. Stay. They know I'm here. I should stay and ask them—

The door springs open and my heart kicks into a gallop.

Cruelty stares down at me, his shoulders back. Not an inch of him disarranged.

"You," I say, my limbs trembling so bad, I know he must see it.

"You," he echoes, regarding me with a small smile.

I spread my toes into the floor, holding my ground, and glance over his shoulder.

The young Flame from my second Test stares back at me, sitting on the edge of a bed inside the room. He gives a small, lighthearted wave — the action so easy and casual, you'd think he wanted to be here. With Cruelty. Alone. Unprotected.

But that's not the most alarming thing about this scene. The boy's burns. . . they're better. Not entirely healed or smoothed over, but the welts and melted skin along his cheeks and forearms appear dry and pink, not at all like the red, bubbling blisters I saw hours ago.

My instincts roar at me to do something, to remove the boy from this room.

The Master leans a shoulder against the door frame, blocking the Flame from view. "Why are you here?" he asks, his voice edged with a sharpness that makes me retreat a step.

I open my mouth to respond, twisting to move around him and get to the boy, when a stitch near my hip rips apart, stealing my words. I bend over with a gasp, my hands splayed on my knees.

Pain captures my limbs, stealing my strength.

I sink to the floor with excruciating slowness, embarrassed by my inability to stand. Hands reach for me, but I push them away. A stupid decision, considering the damage those hands can do if I offend him.

I need to get back to the Flames Quarter. I need to get away from here, from *him* —

"You need to come inside," Cruelty says, reaching for me a second time.

I shuffle away, remembering how brutal he was when he brought me to my Test. I don't want him touching me again.

"Get away from me," I say, my tongue heavy and slow. "I'm fine. I need to get back to the kitchen." I don't know if I say the words out loud or in my head, but Cruelty lifts me into his arms, whispering something intelligible.

I go to fight him off, to tell him to put me down, but I'm tired — so damn tired, that the world blurs, taking me into a darkness I fear I'll never wake from.

It's a small pardon, perhaps, given the torment I'll face if I survive till morning.

Chapter Twenty-Four

Hands touch me, gentle yet familiar. Soothing. They brush the hair away from my face, cooling my forehead with a wet cloth, extinguishing my fever. A deep voice, calm and commanding, calls to me. Screams to me. Or maybe it only sounds that way in my head.

"Nadia, I need you to open your eyes."

Cruelty. He's here. Holding me. Calming me.

I'm too consumed by pain to be afraid.

My body, every inch of it, feels like it's on fire, burning everything from the inside out. I try to open my eyes, but my lids are heavy — so heavy, it's like they're being weighed down by boulders.

Panic swells, hot and incessant.

Where am I? What is Cruelty doing to me? Why can't I move?

A bolt of pain surges behind my eyes, and with it, a memory.

Key. Mountain. Chains. Arrows. I can't get away from them. I can't—

"Open your eyes," Cruelty repeats, his voice my only anchor to the present. "If you want to live, you must wake up. It's the only way you're going to get better."

Although I'm not entirely sure I want to live through this pain, I do as he says.

Slowly, his face comes into view, beautiful and deadly. His features form a placid expression, neither kind nor vicious.

True fear unspools in my stomach as I sink back into the mattress.

A mattress, I realize, that isn't my own.

Though lovely, Cruelty's bedroom is not what I would expect.

Besides an empty bookcase and a small worktable in the back corner, the space is wholly bare. No plush rugs or chandeliers, jewels or ancient portraits, couches or arching windows. Even the walls — a pale blue with chipping paint — are plain and without adornments.

Strange to think that a Master, born and raised in riches, considers *this* to be his home away from home.

And the smell — Emperors above, what is that smell?

A mixture of lemon and something chemical hangs in the air, too sharp to inhale. I hold my breath for a moment. Then I notice the medical supplies scattered across the bedside table, an open bottle of antiseptic and alcohol being the source of the smell.

If I didn't know any better, I'd think these supplies were meant to help me. Cure me. Given Cruelty's reputation, it's more likely they're to be wielded as torture tools.

I start to fling my legs off the edge of the bed, needing to get far away from here.

"I wouldn't try that," Cruelty says, and the moment I shift to my side, pain captures my bones, stalling my movements.

I grunt into the hem of my dress and ease back onto the bed — *his* bed — and wait for the hurt to pass. My vision swims, the world tilting on its side. It doesn't stop me from noticing the back door or how it's propped open.

If I can get there quickly enough, I could slip through it.

"I-I need to get back to the kitchen," I say, hoping he'll let me go. I'm terrified by how weak I am. I don't stand a chance of getting out of here on my own, especially if it comes to a fight.

"I'm not finished mending your wounds," Cruelty says, his face rippling, going in and out of focus.

I don't know why my stitches didn't hold, or how they broke so easily — Tuesday said she was good at mending injuries — but maybe mine were too far gone, beyond the point of repair. Maybe whatever poison was on the bolts dissolved the stitches.

It doesn't matter in the end. I can't stay here. I need to leave.

"You can leave if you want," Cruelty says, plucking the thoughts from my mind, wielding them like a sword. "The door is cracked open for a reason. I won't stop you if you go." He stares at me for a moment too long, his eyes darkening.

I straighten a little, gaze narrowing. "I have a hard time believing you won't run after me." Not that I'm in any shape *to* run. Crawl, maybe. But my current capabilities end there.

Cruelty smiles slowly, disrupting the natural rhythm of my heart. "Lucky for you, I'm not the running type."

His athletic build would suggest otherwise.

"I don't believe you," I say, so sick from my wounds, I've lost all sensibility.

Shut up, Nadia. Stop provoking him!

Cruelty raises a defined brow, his skin radiating gilded light. "Then leave," he says, stepping back from the bed. "Leave and see what happens." He goes to his desk and sits on the edge, giving me more than enough space to escape. A test, to see what I'll do.

I'm not dumb enough to take the bait.

"How long do you think it will take for your wounds to fully heal without my intervention?" he asks, crossing his legs at the ankles. "A day? A week? A month? Would you even last that long?"

As if it matters.

Cruelty says he'll help me, but at what cost? What does he expect in return?

"If you truly wanted to heal me, couldn't you just. . ." I gesture at him, searching for the right words. "I don't know, use your power?"

He laughs, the sound vibrating in my chest. "I may be a Master, but I am not a god. I don't have the power to heal."

I narrow my gaze, practically sneering as I say, "So you just have the power to invade minds and magically summon things from thin air? Is that it?"

He nods slowly, pursing his lips. "Pretty much, yeah."

His good humor does nothing to make me feel safer. I dig my nails into my thighs, trying to remain calm. "I want to leave."

Cruelty leans away from the table and cocks his head to the side — a purely animal motion. "Forgive me for being ignorant, but I just want to make sure I'm understanding. You *don't* want me to save your life?" He says it so quietly, I shiver.

"No," I spit, my vision spinning once again. "Not when I know there's a price attached to it. Leaving me hurt would only help your cause. I won't be able to pass my Tests in this state, so why not keep me this way? What's in it for you?"

Cruelty shrugs, taking a few easy steps toward the bed. "You don't see me questioning you about your motives, do you? Why not show me the same courtesy?"

"No," I repeat, and rest my head against the wall, closing my eyes.

Sky's, I'm tired.

"All right," I hear him say, clasping his hands together, "if you want to let your pride get in the way of living, that's your decision." I hear him pace around the room, his footsteps light as a panther's.

His silence doesn't last beyond a few minutes.

"Is this what you really want?" he whispers, his tone unusually soft. "To die?"

My eyes open at his assumption, and I wish I had something to throw at him.

"That's not what I want," I whisper. "That's what *you* want."

A soft, low chuckle. "You have no idea what I want."

I tense at the fierceness in his gaze, the stillness with which he holds himself. If my vision wasn't dancing, I might've mistaken his quiet intensity for dread.

"The bolts you were hit with," he says, scanning my ruptured stitches, "they were laced with a small dose of poison. Enough to kill you slowly if you didn't receive proper treatment." His usual hostility is gone, replaced by a frankness that surprises me. "Do you know how long you've been out?"

At my prolonged silence, he answers. "Six days. And it will be longer, if you don't get the help you need."

Six days? He must be lying. But if he isn't. . .

"And what is the price for saving my life?" I ask.

Cruelty's mouth tightens into a thin line, his gaze like a brand upon my skin. "I need help organizing some things. It's going to take all day, so you'll be working with me, instead of in the Flames Quarter. I'll need your assistance immediately following your recovery." He peels his eyes from mine to adjust the cuff of his sleeve — a sleeve that doesn't need any adjusting at all. "One day of your help, that's all I ask. You give me one day, Flame, and I will save your life. Sound fair?"

I start trembling again, my heart rejecting the idea of accepting his help. But as I glance down at my dress — wet and sticky from the blood still leaking through it — I know he's right.

I'm dying.

As much as Tuesday tried to help, no one has the cure for my injuries. No one except Cruelty, apparently.

And even if I did ask other servants for aid, they'd all turn a blind eye. Everyone is looking out for themselves — their families. I'd be nothing but a hindrance.

Elisha would push away his pride and risk the Master's price if it meant saving me. My sister would too. As cruel as she can be, she'd risk her life for me. I have to believe that.

"Okay," I say, struggling to sit upright. "You win. In exchange for your help, I agree to provide my services to you for one day, and that's it. Nothing more."

I try not to imagine all the terrible things he could make me do in a single day, but after one week of hardship, what's another twenty-four hours?

"Agreed," the Master says briskly, and with that, he grabs my arm, moving faster than I can follow. He presses something sharp into my bicep — a needle — and there's a harrowing pain followed by a blast of white flaring across my vision.

Cruelty is close, so close I can feel the heat of his body, the curve of his hip. "I know it hurts," he says. He opens the bottom drawer of his dresser, pulls out a clean rag. "Here, bite on this," he says, handing it to me. "Count to ten, then it'll be over."

I stick the rag in my mouth and close my eyes, teeth digging into the cloth. The muffled screams that escape me nearly jolt my bones from their sockets. Every second is an eternity, bleeding me dry of the sanity I try so desperately to keep.

I do as Cruelty says and start counting, focusing on the numbers.

One. Two. Three. Four . . .

Another spark of lighting shoots through my blood.

Seven. Eight.

I don't think I can take any more of it.

Nine.

My eyes droop, blackness staining the edges.

Ten.

When I open my eyes, Cruelty is already bandaging my injected arm, fast at work. "The serum will eat the poison in less than five minutes," he says, his fingers uncharacteristically gentle, not at all like they were at my previous Test. "You should be feeling back to yourself in a short while."

With the grogginess in my head, I have a hard time hearing him, so I watch his mouth as he speaks, catching enough words to understand his instruction.

I never noticed how full his lips were until now. I regret having looked at them.

"You can stay here until you're well enough to walk on your own," he says, finishing with the bandage. "I promise to keep my hands to myself from now on." He flashes a small smile at that, but I'm too busy marveling at the ease in my muscles to be alarmed.

Before I can ask about the antidote and possible side effects, the Master snaps his head to the door, brows raising as he says, "Come in."

We both watch as the door slides open to reveal the young Flame I saved in my Test standing in the doorway, his eyes bouncing back and forth between Cruelty and me.

"Oh. Uh, *ahem*. . ." The boy clears his throat, his plump cheeks turning an unforgiving shade of red. I get the distinct feeling he wasn't expecting my presence. "I'll — uh, sorry. I'll just be — uh .. . bye," he stammers, fumbling for the door as he turns to leave.

And even though I only catch a glimpse of him before he goes, it doesn't take much to notice the difference. He no longer has the burns around his wrist and arms — the marks from being chained are completely gone, as if they never existed.

Did Cruelty heal him? Is that why the boy was here before?

But why? What is he doing? What is his plan?

Can't you just thank me and move on?

Cruelty's voice caresses the outskirts of my mind, a trickle of amusement behind every word.

I open my mouth to tell him to get out of my head, but he addresses the boy, not giving me the chance.

"January," Cruelty says, and the boy stops in his tracks, peeking his head back into the room. "When Sunday is well enough, will you please escort her to the library? I need her help with something."

"Yes, Master," January says, bowing at the hips. "Of course."

Cruelty nods his thanks and leaves the room without looking back.

January watches after him, but unlike most Flames, it isn't alarm or panic coursing through his eyes. It's admiration. Respect. Homage. He must be losing his mind.

"I couldn't help but overhear," January says, entering the room. "But you shouldn't reject his trust. He only extends his assistance to people he likes."

"Likes?" I resist the urge to laugh. "We're Flames. He isn't capable of liking us. Or anyone, for that matter."

January shakes his head, his expression grave. "He's different from the others."

"Different?" This kid must have suffered some serious brain damage over the course of his stay. "Are you willing to believe that? After all that's happened?"

Strands of black hair dip into the corners of January's eyes, and he brushes them back, revealing a gaze that is bright and wide, full of hope. "We can't judge people by their past," he says, taking a seat at the worktable.

I bite the inside of my cheek, summoning every ounce of patience I have left. He's just a child. It'd be wrong to yell at him — to tell him he's too young to understand the Masters and their scheming ways. "And why is that?"

"Because they don't live there anymore," he says. "If you don't let him help you, you won't survive here."

"And how do I know Cruelty didn't tell you to say that? How do I know you two aren't working against me?"

The boy stares at me, shrugging. Indifferent. "Don't say nobody tried to warn you, Sunday, because I did. You can either accept it or deny it. You decide."

Chapter Twenty-Five

After a few hours, the antidote has worked its way through my system, and I'm finally able to get out of bed. I follow January to the library and keep two steps behind him, still shaken from his words. He doesn't explain why Cruelty summoned us to the library, so I don't question it, afraid of the truth.

If you don't let him help you, you won't survive here.

Don't say nobody tried to warn you, Sunday, because I did. You can either accept it or deny it.

You decide.

I try to forget the kid's speech, but the ideas have already been planted, disturbing my beliefs. I try to ignore them, to push away the false promises, but I find it's not that simple.

I don't know why I'm letting him get to me, or how he managed to worm his way into my conscience, but here he is, throwing doubt into the reality I thought I knew. Bloody imbecile. If he had never opened his foolish mouth, I wouldn't have this war for truth raging inside me, pitting me against reason and intuition, impossible to pick between.

Is there any validity to the boy's warning? The question rises from a hopeful place – one I thought long forgotten. Or am I simply being deceived by a lie I wish to believe?

I shake my head.

If Cruelty wanted me dead, he would've left me in the hallway, I'm sure of it, but that's not enough to make me trust him. For all I know, he could have some greater torture planned for me, and making sure I *didn't* die was in his best interest. Not mine.

But if that's the case, why am I not entirely afraid to see him again?

January makes an abrupt turn up a flight of stairs, and I'm thankful for the change in direction, hoping my restless thoughts will do the same.

The sun is up, so the workers are out, the halls swarming with frenzied feet and stern commands. With the amount of hustle that comes with morning shifts, I try to stay out of everybody's way, and they stay out of mine, avoiding setting off each other's tempers like they're some catchable disease.

My only hope is that the library will be empty once we arrive, giving me peace from the chaos that has become my life.

"Where are you from?"

I look down to find the boy staring up at me, smiling faintly. I wish he wouldn't smile. It makes it that much harder to ignore him, but since his question is harmless enough, I find no risk in answering. "Tempus," I say. "You?"

"I was born in Shyro," he says, "but my family moved us to Urie a few months after I was born."

Urie. That's south of Tempus. I don't know much about the village, but I've heard it's well-off, more so than Tempus. I always thought I'd be nice to live there, but after our parents died, we didn't have the resources to relocate.

"So, how many Tests do you have left to complete?" January whispers, his voice swallowed by the servants' commotion, barely loud enough for me to hear.

He leans in, the tips of his black hair brushing against my forearm.

I bite the inside of my cheek, debating my answer.

"It's all right," the boy murmurs, his eyes wide and expressive, full of understanding. "I'm taking the Tests, too."

I almost trip over my feet.

"Your trial in the chamber," he goes on, though I really wish he wouldn't. I don't want to talk about my bargain, and he shouldn't want to talk about his, but I don't know how to tell him to stop without attracting unwanted attention. "It was also my Test. I was given two options before you arrived. The first was to press the blue button and pass the trial, but you would die as a result."

My face blanches at the revelation, at the ultimatum Warfare gave a young Flame.

"The second was to bind myself to the top of the mountain and lay under the Fryer, hoping you'd free me before . . . well, you know." He shrugs his shoulders, underselling the risk he took by trusting me — a complete stranger. "I knew the Tests weren't going to be easy when I agreed to them, so my decision was clear from the beginning. I chose to place my faith in you. And I made the right choice."

The blue button flashes in my mind, and I'm so glad he didn't press it. More than that, I'm glad I didn't either, but the thought doesn't soothe the flip in my stomach.

How in the sky's name could his family let him do this? Why didn't they step in and stop him from engaging in Tests that could take his life? It would've been better to be a servant. At least then, he has a chance of staying alive for longer than a few months.

"Thank you," I say quietly, if only to distract from the horror of his circumstance. "For risking your life for me. I wish you all the best at your next Test."

January bows his head, a faint smile marking his face. "And to you as well. I only have one more left to complete, you know. After that, I get to go home."

I stare at him, mouth agape. The weight of his words ripples through me. If he wins, the information will scatter like roaches, reaching the entirety of the mortal lands in a matter of weeks. Days, possibly. And if all of us, Flames and Soulless alike, hear about January's triumph, the whole trajectory of human existence will change. We'll finally have the proof we've been needing. Proof that shows the Sacred Seven *can* be beaten. They aren't invincible.

January pauses, his hand straying to my wrist to prevent my advancement. "We're here," he says, and gestures to the library's mahogany doors, opening them for me.

He waves me forward, smiling with crooked teeth.

I follow behind him, my expectations high.

It's only now hitting me that we're going into a library — a real-life *library* — which I haven't been in or seen in over a decade. Ever since the Masters tore down every bookshop and depository built by the Emperors, I haven't bothered seeking any out. Why would I, when all the remaining books the Masters didn't ban are about submission, brutality, and war?

I keep this presumption in mind as I enter, trying not to get too excited, for the fear of the library's selection.

Distantly, I sense January on my heels, encouraging me to look around and explore the room, quieting my hesitation.

I drink in the sight as best I can, going dizzy with delight.

The dark wooden floors and gray brick paneling are the first things I notice, the atmosphere so warm and inviting, I almost feel welcome. So opposite of Airabeth's usual environment. Smooth mahogany desks and matching couches circle the middle, illuminated by a ring of candlelight tracing the room. A faint glow from above catches my attention, and when I look up, I find the ceiling is made out of stained glass, the art depicting the night sky and mystery beyond. A visible heaven I can almost touch.

And that's not including the books.

Shelves upon shelves, rows upon rows of stories twist and swirl around the room, covering the majority of the walls from floor to ceiling. I haven't read, haven't *seen* more than two books in over a decade, yet here, tucked away from the entire world, lies more art and history than I can comprehend.

My hand moves to my heart, the muscle pounding in both fear and excitement.

Our books. Our knowledge. Our history.

This is where the Masters have hidden it. All of it. Right here, in this unknown pocket of the universe. My hands shake at the brilliance before me, surrounded by stories the Emperors encouraged us to read, each fairytale detailing the importance of love, courage, forgiveness, and family — a collage of themes the Masters want us to forget.

"You don't have to admire the room from a distance," Cruelty says, and if he hadn't spoken, I would've missed him sitting at one of the working desks, his face buried in a book. "I did invite you here for a reason."

He stares at me over the edge of his novel, assessing from the crown of my head to the bottom of my feet, making me bristle. Though the room is illuminated by an array of candles, he sits in a corner where the light can't reach, cloaked in a shadow I don't dare approach.

"I'll leave you both to it, then." January is already making his way for the exit, leaving before I have a chance to protest. I almost leap toward him when he reaches the door, inwardly pleading for him to stay, to not leave me alone with an enemy.

He must sense my stare because he throws me a look over his shoulder, nodding encouragingly. "You'll be fine," he mouths, and steps into the hallway, shutting the door behind him.

Isolated. With Cruelty. Again.

My head throbs with the remnants of the healing antidote.

The Master lowers his book and crosses an ankle over a knee, letting us sit in a quiet like death. And though his eyes, with a predator's gleam, fix on me, I get a strange sense I'm not the prey he's looking to devour.

"You look better," he says at last, but based on his tone, I would've thought otherwise. "Healthy, except for your shoulder. It's still sagging a bit from when you dislocated it before. Does it hurt?"

"No," I lie. But at least the bone is no longer dangling from its socket.

A disapproving noise is the Master's only response, his gaze darkening as if he can see through my skin, straight to the inflamed joint aching beneath. He doesn't say anything more about it, however, and sits back in his chair, content with silence.

"I don't mean to come off as rude or ungrateful," I say, already tired of whatever angle he's playing, "but I have work to finish in the kitchen, so the quicker I give you what you want, the better off we'll be."

A sharp smile tilts his mouth, the muscle in his jaw tightening. "You're not fond of me. I can appreciate that, so there's really no need for you to be so politically correct. Just say what you're thinking, please. It'll save us a lot of time."

I curl my fingers into fists and resist the urge to grab a book and throw it at his head. "If you want to know what I'm thinking, put a stronghold around my thoughts to find out. You seem to enjoy doing that, Master."

Cruelty narrows his gaze, every shred of amusement draining from his face like a faucet run dry. "It's more productive to hear you say it out loud," he says, giving me a smile that doesn't reach his eyes. "And don't call me that."

"But that's what you are, is it not?"

He glances away from me, withholding whatever retort burns in his mind, though I wish he wouldn't.

How unfair, to know that he can understand my thoughts but I can't understand his.

I clear my throat before I speak, fearing my shaky voice will betray my nerves. "You called me here to fulfill an assignment," I say, not bothering with politeness. "Shall I start working, or are we going to sit here and pretend we aren't enemies?"

Cruelty's shoulders stiffen at that, going still with an emotion I'm afraid to identify.

"I need you to sort through the books," he says, jutting his head toward the wall of shelves, saving me from the brutal cut of his eyes. I could've sworn I saw a glimmer of bitterness within them. Brief, but unmistakable.

I convince myself it was a trick of the light, a shifting shadow dancing over his features.

"They haven't been cleaned or placed in alphabetical order in centuries. Better get to it if you want to finish by morning."

I gaze at the hundreds, *thousands*, of books filling the room, stretching five levels high.

It will take me days, perhaps months, to fulfill the task he's asking. We both know I don't have that much time. "Why can't you do it?" I ask, and Cruelty snorts, brows lifting in amusement. "With the power and athleticism you have, you could clean this place from top to bottom in a matter of minutes."

"I'm busy," he says, his eyes returning to the pages in his lap. "Though I am flattered you've noticed my athletic physique." A small grin marks his mouth, and I'm surprised by the ease in it, his face transforming into something close to lovely.

I try to ignore how the look softens his features. How it lightens the darkness I'm too afraid to glance at, let alone approach.

It does nothing to change how I see him.

It's impossible to forget who he is when every movement is laced with magnificence and power, making even the smallest of gestures look like a deathblow.

When I first saw Warfare, I thought he was the meanest, most majestic creature I'd ever seen, but he doesn't hold a candle against Cruelty. None of the Masters do, and perhaps that's what makes him the most terrifying of the Sacred Seven.

Even with the sleeves of his shirt rolled down to his wrists, I can see how large his forearms are, the muscles stronger and harder than most people's legs — an absolute specimen of a man. The sheer size of him is enough to make a god forget his own name, but it's not his strength alone that scares me. It's his mentality, the unshakable disposition, that makes him truly intimidating.

Immortal or not, it takes a certain discipline to look the way he does, and although I know what it's like to break one's body each and every day and come back for more, I do it out of necessity. Not choice. Hunting for my family and surviving these Tests aren't an option for me, but for him, he goes through pain willingly, just to get stronger.

It makes me wonder if he does it out of preparation or pride. Perhaps a combination of both, given his position. With the strongholds he possesses, he could bend the world to his will if that's what he wanted, and part of me wonders why he hasn't yet.

It's a game to him, I suppose. A game no human will ever truly understand, and maybe that's why I find it strange watching him read. I thought his pastimes would consist of brooding or playing with knives, thinking up new ways to torture humans and adversaries alike.

Careful what you think, there, Flame.

The Master's voice fills my head, low and sharp, disturbingly calm.

I flinch back, my stitches throbbing at the movement. "Get out of my head," I say, but my voice comes out strained, escaping through clamped, aching teeth.

If your shield was strong enough, I wouldn't have found a way in, he purrs, the words a river of arrogance, pushing me to respond.

"You always find a way in," I say, grappling to raise my shield. "You're too strong for us, and you revel in that."

Now, that's where you're wrong, Flame. Your kind are capable of doing much more than you realize, but most don't put in the work to see all they can accomplish.

I look toward the door, wanting desperately to bolt through it, but my limbs have gone taut, too stiff to move. What if this is the end for me?

My dread shifts into an enormous beast that won't stop roaring.

What if Cruelty's face is the last one I see? What if he's done screwing around, and this is the part where he takes my soul, ruining me completely?

As soon as the thought takes hold, I retract my fear, wondering if my destruction would be such a terrible thing. Considering the absolute disorder my existence has become, would submitting to the darkness be more of a damnation or a release? Would falling into the abyss be a finish line or a new beginning?

Perhaps death is the rest I've been seeking, and I just need to find a way to meet it. Let it sweep me away into nothingness, where the quiet, never-ending peace awaits.

I close my eyes and wish for mercy, calling Cruelty to end my misery once and for all, but he doesn't. With my deal still in play, he can't take my mind outright, and the Tests are sport to him. Without this slow form of manipulation, his fun would end, and the Masters aren't finished with me.

Not yet.

Why else would Cruelty release my mind, the pressure in my temples fading, as he frees his hold?

I lean against the nearest bookshelf for support, my head pounding with fatigue, struggling to think straight. I count to ten as I regain control, every sense and thought becoming mine once again, no longer under his control.

I wipe my hands down my face, finding humor in the irony. How rude of the Master to make me plead for death, then refuse to give it to me.

"You need to learn to control your emotions," Cruelty says, lifting his eyes from the book at last. "The Sacred Seven prey on instability. You won't be able to build your shield and keep it strong if your thoughts are out of line." He leans forward in his chair, gaze dark and unwavering. "And if you ever have another thought about seeking death when another Master is around, they'll grant you your wish. Never meditate on subjects you don't truly desire. You'd be surprised how often those wishes come true."

Something strange flashes in his eyes, but it isn't until after it's gone do I recognize it. He steels his face, as if wanting me to mistake his emotion for anger, when really, it's fear. Fear, and something deeper. Something instinctual.

I glare at him, unsure of why he's doing this. Why he's messing with me.

"You should get to work," he whispers, turning back to his reading. "The books aren't going to sort themselves."

Chapter Twenty-Six

I wish the books could sort themselves.

It's not that I hate the menial task Cruelty has given me, I don't, but with the time constraint hovering overhead, I'm not taking my minutes lightly. It's been over three hours since I've started organizing the shelves by author, and I'm only on section C, barely a third of the way through the first level.

Bleeding hell. I'm never going to finish before midnight.

Perhaps if you didn't read the first chapter of every book you come across, you'd be farther along. The voice whispers to me like a secret, distinctly male.

I keep my eyes pinned to the shelves, heart pounding in alarm, and pretend the words never came, resuming my work. Dust and cobwebs mark my fingertips, the stacks so old and untouched their ancientness screams to me, begging to be cleaned. I try not to touch the books too much as I rearrange them, forcing myself to ignore their appeal.

I may not be in Tempus anymore, but I don't think the reading ban on humans has been lifted because I'm in Airabeth. It's better I stay away from the stacks as best I can so I don't lose an eye over them. There's a reason the Masters are hiding this room from us — why they discourage knowledge and learning, forbidding us from expanding our intellect. The dumber the Sacred Seven keep our lands, the easier we are to control, and the less we utilize our independent thinking, the more desensitized to their treatment we become.

Books are wisdom to not only the mind, but the soul, and sky's forbid if mortals got to exercise their minds and grow quicker than the Masters can manage. The Masters' hatred for stories is palpable–– that knowledge is notorious amongst humans, which is why I find Cruelty's silence incredibly puzzling. He hasn't muffled a threat or grumbled his disapproval since I started rummaging through the shelves, even though I've been unable to keep my wandering eyes to myself.

I could chalk up his aloofness to blatant disregard, but he never misses a beat, no matter the tune. He's been trained to know the psychology of mortals. Trained to see and hear, even smell, what a human thinks and desires, using it all to his advantage.

I glance at him now, but he doesn't so much as blink in my direction, eyes glued to the pages of his novel, completely engrossed. I keep staring at him, thinking he's going to sense my look and meet it, but he doesn't. Not even once.

He can't be bothered.

I can't tell if I'm relieved or annoyed by that.

By the time I advance to section E of the library, I'm on a stepladder, no longer able to reach the shelves by foot, and get distracted by a book wrapped in mahogany leather. Before I consider the consequences of breaking the Masters' rules, I open it and rush through it, pausing on pages that catch my attention.

From what I can gather, the story is a murder mystery with a little romance, and although this isn't a genre I particularly gravitate toward, the premise is interesting enough. I'm sure it's something Cruelty would enjoy, given the plot is filled with killings and deception, perfect for an immortal who's a master in both.

My eyes stray back to him then, as if fearing I've caught his attention by merely thinking his name. I grip the top rung of the ladder, worried he's somehow sensed my act of rebellion, then realize that isn't possible.

How could it be, when he hasn't glanced in my direction since I started working? He's too focused on his reading. He doesn't want to listen to my thoughts or engage with my defiance — I'm too insignificant for that — so as I raise my eyes to him, I'm confident he isn't looking at me.

He can't be looking at me.

But he is.

I freeze, unsure if I should glance away or hold his stare.

I decide on the latter, blood rushing to my cheeks as I wait for him to call me out, or invade my mind, erasing every word I've read in these stupid stories. But if the Master noticed my wandering eyes, he doesn't say. Instead, he resumes his reading, mouth set in a thin line, giving no hint to what he's thinking.

And perhaps it's my desire to know something about him — feeling outmatched by his knowledge about me — that has me wondering out loud, "What are you reading?" The question falls out of my mouth before I can stop it, dismay soaring through me as I realize my mistake.

The Master carefully lifts his eyes from the page, as if it pains him to be interrupted, and meets my gaze, saying nothing. The energy in the room shifts with the silence, giving one of us the advantage, though I'm not sure who it is.

My question must've caught Cruelty off guard, and although he's not obligated to respond, he doesn't like that I surprised him, throwing a wrench in the power dynamic between us. Maybe that's why he decides to lift the paperback and reveal the cover, wanting to take back control. I squint through the candlelight to make out the title, the large lettering in an eloquent bold that reads: *Scotch and Bourbon: A Collection of Poems.*

My head tilts. "You like poetry?" I ask, hoping my curiosity isn't as obvious to him as it is to me.

"Didn't think a Master could be capable of understanding the tragic yet beautiful realities of mortal life through the written word?" he muses at my amazement, smiling when I shoot him a scowl. "How very human of you."

I don't believe for one second that he cares or appreciates anything that has to do with what an ignorant human has created. This is all a front, another one of his masks he's chosen to show me. I just don't know what it means.

"What do you like about poetry?" I challenge.

He gives me a long look, then leans forward in his chair, acting as if I — a weak, unintelligent mortal — have the ability to intrigue him. "It still amazes me how deeply humans can feel," he admits, catching me a little off guard with his response. "It's so different from me."

I nearly laugh at that. "That's not shocking, considering you torture people for a living."

His mouth stiffens into a frown, eyes flicking to the bandage on my arm where he injected me with the healing agent mere hours ago. "I'm not going to hurt you, Nadia. I thought I made that clear before." His voice is low, almost guttural with intensity.

Coming from a human, I would've perceived the tone as something honest, but from him, it's nothing short of a carefully crafted lie.

"Well, you didn't," I say. "Just because you helped me once doesn't mean I've forgotten how you treated me at the Test. What's your excuse for that, Master?"

His features are cold and unreadable, with all the emotion of a sitting rock. "How long do you think it'll take before you stop being so stubborn and take a hint?" Even though he doesn't raise his voice, his ire fills the room.

I square my shoulders, jaw aching from clenching it so hard. "I shouldn't have asked," I say, turning back to the bookshelves. "If I had known such a simple question about reading material would ruffle you, I wouldn't have—"

One moment, Cruelty is sitting a healthy distance away, the next, he's standing right beside me, his eyes level with mine, despite my being several steps high on the ladder.

Whatever I was about to say dissolves in my mind, the thoughts replaced with the incessant urge to flee, to look for a weapon.

Cruelty scans my face, his body going so still I think the world stills with him.

"There are certain things books capture," he starts, "that life never could. Maybe that's why humans gravitate toward them. They put into words what we all have trouble explaining. It's intriguing, really. But you already know that."

He narrows his gaze, eyes boring into mine as if he's found a new window to my thoughts. I hold his stare, refusing to back down even though I have no words to offer in return.

"But after reading almost every book in here, I've found that the best writing often comes from the greatest pain. Something honest, something real, is what people truly crave, don't you think?"

When I don't respond, my lungs too tight to allow me to speak, he goes on. "No one likes an easy story where the characters don't suffer or go through hardships, because that's not real life. Real life is difficult and messy, and sometimes unbearable, but the beauty of books isn't to highlight the tough parts of human existence. It's to point out that those tough times can be beaten."

I have no idea what he's getting at, especially since he *is* the essence of tough times in a mortal's life. Even so, there's a candidness in his eyes, a sincerity that makes my gut clench.

"Well," I say, reminding myself that he's had centuries to master such a facade, "for someone who kills humans, you've certainly studied up on them."

Cruelty's snarl rattles the bookshelf, making me jump, though when he spots the fear I'm unable to hide, his eyes soften. An apology on his face. He rubs roughly at the back of his neck, the skin reddening, as if to remove the short burst of temper; the first I've seen from him.

"You want to read something interesting?" he asks, and even though I detect no malice in the sleek angles of his face, I know it must be there, hiding amongst the shadows.

He motions me to one of the bookshelves, and when I make no move to follow, he doesn't react, eyes stark with an incomprehensible patience. "I'm not going to hurt you."

He says it so gently, I can almost feel the words whispering through my body, like a low wind rustling through an evergreen forest. "Look, I'll tie my hands behind my back if that'll make you feel better."

He brings his wrists together and snaps his fingers, producing a thick line of rope that wraps around his hands, taking him hostage. He lifts his arms so I can better see, allowing me to determine whether the makeshift leash is some trick of the mind or a restraint I can rely on. From my limited knowledge of manacles, the rope looks legitimate enough, but I don't dare get too close. If he can bind his hands in the blink of an eye, he can undo them just as quickly.

I try not to think about how effortlessly he wields his power — how far his talents might extend.

The Master leans a shoulder against the shelves, looking up at me, as if sensing the direction of my thoughts. The curiosity embedded there.

I purse my lips at his arrogance. At the quiet smirk inching across his face.

"What do you say, Flame?" The Master's eyes flicker over mine, seeking an answer. "Do you want to enjoy the books spread before you, or would you prefer to spend the rest of your evening moping around, trapped with nothing but the endless sound of your miserable thoughts?"

For a moment I consider denying his offer — I hate the idea of accepting anything from him, decent or otherwise — but for what? I've been isolated from books so long, words have become foreign to my eyes.

If you don't let him help you, you won't survive here. January told me I should trust the Master, and considering the kid has made it to his final Test, maybe he's right. Maybe he's brainwashed, I don't know, and I'll never know unless I make a judgment for myself.

I keep the small kernel of hope in mind as I descend the ladder, my legs shaking as I join the Master by the bookshelf, keeping several feet away from him. The moment I establish my stance, I expect him to obliterate the distance, increase my discomfort, but he doesn't. Not even as he leans away from the shelf, repositioning himself.

"I would show you the book myself," he says, and I don't miss the hint of triumph in his voice, "but considering I have no use of my hands. . ."

"Just tell me what it's called," I say, and keep my eyes level with the shelf, refusing to look at him. He seems to have no problem looking at *me*, however — his gaze burning along my profile, never once roving lower than my chin.

"Right there," he says, and I curse internally when I see the book is directly in front of him. "The one on the right. Three from the bottom. Open the book to page fifty and read it." Cruelty nods to the shelf again, staring pointedly at me.

And even though he speaks the words calmly, it doesn't take much to see that he's the type of warrior used to giving orders instead of receiving.

But he's never been on the battlefield with me, and even though I take the bait and follow his instruction, it's not because he told me to. Cruelty may have a mind of his own, but so do I, and I'd rather die than let him take that away from me.

I stare down at the page, unable to keep the quiver from my voice, as I read the lines out loud:

"I place a rose upon your face,
I give you all my trust and faith.
I will not break. I will not bend,
Believe in me until the end.
Here upon my bended knee,
I promise one day, we will be free."

I blink, staring dumbly at the words.

"Why are you showing me this?" I ask, careful not to reveal my stupidity to him. It's been years since I've read a book above children's level, so anything higher is beyond my comprehension. I'm not about to express my ignorance to him, and I'm certainly not going to admit that I'm too dumb to understand basic writings.

The last thing I want to do is give the Masters something else to hold over me, especially the one I stand beside. I chance a look up at him now, his shoulder an inch away from brushing mine, though I'm not sure why I notice that. "Why are you showing me this?" I repeat, and his eyes, an endless sea of secrets and shadow, shimmer amongst the candlelight, a blue flame of their own.

"Keep the book," he says, and I can't tell whether or not he is ignoring my question on purpose. "Read the rest and tell me what you think. I'm interested in a human's perspective."

Trick. This is a trick, he's tricking me, don't fall for it! Don't!

"There are thousands of books in here," he continues, sensing my hesitation. "No one will notice if one is missing. And I won't tell. Promise."

Even if I were to believe him, which I don't. . .

"What if I get caught with this?"

"Don't get caught."

I bite my lower lip — considering — and Cruelty's eyes go straight to my mouth, lingering a second too long.

I debate calling him out on it, to tell him to keep his wandering stare to himself, but he's already caught his own error.

He steps away from me curtly, the rope around his hands vanishing as he hardens his face, the barrier behind his eyes shooting up like a wall of fire. "I have some work to finish," he rushes, and I wonder if I imagine the sudden huskiness of his voice. "I'll come back to check on you in a few hours." He goes to the door, his hand pausing over the handle as he turns to me one last time. "You're welcome to come to the library whenever you wish. The other Masters haven't been in here for over a century, so you don't need to worry about running into them. I'm sure the books would appreciate your company. It'd be nice not to have them go to waste for a change."

When the door clicks shut behind him, I sigh at the ceiling, my hands shaking in the aftermath of his presence.

What the hell was that?

I close my eyes, trying to forget all the questions ripping at my mind.

Who was that person? That Master?

He wasn't exactly kind to me, but he wasn't terrible either. And for a man of his title, that is not normal. Perhaps I'm losing my mind, thinking him friendlier than he truly is. Is this how it feels before a Flame turns into a Soulless? I bite the edge of my thumbnail, chewing it down to the nub, delighting in the sting. Is this the confusion, the paranoia, one faces before the fall?

I swallow the fears as best I can, knowing everything Cruelty said was lies and nonsense. It doesn't matter how lovely his talk or guise seems, he's a bleeding Master, for sky's sake. Any ounce of decency he shows is for his own benefit. It doesn't matter what he says, or how he says it, this is what he does, what they *all* do, to manipulate and destroy—

Enough, my instinct speaks, putting a halt to my endless spiral of thoughts. Stop giving him your attention. He isn't worth it. But even as I try to forget the Master and his clever ways, I can't get his voice out of my head, his presence disrupting the sanity I try so desperately to keep.

I go to the table and pick up the book he left behind to distract myself. I flip back to the poem he showed me, determined to understand the meaning behind the lines, sick of being outsmarted by the Masters.

But when I find the page I'm looking for, there are no lines. The paper is blank.

I blink, my heart thumping.

What—?

I turn to another chapter, hopeful my eyes are just fatigued, playing tricks on me — but no. The pages are wholly bare.

A chill goes through me, every sense and nerve going on high alert.

Even the flames on the candlesticks go still.

Something prickles at the back of my neck, as if someone unseen has entered the room. I hold my breath, dredging up the stealth of the huntress I left in Tempus.

I scan the library, waiting, listening, preparing, and then—

"I hope you're ready, little Bunny."

I spin wildly, expecting to be met with Sickness's face, but he isn't here, his voice merely an echo in my head. *Because your third Test is about to begin.*

I run to the door, seeking an escape.

I hardly make it five steps before my vision tilts, taking me to the ground.

Dizzy, I crawl forward, head swimming with a sudden onset of vertigo.

Before I have a chance to get my bearings, black dots flare before my eyes, turning my world dark.

Chapter Twenty-Seven

When I come to, I'm afraid to open my eyes.

I'm not ready to face whatever twisted horror Sickness has planned for me. By now, I thought I'd be used to my weekly Tests, thinking six days in between would be enough time to recover, but it isn't. Not even close. I'm too scared to cry about it, a familiar weight growing behind my eye sockets that is stifled by adrenaline.

I force myself upright, my hands raising to defend against any potential threats as I absorb my surroundings. It takes several seconds longer than I'd like for my eyes to adjust to the dim light, catching fragments of what appears to be a living room.

A living room I should not be in.

Bare walls with cracks in the molding. Boarded up windows. Outdated furniture. Warped floorboards from the water damage we couldn't afford to fix. It looks exactly as I remember, every corner and hallway whispering with memories, replaying all the fights and laughs shared within this house. The ghosts of my family are imprinted in every fissure and bend.

I wrap my arms around my torso, wanting so desperately for this to be a dream or figment of my imagination. But no matter how many times I pinch my arm or rub my eyes, the view stays the same.

I stare down at the ripped carpet, mind racing.

I'm in Tempus. My home. Miles away from Airabeth. A place I never thought I'd see again.

It's small — much smaller than I remember — and it's hard to believe we suffered this poverty for over ten years, living in such filth. After staying in the Masters' palace for only a few weeks, my house, where I lived my whole life until now, looks more like a prison cell than a home.

But if I'm truly back in my village like my eyes indicate, does that mean Elisha and Diana are here too?

I look around the house with a newfound hope, then remember how Warfare wiped my existence from their minds, taking every memory hostage.

To them, I'm less than a stranger.

The collar of my dress suddenly feels too tight around my throat. I pull at it, ripping the material, needing to get it off and away from me.

I stumble to the back room and remove the uniform entirely. I rummage through my drawers, grabbing the first shirt and trousers I see, and shrug them on, their fit baggy and well worn.

I inhale the woodsy scent of home, and it fills me with a warmth and comfort I haven't felt in weeks. Once I finish dressing, I hurry to the kitchen to inspect the pantry, picturing shelves upon shelves of emptiness — proof of the damage I've done by leaving my family here, destitute.

It won't be forever. Sasha's voice thunders in my head, as real and inescapable as if he were standing right beside me. *This struggle you're going through has an end, and you will come out the other side of it, but you have to keep moving. Don't be deterred by your worst fears.*

I cling to my brother's voice as I enter the kitchen, checking to make sure everything is in place.

My spine stiffens when I see it.

A jam jar, unused and unopened, sitting on the counter.

Impossible.

Jam is a luxury in Tempus — a luxury no villager can afford unless they're a king, thief, or harlot. I close my eyes, not wishing to know which of the last two applies to my siblings.

I pick up the container of jam to examine every inch of it, the glass cold and smooth in my hands, almost foreign.

I've always wondered what a rich jam like this might smell like, taste like, should I ever get my hands on some. I turn the jar over to open it, to see if I can sniff out the poison Sickness has surely mixed within, when my thumb brushes over the bottom and discovers a texture that doesn't feel like glass.

Paper.

With shaking fingers, I flip the jar upside down to reveal a note taped to the bottom. I pluck it free and unfold, careful not to rip it, and read the lines inscribed there:

Run bunny run, before they drown in the rain,
They don't have much time, for the wolf isn't slain.
The sky is beckoning, their singing too cruel,
For the bunny is brainless, a dullard, a fool.
Uncover me so you might have a chance,
If not, you shall join us in Death's last dance.

It takes everything I have to not tear up the page, my fear turning to anger as I picture Sickness walking through my house, touching my things. Mocking me with this bloody jar; priceless to us, nothing to him.

I read the riddle again, slowly, but I can't make sense of it. Hopelessness clogs my throat, but I choke it down. There's no time to get emotional. I scan over the lines again and again, and the only idea I have is to scratch out my eyes to force them to see what I'm missing.

I almost think I might, as I repeat the first line over and over, waiting for something to stick out in my mind.

Run bunny run, before they drown in the rain. Run bunny run, before they drown in the rain. Run bunny run, before they drown in the rain. Rain. Rain. Rain. Rain. Rain.

It hardly rains in Tempus, and Sickness knows that, so the line must be a clue for something. A location, perhaps?

And what about drowning? In the time I've been alive, my village has only had three deaths by drowning, and all of them happened at the same time. Caused by the same incident.

It happened three years ago, when the Masters plagued our village with a seven-week drought, drying out all our lakes and rivers, cutting off our water supply. For weeks everyone was in a panic, wondering how our village would survive.

Two days after the drought began, a villager discovered that Teeter River was left untouched. I didn't understand why the Masters decided to leave us a reprieve, but it wasn't long before their intentions became clear.

For the next forty-nine days, Teeter River was Tempus's only water source, so the place was overwhelmed with people.

I went with Sasha one afternoon to fill up our buckets, and there were three brothers standing ahead of us in line, all of them dark haired and around my age. They were lingering near the edge of the bank, their buckets already full, when the crowd surged, pushing one of the boys into the river.

The two remaining siblings reached out to catch him, but they lost their balance and fell in, too.

It all happened so fast, none of the onlookers knew how to respond. Even now, I can still see the boys' sputtering faces, begging for someone, *anyone* to help them. But we all just stood there, watching them struggle and drown until they floated downstream, never to be seen again.

Sasha tried to console me in the following days, stating that none of the brothers knew how to swim, so there was nothing we could've done to help. *It's not our fault*, he told me. *It's theirs. If they were dumb enough to stand close to the edge, that's their problem. Forget about it. It's not our issue.*

But even if the brothers couldn't swim, they shouldn't have died in that river.

The currents in Teeter River are known to be calm. Quiet. Safe. And yet, when the brothers fell in, the current picked up in speed, the rapids rising so high, even an experienced swimmer would struggle. Even though I never saw the tides that rough again, I didn't dare fetch water from there for weeks afterward.

Ever since that day, I've carried a greater fear of the Masters inside me. None of us understand the full extent of the Sacred Seven's power. It makes a sick sort of sense as to why they caused the drought, then decided to leave one river alone. They knew people would fight over it. Knew someone would get too close to the edge and fall in. And they knew how effective it would be to leave us questioning the safety of our livelihoods.

I peer down at the riddle again, my stomach hollowing out.

Sickness wants me to go to the river. It's the only place that makes sense, especially since it's one of the last places I'd want to go.

I run for the exit, hands shaking as I push through the door and sprint down the road, rushing for the forest. Outside, the streets are filled with villagers coming and going from the Market, blocking my path. I push my way through them, bumping into their backs and shoulders.

"Hey, watch it—"

"Do you mind—"

"What the bleeding—"

"Ignorant fool—"

I ignore the angry villagers and focus on reaching the river, but a rush of memories whirl in my head, eddying together until they're all I can see.

Images of January and the Amphista blend together, transporting me back to those dreadful moments, sending tremors down my spine. I can't handle such horror again. The best I can hope for is a mental challenge that doesn't have me running for my life or somebody else's.

Clinging to the hope that this Test won't be like the others, I push myself forward, my lungs burning with the effort.

I reach the woodland within minutes, the familiar smells of dew and dried earth welcoming me home. For years, I hated this place. For years, I wanted nothing to do with this town, its people, or stupid traditions. I whined about everything Tempus was and still is today, but after seeing how much worse things could get, I'd take it all back in a second. I wouldn't grumble about anything, and I'd learn to be grateful because I had a lot to be grateful for, only I didn't see it.

I try to outrun my guilt as I weave through the forest, confident in my direction in the familiar terrain. Although it's been months since I've been to the river, I know it isn't far from home. I mark the checkpoints as I go, remembering the large oak at the bend, the bench beside the dead gardens, the boulder before the fork in the path, the Soulless standing on that very path—

Well, that's new.

I skid to a stop, nearly tripping and falling headfirst to the ground, when I see three Soulless blocking the trail, their cool eyes boring into me. With their shoulders hunched and knees bent in a fighter's stance, they seem to be waiting for my arrival.

"Hi, there," says the tall, skinny man on the right, eyes dancing with a madness that has me retreating a step.

"You're making a mistake," I say, deflecting, as if I don't know why he's here. I consider turning around and running back the way I came, positive I can find a different way to the river. But I don't want to turn my back on these people.

"Oh, hun, I don't think we are." It's the girl in the middle who speaks, her voice lilting and sweet, at odds with the hard lines of her face. She turns to the man on the left, who stands tall with a swollen stomach and receding hairline. "Look at her scared little face," she says to him, with a laugh like a crow's cry. "Remember when we used to be that weak? That vulnerable and petty?" The large man nods in agreement, mouth twisting to the side, as if remembering what it was like to be a Flame. "We are forever indebted to the Masters and what they've done for us. Without them, we wouldn't have anyone to take care of us, or tell us what we should do. Why follow the cowardly Emperors, when you can follow power and strength, wisdom and authority—"

The end of her sentence is drowned out by the rush of a flock of birds overhead. I clench my jaw and overlook the noise, suspecting this is another one of Sickness's tactics to distract me. I don't take my eyes off the Soulless, keeping my hands loose at my sides, preparing for a fight. The girl sneers in response, flashing a series of missing teeth, which makes me wonder how she lost them.

I should've realized this was a warning.

The Soulless rush me, attacking from all sides. I hesitate like a fool, unsure of who to hit first, as the three of them tackle me to the ground. I kick wildly and connect with someone's thigh, a string of curses filling the air.

"Grab her arms," says the girl, grunting as she puts pressure on my knees, forcing them down. I cry out, trying to break free, but it's no use. "C'mon, hurry up," she hisses, looking to her companions.

I go to sit up, fending off the two men with my fists, but I'm overpowered. They grab my wrists, twisting slightly as they pin my arms to the ground.

"Grab your needles!" barks the skinny guy, fumbling in his pocket.

The others do as he says and retrieve syringes filled with a thick, black liquid.

I suddenly think back to Sickness clutching his cup, filled to the brim with whatever inky poison he spits into it.

I flail violently, screaming. I glance around the forest, hoping if I make enough noise, an animal will run by and scare the Soulless off, but nothing comes, not even as they jab their needles into my neck, waist, and thigh, shocking the sense from my body.

A wail pulls out of me, vicious and trembling. "Get away from me!" I shout, twisting away from them. "Get away—!"

They let go of me and I scramble away, cursing myself for not bringing a weapon from my house. I know better than to be so careless.

I rise to my feet, readying myself for another attack, but it doesn't come.

Instead, the Soulless retreat, watching. Smirking.

"Good luck, girl. You're going to need it." The portly man on the right winks, and the other two snort, turning their backs on me. They flee toward the forest's entrance without another word.

All I can do is stare at them, raging.

There's no use in overthinking this. No use in wondering what the Soulless injected me with, or why they didn't just kill me outright when they had the chance. Perhaps there's some worse horror waiting for me at the river, and Sickness wants to keep me alive so I can see it.

But never mind that.

I need to *make it* to the river first.

I give myself a second to catch my breath before I advance down the path, the sting from the needles still present.

I realize a moment too late that I'm not strong enough to continue on, the pain from the injections dragging me down.

I glance to the injection site in my side, and my heart skips at the blood spilling from it.

I press the hem of my shirt onto the opening, trying to stop the bleeding, but it's useless. All of this is useless, and it only gets worse when a dark, slimy fluid starts oozing from the small hole.

I go cold at the sight.

I look down to examine the other two places I've been jabbed, and sure enough, both wounds leak the same bubbling goo, sending me into a panic. I should've known the needles were filled with something dreadful.

Sickness would never kill me outright, that'd be too merciful, so I'm not worried about dying. But if this liquid isn't going to stop my heart, what is it going to do?

I get my answer quicker than I'd like, a surge of agony seizing my limbs, digging down to the bone. The pain is short lived, chased away by a coldness that tracks through my blood, shooting straight to my lungs. I wonder if it's possible to freeze from the inside out, and if it is, this has to be it.

There is no worse torture.

Tears burn my eyes as my limbs start to spasm. I attempt to crawl forward, but my fingers slip through the dirt, getting me nowhere. I look up to see where I am, wanting someone to emerge from the trees and help me, but no one is here. No one is coming.

I tell myself to keep crawling, but my body has become too heavy, the world spinning like a wheel. I sprawl on my stomach, completely immobile, and curse the darkness surging toward me, beckoning me into its arms.

NO! Stay awake! I shove away the blackness, refusing to succumb to its tempting embrace. Stay awake. Stay awake. Stay awake. Please, stay—

MY ARMS FLAIL AS I jolt upright, shaking the grogginess from my body.

I don't remember it being cold when I first entered the forest, but it's cold now, goosebumps raised along my skin.

My attention snaps to the birds circling above me, loud as ever. They're the same ones who interrupted the Soulless a while back, still swarming, erratically chirping and flapping. But if the birds are still here, that means I couldn't have been out for long.

Still, I must find a way to make up the lost time.

Slowly, I haul myself to my feet, my usual agility lost to the injections.

One step at a time, I tell myself. That's all I need to focus on.

And I do.

I think about nothing except that simple act until I finally reach the river, limbs shaking with exhaustion. I stumble toward the waterfront, feet catching on rocks and branches, nearly losing my balance.

It's getting dark, almost too dark to see beyond the surface of the water, so I search my surroundings, not entirely sure what I'm looking for.

It takes less than a minute before I realize I'm alone.

Not a whisper to be heard or a shadow to be seen.

My head hollows out at the sight. At the complete and utter solitude.

I got the riddle wrong. I must've, because no one is here, and the rhyme implied someone would be. My temples throb as I try to think of a solution, of an alternative location Sickness would want me to go—

And then, far into the distance, I see them.

Elisha and Diana.

Chapter Twenty-Eight

I stiffen at the sight, my legs trembling as they manage to carry me down the river's bank. I try to get as close to them as I can, not trusting my vision with this drug coursing through me. But even as my mind tries to discredit the scene and every terror it holds, my heart knows this isn't a hallucination.

My eyes are seeing just fine.

Diana and Elisha are there, wrists bound by separate ropes that've been tied to a tree branch, their bodies dangling over the river.

They're far away, too far to reach, but the distance and the darkness aren't enough to make me doubt who I'm seeing.

I'm well aware of the horror I'm stepping into.

This is my worst nightmare, one that takes me back to Sasha and the day he died.

My heart splinters with grief at the thought of losing another sibling.

I tell myself to move, to search for help, to think of a plan, but I'm struck by this fresh horror. I don't know how long I stand still, as if waiting for some divine hand to come down and rescue my siblings, before a flicker of movement catches my attention, pushing me into action.

It's too dark to fully see through the oncoming night, but I spot the outline of a bulky man standing on the opposite bank of the river, lurking behind the tree holding my family. He grips the end of the ropes that anchor them tight in his hands, manipulating how high or low they hover above the rushing water.

He must sense the moment I spot him, because he loosens his hold on the ropes, submerging my siblings ankle deep into the shivering waters below.

He's putting on a show.

Elisha's curses are like a roar in my ears, Diana's sobs like a punch to the stomach, knocking the air from my lungs. I stumble back, as if I've indeed been struck, then glare back at the Soulless, wanting to kill him.

I don't know how much time I have before this Test is deemed a failure, but if my last two are any indication, I have less than thirty minutes before the ropes run out of length and my siblings drop into the river. Limbs tied and all.

Bleeding hell, how did this happen? How did Sickness get them here? Warfare promised my family would be exempt from Airabeth's violence until my Tests were over, did he not? Or was that merely an implication, a hopeful conclusion I jumped to on my own?

"Hey, girl!" I turn my attention to Diana, her eyes wide and bloodshot, even from a distance. "You must help us, please." She doesn't remember or know who I am, at least Warfare kept his promise on that.

"Oh, piss off, you beastly prick!"

Elisha.

My eyes go to him, his face turning red as he screams and spits at the Soulless behind him, demanding to be freed. His long hair is uncharacteristically disheveled — a strange thing to notice at a time like this.

Although the Soulless is bigger, taller, and stronger than me, I won't think twice about engaging him in a fight. I don't need to win, necessarily, but if I can push him away from the rope, just long enough to get my hands on it, I could—

No. No, he's too strong to fight off, he'll just drop my siblings into the river before I get a chance to grab the ropes.

There has to be another way to free them.

I search the edge of the bank, not sure what I'm looking for, when I spot an image carved into the base of a tree beside me. I crouch down to get a better look, finding the image of scythe with an arrow pointing south.

Is this what I need to do? Locate a scythe and cut my siblings free?

There's only one way to find out.

I'm back on the forest's path within seconds, retrieving Sickness's riddle from my pants pocket to look for a clue that might lead to the scythe. Having already uncovered the first few lines, I skip to the middle of the page and analyze the next series of words, trying to make sense of them:

They don't have much time, for the wolf isn't slain.
The sky is beckoning, their singing too cruel.

The letters sway in and out of focus, my head light from the sickness coursing through my system. I order myself to focus, to see through the haze blanketing the world, and for a moment it works, my mind thinking with a lucidity that often evades me.

I lift a hand to remove the sweat gathering on my brow, the moisture falling into my eyes, blurring my vision. I don't think much of the action at first, but when I pull my fingers back and find them drenched in red, my heart drops to my feet, heavy with panic.

Blood. Not sweat.

My head — no, my *eyes* — they're. . . they're bleeding.

But that's not possible.

Confident I'm not seeing correctly, I rub at my sockets again — hopeful this isn't my reality — until more blood smears my palms.

What in the sky's name is happening to me?

Fear tightens its fist around my heart, squeezing until my breaths turn to wheezes.

What is wrong with me? How is this possible? How do I stop this?

I close my eyes to keep the fluid from spilling out, my palms pressing into my eyes, trying to limit the damage. My heart kicks into overdrive as the blood continues to pour, filling my sight, my mouth, my nose, my everything — the world submerging in a sea of red.

I fall to my knees and crawl on all fours, using the ground as a guide. I breathe deeply to keep myself calm, but blood clogs my airways, reminding me how helpless and weak I truly am.

There's no chance I'm making it out of here alive.

As soon as the realization hits, my body goes numb from head to toe, stealing my mobility and everything I have. I rest flat on my stomach, my cheek pressed against the dirt.

A pain I've never known blasts through my skull. Sparks of red and white float in my vision, flipping the world on its side.

My eyes close of their own volition, my surroundings already fading, when a sharp voice jolts me back into my body.

There's nothing wrong with you. Sasha's voice finds me in the midst of my panic, solid and comforting. *Remember your last Test? This is entirely in your head. Get up and keep going.*

"I can't," I breathe into the wind, unsure if the Master can hear me. "I can't move my legs. You don't understand—"

Sickness is tricking you, he responds. Such confidence and power laced within those words. *He's making you believe you're dying, but you're not. Don't give in. You're not weak. Prove it to yourself right now.*

I am weak. I *feel* weak. I can't do this.

Feelings are temporary, he says, and for a moment, I forget why I'm afraid. *You can't let your emotions distract you from doing what needs to be done. Start with your toes.* His tone softens, whispering through every corner of my mind, filling it completely. *Wiggle them and focus on regaining your senses.*

Hating that I have nothing left to offer myself, I take his advice, knowing it's better to take direction from him than to have no direction at all.

At that, my toes start to dance in their shoes, moving furiously.

I feel nothing for a while, then can't help but cry out when a faint prickle pulses through my foot. I don't stop moving my toes until the majority of them can be felt, then move on to my legs, arms, and fingers. Moving each limb little by little, shaking away the prickling numbness.

My eyes remain closed as I picture myself healthy, commanding my body to become the image I hold in my mind.

I'm not sick. I'm not dying. I feel alive and invigorated. I'm not going to succumb to this. I'm strong and I'm able. I know how to survive.

Slowly, too slowly, the trance starts to wear off, and my body awakens, flaring to life.

That's it, Sasha says, his voice becoming more difficult to hear, his presence fading as I return to myself one inch at a time. *Now, open your eyes and stand.*

I do, and when I peer down at myself, there's no blood, no pain or evidence of the horrors I've endured. I almost kiss the dirt in appreciation, thankful to have my vitality returned. I rest on the ground for a moment, enjoying the vigor in my body, the awareness in my mind, no longer slow and thick with illness.

A horde of birds zoom overhead, more crazed than when I first entered the forest. There's at least a dozen of them now. Feathers fluttering, wings flapping, beaks shrieking. All of them flying too close to my head.

I jump to my feet, forgetting all about Sickness and his failed attempt to defeat me, and duck to avoid a swooping crow, its claws nearly gouging my shoulder. The creature screeches in my ear as it passes, then returns to the sky, joining the others.

Shut up, I inwardly tell the flock. Please. Shut up. Shut up. Shut up. Shut up. Shut up . . .

I unfold the riddle again, reading frantically to escape the growing chaos. *The sky is beckoning, their singing too cruel.*

Singing? I don't understand how that could apply to any of—

A bird the size of my arm collides with my shoulder, and I swat it away.

What the hell is wrong with them? Why are the birds being so vicious, so loud?

I don't—

Wait.

I snap my head back to look at them, the flock's presence holding more significance than I originally thought. Perhaps the riddle is referring to them. They are the only singing creatures in the forest, after all, and they're never this blaring, this persistent.

Only a handful swarm above. Strange, considering the noise. From the overwhelming clamor filling the woodland, a passerby would think hundreds were flying overhead. Not the mere dozen above me.

Without another thought, I follow the cries, going to where they grow and swell into an all-out scream. I have to cover my ears once I reach the loudest point, my eardrums ringing with their calls.

My heart thunders as I round the bend and come to a tree surrounded by hundreds — no, *thousands* — of the shrieking, fluttering creatures.

I don't even have time to be afraid of them, because there, lying at the very base of the tree, shines the scythe.

Chapter Twenty-Nine

I grab the weapon and run, telling myself the hard part is over. The finish line is near. I take courage in that — in knowing there isn't much left to do —and hope that if I work fast enough, I can free my siblings without much complication.

When I come to a halt at the edge of the waterfront, I see Elisha and Diana have sunk deeper into the river, their shoulders and necks the only parts that remain above the surface.

They sputter and thrash against the oncoming waves — waves which have grown high and fast, unpredictable in their movement.

I stand helplessly on the sidelines, frozen by the sight.

The waves weren't like this before—Sickness must be controlling the currents. It's the only way any of this could be possible.

With that thought in mind, I take inventory of the river with a new perspective, noting how the waves are rough, but not enough to be dangerous. I can manage them. I'll need to make sure I float with the currents instead of against to not get trapped beneath the swells.

My stomach lurches at the idea of drowning out here, a breath away from saving the only family I have left.

I secure the handle of the scythe into the belt loop of my pants.

If I don't move now, I won't move at all, so before I have time to change my mind, I bend my knees and jump. The sensation of being airborne expands in my chest, dropping low in my stomach, until there's no more room left to fall.

I smash into the river's cold surface and kick wildly, unsure if I'm moving toward the light or into blackness, but I don't stop swimming, swimming, swimming. . .

I gasp, cold air slamming into my lungs.

With chattering teeth, I start into an easy swim, my skin prickling against the unbearable cold. I'm not a great swimmer by any means, but I can hold my own thanks to Sasha. He gave me lessons when I was young. Told me it was a vital survival skill, though I didn't understand at the time. I'm grateful he took the time to teach me. Grateful he didn't let me quit, no matter how badly I wanted to. It's another one of the many gifts he's given me.

I rely on that gift now as a wave rises before me, large and intimidating. I tense at the height of it, wanting nothing more than to shrink away and swim in the opposite direction.

Don't panic, my rationale speaks, calming the terror growing in my heart. Go with the wave. If I fight against it, I'll tire myself—

The wave is on me before I can finish the thought, my ears popping as the water pushes me down, down, down, away from the surface. I make the mistake of opening my mouth to gasp for a frantic breath, suffocating like a fool as I choke down buckets of water.

A newly formed fear rises in my belly.

I can't breathe.

I swim desperately toward the light, coughing and spewing as I come up for air, lungs burning for relief.

"Come on, girl, you can do it!" Diana shouts, and although water clings to my lashes, blocking her from view, the sincerity in her voice makes me paddle faster.

I kick my legs as hard as I can, trying to make up for all the time I've lost. Water fills my nose, my mouth, my eyes, making me feel as if I'm drowning rather than swimming. By the time I finally reach the tree, I'm out of breath and crying, overcome with pain, hope, and debilitating fear.

"Who — who — who — are you?" Elisha stutters through chattering teeth, watching wide-eyed as I swim to his side. Just like Diana, he doesn't know who I am, or why I'm here, but our physical resemblance has his face turning white. I wish I had time to explain things to him, but we can't afford such luxuries. Sickness made sure of it.

I dive a hand beneath the freezing water to retrieve the scythe from my belt loop, careful not to drop it as I raise it above my head. I reach for Elisha's rope — he's the closest one to me – when the Soulless releases the cords another three inches, plunging my siblings chin-deep into the river.

Diana begins trembling, sobbing, as water laps over her mouth and nose. Elisha tilts his head back, neck straining with the effort of keeping his head above the water.

For a moment I'm stunned into stillness, unable to move or blink or do anything except watch my family struggle.

Elisha curses as the river picks up speed, the water rushing over his face in waves. He thrashes determinedly against the rope, defiance shining in his eyes, reminding me of our father. I go to him, my limbs triggering into action, and reach above his head to cut at the cord.

I avoid his face as I work, unable to answer the question burning in his eyes, and focus on freeing him. It takes less than a minute before I notice how dull and useless the scythe is, the blade chipped and overused, too worn to be effective.

I cut faster, refusing to let my fears become a reality.

"Hey, you." I look past Elisha and catch a glimpse of Diana's face, her eyes rippling with something sharp. "Hey, you," she repeats around a mouthful of water, choking. "There is . . . no time . . . to save us . . . both."

I keep sawing, my heart rejecting the words.

We will get out of this. We will. This isn't like last time. It won't be like last time.

"There is no time to save us both," she repeats, but I ignore her, fixing my attention on Elisha's rope. "His rope is too thick, and . . ." She lets the sentence hang, leaving me to fill in the rest. I think I know what she's getting at, but I hope I'm wrong. She continues, saying the words I dread. "My rope . . . it's thinner. It'll be quicker if you . . . save me . . . first."

I don't look at her — *can't* look at her. She's been drinking again. I can hear it in the slur of her words, the huskiness in her voice. She doesn't mean it. Doesn't know what she's saying. She's not thinking straight.

"C'mon," she says, her voice a lashing whip in the air. "Saving one . . . is better . . . than saving . . . none." She says it like saving her life is worth sacrificing Elisha's.

Maybe I should let her die. The idea invades my mind, planting itself into the soil of my heart without invitation. *She's selfish, untrustworthy, unpredictable. Everyone's lives would be a lot easier if she were gone. She's a lost cause. She's never going to get better.*

Diana sneers when I don't stop working on Elisha's rope.

My face grows tense, so unbelievably tense I think I'm going to burst.

"Please, hurry," Elisha whispers, choking on laps of water. I almost forgot that he can see and hear everything that's going on, but I don't think about any of that when I look at him. I think about the last time I saw him — how sick and tormented he was. When I carried him home that dreadful day, I didn't know if he'd make it through the night, but after three weeks of recovery, he looks as well as I could've hoped.

I stare at him, willing his eyes to shift to mine so I can see what he's thinking.

He avoids my gaze, afraid to look into the face that mirrors his own.

Fight back, I want to tell him. *Tell our sister she's being an unfair hag. Stand up for yourself. Say something!*

He doesn't, and even though I want him to prove me wrong, I expected the silence. Elisha would die for our sister — unpredictable heart and all.

Just then, a snap sounds above us, and it's the only signal we get before my twin's rope breaks from the tree, splitting in half.

Emperors above! Finally!

I lunge for him as he plunges into the river, snatching the collar of his shirt before he disappears beneath the surface. I tread water as hard as I can to keep us both afloat, untying his hands and feet so he can swim on his own.

Once he's free, I go back for Diana, every fiber in my being telling me to leave her here, to let her perish.

I bite my tongue, knowing that isn't what I want. Not truly. I have to save her, and I will, but I'm not doing it for her sake, I'm doing it for my mother's. For mine. I couldn't live with the guilt of leaving her behind.

"NO!" Elisha screams, and when I turn to follow his line of sight, I understand his hysteria.

The Soulless behind the tree releases the last few inches of the rope, smiling, dropping Diana into the roaring waters below.

I swim toward her on instinct. I don't have time to think about how this could end.

But as soon as my head submerges, the tides pick up in speed, pushing me up and away from her. I swipe faster at the waves, but the attempt is futile. I scan the currents for any signs of her, but see nothing except blue-white waves and never-ending blackness beneath.

No. No. No. No. No! This can't be happening. Not again. Not like this!

I stay under the surface a few moments longer, hoping I can locate her among the growing chaos.

The waves are too vicious, too strong. I can't swim through them. I can't get to her. Time is slipping by. She can't hold her breath more than a few minutes.

My lungs plead for air, but I don't give in.

I welcome the pain, the sting.

My punishment.

I welcome whatever suffering drowning can give me because I deserve it.

"Nadia."

Chapter Thirty

I thrash against a memory, my exhaustion chaining me to a day I wish to forget. I try to wake from it. Try to escape the trenches of its hold, but sleep keeps me under.

Sasha stands in the middle of our living room, arms folded across his chest, closing me off.

He's been doing that a lot lately.

"I don't know what you expect from me," I say, the words honest but painful, difficult to get out. I wish they weren't true, but they are. I have no clue how we're going to get out of this. How we're supposed to move on.

"I don't want you to worry," he murmurs, pacing in circles. I hate it when he does that. For once, I wish he'd just sit down and say what he's thinking. I'm not a child. He doesn't need to hide things from me anymore. "We'll figure something out. We always do."

Such careful, practiced words.

I shake my head, knee bouncing with restlessness. "This is different, and you know it." The words sounded less sour in my head, but there it is — the truth. Something my family has been lacking recently. "They're never coming back."

Sasha flashes me a hard glare, sharp with impatience, and for the first time in years, I don't like the person I see. Why is he doing this — pretending like what happened doesn't affect him? Hurt him?

"Parents are supposed to die before their children," he says simply. As if losing the people who raised us, the only people loved us, isn't something to sniffle about. "It was going to happen sooner or later. The quicker you come to terms with that, the easier things will get."

My cheeks burn at his harshness, at the cruelty in his tone. "How could you say that?" I lean forward on the couch, too tired to stand. "How can you act like we're not supposed to be affected by this? Like we're somehow weak if we are?" I don't mean to cry in front of him, but I do. It's one of the only times I allow myself to be vulnerable.

"Parents are supposed to die before their children," he repeats, looking away from me. Like my emotion is too much for him to handle. "But siblings are supposed to be there for each other no matter what. We still have each other, Nadia. We need to focus on us, because we're still here. We're all that matters now."

We're all that matters now.

"Nadia?"

I hear my name again, but this time, it's not my brother who speaks it.

I open my eyes, aware of the fluffy pillow resting under my head, and find Cruelty sitting on the edge of the bed. His bed. I debate shuffling away, but he's already watching me, so I stay put.

His eyes are thoughtful, somewhat wary, as I gauge my surroundings, surprised by the familiarity of his room. Perhaps he's waiting for me to scorn him or bolt through the door like I did the first time I woke up here.

The Master's mouth starts to move, but I can't hear what he's saying. I tilt my head to the side, trying to get rid of the clog in my ears, and a sloshing noise fills my head, followed by a wetness dripping down the side of my neck.

Water, I realize. But how—

The Test.

It all comes back to me in short, fleeting flashes, a triggered on-slaught of memories.

The riddle. The birds. The oak tree. The Soulless. Elisha. Diana. Me. The current. And then—

Nothing. Nothing but suffocating silence.

I look at Cruelty again, but unlike before, I'm able to under-stand his words. "How are you feeling?" he asks, his face hard. Cold. Assessing. But the way he tucks a wild strand of hair behind my ear is anything but dispassionate. The intimacy in it surprises me. Scares me.

I sit up and study my lap. His hand falls away from my face, the heat of his touch gone.

"What happened?" I murmur. I stare at my fingernails, chipped and bloody from biting them too low. I never used to do that. My mother used to say gnawing on our fingers was a nasty habit, so I never did it. Never needed to, until after she was gone.

I glance up at Cruelty when he doesn't answer, his hair wet and disheveled as if he's just gotten out of the shower. But that doesn't explain why his shirt is soaked, the material sticking to his chest in a way I find remarkably distracting. He doesn't smell like soap, ei-ther. He smells of fish and musk and something earthy.

He smells of the river.

"You were there," I whisper, fitting the details together. "Why?" My eyes don't stray from his, seeking an answer within them. "Why did you come? Why didn't you leave me there? You should've just left me there. You should've let me drown."

As soon as I say it, I realize how much I mean it. How much I didn't want to be saved. "I didn't. . . ask you. . . to come after me."

I barely get the last couple words out, before I bury my face into Cruelty's pillow, my throat burning as I work to keep the sobs down. I turn the pain into anger — running from the sorrow rising within — and slam my fists into the mattress, picturing Sickness's face.

I can only imagine the things he's doing to celebrate my failure. My sister's death.

We're all that matters now.

We're all that matters now.

We're all that matters now.

It was supposed to be the four of us.

Always the four of us.

Now only two remain.

Life is incomplete with two. Two is lonely. Two is dismal.

We weren't meant to live this way.

But my deal is over now. I lost. I didn't save both my siblings, and now Airabeth will become my permanent home. I can handle whatever suffering comes with working until I die, but I can't cope with the imprisonment of Elisha and the Flames, I just can't.

I start to weep when I think about Sasha — of how his mission was for nothing. Every fear I overcame, every wound I endured, every game I played. . . none of it was enough to beat them. Even with Cruelty's help, I couldn't do it. Couldn't win.

I raise my head from the pillow — eyes aching, welling with tears — and find Cruelty standing by the window. I didn't even sense him get up. Even though I've seen it before, his stealth surprises me.

Though the curtains to the window are drawn, he stares at them, deep in thought.

I wonder what he's thinking.

I hate that I care.

"Get out," I say, the words rough and scratchy.

I'm not sure why I'm being like this. Why I'm taking my hostility out on him.

It's not his fault I couldn't save my sister.

Cruelty doesn't stop gazing at the black curtains, but the slight flicker in his eyes suggests he's heard, thinking up a response. "But this is my room," he says, not a hint of anger or sympathy in his voice.

When he looks over to me, I wish I could read his expression. It might make me less annoyed if I knew his intentions.

I glare at him and throw off the blankets, childishly seeking a reaction. Being angry is better than being sad, after all. "Fine," I mutter. "Then I'll leave." Even though my face feels puffy, and my bones ache with fatigue, I force myself to leave the comforts of the bed.

I use the edge of the mattress for support, the effects of almost drowning still lingering. I hug my arms around my waist to ward off the cold, feeling a bandage through my shirt, wrapped tight around the injection site. I feel over my thigh and hip to discover both of them dressed with gauze, too.

"I'm not kicking you out," the Master says, leaning his back against the wall, face drawn with fatigue and something deeper. If I didn't know better, I'd think he was worried. I distantly wonder how long he's been up, waiting for me to wake. "You don't have to go."

But he doesn't try to stop me when I head for the door, his eyes trailing every movement, as if whatever I do is my choice and no one else's.

It's a freedom no Master has ever given anyone, let alone a Flame.

"Why are you doing this?" I say, pausing halfway to the exit, genuinely curious.

Cruelty's brows pinch together, his mouth a hard line of stubbornness as he says, "You're mad because I won't keep you hostage?" He chuckles lowly, the note sore and full of bitterness.

"No," I bite back. "I'm mad because you're making this impossible!"

He clenches his jaw, a vein in his throat bulging with the action. "Making what impossible?" His eyes narrow slightly, wanting me to say my truth out loud, and admit what I'm thinking. A mocking request.

If I weren't so distraught, I might've withheld the information out of spite or sheer stubbornness, but since my deal with Warfare is done, I have nothing left to hide. "For me to hate you," I say at last, my heart speeding with the humiliating confession. "You're making it impossible for me to hate you, and . . ."

And I don't know what to make of that. I hold his stare and lower my mental shield, letting him listen to my thoughts. I'm only going to say this once, and I can't bear to do it out loud. *I don't know how to trust an enemy I was raised to hate. All this time, I've been waiting for you to reveal your true nature and betray me in the worst of ways, but you don't. You haven't. What in the sky's name am I supposed to do with that? How am I supposed to respond?*

Neither of us says anything for a while, and I don't know what to do, or how I should break the silence. He told me I could leave, so I'm not sure why I stay. Based on the cautious gleam in his eyes, he's not sure either

"How did you know what I wanted to do at the river?" I ask, needing an excuse to stay. To understand why he saved my life when I didn't want to be saved.

"I know what you're thinking," he says plainly, as if that's all the explanation I need. "And if I can't outright read your thoughts due to a mental block, I can sense your emotions. Like now, for instance. You're afraid, and unsure. Utterly repulsed by me."

I fold my arms, uncomfortable with him reading me like this.

"But sometimes," he whispers, a faint smirk on his mouth, "underneath all that twisting hatred, I sense something a little less afraid. A little less unsure. A little less repulsed. Why is that, do you think?"

Warmth creeps into his eyes, and for a moment, I forget why I'm angry with him. Why I ever thought figuring him out would be simple, when he's anything but that. Emperors above, why couldn't he just be evil like the others? Why does he have to complicate things, and confuse everything I thought I knew? Why isn't he cruel? Why isn't he savage?

He isn't supposed to be this way.

"Elisha." I whisper his name abruptly, memories from Sickness's Test pouring in. "What happened to him? I-I saw him before Diana. . ." I can't bring myself to finish the sentence. "And then I went into the water. . ."

"After I pulled you from the river," he cuts in, saving me from spiraling, "I wiped his mind and placed a new stronghold on him. He won't remember anything that happened this evening. Until all this blows over, he thinks he's an only child."

I blink at him. "What do you mean until all this blows over? It's already over. I lost. I couldn't save them both." I struggle to interpret the confusion on his face, but for a brief moment, that confusion gives me hope. Like maybe we still have a chance, and I've misunderstood everything.

"Sickness has deemed your Test victorious," he says. "You passed."

I frown, my face crumpling.

He's lying. This can't be possible. Diana is gone. I couldn't save her.

"The riddle didn't say you had to save both your siblings," he explains, sensing my thoughts. "And since there was only one scythe, you were required to free only one family member in return."

"So, the Test was rigged?" I ask, still not understanding. "I was never meant to save them both?" I know the answer before Cruelty gives it. This is Sickness we're talking about. The slimiest and most morbid Master of them all. "The Test shouldn't have involved my siblings," I say, trying to make sense of the unfairness of it. "When I told Warfare I was going to take the Tests, he implied that my family would remain safe. He said they wouldn't come to Airabeth or be harmed." Didn't he?

"But your Test didn't take place in Airabeth," Cruelty says. "You were in Tempus when Diana died. Warfare told you he would let your family go about their usual, everyday routine, but the Masters are always a part of that routine. They never promised not to harm your family. Diana drowned at the hands of a Soulless, so really, Sickness didn't break any rules."

I rub my hands down my face, the grief hitting me in one fell swoop.

This can't be happening. I was cheated, I was tricked, I was given an impossible task.

"Think about it," Cruelty says, closing the distance between us. He's within arm's reach now, and I have a compelling urge to lean into him, to see what it'd be like to stand close to all that power, that beauty. "If any of the Masters broke your bargain, that would mean we violated the Immortal Law, and violating the Law comes with great consequence. Sickness may be rash and reckless, but he isn't stupid enough to risk putting himself in danger."

I shake my head, disbelieving. "What is the Immortal Law?" I ask, unwilling to put my trust in rules I know nothing about.

"It's part of the judicial system where we come from," he says. "Before the Emperors and Masters came to earth, my people made the Law to protect humans, should any of us decide to abuse our power."

I close my eyes for a moment, trying to understand. Came here? What does he mean came here? Where did the Emperors come from? And the Masters? How did they get their position of power in the first place? Out of all the history textbooks we have on our world's rulers, none of them answer these fundamental questions, and that makes me think the Masters prefer it this way.

I consider voicing my queries out loud, but instead I say, "Protect humans? What does that mean, exactly? When have we ever been protected?"

A ripple of darkness slashes through the glow of his eyes, and for a moment he looks human. Like he's capable of being afraid. "Masters can't physically kill mortals," Cruelty explains, a shadow passing over him. One I wish to understand. "If Sickness wrongfully sentenced your sister to death, the Sacred Seven would be paying for it right now. It's against the Immortal Law for us to physically harm or take a mortal life, so we strictly manipulate humans through their thoughts. It's one of the main reasons the Masters get Soulless to do their killings for them. It's an easy way not to get their hands dirty."

The Soulless from the river rises to the forefront of my mind, and with it, a memory of the Master of Fear. I think back to the first time I met him in the dining room — how he prevented Warfare from punching me when I challenged him after my first Test. I never did figure out why he interrupted. Why the whole room didn't jump me when they had the chance.

"So, the Immortal Law won't allow you to physically harm mortals," I say, "but it allows you to hurt us through our minds instead?"

Cruelty crosses his arms, staring down at me through dark, thick lashes. "No law is perfect," he says. "When the Masters and Emperors came to earth, both groups were given a different set of leadership objectives, but the one rule we were all instructed to follow forbade us from directly interfering with mortal lives. Before the war, the Masters' only job was to implant positive thoughts into human minds and promote good behavior, nothing more. At the end of the day, we give humans the freedom to choose their own actions, and that is the Law we live by."

"I get that," I say, speaking slowly so as to not lose my temper. "But did your people never stop to consider what could happen if the Masters used their mind infiltration *against* us?"

Cruelty clenches his jaw, uncrossing his arms. "If they did, the mortal realm wouldn't be in this predicament now, would it? There is no rule that permits earth's leaders from using their strongholds for negativity, only that we are to never physically intervene with a human life."

I worry my bottom lip, struggling to accept that Sickness did nothing wrong. According to the Immortal Law, my sister's death isn't a violation of their rules, nor the terms I set with Warfare.

Why didn't I make our deal more specific? Why didn't I make more demands?

"You will get through this." The gentleness in Cruelty's voice catches my attention, my heart jumping in an unsettling way. "I know you think you won't, but you will. Grief is like an ocean," he says. "It comes in waves. Sometimes it's calm, hardly noticeable. Other times, it's violent, overwhelming, and unexplainably harsh. But you can't control the tides, or the current. All you can do is learn how to swim through the storm, because eventually, the water will settle. Death is not a thing you just *get over*. It's a thing you learn to live with."

He says it like he knows what it's like to experience great loss. Like he's told himself those exact words a million times before. Perhaps, after centuries of being alive, he has. I can't even imagine the number of people he's met and possibly befriended throughout his life, only to watch them die over and over, forever caged to this world, unable to follow them into whatever comes after.

If I were him, I don't think I'd bother getting close to anyone at all. The pain of losing that many loved ones. . . I couldn't bear it.

Some distant part of me aches at the thought. At the fact that he inadvertently shared something personal with me, whether he intended to or not. I drop my gaze from his, not liking the way the air has changed between us.

"Your knuckles," I whisper, nodding to the bruised and bloodied flesh I've just noticed, diverting the conversation. "What happened to them?"

He doesn't say anything as he stares at the raw skin, his eyes haunted by some unseen horror. "What I do in my spare time has nothing to do with you," he says coldly, his voice hard and full of apathy — not at all like it was a moment ago.

I take a step away from him then, the closeness becoming too much, and realize he's right. I'm losing sight of what this is — of what *he* is — and need to remember that Airabeth and everyone in it mean nothing to me.

Cruelty's business is none of my concern. I don't know why I thought it could be.

Chapter Thirty-One

I immerse myself in work to keep busy, engaging in the same dull, mind-numbing tasks of washing dishes, cooking food, and scrubbing the showers. I volunteer to do chores outside of my jurisdiction, taking on more than I can handle to avoid thinking about my family, Sickness, or the Flames. Even Cruelty.

It's been five days since I've seen him, but it's not from lack of trying. Since Flames aren't known to seek company of the men trying to kill them, it's hard to hunt down a Master without drawing attention. Even so, I've spent every night searching and asking around for him, but no one knows where he is or what he's up to. Perhaps he's left Airabeth to deal with some stately duties, along with Warfare and Obedience.

Even so, why didn't Cruelty tell me he was leaving? Why didn't he say goodbye?

"Sunday, you have to try this and tell us what you think." Tuesday turns away from the stove and motions me over, inviting me to taste the new stew she's been working on.

December stands beside her and retrieves a set of bowls from the cabinet above, helping to prepare the dish.

It looks like he tries not to touch her too much as he reaches for a handful of napkins on the counter, his hand straying to then retracting from her waist. Distancing himself. Tuesday must notice the war waging within him because she leans into his side, brushing her hip against his. It's like a dance when they're around each other, their bodies always in sync.

They aren't usually this affectionate during the day. In fact, they try not to be around each other at all, but since it's well past dinnertime and the kitchen is empty, they're free to enjoy each other's company. Even with me around, they don't feel the need to hide their warmth or avoid each other's advances, which is good, because I'm not going to say anything.

We're friends now.

I'm not sure when I started addressing us as such, but they always seem to have my back, so I have theirs. No one needs to know that Sickness's bride-to-be has fallen for another man.

It's not her fault her heart started beating for a Flame she wasn't supposed to love.

"I'm afraid if you don't come taste this dish," December says to me, a smile in his voice, "our chef will be most offended." Tuesday pokes him in the ribs with a ladle, laughing when he picks her up and spins her around.

I smile back, my cheeks aching from the action. It's been a long while since I've smiled. It's been even longer since I laughed, but for the first time in months, my chest doesn't feel like there's a boulder sitting on it.

"She doesn't need my opinion," I tell him, my heart lifting when he rolls his eyes at me fondly. "I grew up eating frogs, rabbits, and deer. My palate isn't the most reliable thing. . ."

I trail off when I see them gazing at each other, letting them bask in these few stolen moments together, because moments are all they'll ever get.

It doesn't matter how much they crave each other, they can never fully embrace the attraction between them. Tuesday will marry Sickness in less than two weeks, and once she binds herself to him, her relationship with December will be nothing but a distant memory. A hope that'll die before it ever gets a chance to truly breathe.

The door to the kitchen flies open, and the laughter between my friends dies, replaced by a shuddering quiet. December swears and moves away from Tuesday, leaving her shaking by the stove. I wave him over to my sink and shove a plate and dish towel into his hands, making him look busy.

He nods at me — a silent thank you — then glances over his shoulder. He gives Tuesday a comforting smile, and her mouth twitches up in response, wanting to return it. But Sickness is already sauntering into the room, causing her lips to retreat into a thin line, the blood draining from her face.

Something grave and trembling comes over me in the Master's presence, every muscle and limb going taut. I pin my gaze to my shaking hands and clench a plate beneath the dish water, willing my body to calm.

Although it's been days since Diana drowned, I can still see the horror on her face, hear the betrayal in her screams, as she plunged below the waters, too deep for me to reach.

"It smells like vomit and piss in here." Sickness paces about the kitchen, waving a pale hand through the air. "Do you people ever clean it?"

I inch my hand toward a knife on the counter, throat bobbing as I swallow back my fear.

I'm going to kill him. I *have* to kill him, and I don't care what happens afterward, but I need him gone. We *all* need him gone, it's the right thing to do. Noble, even. Sasha would take this chance. My mother would take this chance. I *need* to take this chance.

My fingers fall just inches short of the handle when I peer over to see Sickness, his face mottled with fresh bruises.

I forget the knife and turn toward him, staring at the purplish welts on both eyes, the nail marks crisscrossing the lengths of his cheeks and chin, bringing attention to the brutality of his veins.

His nose, usually straight and pert, has a yellow splotch spreading over the bridge, an indication that it's been broken and reset.

Grim pleasure courses through me at the sight of it. At the suffering he must've endured. He deserves to be wounded, to be tormented and antagonized for everything he's done. I'm sure whoever did this to him had good reason, though I can't imagine what human would be strong enough to. . .

A chill slides into my bones as I remember Cruelty's battered knuckles.

I don't know if I should be glad or unsettled by what he's done. Perhaps this was all some personal act of revenge, or a move he's been planning for a while, but I can't help but wonder if Cruelty took the measure on my behalf.

Sickness surveys the room like a fox, every movement shrewd and powerful, demanding to be feared. His dark yellow eyes brighten when they land on Tuesday, his gaze traveling up her legs, breasts, and mouth, lingering long enough for all of us to know exactly what he's thinking.

My neck prickles at the sight of that feral gleam in his eyes, and when I look at Tuesday, she's rigid as a board. I have the urge to hug her right then because I understand the fear, the feeling of entrapment, rising in her eyes.

I felt it when Warfare showed up at my house three weeks ago. I felt it when I first walked into a dining room full of Masters. I feel it now, as Sickness skips over to my friend, arms swinging like a cheerful child, disturbingly playful.

I force myself to watch as he hugs Tuesday from behind, her eyes wild and frenzied.

This is another reminder, another reason, as to why I need to pass my Tests. There are so many people like Tuesday. So many people who've been forced into a life they don't want because the Masters put them there.

Beside me, December clenches his hands, cheeks red with rage. I consider reaching out to him, to tell him not to do anything reckless, but the darkness in his eyes steals my words.

"Aren't you pleased to see me?" Sickness asks, his mouth sucking hard at a spot near Tuesday's collarbone. She winces at his touch, her eyes squeezing shut.

"Yes, Master, of course." My friend's voice shakes over the words, but she fakes a believable smile, a flicker of brightness reaching her eyes. I wonder how many times she's practiced that smile in the mirror, relying on this ruse to keep her alive.

She does a reasonable job at keeping up the facade, but the moment her gaze flutters to December, we all catch her mistake. The exchange is quick, almost missable, but Sickness catches it.

He yanks Tuesday's arm and spins her around, pressing her chest to his, leaving no room for escape. Her body visibly tenses at the closeness, but she doesn't make a move to back away. She isn't that stupid.

December's nostrils flare, but he doesn't step toward her. He isn't stupid either.

Sickness whispers something unintelligible into her ear, draining the light from her eyes, scaring us all.

December snarls from beside me before he charges Sickness, catching everyone off guard. He violently shoves the Master in his chest, pushing him away from Tuesday.

"December, don't!" Tuesday warns, but he ignores her, swinging for Sickness's jaw.

A crack explodes through the air, and Tuesday pushes in between them, holding December back.

"You little twit," the Master hisses, pointing at December. "I should obliterate you for that." He spits a chunk of black blood onto the floor and laughs, wiping his mouth. "Your mind is mine now, boy."

"No!" Tuesday shouts, and rushes to the Master's side, clutching his forearm.

Sickness raises a brow at her.

"No," she repeats softly, petting his arm affectionately. "It's all right, I can pay for his mistake, Master. Whatever you want." She nods eagerly, eyes pleading for December's sake. "He's just a servant," she adds, growing more desperate, her cover slipping. She cups her palm to Sickness's cheek, drawing his gaze to hers. "It's you I'm marrying, remember? You and me forever, that's all I want."

Sickness looks unconvinced as he glances back and forth between the secret lovers.

I step back toward the sink, looking for that damn knife—

Sickness glares at Tuesday and cocks his head to the side, reaching into her mind to see the truth for himself. My friend doesn't budge at the invasion, barely flinching as he rummages through her thoughts.

Emperors above, I hope her shields are strong enough to block him out, to hide the emotions she doesn't want him to see.

"Of course, my love," Sickness muses, straightening the wrinkles in his cobalt coat. "Anything for you."

But the way he says it, so sharp and resentful. . .

He looks away from her then, a ring of shadow swirling through his eyes. "I have some work to finish, but we'll talk later." He turns away from Tuesday without demanding a kiss goodbye, and that terrifies me.

He doesn't even acknowledge my presence or look in December's direction for one final glare. He just walks to the door, humming a cheerful tune on his way out.

I wait for the door to swing closed behind Sickness before running to Tuesday. "Bleeding hell, are you all right?" I ask her. She nods and December reaches for her, but she waves him off, not having any of it.

"No," she says, her voice breaking over the word. "Just . . ." She doesn't finish her thought, and I don't blame her. She shoves December's chest, eyes blazing, pushing past him toward the sleeping chambers.

I open my mouth to ask if she wants me to go with her, but she squeezes my shoulder, silencing me. "I'll see you again tonight, yes? At the Freedom Celebration?" Tears rim her eyes, but she doesn't let them fall.

"The Freedom Celebration?" I repeat, feeling stupid for asking a question at a time like this.

"It's the one time of year when all servants are allowed to leave the house," she sniffs, rubbing her nose with the back of her hand. "Everyone takes advantage of it. Think of it as our one night without the Sacred Seven's surveillance. There is good food, music, and entertainment. And the Masters won't be there. This is the one time of year they put on a party for us," she explains. "They claim it's their way of showing appreciation for all our hard work, but there's more to it than that. This is a night where the Soulless will be quick to take out the weak and impressionable, which I believe is the Masters' true intent behind the Celebration. The Soulless are hungry for violence, and no one, not even the Flames, will stop them from getting what they want. It's an evening full of abandon, which can be fun, as long as you don't get lost in the crowds and hang around the square. You're welcome to join, if you want."

I pull her into a quick embrace, but say nothing, knowing full well I won't be going.

I don't need to go to the Freedom Celebration and play into another one of the Masters' tactics to keep us foolish and vulnerable. On the surface, the party sounds intoxicating, carefree, and all the things we never get to be with the Masters hovering over us, but how could anyone enjoy such a night when someone at the Celebration — someone we might recognize and work with — could suffer at the hands of a Soulless?

As soon as Tuesday leaves, December runs after her, mumbling an apology to me as he goes. The strain of the evening remains long after their departure, growing stronger as I think about their future.

Tuesday is in danger, more so now than ever before. There has to be a way to get her away from Sickness. I just hope it isn't too late.

TUESDAY WASN'T EXAGGERATING when she said all the servants would be at the Freedom Celebration tonight. From the window in the Quarters kitchen, I watch as the backyard teems with people, the most I've ever seen in one spot. Servants mill around the field in groups, drinking and laughing, dancing wildly to the music coming from the square.

Despite the acres of land reserved for the celebration, there's little room to fit them all, leaving the space feeling small and congested. Tables of treats and pastries are scattered throughout, half of them already empty, waiting to be refilled. Flames willingly serve the crowd, though I'm not sure why they're working on their one night off.

Although I'm separate from the chaos of the party, I feel on edge. Being alone in the manor is a new experience for me, and I'm not sure what an evening of solitude will bring.

The thought makes my breath cut hard through my chest, as if I'm swallowing hot coals instead of air.

I refocus my attention on a group of musicians playing in the grass, the performers clapping, stomping, shouting, and whirling without missing a beat, the melody vibrating in my bones, even from this distance.

The hum of conversation trickles through the transition of songs, a chorus of laughter erupting when a familiar tune spills out from the instruments. It isn't long before the music becomes irresistible, my head nodding of its own volition.

The scene reminds me of the town festivals I used to go to with my family, back when times were much simpler. The memories of laughing, eating, and dancing until my feet hurt come to mind, my siblings a constant presence by my side.

I miss how we used to share our pastries and stay up late. I miss how we used to place bets, play pranks, and encourage each other's antics. I miss their company. Their embrace. The little things.

I lean my forehead against the windowpane, smiling when I spot Tuesday and December in the crowd. By the looks of it, they've made amends, talking and laughing wildly as if they're the only two people in the world. December gestures to the madness surrounding them, noting each and every detail, like it's his first time seeing it.

It makes sense, given he hasn't ventured outside since his designated month. It's a miracle as to how he hasn't gone mad from it. I get to leave the house once a week, and I'm barely keeping my sanity.

I move away from the window and start cleaning the counters to keep busy. With the music blaring across the field, sleep won't find me willingly, so maybe if I work myself into exhaustion, I'll be able to get some rest.

I don't know how much time has passed before I start swaying to the music, my head nodding to the familiar tune, getting lost in the rhythm. Hours slip by as I dance around the kitchen, cleaning and washing anything I can get my hands on, when a whisper at my ear, deep and sensuous, stops me cold in my tracks.

"Why are you dancing alone?" it asks.

Chapter Thirty-Two

I turn toward the voice that shouldn't be here, my blood heating in response to the trouble it promises. Even with the hood of his cloak pulled up to veil the top half of his face, there's no mistaking those shifting blue eyes, the full lips that curve into a tempting smile.

"What are you doing here?" I ask, careful to keep the surprise from my tone, feigning indifference.

"I do own part of this manor," the Master drawls, his voice low and lilting, mixing with the orchestra's song outside. "And this is the best seat in the house." He nods to the window, the party beyond. "I thought I'd come by and keep an eye on everyone. Make sure things remain somewhat tame."

He takes a small step toward me, teetering on an edge he's never crossed before.

I tell myself to turn around and run — his presence will only bring chaos — but I remain still, deciding against it. He'll catch me if I try to run, and what's the point of starting a fight I know I can't win?

"Look," he starts, lowering his hood to reveal the rest of his face. "I don't—"

He stops when a group of drunken servants run past the window, screaming and hollering, laughing at a joke we can't hear. My stomach tightens at the sound, the shouts of pleasure and pain too close to decipher.

The strangers rushing by clumsily are entirely unaware of my watching them, and I turn back to Cruelty to find his hand extended in offering, a playful glint in his eye.

What is he—?

"Would you like to dance?" he asks, a small smile lifting his mouth — the most wicked thing I've seen on him.

For a moment I can only contemplate his proposal.

I find his cordiality to be considerably strange, given how our last conversation ended.

What I do in my spare time has nothing to do with you. I try to forget those condescending words. How empty they made me feel when he said them.

"People only dance when there's something to celebrate," I say, and lean against the counter beside me, trying to feign indifference, when really, I want to put distance between us.

I scan the kitchen, looking for a quick escape. By the time I find one, Cruelty is already beside me, his oversized cloak brushing against my arm as he leans on the counter, mirroring my position.

He crosses his feet at the ankles, the muscles in his thighs flexing. I hate that I notice that. I hate what it does to my heart. How it makes it flip and pound in a way it shouldn't.

"You're alive," Cruelty says from my right, his shoulder bumping into mine. Emperors above, I resent how close we are. It's too hot. I can't breathe. "And you're granted the opportunity to see another day. I think that in itself is worth celebrating."

He smiles, but it's not like any of the other smiles he's given me before. There's an earnestness to it. A warmth I feel in my bones, hitting deeper than I thought a smile could.

"Do you have someone back home?" he asks, and I nearly fall over at the insinuation. At the mischievousness in his tone. I didn't think he had it in him to be coy. "Is that why you're so reluctant to be near me?"

I start to deny his claim, but then think better of it. "Yes," I blurt without thought, not wanting to linger on this conversation. Perhaps if he thinks my heart belongs to another, we can stop whatever game he's trying to play. "We've been together three years now. It'll be four next month."

Cruelty tilts his head to the side, as if preparing to invade my mind and see the truth for himself. I brace for the invasion, anticipating his strongholds to come pouring in, but—

"Liar," he says, and flicks the tip of my nose, startling me. "Your nostrils always flare when you're lying."

"I . . . I'm not lying."

"Then why are you blushing?" His smile widens as my exasperation grows. "If you only had eyes for one man, then you wouldn't be so flush in the face."

Indeed. My face does feel hot. Almost sunburned.

"I'm only flush because you're making me angry," I say, and glance over my shoulder, unable to look at him. Outside, I find Tuesday and December dancing by the bonfire, laughing and drinking, lost in a world of their own creation. Something flares in my chest, and it takes me a moment to recognize the feeling as desire. It does look like fun.

I don't want to make Cruelty angry by rejecting him. Not when he's been helping me pass my Tests. Embarrassing him will only turn him away from me, and the last thing I want to do is jeopardize my chances at winning, which has only been possible because of all that we've been doing together.

What are we doing together?

"All right," I say, my heart dreading what's to come. "But only one dance."

Cruelty bows his head, bending slightly at the waist. "I'll take what I can get." And with that he pulls me into a dance, one hand confidently enveloping mine, while the other goes to my waist, sending shivers down my spine.

He leads me across the kitchen with a smoothness that shouldn't be possible for a man of his size, yet he guides me effortlessly.

The music is a dull bass pounding beneath our feet, the faint light of the kitchen casting shadows over the walls, illuminating our silhouettes. Close. So close, I almost forget the shapes belong to Cruelty and me.

"You're not half bad," I observe, following the Master's lead. "Did a conquest of yours teach you how to dance?"

Cruelty twirls me around before spinning me back into his arms, the heat of his body streaming into mine. "I'm usually not a good dancer. I guess my feet move differently when I'm with you."

A blush overtakes me, and I quickly search for a change of topic, my heart racing. "What do the other Masters think of your little liaisons?" I say, gesturing between us. "I'd think that helping your enemies goes against everything you stand for. Aren't you concerned about getting caught?"

He goes still for a moment, the amusement fading from his gaze. He leans forward, his eyes fixed on mine.

I catch the scent of rosewood and pine. My breath hitches.

"Is that worry I sense, Flame?" His hands press tighter into my lower back, drawing me closer. He smiles. "Thoughtful of you to care for my well-being, but I think I can take care of myself."

And I think he can take care of himself too, but he knows that's not what I'm implying. "Why can't you be honest with me?" I ask, not liking how he knows more about me than I do about him. "Why won't you tell me the truth? I don't understand you."

"You don't want to understand me, Nadia." He whispers my given name — not Sunday, or Bunny, or whatever else the Masters call me. "My truth is scarier than the unknown. It would only frighten you to know what lives in here." He gently brings his hand to the side of my head, his forefinger lingering on my temple. "And I don't like seeing you afraid."

I stare up at him, his eyes strikingly clear despite the night's shadow. I don't know if the last part of what he said is true, or if he only mentioned it to keep me quiet, but either way, it doesn't work.

"I'm already afraid," I say. Perhaps the most honest thing I've said in weeks. "There's really nothing you can share that will terrify me more than I already am."

The Master considers me for a moment, eyes flickering back and forth between mine as if searching for an answer there. Seconds of uninterrupted silence fall between us, pushing us further and further apart, though we couldn't be more physically close.

I get the distinct impression he isn't going to say anything at all, but then his mouth is at my ear, his words a breath of flame on my neck as he whispers, "Don't say I didn't warn you."

And with that, he pulls me into his mind, casting his past and memories onto me, delivering a transparency I didn't think he'd give. Not willingly.

The inside of his head is dark at first, the world submerged in shadow and ink, my eyes blind. Less than a second passes before the door to his thoughts opens, the light within it glowing, beckoning me to enter.

I move swiftly through the passage before he can change his mind, preparing for the worst. I've been wanting to know Cruelty's thoughts since the moment I saw him healing January all those weeks ago.

Besides, he's freely inviting me into something personal, and to pass that up is to pass up the truth, to deny the chance to uncover the Masters' mystery.

I'd be a fool not to seize this opportunity.

The blackness starts to clear as I creep deeper into the room of Cruelty's mind, the smoke around me lifting until I'm no longer seeing through my eyes, but his. The images come then, accompanied by the Master's distant voice, guiding me through the memories.

It used to be an honor to be called a Master, he tells me, presenting a blur of what life was like before the war–– before the Masters and Emperors turned against each other, expelling light and goodness. *Working alongside the Emperors was one of the greatest privileges I could've asked for, and although the responsibility was heavy, it was a burden I carried with pride.*

He shows me brief images of them — the righteous leaders who once ruled over our world. The flashes are quick, barely lasting beyond a few seconds, though I manage to glimpse a pair of luminescent eyes; the golden hilt of a sword; broad hands and even broader chests, each one adorned in a different color. A color that represents their various virtues, I realize.

We grew up together, the lot of us, Cruelty says. *You see, the Masters and Emperors come from another realm, one far from this earth. The citizens who reside in our homeland have various abilities, all of us lucky to have been born in a domain where such gifts are given.*

Through quick-moving images, I catch sight of a glorious city surrounded by mountains, the streets filled with smiling faces and helping hands, laughter ringing in the air. Houses made of black and gray stone stretch for miles, the world rich with community. Outdoor shops line every corner, selling various garments and accessories alike, the town bursting with color.

This is the Emperors' unearthly kingdom, the place they returned to after losing the war. The place they call home.

All of our people have the skill to infiltrate minds, some more so than others. Those who possess the strongest abilities are appointed to rule over various lands throughout the universe, working to keep the realms unified. The ones who aren't quite strong enough to run other lands stay in the kingdom and help govern it, responsible for administering laws and keeping peace amongst the people.

I marvel at the reality of it, of this vibrant, textured world I never knew existed.

When earth was created, it was clear the human sector needed rulers to keep chaos at bay, so my people sent the lot of us, believing we would work well together. When the Masters and Emperors came to earth, the majority of our immortal powers were stripped from us, leaving us close to human. Minus the ability to summon objects and get inside human minds, we were left with mere traces of our power. Our job was to strictly help the mortal lands prosper, so our realm didn't see reason to leave us with our full abilities, lest we let it get to our heads.

I swallow hard, my heart racing at the enormity of the Sacred Seven's power. Since the day earth was created, the Masters have been the most influential beings to ever live among us, and if this is only a fragment of what they can do, I struggle to comprehend the full scope of their capabilities.

The proposition of ruling over an entire realm was a great privilege, but it was also terrifying. A lot of responsibility. Even so, the Masters and Emperors did everything we could to keep humans on the right path. Of course, the work was trying and difficult, I'm not going to deny that, but we were capable of handling trying and difficult things, so we embraced the challenge. Craved it, even. We collaborated well, in the beginning. Each of us — all fourteen outspoken, hardheaded men — understood we had one common goal, and that made us close.

I feel his heart beat a bit bolder at that, his conscience remembering the good things about the men I only know as enemies. Friendship, duty, sacrifice, allegiance, love. That's what Cruelty feels for the Masters — what he *once* felt for the Masters — before everything changed.

He shows me old memories of them, doubled over with laughter, talking about former gambles and recent antics, reminiscing about the past and current affairs. I see brief moments of them all playing chess and drinking wine over dinner, casual as anything.

It's strange, seeing these pictures of them; Sickness smiling with stars in his eyes, skin warm and without those protruding veins. Warfare laughing from a place of love instead of hatred. Fear making jokes about harmless things, not a foul word to be uttered. Addiction radiating with silent delight instead of violent contempt. Doubt offering to set and clean the dinner table, unusually polite. Even Obedience, in all his quiet brooding, manages to crack a grin.

It's a sight I thought I'd never see; the Masters acting as something close to human.

No matter how many disagreements or fights we had over the years, none of it mattered. Cruelty's voice slows to a methodic rhythm, overtaken by the past. *Our task was bigger than us, so we found a way to work out our differences — always. Until one day, there was an argument that couldn't be forgiven.*

The memories twist then, transporting me back to a time that turns Cruelty's heart — *my* heart — sick with dread. I know this part of the story; how it ends. *The Masters got tired of trying to help a realm that went against their influence. They started to loathe the human race, despising how some willingly chose to do the wrong thing, when we encouraged the right.*

The Sacred Seven's whispers fill my head — *Cruelty's* head — and reveal all the vile things they've said about humans over the years.

Mortals are innately born evil, but are taught to be good . . .
Ungrateful twits . . .
They don't deserve to be helped . . .

Let them rot in hell . . .

They're a lost cause . . .

What's the point of trying to change them? . . .

Why encourage virtue when their nature promotes vice? . . .

Perhaps we should focus on their natural instincts; prey on their weakness . . .

It is their choice, after all . . .

Cruelty cuts off the conversation there, having gotten his point across.

I didn't agree with what they were saying about humans being born evil and deserving punishment for it. His chest grows tight with resentment, making it harder for him — for *us* — to breathe. *I didn't have the same hatred they held in their hearts, yearning to destroy every mortal in sight. Humans could be inexplicably frustrating, yes, but I didn't have the mind to hurt them.*

He tried to, though. I can sense the guilt of that in his conscience, festering like rot. Part of him thinks it would've made his life easier to be like the others. Flowing with the current is always easier than swimming against it, but Cruelty chose to do the right thing instead of the easy one.

That fact alone rips the floor from beneath my feet, exposing the lies I mistook for truth.

It took a few years before the Masters' anger grew into a beast so large it couldn't be tamed. No one, not even the Emperors, could convince or stop them from using their influence to cage mortals instead of free them. With both sides working at odds, tempers stirred, prompting the destruction that was to come.

I get blurry flashes of the Masters screaming at the Emperors; the Emperors pushing back against the Masters, both sides throwing punches, ruining each other.

When it became apparent war was on the horizon, I wanted to desert my position and join the Emperors, seeking to help them gain full reign over the mortal world. The only thing holding me back was the Immortal Law, its Act threatening a hefty penalty should any of us decide to abandon our leadership status.

I was prepared to face the price it would've cost me, however. And I feel that truth in my bones, conviction running through every vein. *I would've done whatever it took to ensure the Masters didn't gain rule over the human realm, but the Emperors had a different plan.*

I catch a faint glimmer of one of them — the most ethereal creature I've ever seen — and nearly fall to my knees in amazement, overcome with wonder. With his back turned toward me, I can't make out the details of the Emperor's face, but I see the long strands of light brown hair; the strong shoulders they cascade down.

Kaster, the Emperor of Strength, convinced me to stay with the Masters and join their side in battle. He said I should act like I was as indignant as they were, starving for power and ultimate control. It was a precautionary act — one I'm glad we took — because if I fought for the Emperors and we lost, I'd have been banished from this realm. The Immortal Law disowns us for going against our own, so if any one of us were to desert, we'd be permanently exiled to the Underground Kingdom, a place where corrupt immortals are sent to reside.

The horror of that very place is revealed to me, its environment made of nothing but blackness and silence — a quiet greater than death.

I grew up with the Emperors, he continues, his voice soft with the remembrance of a loved one. *They were my friends. My brothers. Fighting against them was the hardest thing I had to do.*

Red explodes in my vision, the pleas of the injured and dying ringing out; a battlefield unfolding before my eyes. Orders are spat and shouted across the grounds, entirely visceral in their command.

Revulsion rises in Cruelty at the memory of the horrid things he had to do to the Emperors — his friends. I don't get the entire scope of the battle, but I see enough to know the terrors that oc-curred there.

The violent traumas the immortals inflicted on each other were hideous, the wounds ranging from a dislocated kneecap to a broken pelvis and shattered spine — injuries that would kill a mortal in an instant.

I nearly choke on the brutality of it all.

Kaster wanted to ensure that even if the Emperors failed, I'd re-main on earth, working from the inside. He instructed me to help Flames discreetly and keep them from being corrupted by the Sacred Seven's influence. And when the Emperors lost the fight, that's exactly what I did.

The idea seemed clever at the time, but I quickly learned how dif-ficult the execution would be. Since the other Masters' power is linked with mine, I can only help a few Flames at a time or risk getting caught.

And if Cruelty gets caught for interfering, the Masters won't hesitate to get rid of him.

But if Cruelty is gone, there will be no one left to help the hu-man realm; no leader to follow or look up to. Not to mention the unimaginable punishment he'll have to face for breaking the Im-mortal Law, but he doesn't talk about that.

I've had to do some things I'm not proud of to keep up my charade, but the more brutal I am to humans, the more the Masters trust me, and I need them to trust me.

A wave of self-loathing trickles through him, but he covers it quickly, shoving it away.

But we all understood what was at stake, Cruelty says, the mem-ories dissolving into smoke, leaving me in blackness. *We did what we had to. It didn't matter what I wanted.*

He pauses then, an onslaught of emotion — *his* emotion — crashing into me, overwhelming. Pain, anger, regret, grief, suffering, revenge — it all blends together, distorting where one sentiment ends and the other begins.

I don't know how he bears it, living with this burden he didn't ask to take on—

I think you've seen enough.

With that, Cruelty pulls me out of his mind and guides me back into my own, the story of his past now over.

Silence fills my head as I regain my senses, head spinning with everything I learned and saw.

"I told you it was scary," Cruelty says, his eyes still glazed from the memories, the most haunted I've seen him. "Seeing the Masters as they once were can be a jolt to the system. It's difficult knowing the monsters you grew up hating weren't always so vile and vicious. It makes them a little harder to hate, which is the worst dilemma to have."

Indeed, it is. But it's a dilemma I am only just beginning to understand.

Cruelty grew up with the Masters, and at some point, he cared for them all, loving them like brothers. I can't imagine how difficult it is for him to fight against them in secret now, forging a path not many would be brave enough to take. With all the history between them, I don't know how he's been able to stand firm in his beliefs, refusing to fall prey to the Sacred Seven's ways. And to do it on his own, with no support. . .

He doesn't seem to regret his decision to rebel, however. At least, I didn't sense that in his thoughts. If anything, I felt the heavy weight of sadness and longing, wishing to go back to what was, but will never be again.

"I'm glad you showed me," I say at last — and it's true, I am. Sure, it's a bit off-putting to see the Sacred Seven as something more than what they are now, but I haven't forgotten who they've become. What they've done. This doesn't change how I feel about them.

It only changes how I feel about Cruelty.

"Have you tried killing them?" I ask. Perhaps a stupid question, but after seeing the horrors done to the Masters in the war, it's clear the Sacred Seven aren't exempt from physical harm. They may be excused from dying of old age, but maybe there's another way to get rid of them.

"The Immortal Law permits us from hurting each other," Cruelty says, my hope diminishing with every word. "Particularly with our strongholds. If any of us decide to break that rule, it won't be good for us."

"Then why did you beat up Sickness?" I whisper the Master's name, fearing he will somehow appear if I say it too loudly. "The repercussions of harming one of your own sounds too great to risk, but you still acted out. Why?"

Cruelty looks me straight in the eye, and I get the distinct feeling he wants me to see what he's too afraid to say, but I don't budge. I want to hear him say the truth out loud. No more assumptions.

"Some prices are worth paying," is all he says, and the warning in his voice tells me I don't want to know what it was, but I ask anyway. "Nothing too concerning," he answers quickly, shrugging off the words. "I got assigned to take on Sickness's work for the next few weeks. Nothing I can't handle." He winks and I grip his shoulder, not needing him to elaborate. He's already shared enough.

"Well, that's new." Cruelty murmurs the words, the bleakness in his gaze transforming to a heated edge.

"What is?" I ask, my throat dry and thick, suddenly aching.

"That look in your eye. You're looking at me differently than you were before."

He tightens his hold on my hand, his fingers long and warm and not at all like the other Masters. While their hands are hard and crafted for violence, Cruelty's are fine and gentle, designed for swift, clever things.

"How was I looking at you before?" I whisper, my chest inexplicably tight, making it difficult to swallow my unease.

"Like I'm some hideous creature you can't stand," he murmurs, his hand moving higher on my back, drawing me in. "Like I'm the most unpleasant Soul Eater you've ever seen."

My face burns at the truth in that, but the shame isn't strong enough to make me look away from him. I don't *want* to look away from him, and it's been that way for a while now. "Well," I whisper. "If you were a Soul Eater, you certainly wouldn't be the most unpleasant one I've ever seen."

I haven't forgotten about the terrible creature in Tempus, the one who killed the Soulless instead of me. "A few weeks ago," I say, "I ran into this Soul Eater when I was hunting, and it did the strangest thing . . ." I trail off when I see the knowing in Cruelty's eyes, like a spark of recognition. "Is it possible for Soul Eaters to make mistakes?" I ask, suddenly wondering if the Master was responsible for the creature's actions.

He tilts his head to the side, gaze narrowing. "Care to elaborate?"

"The Soul Eater killed a Soulless," I say. "It didn't even bother to go for me. Has that ever happened before?"

Cruelty leans in, his mouth by my ear. "You must've gotten lucky running into one of my pets." At my shocked silence, he continues. "The Masters take turns programming the Soul Eaters and releasing them into mortal villages. When it's my turn to send them out, I reprogram a select few to go after Soulless instead of Flames."

I pull away from him to see his eyes, the truth swimming within them. "Don't the others get suspicious if your Soul Eaters are the only ones attacking Soulless?"

"I only reprogram a few every so often, which makes it easy to blame the Soul Eater's attacks as a rare malfunction."

I'm not sure when it happened, but at some point, my heart started to beat with relief when Cruelty was around — the initial fear of him gone and replaced with a comfort I haven't felt amid the other Masters.

It feels good to finally admit that to myself — to accept that Cruelty is not what I thought, and that isn't a bad thing. For weeks, I worried my affection toward him meant that I was turning into a Soulless, falling victim to his harsh, manipulative ways. But now, after climbing into his head and seeing the truth for myself, I realize how wrong I was.

"Well," I say, doing my best to keep my voice steady, "I was mistaken. You're not a monster." Far from it, actually.

Something glimmers in his gaze then, soft and sweet, undeniably charming. "So, you're not going to stab me in the back the first chance you get?"

I twist my mouth to the side in mock contemplation. "No, I don't really feel like stabbing you anymore." My stomach flips under the intensity of his stare. "But if I did, it wouldn't be in your back." I manage to smile at him. "I'd want to make sure you're dead, so I'd go straight for the heart. Perhaps a beheading, if that's what it took."

He laughs, the sound low and glorious, rumbling deep from within. "That reassures me greatly, thank you." A dark smile of his own dances on his mouth, the hand at my back migrating higher as he closes the distance between us.

I bite my lip, afraid of how delightful this feels–– his chest fully pressed against mine. Emperors above, we're going to destroy each other.

The swing of the music picks up in tempo, urging the crowd outside to be wild and reckless, but Cruelty takes his time, leading me through a series of steps I've never done before.

I mirror his movements without hesitation, his eyes never straying from mine, and try to ignore the change in my pulse, my heartbeats skipping in a way they only do around him.

For a too-brief moment, I allow myself to forget that he is a Master and I am a Flame, and that we are — together — drowning in Airabeth. Tonight, there is only us and the music, and no titles or deals or fear of tomorrow is going to disrupt that.

The celebration blurs outside, obscuring every sight and sound, and I let myself get lost in his touch. In this moment, there is only him, and me, and nothing else. Just us. In the back of my mind, I know this moment won't last forever — nothing good ever does — but it ends far more quickly than I expect.

Before I'm ready for it, Cruelty's body goes still and taut under my hands, his head tilting, as if he's heard something peculiar.

I open my mouth to ask him what's wrong, but the darkness in his gaze silences me. I watch his eyes as they glare at something — *someone* — out the window, his face hardening to stone.

And then I see it.

Chapter Thirty-Three

My stomach hollows at the sight of Sickness walking toward the bonfire, his presence throwing ash on this night. Even from this distance, I can see the green and ivory swirls of his jacket, the colors bringing out the bruises Cruelty gave him. The skin is already healing, thanks to his immortal blood.

He didn't bother to wear a disguise, even though he doesn't belong. He came here to be seen, to be feared, by the crowd.

My heart plunges when I follow his stare, spotting Tuesday and December dancing by the bonfire. Touching. Laughing. Kissing with abandon.

Bleeding hell! Do something, Nadia, anything! Warn them—

Sickness charges for them, practically sprinting to the square to announce his arrival.

Cruelty and I share a quick glance, but I don't have time to explain my urgency.

I take off running, needing to get to my friends before Sickness does.

I take the kitchen's back exit and run down the hall, nearly flying through the entrance to the backyard, joining the crowd. I shove past servants and tell them to get out of my way, but they're so damn oblivious none of them listen.

By the time the bonfire comes into full view, Sickness is already there, stalking toward Tuesday like she's his next meal. Even from here, I can see her face blanch, her hands jerking back from December as she realizes her mistake.

She rushes to the Master's side, her eyes wide and full of terror as she comes up with an excuse to justify her actions. Judging by Sickness's deadpan expression, he isn't having any of her apologies.

He knows she's involved with December.

He knows her feelings run strong for him.

Today's events only prove it.

Emperors above, this won't be good for her. For December. For—

Sickness reaches out so fast my eyes almost miss him shoving December toward the bonfire, pushing him closer to the flames. Tuesday screams in protest, catching the attention of the crowd.

And it's at that sound — that terrified, hysterical *plea* — that pulls everyone from their drunken state. Within seconds, the Celebration goes silent, the music coming to a grinding halt as dread settles into the air, choked with a poison only fear can inflict.

It's a reminder that we're all still in Airabeth.

This night is a ruse.

None of us are safe.

The crowd quickly sobers, the people turning frantic, desperate in their attempt to escape Sickness's wrath. The servants surge toward me before I can make sense of the ensuing chaos, shouting warnings across the field, urging everyone to get back to the manor.

My view of the bonfire gets blocked by the sea of bodies, but I fight against them, determined to get to my friends.

Through gaps in the horde, I see Tuesday, her face broken and pained as Sickness glares at her, his hands bunched into fists. "Lovers!" he shouts over the commotion, his words clearer and louder than any of the human screams. "That's what you two are, is it not? Don't lie," he adds when Tuesday opens her mouth to object. "The next sentence out of your mouth better be the truth."

Tuesday doesn't move an inch, her face starkly pale as she stares at her future husband, afraid to say the wrong thing. But it's that lack of words, the utter silence, that gives Sickness all the answer he needs, confirming his suspicion of her involvement with December.

I hardly have time to let the horror of his moment set in. I'm already thinking about what this means for her. For December. Their bond is unbreakable, untouchable, to anyone who tries to impede it, but Sickness is a Master. He'll do anything — kill anyone — to break their connection.

And considering Tuesday is his bride to be, December will be the one to face punishment. And punishment, in this case, will result in one thing.

Death.

I DON'T STOP RUNNING toward the bonfire, toward the chaos, when everyone else is screaming and scattering back to the manor. Shouts fill the air, so wretched and pleading they make the prior festivities feel like a distant dream. Drinks spill onto the grass, mixing with the pastries people leave behind in their rush to escape.

Within moments, the field divides into Flames and Soulless, the former group fleeing the scene while the latter decides to stay, eager to see what Sickness will do next.

I move to the edge of the field to avoid the thickness of the crowd, my calves burning as I stand on tiptoes in search of Tuesday and December. Fear and panic claw at my throat when I don't find them, the flurry of rushing Soulless and Flames masking them from view.

"Girl, stop! We must leave!"

My heart jumps into my throat when a servant — a Flame — steps out in front of me. She is older than most of the servants I've seen around the house, her hair long and gray, wilting at the ends.

"Don't you hear me?" she cries, her silver eyes crinkling at the corners. "We must leave! Now!" She latches a hand around my wrist and drags me back into the crush of people, undoing all my hard work of getting to the bonfire.

"Let go of me," I yell at the woman, her fingers locked on my wrist. "You don't understand! I need to get back there. My friends—"

A blur of black passes to my right and I halt mid-stride, my focus catching on a small boy slithering through the crowd. The woman tugs at my arm, ordering me to keep moving, but I refuse, unable to look away from the little human zigging and zagging across the field.

January.

His eyes bulge as he charges for the manor, his legs small but swift as he slips out and around the servants, doing whatever he can to avoid being stepped on.

Compared to the full-grown adults stampeding across the grounds, January is tiny and weak. A mouse among lions.

If he gets trapped amid the madness, he'll be trampled. Killed—

No. I shove away the thought before I can finish it. January is small, yes, but he's also fast. Crafty. He'll be fine. He's capable. He'll make it back to the manor, I'm sure of it.

But Tuesday —

I tell the Flame woman to release me again, but she isn't having any of my pleas. I try to be patient with her, I do, but as the seconds drain by, there comes a point where being considerate is no longer an option.

Because of her, I'm losing valuable time to help my friends.

Because of her, I might be too late to be of any use at all.

I reach down without thinking, using my free hand to pry hers away, and twist until something snaps. The woman falls back, a mixture of horror and anger filling her eyes, yelping in pain. Her scream drowns in the chaos surrounding us, and for a split second I feel terrible for what I've done, but she was getting in my way. I did what I had to.

I charge the square for a second time, my heart wild and raging as my eyes land on the bonfire, a horde of Soulless surrounding it.

And there, positioned in the middle of it all, stands Sickness.

"My friends," he announces, arms raised in invitation. "Join me, for it appears we have caught some fleas that need removing." The enthusiasm on his face turns my fury into alarm, and I crouch behind a nearby boulder, shielding myself from view.

He starts to pace around the square, eyes piercing the assembled crowd. "And since we are all dogs living in a ruthless, competitive world, I say it's time we are rid of the lame!"

"Rid of the lame!" the Soulless repeat, their fists high and beating against the air.

"There is punishment," the Master continues, "for those who fail to follow *us* — the true gods of this ruined world!"

"True gods!" the people hail.

"My fiancée." Sickness gestures to his left, and that's when I see her at last — my friend, who has given me comfort and company in a place empty of such things — half hidden behind a group of Soulless.

Her dark skin is sickly. Ashen. But other than the silver lining her eyes, she appears unafraid. Anger builds in her face, strong and steadfast. The Soulless behind her inch closer, waiting to see if she'll make a lunge for Sickness. Ready to punish her if she does.

"My fiancée," the Master repeats, "has fallen in love with a Flame!"

The Soulless erupt at the revelation, bringing a coolness to my skin.

I start to count the number of them but give up after thirty.

Impossible. It's physically impossible to defeat them all.

We're outmatched. Outnumbered.

"It's time we make my bride pure again!" Sickness's voice rises gradually, his chest heaving with every word. "We must wash her skin with the blood of the man who has led her into lust!"

My hand absently drifts to the base of my neck, instinctively reaching for a bow that isn't there. Bleeding hell, I'm running out of time. Out of plans. Out of options.

"I think it's time we penalize the man trying to steal my wife from me. Can we agree?!"

This declaration results in an uproar, every head turning to the right of the field — to where a large, slumbering body lies in the grass hardly five feet from Tuesday.

My mouth dries out at the sight. At the swollen face that's been so brutally beaten, it's unrecognizable, a complete stranger compared to what he was not minutes ago. The slashes mutilating his skin have no beginning and no end, and although blood distorts the majority of his features, his injuries aren't what terrify me the most.

It's his stillness, his non-response to Tuesday's cries, that has me sweating.

Cruelty's voice is in my head, reminding me of the Law and how it forbids the Sacred Seven from committing bodily injury. Masters can't physically harm humans, and if they do, there's a price for it. This can't be Sickness's doing. He loves himself too much to compromise his position.

I look around the circle of Soulless, and eventually I find him — the man behind December's beating. His face is prominent, his features cut with the cruelest of blades, and as I watch, he licks the red from his knuckles, smiling like a fiend. Parts of his uniform are ripped, stained with large, bloody handprints. December's handprints.

Rage blasts through me.

Where are you?

I shout the thought in my mind, hoping Cruelty will respond. I scan the crowd, thinking I might find him among the Soulless, but he isn't there. I lower my mental guard all the way down and reach across it, moving blindly through the darkness to locate him.

Where are you? Where did you go? Why did you leave?

I'm no Master and I have none of their abilities, but I hope Cruelty can hear me, somehow. I'm leaving myself vulnerable with my mental shield down, but there's no other way to call out to him. To ask for his help.

"I was wondering when you were going to show up." Sickness's high-pitched drawl interrupts my focus, transporting me back to the present moment. "Did you grow tired of watching the show from a distance?"

I follow the Master's line of sight, and my heart thunders when I glimpse Cruelty approaching, his steps light and unhurried. I'm not sure what took him so long to arrive – he saw how fast I ran off – but he's here now, his power consuming the entirety of the yard.

My blood hums in his presence, filling me with awe and fear.

No. Not fear, I realize — respect. Respect for his strength. His authority. His boldness.

The Soulless have a different reaction, all of them bowing and praising Cruelty in terror, fearing what will happen if they don't.

My temples pound as Cruelty greets Sickness, the two of them conversing in hushed tones so none of us can hear. I lean forward and watch their mouths, catching a few words here and there:

"Bad move," Cruelty says.

"Worth it," Sickness counters.

"Don't be stupid."

"This is right."

"Be careful."

"She betrayed me."

"Doesn't matter."

"Why do you care?"

A lifetime passes between every phrase, and I wonder how long their banter will last, when a noise — a groan — breaks up their conversation.

I hold my breath and turn to December, his limbs twitching as he rolls on the ground, moaning in pain. My eyes stray to the unstable rise and fall of his chest, laboring but alive.

Tuesday doesn't waste time rushing toward him, her hands outstretched and shaking.

Sickness snarls and stares pointedly at her. "I wouldn't," he growls.

Reluctantly, she steps back.

"Well, this makes things more interesting, doesn't it?" Sickness's ruthless smile returns, his gaze narrowing as he surveys the Soulless. "My friends," he exclaims, his arms lifted in summoning. "It seems the disobedient dog is stronger than we thought. The time has come to rid him from this earth. So go, have fun, rid us of the lame. Remove the filth that's stained my fiancée's purity!"

At the snap of his words, madness ensues.

Chapter Thirty-Four

The Soulless are on December in an instant, their faces red and snarling as they lash into him, brutal and merciless. The slap of fists pounding into flesh echoes across the field. Terror stabs at me, as strong as when my parents were taken, and turns my legs to lead. The Soulless hunch over December, tearing at him like a pack of starving dogs fighting over food.

I lose sight of Tuesday amongst the madness, but I hear her scream — high and keening. I can't tell if it's in response to what's happening to December or Sickness's strongholds, but both are reasons to be afraid.

The Master's power flows easily across the field, its essence rippling with black shadows that choke and blind — a summoning from hell. I push away his influence as it skips along my scalp, refusing to indulge in its sickening lure.

It's too late to save your friends. Turn back and hide in the manor. It's all you're good for.

I rise from my spot behind the boulder, unwilling to cower any longer, and run for the square, blending seamlessly into the crowd. I keep a steady pace as I weave through the mass of bodies, capitalizing on the Soulless' distraction.

With every eye and obscenity directed toward the onslaught, I reach December without much hassle. Fortunately, most of the Flames have already retreated back to the manor, so the Soulless aren't expecting one to be here now, turning me invisible to their scrutiny.

But when I glimpse December's mutilated body through the crowd, I think he might already be dead.

His skin, once smooth and peppered with gold, now bubbles with welts, the wounds oozing blood and something yellow. The sight is so brutal, but I can't turn away, paralyzed by the barbarity of it all.

I don't know if he can see past the swelling around his eyes, but for his sake, I hope he can't. I don't want him to see the wildness of the Soulless, especially as one drives an elbow into his mouth, blood spurting from his teeth.

My eyes water at the atrocity, but I steel myself. I have to— I'm too close to the fight. Everyone can see my reaction. If I show my repugnance now, the Soulless will know I'm a Flame, and I can't have them pulling me away from the scene.

December can't take this beating for much longer, and if the Soulless above him doesn't stop attacking, that'll be the end. I hope he stops, but he doesn't. He just keeps hitting, and hitting, and *hitting*.

I lunge for his back, gripping him like a leech, unrelenting in my pursuit. I wrap my legs around his torso and latch both arms around his neck, his throat bobbing as I choke him.

He stumbles off December like a bad drunk and falters to the side, spinning wildly to fling me off him. "You stupid whore," he seethes, and reaches back to seize my wrists, grappling blindly.

I lean my weight away from him to avoid his touch, but his wingspan is long — much longer than it looked while he was crouching — and he hooks a hand around my forearm.

Although his face is purpling and his body sways from oxygen loss, he bends at the waist, flipping me headfirst over his shoulder, throwing me to the ground. I gasp, the air shooting from my lungs, but I don't have time to rest.

I'm on my feet within seconds, my head spinning from the stars obscuring my vision.

I raise my hands to protect my face.

The daze clears from my eyes in time for me to register the Soulless' lethal gaze, his mouth splitting into a serpent's grin. "You really shouldn't play such games, sweetheart," he growls, his teeth gnashing together. I make a note to keep my neck away from his mouth, not putting it past him to rip out my throat like an animal if given the chance.

He advances on me, every step rushed and sloppy, making him easy to dodge. He throws a right hook to my temple, putting all his power behind the strike. The over-rotation of his hips and torso foreshadows the move, making it obvious.

I duck and avoid his fist, grateful for his carelessness. I spring up and deliver an uppercut to his chin, compressing the nerve connecting the jawbone to the skull.

His eyes cross, gaze distant and far off, gleaming with an unnatural blankness as he topples over and hits the ground hard.

I step back to shake the ache from in my hand, my knuckles singing from the bone-on-bone contact. I move to the Soulless quickly and check his body for weapons, expecting to find a knife or something useful.

I startle when he pushes himself upright, his eyes bright as he drives a large, angry elbow into my rib. I gasp, something cracking inside me. I double over and rest my hands on my knees, trying to find breath, but every inhale is a blade to my chest.

The Soulless flashes a nasty smile before his unusually large and calloused hands lash out and wrap around my throat, squeezing tightly. Light pops in my vision as he forces me to the ground, pinning me beneath him. My head smacks hard against the grass, a terrible pain blooming from my skull.

Something wet trickles from my ear — blood, I realize, as the stench wafts through the air.

"If you wish to act like a witch," the Soulless grunts, his enormous face swimming in and out of focus, "then I have the right to treat you like one." My heart rises in panic as he slides a hand up my dress. I buck beneath him, my body disgusted by his touch, but he hardly notices my struggle.

He smiles again, brushing his mouth against my throat. "Stop fighting me," he says, as if I'm a horse needing to be tamed. "This is what you want, isn't it?" He scrapes his rough palms against my knees and thighs. Higher.

I don't scream. I don't beg. There's no point in giving him the reaction he seeks. Even if I did cry out, no one would help me. I'm surrounded by Soulless. My enemies. There are no limits to what they'll do to me.

Still, I thrash and kick like a rabid dog, but he has already unfastened the button on his pants, drawing closer and closer, despite my fight. I look to the sky to avoid his face, hunting for a solution, when he bears his weight on top of me, trapping my torso.

I react on instinct and drive my knee up into his groin, causing him to buckle. The hit isn't as powerful as I intended, but it's enough to create some distance between us. I crawl backward away from him, digging my heels into the ground for support, and follow up with a kick to his chest, knocking him on his backside.

I sit up to see his glorious flash of surprise, but it doesn't last, his expression fading into a grimace.

It takes me all of three seconds to realize what's happening as a burst of blood explodes from his ears and mouth, his brain dissolving from the inside out.

The Soulless' eyes darken and glaze over as he collapses, looking smaller and weaker now that he's dead.

And there, hovering behind his crumpled body, stands Cruelty.

The Master's eyes are a torch of blue-black flame as he surveys his destruction, every part of him shuddering with a rage I've never seen.

"You killed him," I whisper, staring at the river of blood, too shocked to understand the implications. "But what about the Law? You said Masters can't physically kill—"

"He wasn't human," Cruelty says, kicking the Soulless aside with his boot. "He was a Soul Eater disguised as one. No rules were defied."

The thought alone provides a great comfort, but the relief is a remote thing, my mind divided between December and the horror of what just happened.

I might be more disturbed by the Soul Eater's death if it hadn't tried to defile me, but it's hard to feel guilty after experiencing something like that.

I'm thankful the thing is dead.

It was either the beast's life or mine, and Cruelty chose me.

I need him to choose me again — *now* — before it's too late.

"Help him," I pant through the ache in my rib, pointing toward the square. "Please." I rise to my feet and shake off my daze, clinging to Cruelty's arm for support.

"All right, this is what we're going to do." The Master hunches to meet my eye level, his eyes alive and swimming with power. "But first, I need to know you're well enough. This won't work if you can't run."

"I'm good. I can do it." I'm too tired to make the lie convincing, but if Cruelty's plan will get December out, I will find a way to execute it. I have to.

"Sickness is preoccupied with the beatings," he starts, speaking low into my ear, emphasizing every word. "He's distracted, so I'm going to place strongholds in the Soulless' minds. I'm going to urge them to back off December, just a little, so you can get him out. I can't stop their attacks completely, because Sickness will know I'm intervening, but when you see the violence slow down, you need to run in and grab him from the crowd. I'll keep Sickness preoccupied in the meantime.

"You can't take him across the open field, but there's a path through there." He points to Airabeth's forest, past the tree line. "It circles around and leads back to the manor. Follow it and meet me in my room. I'll be there to help December as best I can."

If he lives. I keep the statement to myself. Sure, Cruelty might have enough supplies to heal a few injuries or a broken bone, but not even *he* has the power to resurrect the dead.

"Nadia." Cruelty shakes my shoulder slightly, his grip desperate. "Do you understand what I'm asking you to do?"

I nod, a wave of dizziness rolling over me.

The Master's mouth starts to move again in response, but I'm not listening, too focused on staying conscious. When I'm positive I'm not going to pass out, I ask him to repeat the sentence, but he's already gone, disappearing into the crowd.

Bleeding hell, this is it. Whether December lives or dies depends on us, and I don't know if I should feel relieved or burdened by that. I don't have time to decide before Cruelty places a stronghold in the Soulless' minds. The moment it happens, their movements slow, shifting with a sudden lethargy they didn't have a moment ago.

I run for Tuesday first — I can't carry December on my own. Two Soulless have pulled her away from December and hold her wrists bound behind her back, but she escapes them easily now that they're under Cruelty's influence. I have to run to catch up with her, my steps slow compared to hers.

I'm out of breath by the time I catch her arm, turning her toward me. She resists at first, thinking I'm a Soulless, but the moment her golden eyes land on my face, she slackens, the tension in her posture draining.

"What are you—?"

"Help me get him out," I pant, and jut my head toward December.

Tuesday's face crumples with confusion, a thousand questions running through her eyes, but she trusts me enough to not voice them.

"I'll explain when we have time, but for now, I need you to do as I say, all right?" At that, I take off running, not waiting to see if she'll follow. I know she will. We're not in a position to argue.

I scan the field in search of Cruelty, but I can't find him, overwhelmed by the downright butchery around us. I should've asked him how we're supposed to save December without getting caught by the Soulless, because surely, they won't let us walk free without a fight.

But then I feel it–– the tremor of power locking around us, buzzing with warmth. My blood thrums at the weight of it, the heaviness secure and protecting, cloaking us in glittering light.

Tuesday must sense something similar, because the lines between her eyebrows soften, the burden in her eyes vanishing, as if her heart's worries have instantly disappeared.

Cruelty is charming us from the Soulless' eyes, I realize — somehow shielding us from sight and sound as we run to the square. Though we're careful not to bump into anyone directly, no one seems to notice our presence, not even as we walk through their line of vision.

It's a blessing to reach December without trouble, but the moment doesn't last. Tuesday steps back, her hand flying to her mouth in horror when she sees the blood. So much blood.

I tell her everything will be all right — we're going to help him — but I don't know if that's true. December is in bad shape. He might bleed out before we get him back to the manor, but we have to try. There's no time to doubt.

"Come on," I urge, needing Tuesday to stay here, in the present, instead of the dark place her thoughts are taking her to. "We have to do this now, before we lose our chance!" I fling December's arm over my shoulder, and she follows suit, lifting the other side of his body.

After we're sure we have a good grip on him, we heave him up by the arms and rush toward the tree line, not pausing to check if someone is following us.

"Don't look back," I tell her when she glances over her shoulder. "Just keep moving."

Chapter Thirty-Five

"**D**o you know where we're going?" Tuesday asks quietly, desperately, her hands shaking as she adjusts December in her arms. She glances sidelong at me, a familiar yet severe concern in her eyes.

I do my best not to show my own distress. "He said — to follow — the path," I pant, lungs burning with fatigue, my mouth thirsting for water. "We should — be there — soon."

I hope.

In all honesty, I don't know how far we are from the house. I regret not asking Cruelty about it. I regret not asking anything at all, being too stunned to think straight.

It's been less than ten minutes since we dragged December into the woods, and we're already tired beyond what we can handle. My body feels like it's been repeatedly kicked by a horse, feet heavy and dragging behind me.

If it weren't for Tuesday, I probably would've paused for a break three times by now, but since she doesn't stop to rest, neither do I.

The sun is just hours away from rising, which means the cool night is gone, and heat is fast approaching, amplifying our fatigue. Sweat soaks the hem of my dress, a sour odor wafting from it.

December's skin is slick, too, but not all of it is sweat.

Blood trickles down his forearms in a maze of red, making him difficult to carry.

I use my sleeve to wipe the fluid from his arm and Tuesday does the same, attempting to improve our grip. We try our best to be gentle with him, but we also can't waste time, so when he groans in protest, we pretend not to hear it. We have to keep moving.

"Who?" Tuesday blurts suddenly, and it takes me a moment to realize she's referring to what I said before. "Who told you to follow the path? It was him, wasn't it?" She doesn't give me a chance to answer. "At the Celebration? You and Cruelty? I've noticed the questions you ask about him. It was him, wasn't it?" She repeats the phrase, wanting to hear the truth from my mouth — to tell her she's wrong.

But the answer she wants isn't so black and white, no matter how badly I wish it was.

Even if I could tell her the facts, she wouldn't understand. Only the Soulless make nice with the Sacred Seven. Only the Soulless pardon their behavior. Only the Soulless would think to take a Master's advice.

If I were to share what I know about Cruelty, she'd think me mad — a Flame who's lost her color. I can't tell her the truth about this, not yet, but I'm also not going to lie to her. She doesn't deserve that.

"If I tell you about it, you'll never believe me," I say, settling for evasion instead of outright deceit.

"Did you hit your head too hard?" Tuesday hisses, the betrayal in her voice stark and raw, stabbing harder than I thought it would. "Did you ever stop to consider why Cruelty told us to go through the forest? This place is festering with Soul Eaters—"

"I know that," I say calmly, "and as long as we stay quiet, we won't draw any attention from them. Just keep walking, all right? We need to get back to safety."

She huffs, and I immediately feel stupid for saying it. We were never safe to begin with, but being in that damn manor is a lot better than being stuck out here, injured and without direction.

"I don't expect you to tell me anything," Tuesday says, her lips pinching together, "and whatever you're doing with Cruelty, I'm not judging you for it. I just don't think it's smart."

"I understand," I say, dancing around a potential argument. "But there are some things that can't be—"

December coughs, drawing our attention to him.

My heart jumps when I see a thick clot of blood fall from his mouth, almost black.

He won't make it.

The thought is so jarring, I physically shrink away from it.

He's going to die, right here in our arms.

December bucks in our hold, his body seizing and thrashing against us. We lurch forward against the movement, attempting to regain our balance, but he doesn't know his own strength. We can't carry him like this.

He slips through our grip and drops to the ground like a bag of bricks, his limbs shivering with a cold that comes from within.

He's dying.

I try to will the thought away, but now that I've had it, it's impossible to remove.

Dying.

The word beats in my heart, hammering brutally against my breastbone.

Tuesday looks the way I feel, her golden eyes dull with pain, completely stripped of their usual vibrancy. She begins to pant, trembling in her fight to stay calm, and wraps her arms around herself.

Her fear reminds me of how I reacted all those weeks ago when Elisha became sick in the forest. I was alone in my dread. I had no one to help me. No one to lean on. Not until I got home to my family. I can be that support for Tuesday. She doesn't have to make decisions on her own.

I kneel down beside December's head and take his hand in mine, trying not to show the worry on my face.

"D." I whisper his name and his eyes crack open, hardly visible through the welts on his face. "I know you're tired. I get it, I do. But we're going to make it out of here. We just need you to—"

The pressure on my hand tightens — a silent interruption that makes me go quiet.

"Thank you," December murmurs, his lips scarcely moving. "You didn't . . . have to come back . . . for me. But I'm glad . . . you did. Thank you."

I swallow hard, refusing to let my emotion win out.

"But now you have . . . to leave," he whispers, tears welling in his eyes. "Make sure . . . you get her back . . . to safety." His gaze flickers to Tuesday. "Promise me . . . you'll get her . . . back."

I shake my head. "I didn't come back for you because I wanted your appreciation," I say, my voice catching on a sob. "We didn't come this far for everything to end like this. You're going to be fine. I swear, you're going to be fine."

You have to be.

"I know you think you're done, but you're not." I say the words I wish I could've said to Sasha. "I need you to stand. Tuesday and I will take care of the rest, all right? I just need you to stand, and then we can make it back to the house, and you'll get treatment."

December doesn't respond. By now, he must be welcoming death, if only to escape this pain. But he can't leave Tuesday, not like this. Not so soon. He'll fight for her, I know he will, he just needs to be reminded of it.

"Please, D. I know you can . . ." I trail off, my blood stilling as an ominous presence prowls by, hovering around us.

I scan the forest, searching for signs of a threat.

When I see none, I think I imagined it. A mere trick of the mind, feeding off my fear.

But then it comes — a swishing noise, like the unsheathing of a weapon.

Tuesday must hear it too, because she looks to the tree line, her eyes flickering back and forth. "What do you think that was?" she whispers.

"I don't know," I breathe, looking behind us to make sure no one is there. "Let's leave before we find out."

December cries as we go to lift him, his hand moving to his abdomen, suggesting a broken rib.

Bleeding hell, we can't keep doing this to him. We're making his wounds worse by dragging him through all this dirt and grime, increasing his chances of injury and infection. Emperors, help us.

"Tuesday." I look at her. "Together on three, all right? One. Two—"

On three, we lift December by the underarms, and I instantly sense Tuesday's anguish from beside me at his pain. I fix my eyes on the path ahead, wondering how much longer we have until we reach our destination.

We must be close to the manor by now. We have to be.

If we're not, that means I've been lied to — betrayed by the Master I was starting to trust.

I GLANCE OVER MY SHOULDER every five seconds, checking for and somewhat expecting to find someone standing there. Each time I look, I'm greeted with darkness. Each time I look, I lose a shred of sanity, seeing and hearing things that aren't real.

"Where do you think that noise—?"

"Hush," I say to Tuesday, cutting her off.

I don't want to talk about what we heard. I don't want to talk about anything, for fear of drawing attention to ourselves. We need to stay quiet and move in silence, because if something does come after us, I want to be able to hear it.

And at some point, I do.

A crunch, like the snapping of twigs beneath heavy feet, comes from our right.

I whip in the direction of the sound, eyes darting for signs of an attack.

Wolf. Bear. Fox. Soul Eater. These are the possible attackers that come to mind, but I don't have anything to defend against them.

Maybe it's a rabbit. Emperors above, please let it be a rabbit.

Just then, a flash of silver twinkles against the black of night — definitely not a rabbit — and zooms straight for Tuesday, aiming for her side.

I don't have time to react.

I blink, then hear a terrible yet subdued sound, a mix between a gasp and a scream.

I look to the ground, expecting to find Tuesday bleeding out and gasping for air. I nearly jump out of my skin, shocked beyond reason, when I realize my expectation is wrong — so unbelievably wrong.

It isn't Tuesday who lays with the blade buried deep in her side, wrestling for life.

No.

It's December.

I didn't see it happen.

I don't know how he reacted so fast – how he angled himself in front of her, taking the blow.

I lift my eyes to who ambushed us, and although I don't know him personally, he's a Soulless from the Celebration, guaranteed. He must've found a way around Cruelty's strongholds and followed us here.

From what I can see, he has a rough face and buzzed scalp, his eyes black and without kindness, fusing with the night. It's hard to guess his age from this distance, but judging by his stature, he can't be much older than us. He doesn't have the build of a full-grown man, but he certainly isn't scrawny, either.

I advance on him, wanting to smash his face, but Tuesday beats me to it. She's already rushing him, the knife from December's abdomen in her hand, swinging for his head.

I didn't even see her grab the blade.

Rage overtakes her, giving her a power she doesn't naturally possess. She pushes the Soulless to the ground, attacking with a vengeance that turns feral.

I inch toward my friend, but I don't intervene.

Not even as she anchors the knife above her head, plunging it down.

It all happens so fast. I look away, cringing as the blade digs into the Soulless' chest, crunching through bone. Tuesday brings the knife upon him again, again, again, again, again, each strike accompanied by spurting blood and grinding cartilage.

The Soulless screams, wild and hopeless.

It isn't long before those screams dull to groans, and the groans to whispers, and the whispers into silence, leaving nothing but Tuesday's erratic breaths and my own hammering heart in my ears.

I turn to her slowly, not daring to make any quick or sudden movements. I watch her rise from the Soulless' dead body, her hands shaking, dressed in red.

I think to touch her, to comfort her in some fashion, but the way she stands — so still and not quite of this world — warns me to stay away.

Her golden eyes seem to glow in the darkness, fixing heavily on me.

For the first time since I met her, I fear the person I see.

Tuesday is something untamed, something vengeful and un-feeling.

I feel small under her gaze.

She dries her palms on her dress, calmly removing the blood like she's done it a thousand times before, and walks over to her true love.

She doesn't drop the knife, as if forgetting she was holding it at all. She stares down at the weapon like she's surprised to see it there. Surprised that she could do such a violent thing.

I should say something — should offer words of support — but what could I possibly say at a time like this?

"Sunday!"

Emotion rises in my throat at the sight of him, relief filling me at the sound of his voice. His presence.

He came back for us. For me.

"Are you okay?" Although Cruelty stares straight at me, he goes to D, kneeling by his side.

"How did you find us?" I ask, joining the Master on the ground, wincing at the blood oozing from December's side.

"I went back to the manor and you weren't there," he says sim-ply, examining December's wounds, hands quick but gentle.

"I thought we'd be back at the manor by now," I say, "but we were attacked and –"

"You're kidding, right?" Tuesday raises the bloody knife, point-ing it at Cruelty.

The Master's gaze drifts behind her, his expression unreadable as he catches sight of the dead Soulless.

I rise to my feet and take a step toward her, gesturing for her to lower the knife. "We can trust him," I assure, approaching her slow-ly, like I would a spooked animal. "Just give him a chance to prove himself, please."

"I don't want to give him a chance!" she yells, her hand shaking around the knife's handle. "After everything they've done to us, Sunday . . ." She shakes her head, mouth tight with disgust. "How could you take his side?"

"It's not about taking sides," I reason. "We aren't strong enough to carry December back to the manor, not like this. We also don't have the supplies he needs to get better, but Cruelty does. We need help, Tuesday. Let him help us."

"Help us?" she repeats. "Like how he helped us here, down this path? He told us to come this way, Sunday, don't you get it? This was all part of his plan. He sent the Soulless here to ambush us!"

I shake my head, willing her to understand. "That was an accident –"

"Do you hear yourself?" she whispers, her voice suddenly hushed with fear. "Are you a Soulless now? Why are you defending him?"

"I'm not defending him. I want December to live, and Cruelty can help us. Please, just listen to me. He's dying, Tuesday. Look at him. We don't have much of a choice."

She takes her attention off me for a moment, tears filling her eyes as she stares at her true love, bloody and barely breathing.

She shakes her head once. Twice. Three times.

"If he dies," she says at last, lowering the knife. "I'll kill you myself."

I take a tentative step closer, refusing to break eye contact. "If he dies," I repeat. "I'll give you the dagger."

Chapter Thirty-Six

After the Freedom Celebration, Tuesday refuses to talk to me. It doesn't bother me at first. I understand she needs time to cope with everything that's happened.

I haven't known the girl long, but I'd bet she's never killed a human before, so I'm sure all of this is just as disturbing to her as it is to me. I understand why she did it, though. I'd be a hypocrite to say I would've acted differently in her place. I've thought about taking someone's life before. I've thought about doing a lot of despicable things, if it meant protecting the people I love.

I'm sure Tuesday doesn't regret killing the Soulless — it was either him or us — but even if she does, that's not the only thing weighing her down.

Cruelty has been watching over December since the attack, and Tuesday refuses to believe it's in good faith. She thinks I'm in league with him — that it was somehow my plan to hurt December. She's formed this wild conspiracy that Cruelty is working with Sickness to keep her and December apart – as if the Master is healing December privately to keep them from seeing each other.

I don't know how long it'll take for her to trust me again, but after five days, I'm tired of waiting for it to happen. In Airabeth, we are nothing without each other. How can she still believe I meant her harm, after everything we've been through?

I abandon my duties to find her, slipping out the kitchen's back door and heading for the main foyer.

The hall is busy when I enter, crowded with servants. I tune out the chaos and practice what I'm going to say, searching for the right words.

I've never been good at confrontation. I grew up thinking it's better to bottle up your emotions than speak them out loud. I care about Tuesday, and I don't want to fight with her, but I'm not sure how to convey that truth in words.

I'm halfway down the corridor, mind racing, when I see Cruelty sitting against the wall, fingers drumming against his thigh. His head hangs between his knees, black hair ruffled as if he's been running his hands through it all night. Exhaustion is written in the hunch of his shoulders, the heaviness in his posture.

How long has he been sitting there like that?

My stomach lurches when he looks up at me, his eyes striking, even from a distance.

"Hi," Cruelty says, and rises to his feet with feline grace. He's exchanged his usual embroidered jacket for a plain blue shirt and baggy pants. They do nothing to hide the enormity of him, his presence stifling in the narrow hallway.

"How's he doing?" I ask, getting straight to the point. Cruelty has been sneaking away from the other Masters to update me on December's recovery. The last I heard he's in a coma, which is better than being dead, but not by much.

"I checked on him this morning," the Master says, eyes drooping and bloodshot. He looks like he's gotten even less sleep than I have, and I'm only managing a few hours a night. "He has severe head trauma, but it's still too early to tell what kind of an impact that'll have. Good news is that his breathing has become stable, so that's something."

"Good," I say, and desperately cling to that one piece of uplifting information. "That's good."

We stand there for a moment, both silent and keeping our distance.

I cross my arms.

Cruelty shoves his hands in his pockets, looking equally as uncomfortable as I feel.

I rack my mind for something to say, but he's reported all I need to know, so technically we're done here.

I should leave.

He should leave.

Neither of us stirs.

It's strange, this shift between us. I can feel it deep inside myself, like a stone sitting at the bottom of my stomach. Whenever I see him, I pretend not to notice it, but we're reaching a point where ignorance is foolish.

"How are you?" Cruelty asks.

"I'm good," I say, but the words come out forced. I try again. "I feel fine, truly I do." The Master raises a brow, accepting none of my lies. "Everything is fine, given the circumstances, and I'm doing all right. A little tired and anxious, but overall, I feel . . ."

"Guilty," he fills in.

I shrug, not sure what to say. He's right, of course. "If I hadn't dragged December into the woods, maybe he wouldn't have—"

"I'm not talking about December," he says gently, probing an emotional wound better left untouched.

I take a step away from him, physically distancing myself from a topic I have no interest in exploring. I don't want to talk about what happened to Sasha. I don't want to talk about what happened to Diana either, no matter how strained our relationship was. I didn't want her to die. I didn't want anyone to die, but life doesn't always give us what we want.

"Now isn't the time to confront everything that's happened to you, I know that." Cruelty's eyes are still and patient, a wondrous sight that soothes me more than I'd like to admit.

He removes his hands from his pockets, but doesn't reach out to me, keeping his distance. "But there will come a time where you'll have to face the past and deal with it," he says. "When that time comes, it's important you have someone to talk to, and although that someone will probably be Elisha or Tuesday, I'm just a thought away, if you need."

He stares at me, his gaze pensive. "I find it's sometimes easier to be open with someone you don't know very well, or might never see again, because who cares what a person you don't have a fondness for has to say, right? You have nothing to gain or lose if the conversation goes awry, but at least you're talking and getting the words out. That's better than nothing, I believe."

I stare at him for a speechless minute, a strong emotion drifting through the air between us, though it isn't from his power. I fall back against the wall, my legs a little too weak to stand on their own.

"But I see you every day," I counter, rejecting his proposal. "How can I have no fear of judgment or ridicule if I bare my soul to you, a Master I see at every turn."

"It won't be like that for long," he says, his tone passive. Difficult to decode. "To be quite honest with you, I pray for the day I never see you again. Because that'll mean you passed your Tests and you'll be gone, living your life out there, where you should be." His shoulders curve a bit, as if the words have somehow made him feel small. Perhaps a little unhappy.

I straighten my own shoulders in response, fearing the weight bearing upon them. The sensation is odd, given everything he's said. There isn't a thing he's mentioned that I wouldn't want for myself, yet there's a heaviness to my heart — a dread I can't explain.

I push the emotion aside, afraid to examine it.

"Why are you so willing to fill the position of a stranger I care nothing about?" I ask.

The Master tilts his head to the side, chin lifting in a challenge. "I thought I was already filling it."

"The position is, indeed, taken," I agree, turning on my heel to leave.

I need to get out here, away from him. I don't like the heat rising to my cheeks. I don't like the flutter in my stomach. And I certainly don't like the look in his eye — how it makes me crave and want in ways I shouldn't.

"But it's not by you," I add over my shoulder, not daring to turn around. I'm too embarrassed — too surprised by my admission — to hear a response, but I swear I feel it in my mind, an echo of the lowest laughter.

I have no idea why I said that.

I have no idea what possessed me to reveal a small truth to him that I wasn't ready to even admit to myself, but Cruelty makes it easy to be honest. To be vulnerable.

I hope it doesn't come back to bite me.

I FIND TUESDAY MOPPING the stairs in the main foyer, hard at work. I know her well enough to suspect the focus in her eyes isn't related to her job, but to December's recovery. She's no doubt anticipating the worst.

"Tuesday!" I call her name with as much cheer as I can muster, hoping it's enough to lift her spirits. Maybe if I smile big enough, she'll drop her guard and talk to me.

As soon as she turns to me, she scowls, her eyes dark with hostility.

My stomach tightens into a knot. We're not off to a good start.

"Look," I say once I reach her. "I know you're mad at me, but please, I—"

"Stop." Tuesday cuts me off. "You're embarrassing yourself. You're a coward and a fraud, and I don't want to be associated with you anymore. Leave me alone and get back to work. I have nothing to say to you."

She turns and heads out the front door, but I follow right behind, refusing to let our conversation end like this.

"Please," I tell her, "just listen for one second—"

I reach for her hand, but as soon as I step over the door's threshold, I'm blinded by a flaring light. I hiss and shield my face, rubbing my eyes to adjust them to the brightness.

It takes several blinks before the dots in my vision fade, allowing me to behold a scene I'm unfamiliar with.

A scene that turns my insides watery, inducing a fear I desperately wish to escape.

Bleeding hell. It's happening again.

Chapter Thirty-Seven

Airabeth's desert. That's where I am — where I've been transferred — to complete my fourth Test. With the sky almost dark, I don't know how the Masters managed to get me here so quickly, but alas, the bastards are getting more and more creative with their testing environment.

I fold my arms around me to ward off the winds, forbidding any fear from taking root. I've won a Test before, I can do it again.

Clinging to that small kernel of hope, I take in my surroundings quickly, staring straight into the wide expanse of nothingness. I soon spot a faint outline sitting in the distance. The silhouette is slim and tall, its edges rippling against the heat.

At first glance, I think it's a cactus, but the closer I look, the more alien the object seems.

The Masters must've put this thing here for me to find. A clue of some sort.

I go to it with dread, feet dragging.

A tendril of dread claws down my back when I discover the outline is a wooden plank erected in the sand, a series of words inscribed into its middle.

I shield my face with the back of my hand and lean in, squinting to make out the writing:

You have one hour to make it to the other side of the desert. Your destination will be marked by a red flag. Take it, and you will be declared victorious. Failure to live out the tasks required will result in ultimate defeat.

— *Master of Doubt*

One hour. That's it? That's all I'm given?

A chill sweeps through me, reaching all the way down to my soul.

This desert has no trail, no direction, and could easily be over fifty miles long on either side. How am I supposed to navigate all of that in less than an hour? The farthest distance I've ever traveled by foot in an hour is only six miles.

Stay calm, Nadia. Sasha's voice echoes distantly in my mind, his voice certain and strong, so opposite of how I feel. *Don't let fear get in the way of observation. Look around. Find another clue.*

But how am I supposed to find a clue among this unending empty terrain? I thought searching for the key in my second Test was bad enough, but at least I was in a contained environment back then.

This is a whole new level of insanity, one where the possibilities are endless.

Keep moving. An inborn part of me stirs. *The answer could be much closer than you* think.

And that's when I see it, a glint of metal sticking up from the ground, barely two feet ahead of me. I drop to my knees and push away the sand to uncover it, my heart pounding. As soon as my fingers bump against something solid and cold, I pull them back to investigate, not entirely sure what to think.

A treasure chest? That's what the Lord of Doubt has left me?

Before I can overthink what possible horrors lay inside, I open the lid to reveal a mace club, spear, and line of rope.

I don't have the time or energy to think about what I'll have to do with these supplies, but they're here for a reason. I'm not taking any chances by leaving them behind. I grab the tools and move on, not wanting to waste whatever minutes of sunlight I have left.

I look around the desert and debate which direction I should go next, then realize there's no point agonizing over it. I just throw the line of rope over my shoulder, grip the weapons in either hand, and run.

I have no idea what I'm surging toward, or if I'm even moving in the right direction, but I have to go *somewhere*, so I go east.

I pump my legs at a decent pace, adamant on preserving my energy, but no matter how slow I go, my lungs burn, suffocating under the conditions.

Less than ten minutes of jogging go by, and I'm already tempted to take a break, my calves cramping to the point of pain. I find a way to resist the temptation, however, reminding myself of all that's at stake — of everything I can't afford to lose.

Now isn't the time to get comfortable.

I repeat the thought over and over in my head, relying on its strength to propel me forward. It works for a time, but soon, thinking becomes too tiring, and I have to depend on sheer willpower to push on, hoping my body doesn't betray me. But after miles and miles of aimless running, my legs start to buckle, my feet begin to drag, and something horrifying spins in my vision.

I take a deep breath, telling myself the dizzy spell will pass, but it doesn't.

It only gets worse.

Not only am I drunk on vertigo, but apparently, I'm hallucinating things now, too.

At least, I think that's what's happening when the sand starts to hiss and swirl beneath my feet, scattering as if blown by a powerful wind.

I frown at the tendrils of sand, watching in horror as they begin to drift, lift, and rise from the earth — a spirit awakening.

I blink several times to remove the vision, but it doesn't change.

I'm not hallucinating.

Emperors above. This is really happening.

The sand builds and builds, taking on the form of a ghostly human, only its eyes and mouth visible.

I retreat, horrified and confused by what I'm seeing, and sprint back the way I came, the wraith racing at my heels.

Think. Think. Think. Think. Think.

The sand ghost gains on me, blowing hot air against my back, going for the kill. I drive my legs as fast as I can, but I can tell it won't be enough. The aggressive winds pick up sand from the ground, clouding my sight. I lose sense of everything around me, my momentum waning.

The gales are too fast, too powerful. I can't outrun them.

It isn't long before I'm on my knees, crawling.

I drop the supplies and risk a glance up, my heart plummeting as I take in the unfolding horror. The spirit has created a sandstorm, the vicious winds trapping me inside the eye of a tornado, lashing and violent.

I gasp at the sight, the twister ripping the air from my lungs, leaving me breathless. I bend my head toward my lap to defend myself, my hair whipping around my face. But through the frightening strands of chaos, a shadowed figure appears out of the corner of my eye, begging for attention.

I instinctively lift my head toward it, squinting through the sand clouds . . . And then I see him, standing outside the twister, too far for me to reach.

Sasha?

I blink and rub my eyes, a cry sitting in my throat.

He's gone before I can call to him, his face replaced with someone else's — a face I know better than my own.

Elisha.

Despite the brutality of the wind, my twin's long hair doesn't thrash around his face like mine, but rather remains static. Even his clothes, baggy and hanging off him in tatters, do not billow.

I lift my eyes to his, desperate for connection, but the moment I glimpse the bolt of blue so similar to mine, the color morphs into something deeper — a rich golden brown I've come to know well.

Tuesday.

She stares back at me, her anger and hatred more potent than ever. She says nothing as I struggle to get to her, but I don't have time to be hurt by her apathy. I blink and she's gone, her face shifting into December's.

Next is Diana. January. My mother. All of them disappearing and reappearing before I can get a good look at them. Their shifting faces hypnotize me into a trance, distracting me from the bits of sand cutting into my skin, leaving blood smears behind.

My heart is beating too fast. My mind is racing. I need to calm down.

This isn't real. You can overcome this. Cruelty's voice breaks through my growing hysteria, but his presence is so removed from this wretched place, it provides no solace.

I'm alone. No one is coming for me.

I hide my face in the hem of my dress and cover my ears, the tornado so loud it's like thunder cracking inside my skull. I press my mouth into a thin line to prevent sand from swirling down my throat.

A sob escapes me as the winds knock me to the side, my head inches from the tornado's edge. I shuffle back, my cheeks scratched and bloody, the small grains shockingly painful.

Calm down, calm down, calm down, calm down. Use your brain. Get out of this.

I think back to my previous Tests, remembering how Sickness made me believe I was bleeding from my eyes and Warfare made me think my bones were snapping, when in reality, I was fine. The Master of Doubt must be using a similar tactic now, which means it's only a stronghold — a lie the Master has placed inside my head.

The truth in the statement relaxes me, my limbs loosening of their own accord.

This is all a trick. None of this is happening. You're under their influence, you must escape!

I close my eyes to shut out the Sacred Seven's illusion, submitting to the tornado's power and control. I let the ferocious gales push and pull me in whatever direction they please, refusing to fight against their strength.

My heart spikes every time my body wavers to the edge of the twister, trying not to panic. Warm. Quiet. Gentle. Serene. Beautiful. Undisturbed.

This is the desert I envision; the one I speak and welcome into existence, calling it forth.

I sense a shift in the atmosphere then, like a turning of the tides, the change discernible. Slowly, the sting of the nicks and scrapes along my skin begin to dull, my injuries improving as the image in my head becomes more detailed.

I keep my thoughts in check, refusing to let them scatter in fear, and shove Doubt's strongholds from my mind, building a mental barrier brick by brick. My mental shield rises gradually, slower than I'd like, but once the wall is up and the corruption is out, I open my eyes.

The tornado is gone.

Everything is still and silent, undisturbed.

My limbs shake as I rise to my feet.

I rub my palms together to stop their shaking, a mixture of fear and relief pulsing through me.

It's over. I have to keep moving.

I quickly find my supplies lying among the sand, my eyes aching as if they've melted into the back of my skull. Although I'm still dazed from the phantom tornado, there's no time to recover. My second obstacle could arrive at any moment, and I need to be ready.

I barely have a handle on the spear when a piercing shriek comes from my right, paralyzing me.

My throat closes up at the sound — a warning.

In all my years of hunting in the forest, I've learned to recognize all kinds of noises, but this is a new one. I've never heard any deer, bear, or large animal scream like that, but that doesn't make it unearthly, right? I'm sure there are lots of mortal creatures who are capable of making that sound.

Every beat of my heart chants for me to *run run run,* but I know it won't do any good. I didn't come this far to flee, and even if I wanted to, I don't have a choice. The faster I overcome this obstacle, the faster I pass my Test, and right now, that's all I want.

Slowly, I turn, my heart pounding with all kinds of fear, and meet a pair of cunning green eyes. It takes me a second to realize what I'm staring at, my senses overwhelmed by the wondrous sight.

I've never witnessed a cougar in real life, but I've seen them in paintings. Slender bodies. Pointed ears. Sharp jawbones. Carnivorous teeth. If it weren't for the sheer mass of this creature, I'd think she was some sort of wildcat, but she's many times larger than the average feline. Terrifyingly beautiful.

I avert my gaze to avoid the intensity of her stare, afraid of provoking her into action. I can't help but take a selfish moment to marvel at her gray-brown fur, however, every inch of her rippling with power and brawn.

If I were back in Tempus, I bet I could have sold her pelt for an excellent price. By the looks of it, she must be at least ten feet long, and that's not including her tail. She's at least two hundred pounds and her paws match my skull in size.

I am distracted from her intimidating stature by the humanistic awareness in her eyes, bringing gooseflesh to my skin. She stares at me with wit and understanding, like she knows exactly who I am and why I'm here.

I get the compelling sense she's been awaiting my arrival.

I pick up the spear, assuming this is what I'm supposed to use it for, and place the other two supplies on the ground. I lift my weapon to eye level, the handle large and awkward in my hands, preparing for the battle to come.

But when the cougar snarls and crouches to the ground, I know nothing will ready me for her attack.

She lunges, her speed surpassing that of the Amphista, and swipes for my head, going straight for the kill. I pivot backward and clumsily thrust my spear forward. She dodges it easily, her eyes laughing at my pathetic attempt to fight back.

She growls hungrily, stalking toward me with a predator's intent.

I take off running, thinking it'll give me the best chance at survival, but it won't.

I'm not nearly as fast as she is.

Not a second later, the cougar bounds for my heels, her strides outmatching mine three to one. I risk a quick glance over my shoulder and catch her leaping through the air, her body outstretched and soaring, moving to jump on top of me.

I pick up my pace to outrun the length of her pounce, but she's too big. Too fast.

In a flash of brown, she descends from the air and knocks her heavy paws against my back, pushing me face first into the ground. Breath shoots from my body as I smack to the earth, eating a pile of hot sand. I lose hold of my spear and hear it fall to the ground beside me, cursing its absence.

I'm coughing and spitting up grit when the cougar pushes me with the tip of her snout, forcing me onto my back. I try to scramble away from her, but she cripples me with her massive paws, pinning them on either shoulder. A pop erupts near my collarbone as she sinks into me with her weight, pressing my body deeper and deeper into the sand.

Red explodes in my vision, but I bite back the scream, afraid of how the creature will react. I twist my head to the side, grappling for my spear, but it's too far away from me.

It doesn't matter. I need to get it. I have to get it, or else—

The cougar slaps my cheek, claws slicing through delicate flesh.

Tears prick my eyes, but I don't stop stretching for my weapon.

The cougar slants her head toward me and opens her mouth, wide as a cave.

I gag at the smell of her breath, reeking of rotting flesh.

I angle my body toward the spear, the handle knocking against my fingertips.

It's still too far away.

I lean closer to it, my shoulder popping once again, until finally, *finally*, the handle is in my palm.

I pick it up and turn to the cougar, her teeth flying at my neck.

I arc the tip of the spear upward, agony traveling from wrist to shoulder, until the spear smashes straight through her skull and out the other side.

A vibration rattles through my body, and I stare wide-eyed as the creature slumps forward, blood dripping from her head and onto my chin.

Tears blur my vision, and I close my eyes as I struggle to escape from under her belly, my body trembling. I use the side of her body for leverage and push against it, wiggling free.

Don't cry. Don't cry, don't cry, don't cry, don't cry.

I roll to my feet, the tremor in my legs more prominent than ever. I bury my face into my hands — no, hand. I can't lift my right arm. It feels heavy, as if someone has pinned it to my side.

I peer down at my shoulder, but it doesn't look crooked or dislocated, like I expect. The skin is only swollen and bruised. I assume the ligament is torn. I know I'll be fine. I've suffered worse injuries.

Gingerly, I reach down and pick up the club and rope, my body aching as I start into a jog.

I try not to look at the cougar as I pass, but I find myself staring at the spear protruding from her skull. Should I take it with me? It might be of use later on.

As soon as I have the thought, the weapon dissolves into thin air, turning to dust. For a moment I think I'm hallucinating again, but when I go to the cougar and swipe a hand over her temple, nothing is there.

It's gone. The spear is truly gone.

The Master of Doubt doesn't want me to use my weapons more than once, it seems.

I hope I've used the right weapon for this obstacle then, because otherwise I won't have the right tools to complete the rest of my challenges.

I push the thought from my mind and continue east, assuming it doesn't matter which way I go. The Masters will make sure my trials find me, no matter what path I take.

"Kiddo? Is that you?"

My spine locks up at the voice, the *name*.

I slow my walking, waiting for another sentence to follow.

When nothing comes, I move on, afraid I'm imagining things again.

"Kiddo, it's me." There it is again. Louder, this time. "Turn around. Let me see you."

Kiddo.

My heart collapses at the nickname. There is only one person in the entire world who ever called me that. One person I haven't seen in ten years. This can't be real. It can't be.

Still, I turn.

And there, standing before me like a ghost, is the first man I ever loved.

I shake my head at what I see.

This is ridiculous.

A fantasy.

A dream.

Yet here he is, standing five feet away from me.

Impossible.

I call out to him against my better judgment, my mouth stumbling over his name. It's been a while since I've said it.

"Dad?"

Chapter Thirty-Eight

"Nadia! What — how did you get here?" My father takes a large step toward me, his hand outstretched in earnest, beckoning me to go to him. When I don't, the eagerness in his voice dwindles, a glimmer of disappointment in his gaze. "Kiddo, what's wrong?"

He blinks hopefully through eyes that look like mine, but the resemblance is off-putting, almost frightening in its accuracy. "There's no reason to be afraid. It's me."

But it's not, I warn myself. My parents are dead. They died ten years ago.

And seeing the illusion of my father now only brings back painful memories, turning my insides sour. It isn't hard to remember the tears I cried, or the denial I felt, after realizing I'd never see his face again, his death the first of many losses to come.

And it doesn't matter how much time has passed, or how mindless I get, I haven't forgotten the strength of his hugs, the wit in his jokes, the fullness of his laugh.

I wish I could forget those things. Perhaps then, I wouldn't be able to conjure the other memories either. The darker ones.

Like how the Soulless ripped my father away from us like he was less than cattle, beating him into submission. Or how my mother bellowed and cried when she was next, desperate to escape. Or how the silence following their capture was somehow worse than the scent of their blood, trailing splatters from where they were brutally pulled—

"What's going on in that head of yours?" The man's voice — my father's voice — hits me like a punch to the throat, stealing my breath. "Sweetheart, why are you crying?"

The impersonator approaches me, the gap between us nearly gone, and gestures to my face. The tears. He frowns softly at my sadness.

The look is so uncanny, so familiar, it makes it harder to accept that he isn't real.

"How are your sister and brothers doing?" he asks. I don't like the intimacy of his question. I don't like how it throws me off guard, making me see him as family, when he's nothing but a lie. "What have they been up to? Is Elisha keeping his hair short?" He laughs to himself, transported into a memory. "I suppose Sasha is keeping him on track, yes? He always ragged on your twin for his choice in hairstyle."

I flinch when he reaches out to tuck a strand of hair behind my ear.

"They're dead," I say flatly. "Everyone is gone, except Elisha. It's mostly my fault."

My father quirks a brow, seemingly pleased with my confession. It's an odd reaction, given what I just revealed.

"At least you can finally admit it," he says, his tone hardening. "You've spent years pretending to be the savior of our family, so I can only imagine how good it must feel to be honest with yourself."

The contentment in his gaze puts me on edge. I've never seen him wear a look like that, least of all around me.

"My darling Nadia." His voice shifts then, turning into a thick, gurgling sound. "I'm your father. I know you better than you know yourself. I know the pain inside your heart. I know all the shame and regret you've been carrying. It's not healthy to live with such deprecating emotions, my dear." He smiles, subtle and dark. "I can help you get rid of all that, if you'd like."

He hardly finishes the sentence before he changes, the strands of his hair lightening to an unnatural green.

I cover a hand over my mouth, suddenly sick.

Sky's, why did I come this close to him? I knew he was trouble, I knew, and yet I am inches away as his physique — previously tall and lean and on the brink of underweight — becomes stocky and built, so opposite of my father's famished body. The familiar glint in his eye darkens to a colorless black. Wickedness brightens his smile, mouth wide and red and glowing, ready to devour.

I should've taken that as my signal to run, but instead I wait for him to pounce.

Although large and frighteningly morphed, the creature retains the overall shape of a man, making me think he can be beaten.

I jump back, my limbs caught between fleeing and staying, and stare into a mutated face stuck between human man and demonic jester. An unpleasant combination.

The creature lashes out with unparalleled speed and wraps his unusually large hands around my neck, squeezing tightly. I gape at the pressure, his thumbs pressing mercilessly into my windpipe, cutting off the airway.

I thrash, straining to escape, but I don't know how to break his hold.

I drop the rope and club to free up my hands, smacking aimlessly at the creature's arms.

Tightness builds in my chest, growing worse and worse when he doesn't let go.

True panic starts to set in as I realize I'm not strong enough to push him away.

Struggling is getting me nowhere.

I'm going to pass out.

I need another plan.

I relax my body, going limp in the creature's hands. Every fiber of my being tells me to keep fighting, but I submit, keeping my limbs loose and floppy. I close my eyes and hang my head forward, my throat suffocating beneath the creature's brutal hold.

One minute, I tell myself.

Just hang on for one minute, and then it'll be over. He'll think you're dead and let you go.

Although my airway is being crushed and I can't get a single breath down, my heart pounds stubbornly in my chest, urging me to act.

Thirty seconds pass. Then sixty. Eighty.

This is taking much longer than I anticipated.

I start to worry as life begins to truly ooze out of me — slowly, then all at once.

My consciousness drifts in and out, walking toward the blackness.

I crack my eyes open and seek out the sky, desperate for something beautiful. I don't want to die in the dark. I stare pointedly at the heavens, wondering if that's where I'll go after I die, and start praying for a miracle.

I haven't prayed much since my parents passed away, but in times of crisis, it only feels natural to cry out to the sky's above. I sometimes question why that is, why we only ask for help when we're on the brink of disaster.

Either way, someone must be listening to my call — they have to be — because I don't know how else to explain why the creature's hands begin to slacken around my throat, the pressure on my windpipe easing.

He thinks he's killed me. He's going to let go. I can't believe he's going to let go.

I use his mistake to my advantage and strike, driving my knee up into his groin.

He yelps, the sound clotted and feral, as he releases me.

I fall to the ground in a blur of pain, gasping as my hip claps against the sand.

The desert air is hot and choking when I first suck it down, but my lungs adjust quickly, delighted to be functioning again.

I'm back on my feet within seconds, frantically searching for the club, but I don't see it. I settle for the line of rope instead, my fingers shaking as I unravel it to its full length.

I lift my head to see where the creature has gone — why did I take my eyes off him? — and the next thing I know, I'm on the ground, pinned beneath his body. I hardly have time to register his attack as he punches my face and the world spins on its axis. He follows up with jabs to my stomach, ribs, and side, stunning me.

He reaches for my neck again, determined to end me, but I don't give him the chance.

Before he can press his thumbs into my jugular, I thrust my arms up through his, pushing my forearms against the inside of his wrists. The momentum forces his hands off my throat and he spins away, his back to me.

I crunch up to a sitting position, getting as close to the mutant as I can, and wrap the rope around his neck, pulling tightly.

By the time he registers what I'm doing, it's too late.

I yank the rope backward with all my strength, forcing the creature's back into my stomach, trapping him against me. He twists to get away, flailing wildly, but it doesn't work. I finally have the upper hand.

I grimace when his skin begins to rip under the cord's rough edge, leaking blood onto my hands. At this proximity, I notice how coarse the rope's fibers are, unnaturally prickly. Perfect for slicing through this monster's throat.

I dig my heels into the sand for extra support, arms shaking as I pull the rope harder.

The creature reaches behind him, grappling for me, but he's weak. Dying. It's only when his thrashing starts to slow, the life draining out of him, do I find the courage to snap his neck to the side, screaming as I do it.

Once his head hangs limp, I pull the rope taut, slicing deep into his throat. I need to make sure he's dead.

I'm not taking any chances.

I don't let go of him until my strength gives out and the rope loosens, setting the creature free.

He slumps to the side, eyes open, chest unmoving.

Dead.

I WISH THE SUN WERE hotter.

It's been forty minutes since I killed the creature impersonating my father, and that's the first thought I have. The heat, once boiling and baking, has abandoned me, replacing itself with another temperature unfit for a mortal.

As my time to complete this Test runs down, night creeps in, stars appearing overhead — my only company in this freezing pocket of hell.

I wrap my arms around my waist to lock in some body heat, hands shaking as I rub them up and down my sides. The blood splattered from my fingertips to my elbows gradually peels off, leaving a trail of black flakes behind me.

I dig my palms into my eyes to block out the image of the horrific creature that wore my father's face, refusing to succumb to the terror growing within. It's a difficult task, given how my mind is withering. Weakening.

I'm alone. Tired. Wasting away.

I don't know how much longer I can do this. I don't know how much time I have left before—

I need a distraction. I pray for a distraction, and at some point, I get one.

I gasp when my foot catches on something — a hole — and lean all my weight backward to prevent a face plant. I flail my arms to regain my balance, trying to move forward, but my feet don't go with me, completely immobilized from calf to ankle.

My heart plummets when I glance down and identify the problem: quicksand.

A strangled sound erupts in the back of my throat, igniting a surge of fear.

I tell myself not to overreact or lose my wits, but that's easier said than done. The sand is rising faster than I can think, already reaching all the way up to my waist, pulling me under.

I try not to fight it. Fighting will only make this worse.

I keep my arms high and grip the club in my hand, mind racing in search of a plan.

I scan my surroundings for a solution.

I find one a few feet away from me, a three-armed cactus being my possible savior.

If only I had the rope, I could lasso it over one of the limbs and pull myself out, but the rope is gone. I need to figure out a way to use the club. It's my only option.

I examine the weapon — particularly the circular head — and touch one of the many spikes protruding from it. A small pinprick of blood oozes from my forefinger upon contact, stinging slightly.

It's good to establish that the spikes are real and painfully sharp, but I don't know how that's going to help me.

My mind spins in a thousand different directions, telling me victory isn't possible, when a memory emerges amid the chaos. I think back to my second Test, remembering how the Flames' arrows weren't ordinary forms of weaponry. They were charmed with the Sacred Seven's strongholds. Powerful. Otherworldly.

Is it possible the Masters have done the same with this weapon?

There's only one way to find out.

I stretch out my arm as far as it'll go and pierce the club's head into the dirt, pushing it down, down, down, until only the handle is visible above ground. Once I'm sure it's buried deep in the earth, I tug on the hilt to make sure it holds.

I try not to marvel as the sand hardens around the handle, turning the club into an anchor.

Arms trembling, injured shoulder screaming, I pull myself upward, relying on nothing but upper body strength to draw closer to the club. I cry out when something in my shoulder pops, but I don't stop climbing.

I rise out of the sand, my chest halfway free.

Emperors above! It's working.

I continue to pull myself up, up, up, clearing my torso. I fall forward on my stomach and dig my hands into the dirt, trying to crawl the rest of the way, but there's nothing solid to hang on to.

I bury my palms deep into the sand to get a better hold, squirming to break free.

By the time I'm able to clear my feet from the quicksand, I'm shaking and out of breath, my vision spinning.

I take a second to catch my breath and lay on my back, staring up at the sky.

I wish I had time to rest — to grasp everything that's happened — but I don't.

My hour is nearly up.

I have to keep moving.

I roll to my feet and stumble forward like a toddler learning to walk, cradling my wounded shoulder to my stomach.

I can no longer run — my feet simply won't allow it — but I'm walking. Barely.

Find the flag. Find the flag. Find the flag. I repeat the words like a mantra, sensing the end is near. Considering all the supplies Doubt gave me are gone, this has to be it. I have to be close to the finish line, because if I'm not . . .

I resist the urge to drop to my knees when I see it.

In the distance, waving gloriously in the wind, stands the red flag.

Chapter Thirty-Nine

When I open my eyes, the first thing I see is the curtain. I've learned that June, a middle-aged woman with black hair and almond eyes, sleeps behind it — my adjacent roommate. I never thought I'd see the day where I delighted in her snores and bursts of sleep talking, but tonight is different.

I don't remember losing consciousness, but being back in the Flames Quarter means I'm no longer stuck in that hideous desert, trapped with those unearthly things. Since I'm here — alive — I must've passed my Test.

I sit up, almost screaming from the pain of it, and prop myself against the back wall, shaking the daze from my mind. Everything hurts. Blinking is a chore. I try not to cry about it as I situate myself into a comfortable position, my bones shrieking as if they've been hacked through by a jigsaw. Unbearably painful.

I look down to examine my shoulder — most of the torture is coming from there — and check for injury or infection, dreading what I'll find. I've seen what happens when broken bones go untreated. I've smelled the spoil and disease of gangrene, and I hope that isn't what's happening to me now.

There are no protruding tendons or infection-filled wounds, but there is a black sling wrapped around my hurt shoulder. The cloth is comfortable and intricate, sewn by a swift, nimble hand. The strap does much to relieve the ache of the broken cartilage, but it's also a reminder of my diminishing strength.

Knock. Click. Pat, pat, pat. Click. Knock. Pat, pat, pat.

Fear coils in my stomach at the sounds of doors closing, locks snapping, footsteps shuffling.

I glance toward the Quarter's back entrance.

No one, not even the Masters, enters the Flames sleeping chamber after midnight.

Pat, pat, pat, pat, pat . . .

The footsteps echo louder. Closer.

Pat, pat, pat, pat, pat . . .

I go to stand from my cot.

"Nadia?" Someone breathes my name into the quiet, and I instantly relax at the familiarity of the voice, the tightness in my chest loosening.

A moment later, Cruelty steps into the room, his eyes finding mine in the dark. He shrugs off his formal jacket, then tosses it to the foot of the bed, crouching before me.

He rolls up his shirt sleeves and unfastens the top two buttons near the collar, trading in the Master he hates for the one he truly is. "This may be a stupid question," he starts, and I don't need to see his face to notice the trouble in his tone or the stiffness in his posture. "But how are you feeling?"

"I'm all right," I lie. "Just tired." It's an effort to speak, to swallow through the dryness in my mouth. I can already feel the bruises forming around my neck, the phantom touch of the creature's hands still pressing against my windpipe.

"Your nostrils just flared," Cruelty says, flicking the side of my nose, chuckling at my half-hearted scowl. "May I?" He gestures to my wounded arm, and at my nod, he gently unwraps the sling.

I grind my teeth, heart pounding, as he places a soft, delicate finger on the broken bone. It takes everything I have not to scream.

"Bleeding hell," Cruelty mumbles, his mouth slashing into a grim line. "I need to make you a better sling."

Make? He *made* this for me?

"And bandages," he continues, "I need to patch up those cuts on your face and arms. Now that you're awake, I'll also bring you some water." He rises to leave, and my chest tightens.

I lurch forward and catch the Master's wrist between my fingers. My insides trip over themselves when he turns to look back at me, something raw and overwhelming in his gaze.

There's so much I want to say to him. So much I want to ask, but in a moment of panic, I end up voicing the least important question. "How did I end up here?" I drop his hand, terrified of the heat where we touch. "I don't remember grabbing the flag or losing consciousness. And December!" I can't believe I forgot about him. "How's he doing? Do you have any updates?"

Cruelty runs a hand through his hair, looking as tired as I feel.

I have the sudden urge to reach out again, to apologize for putting him in this position. He's always taking care of everyone else. I wonder how long it's been since someone took care of him.

"December is doing well," he whispers, careful not to wake the other servants. "He woke up today and has been responding to treatment. He hasn't said anything aloud, but he's able to nod and shake his head. All great signs. I tried to tell Tuesday, but I can't get her alone. Sickness has increased his watch on her since the Rite."

I can only imagine.

After confirming that Tuesday and December have been romantically involved, I wouldn't be surprised if Sickness shackled himself to her, demanding they spend every waking moment together. She still has one week before she marries him, and although Sickness is coarse and lecherous, he's waiting until marriage to consummate their relationship.

He won't lay a hand on her in a sexual way, but he'll mar her skin. Take her fingers.

I have to make sure she's all right.

I open my mouth to tell Cruelty I'm leaving to find her, but instead of coughing up words, I cough up blood, my throat burning with the metallic taste of it.

I go still, my heart pounding so hard I feel it in my head.

Cruelty leans in and wipes the corner of my mouth, removing the blood with the edge of his thumb. "It's all right," he assures, and although I know it isn't, I'm soothed by his words. "You're going to be okay."

Something heavy builds in my chest, primal and knowing.

How many times have I said those exact words to the dying? To those I knew weren't going to make it?

Cruelty's eyes search mine, troubled.

My chest aches at his distress.

"I'll be right back," he says, breaking away from the bed.

He scrubs his hand on the back of his pants to rid them of the blood. My blood.

"Tuesday." I mumble her name through the clots in my mouth, "I need to make sure she's all right."

"I'll do it," Cruelty offers, turning for the door. "I need to get her opinion on something anyway, so I'll ask how she's doing while I'm there." When I blink and raise a brow, he elaborates. "Before she got captured and taken to Airabeth, she was training to be a nurse. I'd feel better getting a second opinion on what I should give you before . . ."

I tune out completely, my mind caught on the small revelation.

A nurse. Of course. Tuesday would've been a great nurse. It also explains how she knew how to stitch up my wounds after my second Test, even without the tips of her fingers to guide her.

". . . which means you must stay here, all right?"

I look to Cruelty, tuning back into his voice. His face is calm but determined, a storm brewing behind his eyes. It reminds me of how I felt when I tried to save Sasha. My sister. But I don't want to think about my family right now, and if this is the last time I'm going to see Cruelty, I don't want to waste it thinking about death.

"Are you trying to make a deal with me, Master?" I smile at him, trying to lighten the mood.

To my relief, he does the same, the lines around his mouth softening as he walks to the door. "I don't make deals with mortals," he says, and for the first time since we met, my heart sinks at the sight of him leaving.

MY EYELIDS ARE HEAVY, but I don't sleep. I'm afraid to close my eyes, fearing the darkness will be the last thing I see. It's been over ten minutes since Cruelty left, and I've already coughed up blood six times, my face hot with fever. I keep a hand on my chest to measure every heartbeat, worrying the pulses will eventually stop.

I tell myself that everything will be fine — Cruelty will be back soon — but the idea doesn't lessen my fears. Still, I have to try to be positive about it — being stressed and afraid will only make my condition worse.

I remove the sheets from my bed to cool off, but it's like my bones are on fire, the heat unending.

Don't panic. The Master will be back soon. He said so himself. He's going to help me. He won't be much longer.

He won't be much longer.

He won't be much longer.

He won't be much longer.

I repeat the words over and over until I hear him reenter the Quarter, his steps swift and light.

I pull myself upright and adjust my pillow, moving to greet him, but he beats me to it.

"I expected you to be asleep."

I freeze at the voice. At the arrogance and hostility laced within it, none of it Cruelty's. A silhouette of a man steps through the door, filling the entryway for a brief moment before shutting the shadow of the door behind him soundlessly. For one gorgeous second, I convince myself that delusion's got the best of me — I must be going mad.

But my eyes and ears are working just fine.

The Master of Sickness steps into view, a vicious glint in his gaze.

I scoot to the far edge of my cot, hot tears rising to my eyes, threatening to fall. I push them away as quickly as they come, refusing to show my alarm. Crying isn't going to get me away from this beast, and it certainly isn't going to give me the upper hand, so I choose to do something that will.

Releasing my hands from beneath the covers, I shift into a defensive position, my collarbone howling from the sudden movement. I bite the inside of my cheek to hide the wince, but Sickness sees right through it, his eyes brightening at the sight of my ruined shoulder, the bloody sheets.

It doesn't take a genius to guess what he's thinking. Hurting. Weak. Defenseless. Easy. "Now *that's* deliciously dreadful," he mutters, gesturing to my arm.

I go to move away from him again, but I'm already on the opposite end of the mattress.

There's nowhere to go. Nowhere to hide.

I should stand up for myself. Say something, do something, before—

Sickness strikes out a hand, his large, burly fingers clamping down on my collarbone, squeezing the torn cartilage. I shriek at the brutality of the touch, my vision exploding with white sparks, nearly knocking me unconscious. I close my eyes to keep the nausea down, but vomit still climbs up my stomach, leaving acid in its wake.

The Master draws closer to me, leaning over the bed. The heat of his body fills the air around us, disgustingly hot. I kick him in the gut, increasing the distance between us. He staggers back, more out of surprise than anything, and clicks his tongue.

"I'm surprised to see you alive," he whispers, his expression dark and unhinged.

My head lolls to the side, ear resting on my shoulder. It's getting harder to keep myself upright, every inch of me growing heavier and heavier as the seconds tick by. "What are you doing here?"

"You're more than halfway through your Tests," he says, as if this is news to me. "If I were being totally honest, I'd tell you how unexpected that is. You're only three trials away from victory." Whether he shakes his head in disappointment or awe, I'm not sure. "That's quite a feat."

"Afraid I'll win, Master?"

He quirks a grin. "Wolves aren't concerned with the opinions of sheep, little Bunny."

"True," I say, feeling the heaviness in my tongue. "Wolves aren't afraid of sheep either, so which animal does that make you?"

The veins in his neck pulse, crawling with disease. "Neither," he replies, the words so quiet I could've imagined them. "I'm the fox you didn't see coming."

And with that, he whips out a hand, catching my wrist. I yank my arm back, thinking his grip will be strong, but it isn't. He lets me go easily, my momentum throwing me off the bed and onto the floor.

Everything inside me shrieks when my stomach smacks against the cold ground. I tell my legs to stand, to run, but they won't work. I hardly feel anything below my knees.

I crawl toward the door, begging for someone to help me, but the surrounding Flames remain quiet, blocking out my pleas. I like to think I wouldn't be so heartless as to let a fellow human suffer in plain sight, but if the roles were reversed, would I intervene?

Sickness takes his time as he flips me onto my back, enjoying the fight. I try to push him away with my good arm, but it's pointless. I'm in no shape to fend him off.

"You were getting too close," he murmurs, his mouth at my ear, tickling my neck. He lets go of my wrist for a second — hand reaching for something I can't see — and returns with the pillow from my bed.

"You were going to pass your Tests," he says, and although he flashes an easy smile, there's savagery in his gaze. "Your spirit is strong, I can see it in you. But I can't let you win. No matter what the others say." He stares at me, as if contemplating what to do next. "Do you remember January?" he asks, his voice strange and creeping, prickling through the air. "He died, you know. At the Celebration. He got jumped. A group of Soulless beat him so badly, he died on the field."

I blink, the words refusing to sink in.

He's lying. He must be lying, because January can't be dead. It's too cruel. He's survived six of his Tests, just one away from freedom, and after all he's endured, it's impossible to think he could die so senselessly.

"It should've been you who died on that field." Sickness shakes with a century's worth of rage, his face reddening. "I ordered the Soulless to kill you, but they got the wrong Flame." He laughs to himself, low and guttural. "Why do I have to do everything myself?"

He brings the pillow to my face, and I jerk beneath him, trying to push him away. He counteracts every move, deflecting me easily.

*What are you doing? No. No! NO! Get off me! STOP! Get off.
GET OFF —*

I scream the words in my head, unable to shout them out loud
as he holds the pillow over my nose and mouth, smothering all airways. I claw for escape and scratch at Sickness's arms, but my fingers
are like twigs against his hands.

There's no way out of this.

He's on top of me, shaking, arms trembling, breath quickening,
as he pushes the pillow harder and harder into my face. My nose
snaps under the pressure, the explosion of blood choking me further, thick and never-ending.

I open my mouth for air, but nothing comes, my lungs tightening against their will.

I used to think a quick death was cruel and unnecessary, but
now I wish for it. Beg for it.

People say the best moments of your life flash before your eyes
as the end nears, and they aren't wrong. Memories from childhood
and adolescence materialize in my mind, playing out a series of
events, new and old, forgotten and kept.

But as death approaches, the good times dissipate and replace
themselves with the darker, crueler points of my existence.

I see my mother sobbing after Grandad died, her limbs frail and
shaking as she lies in Father's arms. I watch a teenage boy scream in
hopeless rage as a Soulless drags his little brother to Airabeth. I re-
live the first time I killed an animal, the blood sticky on my hands,
forever dirtied.

The memories race by, unbearable in their intensity.

And that's when the voice comes.

Cruelty says my name inside my mind — no, *screams* it.

I try to reach for him, to respond with a plea of my own, but I
can't find the strength.

The energy.

The breath.

His voice is the last thing I hear before the world goes dark.

Chapter Forty

The Master of Cruelty

Tuesday's thoughts are a minefield of fury and insults, surprisingly coarse. She leaves the door to her mind wide open, exposing all the fear and hostility she feels toward me, leaving no question about where we stand.

I keep my comments to myself as she increases her distance, putting ten feet between us, as if the space will protect her. The point of my visit is to get her to trust me, not fear me, and the quicker I do that, the sooner we can get on with our lives.

"I've told you what you need," Tuesday says, her hands shaking as she slides a vial of medicine down the kitchen counter to me.

I pocket the bottle as soon as it hits my fingers, amazed by her compliance.

After our little altercation in the forest following the Celebration, I didn't think she'd be particularly eager to assist me. But as soon as I told her Nadia — Sunday — needed our help, her attitude changed, becoming more cordial.

"Is there anything else I can do for you?" The Flame's voice is aloof and casual, somewhat confident. If I were human, I might've fallen for the front, but I can hear the speed of her heart, the pounding of her blood.

I'm not offended by her reaction — I'm used to humans fearing me — but the blow still hurts, no matter how many times I've taken it.

I can't believe I'm helping a Master. My ears echo with her chorus of thoughts, my power naturally linking us together. *He's a slimy bastard, no better than Sickness. But if he's going to save Sunday's life, I have to give him what he wants. There's no other way. Emperors above, if he hurts her, I'll cut off his—*

I consider breaking the line that ties my mind to hers, but Tuesday is a difficult human to read, and we're not done talking just yet. I can't ease her worries if I don't know what's bothering her, and since she isn't going to tell me outright, I need to do a little prying.

"I appreciate your professional opinion," I say, and prove the sentiment by giving a small bow, my spine aching at the movement. I'm not built to submit myself to others — my title makes sure of it — but I do it for Nadia's sake, setting my pride aside.

The action makes Tuesday's eyes widen, her hand flying to her mouth.

It's just the reaction I was expecting.

Masters never earnestly bow to anyone. Ever. Especially not to Flames, but I need to show her we're on the same side. That I have no interest in harming her.

"You're going to save Sunday's life," I add, nursing the tendril of hope burning in her gaze, wanting her to trust me.

Although she doesn't admit it, I can sense her concern for Nadia, almost as strong and unconditional as that of a loved one. A sister.

"How bad is she?" The pain in Tuesday's voice is visceral, broken in its softness. "What did she tell you?"

"She's worried about you," I say, sensing her peace of mind is dependent on my response. "She wants to make sure you're doing well. She requested I come here to update you on December's health." Tuesday stiffens at the sound of her lover's name, triggering a defensiveness within her. "He's recovering well, but I believe his rehabilitation would be quicker if you came to visit him. He's been alone for an entire week, and you haven't seen him once."

Tuesday narrows her eyes, and all hope of creating a civil relationship dies.

"I'm not the one who put him in a coma," she chides.

"Nobody put him in a coma," I say calmly, but not kindly. "What happened in the forest was an accident. Things like this happen all the time, and I thought you of all people would understand that."

"Do you have any idea what it's like to watch a loved one suffer?" she asks, her tone lowering. "Do you know what it's like to not eat or sleep because you're wondering if the most important person in your life has been taken from you forever? Do you know how consuming a terror like that can be? How debilitating?"

To her, I don't know what it's like to care for anything or anyone, but she doesn't know my past. My suffering. Over all the years I've been alive, I've lost so many friends and family to war, sickness, and age that there weren't enough graves to bury them all, but I don't tell her any of that. None of it matters.

Tuesday is going to believe what she wants, regardless of what I say, but I stick with the truth. It's the only way to get through to her. "I may not love someone as strongly or passionately as you do December," I say, "but I think I could." I tremble at the realization, my hands slick with sweat, though the kitchen isn't hot. "I think I can imagine what it would be like to care about someone that deeply."

Tuesday goes silent for a moment, her head shaking with disbelief as she paces around the kitchen. She glares at me, debating where she stands with me after my confession.

I don't regret what I said. There's no shame in speaking the truth.

I only wish I would've told it to the girl my honesty is referencing.

"I want to speak with Sunday," she says finally, her eyes shifting to the exit. "Is she well enough to see me, or are you keeping her all to yourself?" Her implication is blunt, suggesting an impropriety that churns my insides.

I roll my neck to relieve some of the tension, unable to stand this conversation for much longer. I consider ending it — we've overspent our time together — but a scream from the hallway stops me short, the shrill sound harsh and familiar.

I'm already running down the hall toward Nadia's room, her pleas growing louder and fiercer as I step into her mind. I sprint down the corridor and round the corner leading to the Flames Quarters, my mind reeling.

Nadia! I bellow her name to her mind, my heart thrashing in warning as I wait for a response. When nothing comes, I call out to her again, more panicked than before. *Nadia, what's going on? Say something!*

I try to strengthen the line linking my mind to hers, but a layer of shadow clouds our connection, making it impossible to pluck out a single thought.

I can feel her panic in the pit of my stomach, her distress hiding her from my strongholds.

When I reach the Quarter door and find it open, my heart stalls, expecting the worst kind of trouble. I jog through the entrance and hurry to Nadia's cot, my hand shaking as I push back the curtain.

My world slows when I find her mattress empty, the blankets ruffled and unkempt, showing signs of a struggle. I look around the room, hunting for something out of the ordinary, but nothing sticks out.

After a moment, the shift becomes apparent.

The Quarter is uncommonly quiet. Not even June, Nadia's neighbor, is snoring or talking in her sleep. There's only a pulse to the air, the room prickling with an electric liveliness that's typically felt in the presence of—

A flash of blue fabric glimmers from the other side of Nadia's bed, and I go to it, my fury soaring when I see Sickness kneeling there, hunched over the floor like a carnivore ready to feast.

His back faces me, so he doesn't notice me as I peer around him, my mind whirling as I assess what he's doing.

It takes me several moments — an eternity for my slow-moving mind — to understand the mess he's made, the damage irreversible.

My lungs tighten beyond control, struggling to work properly.

I'm not sure how I get myself to move, but my hands find Sickness's collar and throw him across the room, seeing red. His back cracks against the far wall, damaging his spine.

Vicious delight pours through me at the sound he makes, his agony better than music.

He rolls to his side and rushes to his feet, his rage miniscule compared to my own.

When he recovers from the blow and sees my face, he abandons his fighting stance, the pink in his cheeks fading.

"Cruelty," he says, exhaling like he's glad to see me. "What are you doing here? Why did you push me?" After a beat of silence, he smiles weakly, rubbing at the pain in his lower back. "Ah, I see the problem. You're jealous you didn't get to partake in the show. I know she was your whore and all, but you'll get over the loss, I assure you."

He glances behind me, his eyes directed at the floor. I turn, and when I see her, my heart drops to my feet, my blood like lead in my veins. Though my first instinct is to look away, I force myself to stare at her, refusing to let Sickness see my devastation.

With her arms splayed out to the side, Nadia looks like a discarded doll, her limbs twisted and unnatural.

My mind rejects it — she can't be dead, it isn't possible — but I've seen enough corpses to know Nadia's stillness isn't temporary.

Humans aren't capable of being so silent. So motionless.

That doesn't stop me from sinking to my knees to check her pulse, her wrist cold and slack in my hand, pale as Sickness's. Gently, I place my thumb over the delicate skin where her heartbeat should be felt, praying for a miracle.

I don't get one.

I don't understand. How is this happening?

"What did you do?" I grind out the words as I rise to my feet, digging deep inside myself for that callous, unfeeling Master who's been trained to hate Flames. I'm hyper-aware of the way I set my jaw, tilt my head, harden my eyes, each movement tactical and designed to mask the disbelief washing through me.

Gone. Nadia's gone.

I take extra caution to hide the essence of my spiral, but I don't bother leashing my rage. Sickness expects it. He killed a human with physical force, making himself a traitor and a criminal to our kind, violating the Immortal Law.

"I did what needed to be done," Sickness says, his eyes looking everywhere but at me. A coward in his truest form. "She was getting too far," he adds, voice quiet and trembling. The shame in his eyes is starting to show. I wish I had the presence of mind to revel in it. "You know she was going to pass those Tests. I had to do something."

I can't help what happens next.

My reaction to his confession is purely animalistic, urging me to attack with an instinct I've spent centuries suppressing. Without much care for consequence, I seize him by the throat, choking him until his eyes bulge, until they plead for me to let go.

I wonder if Nadia wore a similar expression before he smothered her to death. I wonder if he felt the same pleasure I feel now, watching him suffer.

I drive his skull into the wall, not caring if I immobilize him, and watch as blood pools near his temple.

"Cruelty, calm—"

I hammer my fist into his nose so hard, his eyes momentarily cross. He falls to the ground and clenches his snout with watering eyes. Satisfaction swims through me.

"What were you thinking?" I kick him with my boot.

"C-calm down," he begs, crawling back to the wall.

Is that . . . terror running through his eyes?

Oh, how I wish I could capture this moment.

"Why?" I keep my emotions under control. "Have you lost your mind?"

"We couldn't risk her passing the Tests," Sickness claims, spit flying from his mouth. "It would destroy everything we've built." He tries to scoot closer to the door, but I crouch before him and snatch his wrist. Without thinking, I twist the bone toward me, watching as it beautifully snaps, causing an uproar of curses. The best I could've asked for.

"Stop, Cruelty. Please," he moans. I almost laugh at the sight of him begging. "Her mind was incredible. Even after all we've done to her, everything we've put her through . . ." He wipes his good hand over his mouth, considering. "Her mind was impenetrable. It didn't matter what we did to her, she overcame it. I couldn't stand around and watch her win. Could you imagine the consequences? A Flame running wild and telling others how to defeat us? That would be the end of our existence."

The end of *your* existence, I want to say, but I keep the remark to myself.

He cringes away from me, as though sensing the instability stirring within. "You should be thanking me for doing what you were too weak to do yourself. The threat has been eliminated. I thought you of all Masters would be happy about that."

I lose my temper at his assumption, blind hatred overwhelming me, spiraling out of control. My fists smash into Sickness's face, his stomach, his ribs; anywhere I can reach. Bone crunches and blood splashes up to my elbows, my sleeves soaked in red.

He bellows for me to stop, but I don't listen.

I kick him in the ribs and crack them, marveling in his screams. A rational voice hums inside me, telling me to stop — let him go! — but I push it to the back of my mind.

I haven't had enough.

I strike him hard in the mouth, knocking teeth loose.

Stop, he gets the point.

I elbow him hard in the face. His eyes roll to the back of his head as he loses consciousness.

He's suffered plenty, get off him.

I punch him again in the temple, the light in his eyes darkening. My greatest dream comes true.

For sky's sake, Cruelty, you're going to kill him!

Good.

I hope I do.

Chapter Forty-One

Without warning, the Quarter door opens behind me, announcing the arrival of another enemy. With my eyes still fixed on Sickness, I'm too distracted to turn around to see which of the Masters has come to stop my outrage.

Since I first laid hands on the coward writhing beneath me, his face has transformed into something ravaged, his features crooked and unrecognizable beneath the broken skin and outpouring of blood.

I can't help but savor his pain. His blood splattering up my arms. I snarl with pleasure as his jaw cracks beneath my fist, his entire mouth twisting to the side, knocked out of place.

Enough! That's enough, Cruelty, get off him!

The words echo distantly in my head, but I'm not sure who speaks them. My conscience isn't moral enough to experience guilt toward Sickness, and I've been waiting over fifteen centuries to kill him. I'm not going to let him go now.

"Get off!" The words roar in my ear, spoken out loud this time. "Cruelty, stop!"

Hands tug at my shoulders, dragging me back.

"Bleeding hell!" Warfare shouts and shoves me against the wall. It takes every ounce of restraint not to spit in his face or pluck out his eyes, cursing him for interrupting my bloody spree. "What do you think you're—?"

I swing my arm back and punch him in the face, hardly aware of my decision to do so.

Warfare teeters to the side, completely stunned, clenching his nose.

I return my attention to Sickness and watch him crawl to the door. He leaves a trail of blood in his wake, growing weaker and weaker as the life drains out of him.

I let him get halfway to the exit, following him slowly, before I stomp on his back, pinning him to the spot.

Pathetic. So utterly pathetic, when he isn't fighting a mortal.

"You can't kill him!" Warfare yells, and grabs at me a second time, pulling me away.

"I'm not going to kill him!" I growl, throwing him off me. "I'm not going to kill him," I repeat, though I'm not sure who I'm trying to convince. "I just wanted him to remember that I could."

"And why would you feel compelled to make such a statement?" Warfare's challenge ripples with condescension, every word filled with conceit and self-importance, making me see red.

If it weren't for the centuries of practice, I would've lost my temper and obliterated him, but I make myself give a slow, displeased nod in Nadia's direction. "Take a look," I say.

Warfare's eyes turn grim as he pops his head around the bed, spotting Nadia dead on the floor. "What — what have you done," he breathes, his head snapping in Sickness's direction. "What in the sky's name were you thinking?"

I don't expect him to respond — I've beat him too badly — but somehow, he finds the strength to speak. "She was going to pass," he slurs, cowering against the wall. He opens his mouth to continue, but Warfare raises a hand, silencing him. He jerks his head toward the hallway.

"In private," he seethes, and for the first time in two thousand years, I agree with him.

The last thing we want is to discuss the Immortal Law around mortals. I'm not surprised they've remained hidden behind their curtains all this time, waiting for us to take our business elsewhere.

I certainly wouldn't intervene in an immortal fight if I were a Flame.

"WHAT DO YOU MEAN SHE'S dead?"

The Master of Obedience grips the edge of the dining room table, his hands trembling as he fights not to snap the wood in two. His umber eyes are a flame of ice as they settle on Sickness, every inch of him shuddering with a fury that shouldn't be provoked. Even his tattoos, dark and twisting with demonic designs, seem to shake with untamable madness.

"I had to do something," Sickness huffs, the bruises along his cheekbone pulsing in time with his veins, the wounds barely visible. It's been less than twenty minutes since Warfare gave him a healing antidote, and the broken bones are already recovering, erasing all evidence of the previous hour.

Too bad. I liked seeing him shattered.

But conflict is coming, and when I finally get my chance to turn against him on the battlefield, I want him fighting at his best. It's the only way to ensure my victory is earned.

"Think about what would've happened if . . ."

I tune out, tired of the conversation.

For a moment my mind is lost in thoughts of war and survival, but that doesn't last beyond a few seconds. Nadia pops into my thoughts, her presence rooted in my subconscious. I stare out the window and into the gardens, trying not to think about her.

I fail miserably, picturing her face in everything I see. It doesn't seem to matter what I look at — the moon, the flowers, the stars

— she's somehow there. I don't know how to get rid of her. I don't know if I want to, either.

I think back to the day in the library, remembering how exhilarated she was. I couldn't take my eyes off her. Couldn't imagine how someone could find such joy in a book. Her excitement made me want to pack up every single one and give them to her, if only to keep that smile on her face. It was a smile I couldn't get enough of at the Freedom Celebration. It filled me with longing and hope and endless possibility.

"This wasn't for you to decide," Obedience says, rubbing a hand over his jaw.

"She was going to pass the Tests, and you know it as well as I do." Sickness is quick to continue his rant once we settle into our usual seats around the dining table. He slides down in his chair, about to fall off, when Warfare leans over to help him sit upright, not bothering to be gentle. It's a small victory I can't bring myself to enjoy.

With Nadia gone and the Law broken, my thoughts are divided between the obstacles set before me and the tragedy left behind. Though I tell myself not to brood over what could've been, or should've happened, the past and present are inextricably linked.

The moment Sickness laid his hands on her, the Law's consequence was put in motion, disrupting the natural order of the mortal world. I once told Nadia that if a member of the Sacred Seven were to kill a human with physical force, they'd have to face a hefty punishment.

What I didn't tell her was that the punishment grants the Emperors' re-entrance into the mortal realm, changing the entire trajectory of human existence. Their return is the blessing I've been waiting centuries for the world to receive, praying for a miracle I didn't think would come.

But the miracle *did* come, and there's no denying the battle that's about to transpire.

"We beat them once, we can do it again." Sickness's voice drags me from my thoughts.

"I don't want to hear your excuses," Warfare says to Sickness, rubbing a hand over his jaw. "We don't, *we can't*, physically kill anyone belonging to the mortal realm. The Sacred Seven's sole purpose is to destroy human existence by invading mortal minds and planting strongholds. We are not to materially intervene. *Ever*." He lets out a long breath and pinches the bridge of his nose, brooding over Sickness's mistake.

Nice to see him fuss for a change.

"We will win, I swear it." Sickness's promise is based on pride and nothing else. "Think about it. We are even more powerful than we were thousands of years ago. We have collected millions of souls. Our bodies — our strongholds — are overflowing with strength. It'll be easy this time."

Easy?

It takes everything I have not to laugh at that, as if this is all just a fluke and the Emperors won't be ready. I'm sure that they have spent the last few centuries preparing for this eventuality.

When the leaders in our homeland made the Immortal Law, they made it illegal for the Sacred Seven and any immortal leader to end a human's life through bodily force. They went on to explain that the violation of this Law would result in impeachment, granting the Emperors re-entrance into the mortal lands. Considering our past, I have no doubt the Emperors will come down and eliminate the Masters.

This consequence shines a shameful light on the Sacred Seven's failure as leaders, a fate the Emperors have known we were doomed to face since the moment we cast them out the first time. It promises that the Masters will be sent to the Underground Kingdom — a place where all evil from our realm goes to live — should we lose. And it is very likely that we will lose.

I don't know what awaits in the Underground Kingdom, but it's a place I must prepare myself to go, considering the circumstances. Although my values differ from the others, I'm a member of the Sacred Seven. I am not perfect or blameless. I've made mistakes and done things I shouldn't have, and I'll have to pay.

"You imbecile!" Warfare shouts at Sickness, the table rattling with his rancor. For a moment, I think he's going to strike Sickness across the face, but he doesn't. If the Sacred Seven want to win against the Emperors, they need all the help they can get, and killing Sickness prematurely won't benefit their cause.

"You've released the Emperors from our kingdom," Warfare sneers, every word laced with anger. "They will arrive in Airabeth soon, and they *will* attempt to reclaim their position as leaders of this land. They were expecting us, or better yet, expecting *you*, to do something like this. Don't you think they've been preparing for this moment? Don't you think they'll be ready for us this time?"

He stands abruptly, knocking over his chair. "Congratulations, Sickness. You've just signed our death sentence."

"She was already dying." The Master of Addiction digs his fingers into the armrests of his chair, preventing himself from jumping at Sickness's throat. "She wouldn't have gotten past the fifth Test."

"Clearly, you and I have a different way of seeing things," Sickness replies, leaning forward in his seat. "She wasn't giving up. Her soul was still full of color, and after everything that's happened, she didn't change. We tried to break her down, but we failed. I had to step in."

"Why kill her with physical force? Why not ruin her with your strongholds so we wouldn't be in this mess?"

"Is your head made of rock? What are you not understanding?" Sickness raises his voice, igniting more than one Master's temper.

"She. Was. Too. Strong. To. Listen. To. My. Strongholds. It. Wouldn't. Have. Worked."

Addiction's face purples with rage.

I sit up in my chair, fascinated by how this might unfold, but Fear jumps in, preventing a brawl. "How much time do we have before the Emperors arrive?" he asks, steering the conversation back to what's relevant.

"Three days." It's Warfare who responds, but I can't gauge his tone. Irritation? Nerves? A combination of both? "What about you, Cruelty?" He stares straight at me, and I have to control my reaction. Having practiced it a million times in the mirror, I force my mouth into a frown, masking my delight at the Emperors' imminent return.

"You haven't spoken a word since this conversation started," he adds, and I don't like the suspicion in his voice. The implication in his words.

I recover quickly and spin my questioned silence to my advantage. "What do you want me to say?" I ask and wring my hands to feign concern. "We have a battle to prepare for. I suggest we stop arguing and start strategizing."

That night, a plan is made.

Chapter Forty-Two

Nadia's been dead for five hours, and if we don't do anything about it, her corpse will begin to stink. We're nowhere near the Flames Quarter, but I can imagine the potent odor of decaying skin and rotting insides grow stronger by the minute, filling the house with its horrid stench. We'll have to open every window and door to air out the space, and even then, it might not be enough to mask the evidence of what's been done.

One of the Masters — I can't remember who — orders someone to burn the body and dispose of it in the cremation chamber. Sickness looks like he might volunteer, the only Master disgusting enough to be comfortable around such putrescence, but I beat him to it. With both hands clasped behind my back, I play the part of the dutiful Master and step forward, offering to do it. No one objects, and the group goes back to discussing war strategy, indifferent to my departure.

He won't touch her again. None of them will.

The sun is already rising when I dismiss myself from the dining hall, so I know I must hurry. I don't want to risk bumping into any servants — least of all Tuesday — when I go to retrieve Nadia's body.

What will I say when she notices her absence? How will I explain?

My hands are trembling when I reach her room, and even though I prepare myself for what's to come, I still gasp when I see her. I'm not sure how I get my feet to move, but before I'm ready, I'm by her bedside.

I bend down with weak legs and scoop her into my arms, unable to fathom that this is my reality.

I stare down at her quiet face, wishing it would look more peaceful and less afraid. Her skin is pale. Bloodless. I squeeze her hand until my fingers go numb. Until I can no longer feel her cold skin against mine.

I don't know how long it takes before I realize nothing is going to happen — that this is the end, and she is gone. I release her hand for a moment, then grasp it once more, unable to let her go.

This isn't Nadia anymore. I repeat the words inside my head until I believe them. Without her soul, this thing — this body — is just an empty vessel of flesh and bone.

Still, I take her in my arms and cradle her to my chest, hating how cold she is. I flinch at the memory of her being alive, of how soft and warm she was when we danced.

I want to stay here, locked in the past of what was and could've been, but as time speeds by, there comes a point where I can no longer delay the inevitable.

I rise to my feet and carry Nadia through the Quarter's back door, praying I don't run into anyone as I rush to the cremation chamber.

Cremation chamber.

I stop short, the weight of the words hitting me like a blow to the chest.

The Masters expect me to burn her body, erase her existence, but I can't do that. It seems wrong somehow. Like I'm gambling with her soul. Can spirits feel pain in death? I don't know, but I'm not willing to risk it.

I change my path and go to the rear of the house, toward the catacomb. At least there, I know some part of her will remain whole.

I walk down six corridors and several flights of stairs before I finally reach the dark stone hallway leading to the crypt.

The second I crank open the catacomb's metal door, I'm blasted with a biting chill. Clouds of frost puff around me, temporarily distorting my vision.

Once the fog clears, I step into the room.

Besides a few crates and stone tables, the catacomb is empty. Haunted.

Exactly as I remember.

Returning to this wretched place only brings back a wave of horrid memories, each one rising before me in the shape of living nightmares. Vivid as ever.

Dried blood still dirties the walls, marking the trials the Masters did in this room when we experimented on humans.

Back then, we'd collect the bodies of dead Flames, take them here, and cut open their skulls to examine their frontal lobes — the place where thoughts and emotions originate. The Sacred Seven were determined to find a certain gene or cell mutation that explained how Flames overcame strongholds, but after years of testing, we found nothing.

Every single mortal — both Flame and Soulless alike — has the ability to overcome our power, except they don't know how. Contrary to popular belief, defeating the Sacred Seven has nothing to do with the brain, intelligence, or natural instincts. It has to do with the mind — the transcendent world where thought, attitude, feeling, belief, and imagination dwell.

Mortals have a choice to fight and cast down every stronghold that comes to attack, but they need to be taught on how to do it.

For this reason alone, I'll fight with everything I have to make sure the Emperors win this war and return to the mortal sector.

With them, the path toward truth, redemption, and light is possible.

Without, we get what we have now — a world full of brainwashed Soulless trapped in the Masters' deception.

Searching for a light source, I scan the room and spot a set of candles on a nearby side table. I go to ignite them, but they don't work, the wicks wet with condensation. I try to think of another way to brighten the room, but I can't focus on anything other than the dead woman in my arms.

Without overthinking it, I lay Nadia down on a table and start prepping her body for rest. I don't look at her face. I try not to touch her too much. But before I can even finish covering her body with a white sheet, my heart catches.

I quickly cast my eyes down and memorize the lines of her mouth, her jaw, her cheekbones. My vision blurs when I lean down to kiss her forehead, knowing this will be the first and last time I get to do it.

I store her in one of the crates, looking away as I close the lid, taking comfort in the fact that Nadia no longer belongs to this hateful world, but rather to the world up there — the one made up of stars, clouds, and never-ending sky.

I can't give myself time to mourn. The Masters will come looking for me if I stay too long, and I don't want them finding me here.

THE PLAN IS SIMPLE.

Get to Airabeth's main field before dawn. Initiate a direct attack through the forest's tree line. Charge the Emperors head on, and never, under any circumstance, retreat.

The Sacred Seven's strategy is mediocre at best, but I'm not going to be the one to point it out. If they want to let their pride and arrogance get in the way, so be it.

"Fear, you go after the Emperor of Truth," Warfare says, assigning each of us a target. "You're stronger than him, so you should have no problem eliminating him swiftly. Doubt, I think it's best you go after the Emperor of Purity. He's smart, but if you attack quickly and catch him off guard, you'll be fine. Sickness, you're in charge of the Emperor of Wisdom. Don't be afraid to play dirty. You do that, and you'll banish him in seconds. Cruelty, the Emperor of Strength is all yours. You know him best, so it's your job to use his weaknesses against him, whatever those may be."

I nod, working my face into an emotionless mask. I sit back and let them speak, listening as Warfare devises a plan to keep everyone on track.

Just a little bit longer, I tell myself. *You only have to pretend a little bit longer, and then you're free.*

An hour passes before Warfare addresses me again, as if remembering my presence. "Why so quiet, Cruelty?" He shoots me a hot glare that makes my skin itch. "Don't you have anything to add?"

"You've already said everything that needs to be said. Including anything else would be foolish on my part." Even after all these years, it frightens me how easily I lie.

"That's reassuring," Warfare says, sounding anything but reassured. "I was starting to worry. Sickness mentioned you might have feelings for the girl, considering how upset you were after her death. Is that true?"

I brand Sickness with a hard, but fleeting scowl.

Play it off, instinct demands. *Don't show your nerves.*

I cover up my mistake by forcing a deep, hearty laugh. "And you're going to believe him?" I say, "Given his reputation? Did you ever stop to consider that perhaps I was upset because the Emperors are coming back? They're the only living creatures who threaten our rule, so pardon me if I seem a little pissed off about their return."

Warfare watches me for a moment, the air curdling with uncertainty. "Excellent," he says at last, regarding the rest of the table. "I just wanted to make sure we're all on the same page."

THREE DAYS HAVE PASSED since the Law was broken, and the Masters are as restless as ever.

We stand outside the manor, the atmosphere sparking with a rare unease, and go over the plan one more time.

I listen, aching to get this over with, but my thoughts travel elsewhere, pulling me from the moment. I glance back at the cluster of servants surrounding the house, guilt eating at me for helping Obedience place a stronghold in their minds.

For now, the servants are bound to the estate. As soon as the Emperors win the battle, however, they'll be free and the stronghold will be lifted, releasing them from this eternal hell once and for all.

The notion makes me look around to each of my adversaries, staring at the weaponry dripping from their belts. We all wear the same armor and daggers. The same swords. I peer down at my hip and stare at the lethal blade swaying there, the reality of war setting in.

This sword is the only weapon that can return the Emperors to their unearthly kingdom, and since I know I won't be using it, it feels too heavy somehow.

The Sacred Seven huddle together and discuss strategy, so I pretend to care. I nod when the conversation calls for it, speak when necessary, and force a sadistic light to my eyes when the Emperors are mentioned.

I stand as tall as I can to feign confidence, and my spine aches from the effort.

I can't wait until all this is over. Until I can slouch, and relax, and stand however I want. Until then, I have to sustain a Master's image.

Make the humans fear me. Badmouth the Emperors. Be arrogant. Wield my strongholds. Corrupt mortal thoughts. Don't fall in love with the Flame. These are the things I have to remind myself of each morning, but if this battle doesn't go as planned, I fear I'll be reciting them for the rest of my life.

I shake my head. I need to remain hopeful. I need to believe we can win.

And I do.

Once I join the Emperors on the battlefield, the Masters will be outnumbered, and we'll have the advantage. There's no other way —

A loud crack sounds above me, jolting every thought from my head.

When I look to the sky, beams of blue, yellow, red, white, green, purple, and gold cut through the clouds, one after the other.

The colors only last a few seconds, but when I look to the Masters to gauge their reaction, I know we're all thinking the same thing.

The Emperors. They're here.

Chapter Forty-Three

When we reach the edge of Airabeth's forest, we're surrounded by nothing but open land. The Emperors aren't here yet, but it's always in moments like this, right before the battle, where emotions run their highest.

Doubt. Fear. Hope. Aggression. Rage. Timidity. Desire. Faith — all of it swarms within us, each one fighting for control. I do my best to ignore the meeker, less helpful feelings, and try to match my mentality to the calmness I practice in meditation, finding confidence in the quiet intensity.

Alone, I jog forward to scan the mile-long terrain and study its details. It's strange being back here on the same battlefield where the previous banishment took place. I suppose it's only fitting we meet here again. It'll be a poetic end, defeating the Masters in the very place they first seized the mortal realm.

Uneven ridges. Boulder-sized craters. Lines of trees surrounding the land. The scene is nothing special or unexpected, which is good, because the fewer surprises we face, the better.

As the Masters get familiar with their surroundings, I go over all the war tactics and combat moves I can think of in my head, using them to stay sharp and focused. I get lost in the imaginings, fantasizing about what I plan on using, particularly against Sickness.

Oh, how satisfying his end will be. How deserved.

I delight in the vision, enthralled by the idea of spilling his blood and banishing his soul to the Underground Kingdom.

Perhaps that's why I'm not entirely ready when seven figures emerge from the western trees, each approaching with the stealth of a leopard, unmatched in agility and power.

I blink hard to make sure I'm seeing correctly, and when I find that I am, something strange blossoms inside my chest — a lightness that feels a lot like relief, though I can't be sure. I hadn't allowed myself to fully imagine the moment where the Emperors returned to earth. Such a fantasy was too painful to think about — a dream that was always far out of reach — yet here they are, advancing with a dominance and grace only they can carry.

I have to control the fire in my eyes as they draw near, my feet itching to stand by their side — to reunite with my brothers.

The clink of armor and metal sounds from my left as the Masters ready themselves for battle, removing swords and daggers from their sheaths. I refrain from following and opt to hover my hand above my holster, feigning mental preparation.

It's a sign I know the Emperors will catch, proving my loyalties. It's been centuries since we've seen each other, and after all this time, I don't want them doubting my allegiance.

As planned, Warfare and the others set back into a V formation, but I don't situate myself like I'm supposed to. Instead, I stand off to the left and angle myself away from them — another subtle sign my friends won't miss.

The Emperors take their time in approaching, building tension among the Masters. By the time they're in front of us, every member of the Sacred Seven is still, their mouths thin and bloodless, twisting with unease.

I'd be lying if I said I didn't take pleasure in their fear.

"Well, you all look considerably better than the last time we met." It's Warfare who breaks the silence from the point of the V, his tone exuding a calmness that doesn't reach his eyes. "If memory serves me correctly, you were left with some pretty severe injuries during our previous encounter. I'm glad to see time has healed most of the damage."

Glimpses of broken bones and bloody armor fill my head, taking me back to the first battle. Crooked spines, shattered hips, dislocated elbows — all horrific injuries a mortal would die from, but the Emperors were lucky enough to survive.

Though centuries have passed since I was forced to fight my friends, there are some wounds that not even the gift of immortal blood can heal. Various scars and deformities still mar the Emperors' flesh, their past injuries so grave they caused permanent damage.

If I look close enough, I can still pinpoint which marks I inflicted. The injuries I caused. Kaster, the Emperor of Strength and my most trusted friend, got the worst of it. Our confrontation was supposed to be for show — a halfhearted attempt at a fight neither of us wanted.

Our plan changed as soon as the Sacred Seven gained the upper hand, mere moments away from winning the battle. That's when Kaster told me to injure him, to fight without hesitation.

They'll know we aren't trying, he said.

You have to do this, he said.

We've already lost, he said.

The humans need you, he said.

Trust me, he said.

And I did.

I broke his nose, hand, and ribs.

The memory makes me look at him now, my heart heavy with guilt, but he hardly notices my stare. The other Emperors follow suit, standing unmoving with their eyes on Warfare.

I don't let their avoidance bother me. They're just playing their part.

I should be doing the same.

"It's been over two thousand years," Warfare says, his knuckles moonstone white as he clenches his sword. "Don't you have anything to say to me?" He addresses the group with a broad wave of his hand, but his gaze is unwavering, set on Kaster.

I try to obey the disciplined part of me that refuses to glance at the other Emperors, but the temptation is too great.

It's hard to believe I haven't seen my friends in over a millennium, but the distance and time spent away from earth hasn't altered their appearance. They all have the same unnatural eyes that glow with a tint of silver, their statures alike in height and brawn, though that's where the similarities end.

Each Emperor wears a signature piece of clothing that corresponds with their ray of color, their attire crisp and shaped to their bodies like artwork. A variety of blades are strapped to their hips, thighs and torsos, yet the swords locked down their spines are the only weapons that'll banish the Masters to the Underground Kingdom.

"As much as I've missed these conversations," Kaster starts, his eyes flashing like freshly sharpened steel, "I'd prefer if we jump straight to it." There's a vitality to his voice that brings a sense of comfort.

Though I've never forgotten his authority and strength, listening to Kaster only revives an excitement I thought long gone, reminding me that there are leaders worth fighting for. Leaders who I'd be proud to stand by.

"Since you're our *guests*," Warfare sneers with an edge that makes my blood pound, "your wish is our command."

And with that, blades on both sides raise.

Kaster's face is unreadable as he bends at the knees, limbs loose and ready to shift in either direction. He nods for Warfare to give the order, not wasting any time.

At the last second, I remove one of my daggers and wait for the command to be given, my heart thrashing in its cage.

This fight won't be easy, and it won't be simple, but the greatest victories never are, so when Warfare raises his hand as the signal, I find myself running into battle, ready to change the course of history.

Chapter Forty-Four

I move across the field with nothing but a dagger in my hand and revenge in my heart, overpowered by a pure, raging madness that consumes me.

I use the surge of insanity to sprint after Addiction, my first and closest target.

Unlike the Emperors, I don't have a sword that'll banish my kind from earth, but I don't need one to be useful. War is about more than just weapons and brawn and cunning. It's about mental fortitude — about who can handle more setbacks, more pressure, more pain than the opponent.

Addiction charges toward Kaster, but I speed ahead, meeting Addiction within seconds. Before he gets a chance to understand why I'm charging him, my dagger is already cutting through his hip, deep and merciless.

A feverish joy courses through me as a stream of blood splatters to the ground, robbing the grass of its purity.

It takes Addiction two tenths of a second to realize what's happened before he lets out a curse so colorful, my blood sings.

This outcome has turned out much better than I expected.

He drops to his knees and grasps the gash in his side, losing mobility below the waist.

Kaster comes up from behind me and kicks the Master in the abdomen, forcing him to his back. We get a good look at his face then — at all the anger and hurt and devastation, more rewarding than I could've dreamed.

Addiction remains silent for a moment, his mouth opening and closing like a puppet, seemingly incapable of forming any words.

"You'll rot for this," he says finally. "Going against your own men . . ." He shakes his head and looks to the sky, laughing to the heavens. "And I thought Sickness was the imbecile."

A slight quirk of his mouth is my only warning before he swings at me, nicking my bicep with his blade.

Kaster snatches the weapon from Addiction's hand and stabs it through the Master's arm, pinning him to the earth.

Addiction lets out a howl, crying for mercy. He droops, my heart dancing at the sight of his pathetic form.

Kaster moves around me and places his banishing sword over the Master's throat, ready to end him.

He's much kinder than I am.

I want to drag this out, to watch Addiction bleed and experience a century's worth of pain, but we don't have time.

I kneel down beside him and choose the next best thing. "Give the devil my greetings, will you?" I say, and pat his cheek tauntingly, content with the glorious view of him struggling.

"You'll be seeing him soon enough," the Master bites back, spitting in my face. "Say hello to him yourself."

And with that, Kaster plummets the sword deep into Addiction's neck, twisting aggressively. The Master's eyes protrude, his mouth involuntarily yawning as his Adam's apple explodes, bursting into a thousand pieces of . . .

Nothing.

I blink.

Rub my eyes. Look again.

Gone.

Addiction is gone, his body disintegrating into a pile of ash, drifting off with the winds. Not a wisp of his existence is left behind.

But as Kaster wipes the Master's ash from his sword, I let out a breath, understanding that this is how the banishing happens. Fast. Easy. A modest escape. That is how each of the Masters will go, and although they deserve worse than what they're getting, we can't do anything more.

Not in this life.

"Cruelty."

Kaster tugs on my shoulder and spins me in the direction of our next opponents, pointing to where two Emperors launch into a fight against Obedience and Fear. The battle is a savage mess of bloodied faces and swollen knuckles, the injuries grave in their severity.

Kaster and I sprint across the field toward them, the stench of blood, sweat, and steel growing stronger as we approach.

We break off, Kaster going to the left, me to the right, to each take on a Master of our own.

I run for the Master of Obedience, who kneels above Toby, the Emperor of Freedom, and charge him as fast as I can, not liking his advantageous position. Obedience has his hands wrapped around the Emperor's neck, strangling him to the point of blackout, winning the battle.

If it weren't for Toby's iridescent fatigues shining a dozen shades of violet, I wouldn't have seen his sword reflecting off the ground, nearly five feet away from him.

I run and grasp the handle, enjoying the immediate power it gives me.

I sneak up behind Obedience and focus on the chain tattoo snaking up his neck, my hands itching to rip it off his skin.

With his gaze pinned on the Emperor below him, the Master doesn't have the awareness to notice me as I drive Toby's sword through his throat, pushing it straight through his tattoo and out the other side.

A part of me wishes I would've attacked him from the front, if only to see his shocked expression, but I hear it in the sharp intake of breath, the gurgling as he tries to scream.

Red spurts from the open wound, staining my face, neck and collar; the most blood I've seen in years. Similar to Addiction, the Master of Obedience disintegrates into a heap of ash, leaving no stain of his existence behind.

Toby props himself up by his elbows, breathing hard.

Alive.

He watches me with wide-eyed amusement, his mouth slightly agape, before flipping onto his feet, agile as a feline. He slaps me on the back and briefly credits my skill with a blade, but I don't respond.

We both know now is not the time to get affectionate.

The clash of blades and violent grunts echoes to my right.

I decide to go for the Master of Doubt, who engages in hand-to-hand combat with Oliver and Ben, the Emperors of Love and Truth, their weapons nowhere in sight.

With Toby's sword still in my hand, I move toward them, but Toby puts a hand on my arm, wordlessly signaling that he'll take care of it. I go to give my friend his weapon back, but he tells me to keep it.

He's gone before I can protest, leaving me to search the field for Warfare.

I hunt for a streak of long silver hair among the red and black of war, spotting him almost instantly.

My heart spikes as I run in his direction, to where the real fun awaits.

"TRAITOR!"

Warfare screams across the field, warning the others. He must've seen me stab Addiction, or maybe it was Obedience. I don't know, but either way, everything is officially out in the open.

The first two banishments were easy. I had the element of surprise on my side, and simply put, the Masters weren't expecting my attack. They are now, and the advantage I had is slipping away.

Nothing I've done up to this point matters, because the real work starts now, when there's nothing left for me to hide behind. With my loyalties exposed, there's little room for error, but I trust in my training.

I sprint across the field to Warfare, where he clashes swords with Daniel, the Emperor of Purity. My friend's ivory fatigues are already stained with generous amounts of blood. I can't tell if it's his or someone else's.

If he's anything like I remember, he prefers the mess, the grit, the disorder. He fights better under pressure, and when a battle gets tough, he gets tougher with it. Based on how well he looks, he hasn't quite reached that point, and neither has Warfare.

Each of them strikes with vigor and certainty, showing no signs of hesitation or fatigue, their blades sparking each time they meet.

Daniel slashes low for Warfare's knees, but the move is rushed and impatient.

I can anticipate the Master's reaction before it happens, his elbow flying toward the Emperor's stomach, pushing him back.

Warfare tenses, sensing the advantage.

I don't let him capitalize on it.

I charge him from the side and tackle him, knocking us both off balance. We hit the ground hard, but the moment passes quickly. We're back on our feet in moments, swords raised and ready for blood.

"Daniel, go help the others." I don't take my eyes off Warfare as I say it. "Now," I order, when the Emperor doesn't make a move to go.

I don't want or need anyone's help to win this battle, and finally, Daniel listens, escaping to the left of the field to join another fight.

Warfare holds my stare, his death gaze world-ending, I think the ground trembles. "How noble of you, Master, to fight your own battles without the help of your friends." He raises his sword. "Noble, but foolish."

And then he pounces, slashing for my neck.

I bring up my blade to deflect, barely blocking him, and respond with a swift kick to his knee, driving him backward. He changes his stance, the shift small and almost missable, but it's enough to give me an opening.

I swipe for his abdomen and connect, drawing a thick line of blood that leaves him groaning.

I salivate at the sight, but my delight is short lived.

Warfare recovers quickly and resumes his position, motioning me forward. I take the bait to keep the advantage, but the Master is already slicing his weapon down on an angle, aiming for my arm.

Although I dodge the brunt of the attack, the edge of his blade catches my shoulder, drawing blood.

He advances again and launches off his back leg for momentum, reaching for my bicep. I sidestep to avoid the hit. I'm not quick enough. Blood explodes from my muscles upon impact, my skin splitting.

I rear back on instinct, my flesh screaming, but it only lasts a second, the healing quick.

I run forward at the same time Warfare does, and we come into a bind, our swords crossing, pushing hard against each other. My arms shake from the force of the attack, but I break off, rushing ahead.

I push Warfare's raised elbow toward his chest, exposing the left side of his face. I drive the hilt of my weapon into his nose, forcing him away from me. From there, I disarm him easily, stealing his weapon as he grabs his face in agony.

Now would be a smart time to end this — to stab him while I still have the advantage.

But I'm not feeling particularly smart at the moment, and I don't need to rely on anyone, or anything, to win. When I expel Warfare, it'll be because I'm the better fighter, but in order to prove that, our advantages need to be the same.

I toss my own sword to the side to level out the playing field, enraged by the Master's smug grin. He takes the challenge without hesitation and charges first — out of eagerness or impatience, I don't know — and delivers a rapid one-two jab to my jaw.

The strike is so quick I have no choice but to take it, my head flopping to the side like a ragdoll. A flare of pain sparks through my skull, but I ignore it as best I can, working my breaths into a steady rhythm.

Warfare smirks, his mouth tilting into a slash of white tinged with blood.

I raise my hands to protect my face — I won't make the same mistake again — and execute a high kick to his temple.

He stumbles to the right as my foot connects with the side of his head.

I search the ground for my sword and find it – the bastard has suffered enough – but Warfare is already back on his feet, darting toward me. I hardly have time to think as I grab my weapon and anchor it behind my head, throwing it like a javelin.

One moment, the steel is shining through the air, reflecting the morning light.

The next, the blade is lodged in Warfare's breast.

He comes to an abrupt stop, eyes widening as he looks down at the hilt protruding from his chest. He crashes to his knees. Falls to his back. Mouth gaping as blood pours out of it.

I'm on him in an instant.

With my forearm pressed against his throat and my free hand clenched around the sword's hilt, it's easy to keep Warfare down. He twists uselessly below me, his waist trapped beneath my legs.

"You could've ruled the earth, Cruelty."

All the pain and tiredness from this day evaporate as Warfare speaks, uttering what are about to be his final words. I should end his existence as quickly as I did the others, but I let him talk.

There's something cathartic about watching an enemy spew nonsense during their final moments.

"You could've had everything you've ever wanted," he says, rather calm. "Wealth. Women. Power. You could've had it all, but you just threw it away, and for what? Some moral code?"

He looks away from me and gazes up at the sky, eyes watering against the sun. "All humans are born evil, but are taught to be good. They can choose to be kind or malevolent, but they always choose malevolence. Why is that, do you think?"

He pauses for half a second, not wanting my answer. "Because it's easy, Cruelty. It's easy to be selfish, and mean, and cruel, and un-caring, because that's how mortals are, and sooner or later you're going to realize that we did the right thing —"

I yank out my sword and slam it back down through the center of his heart. I dig the sword deeper and deeper, until the point shoots straight out his spine, impaling him to the dirt.

Warfare goes still, his eyes darkening as his body prepares for banishment.

For a second, I consider saying something clever or boastful, if only to rub my victory in his face, but my mouth is paralyzed.

My words entangled. There are too many things I want to say. Too many thoughts I can't keep track of.

I remain quiet, keeping it all to myself.

And then he's gone. His body exploding into ash.

I feel strange about his departure. It doesn't excite me as much as I thought it would, and I don't have time to process why.

I'm barely on my feet again when a scream rings from the right of the field.

I whirl to find Jaxon and Pierce, the Emperors of Wisdom and Humility, ganging up on Sickness, outmatching him in intelligence and brawn.

I scan the field quickly, getting a clear view of Kaster digging his sword into the base of Fear's throat, banishing him instantly. Not far behind him, Ben, the Emperor of Truth, jogs forward, blood leaking from a gash in his forearm. I peer over his shoulder and spot the Master of Doubt slumped on his side, a sword protruding from his chest before he disintegrates to ash.

That only leaves Sickness as the Sacred Seven's sole survivor.

I run to the Emperors, telling them to stop, to let the Master go. Sickness stumbles away immediately, disappearing into the trees without a backward glance.

When the Emperor of Wisdom opens his mouth to protest, I cut him off.

Out of all the Masters I yearn to banish, Sickness is at the top of the list, and though his leg is broken, and his hips are displaced, he hasn't suffered enough.

I want to be the one to change that.

Chapter Forty-Five

I count to fifty and then go after him, giving him a generous head start.

With all his injuries, Sickness doesn't get very far, but at least he can't say I didn't give him a chance. I suppose I was looking forward to the chase. The fight. The satisfaction that comes with earning something that doesn't come easy.

Oh, well. Maybe in another life.

Sickness doesn't turn as I approach, but I hear the small groan of exasperation as he senses my presence, trying to stay ahead. He falls to his knees and drags himself forward on all fours, grunting with the effort it takes to keep moving.

Some grim creature smiles within me as I take in the trail of blood flowing from his abdomen, killing him slowly. The severity of the gash only makes me think of Nadia — of how hopeless she must've felt when Sickness brought that pillow to her face, smothering her.

The image quickens my steps, prompting me to end the chase sooner than I planned.

I catch up to the Master's crawling form and stomp on his ruined calf, acting out of instinct. Sickness screams as I dig my boot deeper into his leg, crushing the injured muscle and halting his progress. He hardly musters more than a whimper as I kick him in the ribs, pushing him onto his back.

I kneel down in front of him and dig my knee into his chest, delighting in his pain.

"Where are your comrades?" Sickness croaks, his gaze darting over my shoulder as if expecting the Emperors to come following behind me. What a mercy that would be for him, to have my friends take over and finish him off quickly.

"C'mon, Cruelty. You're not playing fair," he says. "I'm injured and incapable of defending myself. This is hardly a righteous victory, don't you think? We should save this moment for when we're both healthy and fighting at our best. That's the only way to prove—"

"Fair?" I interrupt, my voice low. Rough. Hardly recognizable. "You want to talk about what's fair?" I scratch my brow with the pommel of my sword, trying to forget Nadia, but I can't.

For sky's sake, I only knew the girl for four weeks, but every time I blink, I see her face, hear her laugh, sense her touch. "Bleeding hell, Sickness, if you were going to kill the Flame, you should've at least given her a fighting chance."

The Master cocks his head with primal fascination, a corner of his mouth lifting. "Interesting to know that after all these years, she's the one to make you loathe me." He laughs at the idea of it — a terrible, gnarled sound made of blood and corruption. "She screamed for you. She screamed for your help. When I had my way with her, she prayed you'd return, but when you didn't . . ." He bites his bottom lip, stifling a grin. "Oh, you should've seen the disappointment on her face. Such an ugly look for a beautiful girl."

Despite my mask of cold indifference, Sickness gives a sly smile that suggests he knows exactly how sore this topic is for me. "Banishing me won't bring her back," he says. "She's dead and she's never coming back, and you'll never know what could've happened between the two of—"

I reach out and squeeze his neck, turning his words into a wheeze. He bucks uselessly beneath me, thrashing to escape. For a moment I wonder if Nadia struggled in a similar way when he knelt on top of her. I wonder if she looked just as scared as he does now.

"You . . . you . . ." Sickness wrestles to speak under my hold, so I ease off a little. I want to hear what he has to say. "You can never get rid of us," he gets out. Barely. "We will always be here. We will never stop infecting human minds. Whether we're in the earthly realm or not, we have ways of spreading our strongholds."

"I know that," I say calmly. It's a reality I've known for a long time, but . . . "But as long as you're gone, humans will have a freedom they haven't had in centuries."

I raise the Emperor's blade above my head, ready to end him.

"Freedom?" Sickness sneers, biding his time. "Freedom for what?"

"Freedom to choose."

"You fool," he mutters. "Humans have always had the freedom to choose, and they always choose wrong. Being bad is easy. Being bad is fun. Being bad is simple. You of all people should know that."

"Shut up," I growl, and grip the sword tighter, losing my patience. "You have no authority to speak to me like—"

"You think banishing me will erase every terrible thing you've done? You're not the good guy, Cruelty. The darkness will claim you, as it does everyone else, and time will force you to accept that truth."

"My destiny is within my control," I say, convincing him as much as myself. "It is a matter of choice. Not chance."

It has to be. I have to believe that, otherwise what's the point of all this?

"Is that what you truly think?" Sickness asks. "Is that what you made her believe? Let me ask you something." Satisfaction jolts in his eyes, and I must admit, it puts me on edge, shaking my confidence. "Did she know that you, her dear and only confidant, were the one working with Sasha?"

I pause.

Impossible. He doesn't know. He can't.

We were so careful.

"Did she know that you were the one who put his life at risk by giving him those lists?" He smiles at my silence, at the shock trembling through my hands. "All this time you've been protecting the Flames, am I right? You've been searching for them outside of Airabeth to continue the Emperors' work."

He laughs at the look in my eyes — a look I'm sure reflects the distress swirling deep in my belly. Our eyes hold for several heartbeats, and when I don't so much as breathe for fear of what he'll see, he continues on, enjoying this.

"You used the mortal boy as a pawn in your greater plan. Used him, because you couldn't afford to be out of our land for more than a few hours without drawing suspicion. He didn't know you were a Master, did he? He wouldn't have helped you otherwise, so you must have hidden it from him. How did you do it?"

At my silence, he smiles, catching on. "Did Sasha think you were a Flame?" He cackles. "Of course he did. He wouldn't have worked with you, otherwise. What was your plan, Cruelty? Locate as many Flames as possible and form an army against us? How poetic of you, Master."

He inclines his head in mock honor.

"Tell me something, when you first saw Nadia walk through those dining room doors, did you know she was Sasha's sister? You must have, right? I bet you thought you could make up for his death if you helped her survive the Tests. That's why she got as far as she did, yes? Because of you?"

I don't answer, but as our eyes hold, I know the truth is written there.

I can feel my mask slipping, my energy draining.

"I'm impressed," Sickness drawls, nodding in earnest. "You're a sneaky little prick, I'll give you that, but your betrayal to the Masters will have greater consequences than you think."

I stop listening, unable to focus on anything beyond the two-syllable word that makes my head swim.

I try to move my mouth to respond, but it won't work.

I feel slow.

I wish I had somewhere to sit down. Something to lean against—

"Milo."

Sickness says it again, and I wish to the sky's above he wouldn't.

"Milo, are you listening—"

Milo.

My name.

My *real* name.

I haven't heard him speak it out loud since we changed our titles and became the Sacred Seven, leaving our past identities behind. The only person who's used my name since becoming a Master is Sasha and Sickness knows that, though I don't know why he's waited until now to tell me.

"You've hardly been at the manor before these past two months," he explains, pulling the questions straight from my eyes. "But then Nadia shows up and you never leave. I found that to be quite strange."

He twists to the side to free up his right hand, reaching for something in his jacket pocket.

As soon as he finds what he's looking for, I raise my sword and plunge it straight through his chest, not taking any chances. Sickness hardly flinches upon impact, his eyes flashing.

Anger stifles me as he laughs. A pang in my gut tells me something isn't right, but I ignore it, anxious to get rid of him once and for all.

In an attempt to make his final moments memorable, Sickness retracts his hand from his pocket to show me what he retrieved, revealing several crumpled pieces of paper, the ink smeared with age.

He shoves the pages in front of my face, forcing me to read the words.

My insides tighten when I scan the top line, recognizing the name written there. I know the second one, too. And the third. The fourth. Fifth. Sixth. Seventh. Eighth. Ninth.

I'm familiar with all these names because I'm the one who wrote them.

Harley. Sarah. David. Michael. Billy. Stephen. Colleen. Rebecca . . .

The record goes on and on, identifying hundreds of Flames I haven't gotten a chance to meet or save.

These are my lists. The ones I planned on giving Sasha before everything changed. How did Sickness find them? How long has he known? Why didn't he tell the others? I've been successfully hiding my lists for centuries, so I don't understand how he stumbled across them. Every other day, I move the lists from place to place, constantly stashing them in new spots to make sure they don't fall into the wrong hands . . .

No. Wait. I haven't been relocating them. Not recently, anyway. I've been so focused on Nadia, I completely neglected them.

When was the last time I even looked at one of my lists? A few days? A week? Longer?

"After Nadia's second Test, all of us knew she wouldn't be able to recover in time for her third," Sickness says, speaking quicker, sensing his end is near. "And yet, she was healed. She wasn't wounded to the extent she should've been."

He smirks from ear to ear, and I feel myself frown, already knowing his next words before he says them. "As time went on, I noticed Nadia's health wasn't deteriorating as fast as it should've been, and it became clear someone was helping her. Considering she's young and relatively healthy, I was able to shrug it off at first, not thinking much about it. You're a fool to think that I — the Master and expert of all disease — wouldn't notice a thing like that. It's insulting, actually, to know you think so little of me."

I open my mouth to protest — to at least try to make the truth less believable — but he rushes on. "Didn't you think I'd notice she wasn't afraid of you? Every time she looked at you, there was calm in her eyes, and that, my friend, is not the emotion Masters are supposed to evoke. Shortly after the Celebration, I searched your room to see if I could find anything that would support my suspicions, and . . ."

He waves the paper in my face, flaunting it like it's some prized possession. "Mystery solved."

The ground tilts, spinning out from under me.

"Steady, my friend," Sickness says, his entire face lifting into a dreadful smile, worse than death itself. "I haven't even told you the best part."

I can feel my blood pounding in my veins, thick and slow, as if replaced by lead.

"After I found your little secret, I did some more digging, and although Nadia's mental shield was strong, it wasn't strong enough to keep me out while she slept."

"What did you see?" I ask, every part of me chanting to *kill him, kill him, kill him* and be done with it, but—

"Everything. Starting all the way back from when Warfare broke into her family home, to the day she took her last breath." He leans forward a bit, trying to get closer to me. "I saw it all. Heard it all. Felt it all." A sick sort of glee overtakes him.

"I'm sure you can imagine my surprise when I heard her talking about this infamous Milo who recruited her brother, created lists, and used them both in an attempt to build a rebel army against the

Masters. Milo was close to Sasha, practically friends. They must've cared for each other. Probably cared for each other's families, too, should they have any."

He spits out a chunk of black phlegm, smiling with charcoal teeth. "I found it strange how quickly you took a liking to Nadia. It didn't take long before you convinced us she was your plaything, giving reason as to why you spent so much time with her. I believed it, at first. But I know you, Cruelty. You played her off as your new pet, yet I've never seen you take an interest in any human girl. And after Nadia died, I saw the look on your face, and my suspicions about you and your loyalties grew."

He narrows his gaze, voice quickening as he pushes for my confession. "You not only cared for her, but Flames in general, right? Sasha got away with his mission for years, slipping past the Masters' detection, which is a near impossible feat. Unless, of course, a Master himself were helping."

He laughs, a sloppy, wet sound. "I didn't have any concrete evidence to prove that these lists were written by you, and I didn't want to risk Warfare's prosecution if I was wrong, but after your betrayal on the battlefield today, my theory has been confirmed. It wasn't hard to put two and two together after that, and well . . ." He waves the lists again for emphasis. "You're smart. I'm sure you can fill in the rest."

I don't realize I'm leaning forward until I swipe for the pages, determined to get them back.

Too late.

My hand catches no more than a fistful of wind as Sickness disintegrates into a heap of embers, leaving nothing but the echo of his laugh and his cruel words behind. I quickly look around for the lists, praying they somehow managed to escape the Master and stay in this realm, but no.

It's gone. He took them with him.

I sit back on my heels, my heart pounding.

I wish I had the energy to lay down, stand up, pace around — *anything* except kneel like a beggar, but my legs have turned to wood, refusing to move.

Two weeks. Sickness knew for two weeks that I was the one working with Sasha, yet he said nothing, did nothing, to punish my actions. He figured out my betrayal, knowing damn well I was on the Emperors' side, and still, he let the battle happen.

I could chalk up his choices to stupidity and arrogance and leave it at that, but that's not what this was. Sickness may have been a fool, but he wasn't stupid enough to miss an opportunity to reveal my disloyalty to the others, that I'm sure of. He let my treason slip by without a word, refusing to speak out about any of the things I've done.

But why would he do that? Why didn't he turn me in for double-crossing the Masters? Why would he risk the Sacred Seven's banishment if he knew I was going to fight for the Emperors?

There's a purpose behind his plan — a purpose I have yet to decipher — which makes me think *this* is the result he wanted.

He wanted to give up his position of power.

He wanted the Emperors to win.

He wanted the Masters to go to the Underground Kingdom.

And that bloody bastard has left me to figure out why.

Chapter Forty-Six

I clench the grass as I vomit, throwing up everything but a lung, trembling with exhaustion.

The Masters are gone and the battle is won, but the victory isn't ours. Sickness has my lists, and though his plan for them remains unclear, he has them nonetheless. The Sacred Seven's banishment was never meant to completely rid their strongholds from the mortal realm, but it *was* supposed to make them weaker – or so I thought.

With Sickness's parting words ringing through my head, I worry the Masters will enjoy the Underground Kingdom — a place where corrupt immortals are banished to reside — and somehow use its wickedness to their advantage. It's a possibility I never considered and one I fear to look at too closely, fearing the consequences.

The speculation alone is enough to make me heave all over again, my throat burning from the acidic taste.

I don't mention any of this to Kaster when he finds me some time later. I'm not in the mood to share or explain what I know, so I pretend it doesn't exist.

Kaster places a hand under my arm, attempting to get me back on my feet. I resist him, weighed down by the burden of my thoughts.

Leave me here, I want to say. *Let me die. I don't care anymore.*

But the Emperor of Strength doesn't let me go so readily. "Get up, Milo, we need to get out of here." He pulls on my shoulder, trying to get me to move. Kaster is strong, much stronger than I am, but his energy is diminishing. A consequence of combat.

I yank my arm away from him, still staring at the ground. "Don't call me that," I say, and the voice that comes out of my mouth isn't my own. If Kaster notices, he doesn't let on, no doubt excusing my rudeness by the fatigue racking my body.

"Call you what?" he asks, trying to understand.

I turn away from him, my chest caving under his forgiving stare.

"Where are the others?" I ask, and pick at the blood beneath my nails, undeserving of his goodness.

"I told them to wait by the forest entrance," he says, voice firm yet insufferably gentle. I wish he wouldn't speak to me like that. Like I don't warrant a lifetime of misery, when that's all my existence has earned me. "Said I'd meet them there after we talked."

A long, excruciating pause aches between us. Kaster is the first to break it. "I hope you don't mind we stayed back while you took care of Sickness. We assumed you wanted to deal with him alone, considering—"

"I don't need your consideration," I interrupt, not sure why I do it.

Kaster frowns and rubs a hand over his face, bloody palm and all. Saying nothing.

The air between us shifts, turning strained and hateful, and it's all my doing.

I don't know what's wrong with me.

Kaster is my best friend — my family — and this is how I welcome him back?

Maybe Sickness was right about humans. About me. Perhaps we all choose the easy wrong over the hard right because it's simple. Painless. When Kaster looks at me, all he remembers is the kid who used to chase after girls, place stupid bets, and spar in the training ring for hours, believing competition was all that mattered.

But the things that used to define me no longer hold a spot in my life, and have since been replaced with the title of Cruelty. From the time the Masters came into power, dark, ugly things have infected my heart, growing and manifesting into a beast I can no longer tame.

"You didn't do anything wrong, Milo." There's pleading in the Emperor's voice, and though he sits down beside me to show support, I scoot away, his closeness unbearable. "It's not your fault," he continues, telling me lies that make me feel worse. "I know you think it is, but it's not. None of this—"

"You know what I've done," I say, and glance up at the sky, my eyes stinging against the sun. Maybe if I stare at it long enough, the image of Nadia's lifeless body will burn from my mind forever. "You know everything that's happened since you left, and yet—"

"That's why I'm telling you this isn't your fault," he says, impatient now. "We've been watching everything that's been going on for the past two thousand years, and you've always tried to do right by us. Did you screw up along the way? Of course you did, but that's life, and you need to get over it."

I should kneel on all fours, press my forehead to the ground, and beg for forgiveness. Beg, because it's the only form of apology I can offer.

Sickness vanished with my lists, taking the only advantage I had. There were hundreds of names written down, probably close to a thousand. There's no way I'll be able to remember all of them. I'll have to start from scratch if I want to find and protect those Flames from whatever Sickness has planned.

Guilt envelops me, my body heavy and hurting. The feeling prickles in my veins, traveling all the way down from the crown of my head to the bottom of my feet.

I gave Sasha the wrong name to investigate — a spelling error that led him to a Soulless instead of the Flame I had planned for him to meet. Jayden Mckenzie. That was the name of the Flame I wanted Sasha to see, but I misspelled his last name, adding an "A" where it didn't belong.

One letter difference.

The Flame and Soulless had a one letter difference to their name, and I mixed them up.

It was a careless mistake, an oversight I've never made before, because I was always careful — so careful not to make these types of errors. I did not suffer for my failure, but Nadia did.

I shouldn't have asked Sasha to help me with those lists. I shouldn't have put him in a position of attention, especially as a Flame. And then I did the same with Nadia when she came to Airabeth. I shouldn't have healed her or paid her any heed.

She'd still be alive if I hadn't interfered.

I shouldn't be protecting anyone.

"The girl," Kaster says, his voice dragging me from my thoughts, which grow darker by the second. "Did you preserve her body, or burn it after she died?"

When I tell him I took her to the tomb, he nods. Pondering.

"Take us to her," is his only reply.

THE TRAVEL TIME BETWEEN the battlefield and manor should be less than fifteen minutes, but it takes us forty. With our adrenaline gone and the battle won, the Emperors and I move much more slowly than usual, bogged down by injury and fatigue.

We hurry through a back door that leads straight into the tomb — the last thing we want is to bump into a servant — and trudge down an ancient corridor festering with termites.

The Emperors hardly speak as we go, and although I'm not exactly in a talkative mood myself, I want to know why they wish to see a dead girl they've never met.

I will my heart to ice as I retrieve Nadia's corpse from the tomb and lay her down on an examination table, displaying her before my friends. Parts of her body have already begun to blacken, her skin blistered and peeled as if set aflame. Chunks of her hair have fallen out, too, leaving bald patches along her scalp.

I clench my jaw and look away.

The seven men surround the table, and Pierce — the Emperor of Peace — is the first to study her. His gold armor casts a luminous glow over the shadowed room, providing our only source of light.

I have no idea what he plans to find by studying Nadia's body, but when he looks up from across the table, I'm thrown by the gravity in his gaze. "Are you aware of what happens to the human who is sacrificed at the hands of a Master?"

Pierce looks to me as if we're the only two people in the chamber.

I shake my head, unable to verbally respond.

"The mortal who is physically murdered by the Sacred Seven is considered an offering," he says. "And since Nadia gave up her life to allow our reentrance into the earth realm, her demise is declared unnatural, outside of the natural laws of human death. It is in this circumstance that we are able to bring her back to life."

I still at the revelation.

Impossible. It can't be possible. It's too good to be true.

For a moment I forget how to breathe, my mind reeling, rejecting the idea that she can be revived.

The possibility of resurrection only exists in fairy tales.

Death is final.

There are no second chances.

And yet, the Emperors' very existence is an impossibility to most, and they're standing right in front of me. How do I explain that?

"However . . ." Pierce continues, his voice a distant, muted sound amid the chaos in my head, "the Law affirms that this act can only be performed if *all* Masters are banished to the Underground Kingdom." His eyes bounce from Emperor to Emperor, as if he is begging someone to interrupt and prove him wrong. No one does. "For the mortal realm to fully accept the Emperors as their leaders, every member of the Sacred Seven must be banished, and since you, Milo, are still here . . ."

He doesn't need to elaborate.

I understand what he's saying, what he needs, to bring Nadia back.

I'm overcome with an odd mix of fear and relief.

Nadia has another shot at life. With the Emperors' gift, she'll be able to grow old and pass on the way she was supposed to, well-lived and surrounded by loved ones.

The only disappointment is that I won't be here to greet her when she wakes up.

I look down at the sheath fixed to my hip, Toby's banishing sword still hanging from it.

Will it hurt when the blade pierces my heart? Will my banishment to the Underground Kingdom be quick and easy, or long and suffering, like I hoped for the other Masters?

In the end, it doesn't matter.

I know what my choice is. It's the easiest one I've ever had to make.

I free the sword from its holder and bring the blade to my chest, sweat beading on my brow. I haven't given much thought to how it would happen, but this seems like the best way to go, given the choice.

My life for hers. Her happiness for my misery.

The trade is fair, considering all the pain I brought into her life.

Now is the time to pay my debts.

"I'm sorry, Milo," Kaster says, eyes heavy with an emotion I can't quite place. Guilt? Sadness? Anger? A combination of all three? I suppose it doesn't matter now. My title has earned me a spot alongside my enemies, and after my betrayal, they will make me suffer in ways I don't care to imagine.

"It was a pleasure to see you all again," I say to the Emperors, failing to keep the emotion from my voice. "Tell her I'll miss her, and that I'm sorry."

Sorry that I couldn't save her. Sorry that I have to leave. Sorry that Sasha is dead and it's all my fault.

If she ever finds out who I truly am, I hope she never forgives me. It makes what I'm about to do that much easier. I couldn't bear to be in the same realm as her if she knew the truth about who I am. What I did. How I ruined her family.

With that, I look to each of the Emperors, wishing I could lead and serve with them, but I know this is for the best. Kaster nods and bows with respect — his parting goodbye, and that's when I know this is it. No more messing around. It's my time to go.

I apply pressure to the blade, a trickle of blood appearing over my breast, the sting growing every second. I don't let the pain deter me and take a deep breath. Close my eyes. Count to three, and plunge the sword into my chest.

SHARP, VIOLENT TALONS pull at me, dragging me down, down, down into blackness, tearing at my clothes, my arms, my face, relentless in their pursuit to entrap me. The sensation of falling sinks deep in my stomach, stealing my screams, my breath. My body burns from the inside out, my veins pumping fire instead of blood, unbearably painful. Although fighting is useless, my instincts kick in and I thrash, determined to escape the eternal darkness, which meets me too soon.

Chapter Forty-Seven

My skin stings when the banishment is complete, the fabric of my shirt sticking to my back, covered in sweat. I touch the tender flesh on my forearms, expecting to find welts bubbling, but I find none. I peer through the darkness surrounding me, unable to see or hear much of anything beyond my own breaths.

Instead of creeping forward through the Underground Kingdom to meet my grim fate, I sit on the hot ground, my face buried in my knees.

At some point I hear the Masters in the distance, sensing my arrival.

I close my eyes to block out their muffled chatter, stretching my strongholds to the Emperors above. Nadia's life is in their hands, and no matter how badly I want to help, I can't, so I stay where I am, let them work, and wait for them to give me a signal that she is alive.

IT FEELS LIKE HOURS have passed since I banished myself, and there's still no sign of Nadia's resurgence.

How long is this supposed to take?

Although my question goes unheard, I wish someone would answer me. I don't know how much longer I can wait like this, staring into the void with nothing but my own breathing to fill the silence. Every so often, I envision Nadia's face and try to place a stronghold in her mind to see if she's alive, but I'm met with eternal blackness, her lungs empty and unmoving.

The Emperors said they could bring life back into Nadia's revenant heart, but every power has its limits, even an immortal's. What is their plan? How are they going to accomplish the impossible? What if it doesn't work?

Bah . . . . boom. Bah . . . . boom. Bah . . . . boom.

Blood thrums in my ears, producing a brutal headache in my temples.

Given my lack of food, energy, and sleep, I'm not surprised.

I rub my fingers over the small throb, trying to soothe the—

Bah . . . . . boom. Bah . . . . . boom. Bah . . . . . boom. Bah . . . . . boom.

The headache intensifies with every breath, blood pounding against all sides of my skull.

Bah . . . . boom. Bah . . . . boom. Bah . . . . boom. Bah . . . . boom. Bah . . . . boom.

The blood rushes faster. Harder. Dizzying my vision. For a moment, I think I might—

Bah . . . boom. Bah . . . boom. Bah . . . boom. Bah . . . boom. Bah . . . boom. Bah . . boom.

I cover my ears and waver to the side, unable to—

Bah . . boom. Bah . . boom. Bah . . boom. Bah . . boom. Bah . . boom.

I bury my head between my knees, terrified I'm having some sort of brain aneurysm, when Kaster speaks into my mind, urging me to listen.

Do you hear that? he asks, the throbbing in my head refusing to cease.

Bah boom. Bah boom. Bah boom. Bah boom. Bah boom.

I cover my ears to block out the beating in my temples, straining to hear above it, then realize the throbbing isn't in my head.

No.

The pounding . . . it isn't a headache.

Bah boom. Bah boom. Bah boom. Bah boom. Bah boom. Bah boom. Bah boom.

It's a heartbeat.

Chapter Forty-Eight

Nadia

Though my eyes are open, I'm blind when I wake, blinking rapidly in a sea of darkness. Low voices, hushed and frantic, hum around me. Entirely unfamiliar.

Approaching footsteps sound nearby, but I can't tell if they're coming from behind me or in front.

Everything is black. Hulking. Unidentifiable.

I don't know where I am.

My mind races at the realization, struggling to make sense of things.

Cold nips at my spine, skull, and hands, but no pain from my fourth Test lingers.

Something is wrong.

I blink again, the darkness dispersing in waves, and stretch toward consciousness, clinging to life.

I prop my hands against something metal and push myself upright, hissing as the ceiling lights burn my eyes.

No.

I reassess.

Not the ceiling lights. There are no ceiling lights. The glow, it's . . . It's coming from me.

My fingers. Hands. Arms. Legs . . . all of it is soft and smooth, gleaming with a gentle, reverent light.

Dreaming. I must be dreaming.

I cast a quick glance around the room, my heart racing as I take in the dark stone walls and dried blood splattered across them. The stench of rat feces and something damp hangs in the air.

Flames Quarter. Why am I not in the Flames Quarter?

"Nadia?"

Pain lances down my spine as I jolt forward, aware of the fact that I'm not alone.

I squint through the shadows with my nerves on high alert, every limb pulsing with terror and warning, ready to fight.

"Who's there?" I hunch down to get a better look, to make sure I'm not hallucinating.

The shadows by the door seem to move closer, the blackness taking on the form of a human — no, *seven* humans, all of them handsome and young, dressed impeccably in shimmering fabrics. Dark, bloodstained armor covers each of their chests, their faces wan and dirty, covered with sweat.

I jump off the table and retreat a step, my thoughts struggling to keep up with the vision before me.

With their expressions entirely unreadable, the men watch me, their eyes glowing like stardust, the colors ever-changing.

My breath turns shallow under their stares, reminding me of the first time I stepped into the Sacred Seven's dining room. Outmatched and outnumbered.

"We're not going to hurt you." The man dressed in blue steps forward and extends his hand to me in greeting, his smile forced and overly kind. "You have nothing to fear."

A laugh almost bursts out of me at that.

Nothing to fear. As if I can remember what being unafraid feels like.

"It's a pleasure to meet you, Nadia," he goes on. "My name is Kaster." He doesn't look much older than the other Emperors, but his gray eyes give off a maturity that exceeds his appearance, warning me that there's something ancient —unpredictable — stirring behind that handsome face.

Still, I reach out to shake his hand, his touch unnaturally warm and gentle, despite his intimidating size. As our palms meet, his face softens with a genuine smile, startling me into returning it.

When his hand breaks away from mine, I'm unsettled.

I meet his stare with disbelief, an odd energy prickling through my veins.

"My name," I say, oblivious to how I manage to speak through my panic. "You said my name, but I didn't tell you what it was. How do you know me?" My heart pounds painfully in my chest, and I become distressingly aware of how fast it is. I lean back against the table, my body trembling, and gaze pointedly at the other men, waiting for someone to explain.

All of them stare at me with concern — saying nothing.

I dig my nails into my thighs to gain control. I'm on the verge of screaming, of demanding they tell me what the hell is going on, but the strangers just stand there in their armor and shimmering fatigues, offering nothing.

Yellow. Red. White. Green. Purple. Blue. Gold.

Such odd shades for a team to wear. So random. So out of order.

The only time I've ever heard of those specific colors being together is—

No.

I shove the absurd thought away, but it doesn't leave, pushing back with a deep conviction that wraps around my heart, conveying its truth.

I shake my head.

There's no way. It's impossible.

I scan the line of seven men again, and whatever dumb shock is plastered on my face must be apparent, because Kaster ushers me to sit, moving closer. "Allow me to explain," he says, the words slow and careful. "You have been resurrected. There is a lot we must cover, but please, sit down."

Resurrected? What in the sky's name is he—?

"Cruelty." I whisper. "Where is Cruelty? What happened?" I ask, my voice rising with the terror rushing through me. I hug myself around the waist, fingers digging into my forearms. . .

Arms.

I remember lying in Cruelty's arms, but I was limp. Heavy. Immobile. I couldn't feel anything as he scooped me to his chest and carried me out of the Quarter, but I *saw* it happen, as if watching the scene from somewhere far above.

Dead.

I was dead in Cruelty's arms, and—

Sickness.

An image of him walking into the Quarter flashes through my head, my heart pounding at the vivid memory. I was alone, terrified. I tried to get away, but he grabbed the pillow, smothering me.

"Dead," I whisper the word, as if saying it quietly will make it any less believable. "I died." I remember it now. The darkness I emerged from, blacker and heavier than anything I've ever seen. I shy away from the memory, focusing on the present. "And now you're all here . . . and my skin is . . . but how . . . ?"

The thoughts tumble out of me unfinished.

"I'll explain everything," Kaster promises, and although I didn't voice my concerns out loud, he knows they're there.

I don't know why I'm surprised by that. It's his job to know everything about me.

He is an Emperor, after all.

"Where is Cruelty?" I repeat, my eyes brimming with tears.

If the Emperors are here on earth, does that mean —?

"Please, sit down." Kaster repeats, gesturing to the table. "This might take awhile, so you should make yourself comfortable."

Chapter Forty-Nine

"I'm sorry, but I don't understand what you're saying."

I stare at Kaster and wait for a revised explanation, my mind lost in the avalanche of information he's shared. It's not that his initial retelling of the past few hours wasn't precise or easy to follow, it was, but with my mind in overdrive, it's hard to comprehend all that's happened in the short time I was dead.

Dead. It still doesn't seem real. None of this does, but who am I to question an immortal battle, the Sacred Seven's banishment, and my newborn existence, when the proof is standing right in front of me?

Kaster tells me they couldn't have achieved any of their success without Cruelty's help, but that's not surprising. He gave everything to keep me alive, including trading his existence on earth for mine. What are the Masters going to do to him in the Underground Kingdom? How will they punish his betrayal?

My blood boils at the possibilities.

"As I'm sure you've realized," Kaster starts, towering over me, a total specimen of a man, "there's something different about you." He gestures to my slightly glowing skin — more golden and healthier than it's been my entire life — and uses it to prove a truth my mind has difficulty grasping.

"Since the Master of Sickness took your life through physical force, your death was deemed unnatural, which is a violation of the Immortal Law. Due to this, we were able to give you another chance at life. A new life. One where you are more like us. Immortal in every way."

Immortal.

I go still at the proclamation, and wish I had the power to disappear. To escape.

"How is this possible?" I ask. I know the Emperors have extraordinary abilities, but to raise the dead? They don't possess that sort of power.

I bet if I screamed or cried or shouted folly about this entire situation, I'd feel better, but I can't bring myself to find that release. I'm numb. Incapable of doing anything except stare mindlessly into the endless depths of Kaster's silver eyes.

The Emperors exchange a look. "It's better if we show you, rather than tell you," Kaster says. "But there's time for that yet. For now, rest. Go home and see your family."

Elisha.

Whatever fear I felt diminishes as my brother's name jars through my mind, crackling like thunder. "Will he remember me when I see him again?" I ask, already going for the door, eager to find him. "With the Masters gone, do their strongholds still have power over him?"

The Emperors shake their heads in unison, but it's Kaster who answers. "With the Sacred Seven gone, the stronghold capturing his memories has been lifted. You'd better hurry back. He's waiting for you."

I pause by the door, gesturing to the space between us. "What about this? About us?"

"Don't worry about that," Kaster says, crossing his hands behind his back. "We know where to find you. We'll keep in touch."

Chapter Fifty

I follow the Emperors to the main level of the manor, a cacophony of noise erupting from every hall.

Blood, sweat, and the aura of war still cover them from head to toe, the effects of battle lingering, despite the victorious outcome. I envision Cruelty, what he must've looked like before he banished himself. He sacrificed too much of himself — his health and soul included — for a purpose he believed in.

For centuries, the Emperors looked to Cruelty to be strong and stable on earth, confident and leading in his mission to help the Flames. With a position like his, there was no room to get weary, and he never did. The selflessness he's shown not only me, but the entire human realm, is astounding, and I hate him for that.

I hate that he's gone. I hate that he left without saying goodbye. I hate that I never got to thank him. More than that, I hate that we'll never get to see what could've happened between us.

When I round the corner to the main foyer, my enhanced vision blurs at the chaos — at the servants bustling down every corridor and up every staircase, muttering amongst themselves. My knees nearly knock at the frenzy, the room pulsing with hushed conversation and frantic whispers.

I push through the crowd, my arms itching against the stuffiness, confused as to why and how everyone has gathered together so quickly.

It doesn't take long before clarity hits.

They know the Emperors are here.

Kaster walks to the front of the foyer and clears his throat to silence the crowd, the commotion growing as the remaining Emperors follow behind, taking positions beside him.

I stay behind.

This is their moment to reveal the truth — to prove their loyalty and virtue to the Flames — and I don't want to distract from that.

The Sacred Seven have been pushing a narrative of lies for far too long, but with the Emperors back in control, we have a chance to see the world for what it truly is, without the influence of evil.

"I know this is a confusing time for everyone, but please, if you'll all quiet down, I'll be happy to explain." The crowd's chatter comes to an abrupt halt, conversations pausing mid-sentence as Kaster's powerful voice travels across the room. "You're more than welcome to ask questions, but for the sake of time, it's best to leave them until the end, if that's all right?"

The Emperor nods gratefully at the silence, folding his hands behind him, opening his stance. "Very well. I suppose it only makes sense to start from the beginning, so let's backtrack a few days to when the Master of Sickness took a human life."

I stop listening after that, not caring to rehash events I already lived through. I catch pieces of his words here and there, scraping up just enough information to get the gist of what he's saying.

Can it be possible?

If I strain hard enough, I can almost hear the servants' thoughts, each one hitting louder than the one before.

Are these men truly the Emperors? Is Cruelty really a betrayer of the Masters? Can a human girl be made immortal?

The doubts sprout from their minds like weeds, creating a tangle of confusion I'm far too familiar with. It took me three weeks to believe Cruelty was the man he claimed, and even then, the reality of his mission didn't hit me until I woke to the Emperors, their presence testimony to what he'd told me.

I'm hoping the servants will be easier to convince.

I'm hesitant as to whether Kaster's speech is going to win over the crowd — mortals aren't so easily swayed — but to my delight, a miracle happens. One after the other, the servants start to believe, their skepticism diminishing as the truth unravels before them.

With his storyteller voice and comforting presence, Kaster is a convincing man. He lures us in like a horse to running water, explaining a truth he manages to make us feel in our marrow.

Gently, like a father soothing his child, he patiently coaxes the doubt from the peoples' eyes and makes them see the truth in his. One by one, he looks into every human face and speaks to them like a friend, empathy warming the silver in his eyes.

Gradually, the crowd begins to press closer around the Emperors — some sobbing, others cheering — as they realize their freedom. Kaster nods and smiles through it all, accepting everyone's hugs and kisses, prayers and bows, like he was born to receive them.

And despite the hole in my heart that's reserved for Sasha and everything else I've lost, I smile too. Today was a step — a small step — but it was taken in the right direction, pushing us toward the world I always dreamed of, but never thought possible.

KASTER LEADS THE SERVANTS out of the manor through Airabeth's forest, explaining that this is the only route back to our homes. For a startling moment, I think we're going to have to walk hundreds of miles to return to our various towns and villages, but then Kaster raises a hand, stopping us at a fork in the path.

"Here," he says, and leans down to the road, the horde of servants surrounding him to get a better view. "It should be right around here . . ."

He runs his hands over a large mound of dirt, pushing it aside to reveal a smooth slab of wood, the edges chipped and worn with age.

A trapdoor.

I blink. Unmoving.

Bleeding hell, this has to be some sort of a cruel joke, right?

I don't know why I'm surprised by it. I should be used to the Masters' secrets and trickery by now, but I didn't expect an unknown passageway in the middle of a forest.

Kaster opens the latch smoothly, gesturing to the stairs that spiral down, down, down into the darkness below. "There's an underground train that runs from here to the human lands," he says, my mind struggling to comprehend that information.

A train? The masters have been using a train this entire time?

"Each of your destinations have already been programmed from when you were taken to come to Airabeth," Kaster says, explaining how Warfare got me here— got all of us here— and how the Masters were able to travel to different villages so quickly. "Inside the train, there's a map on the wall that'll help you navigate, so make sure you pay attention so you don't miss your stop."

"Aren't you and the other Emperors coming with us?" I ask, genuinely curious as to why they're choosing to stay behind.

"We need to sort some things out first," Kaster says, already turning back the way we came. "Don't worry about us. Go home and reunite with your family. Spread the good news that the Emperors have returned."

We don't need to be told twice.

The servants practically jump through the trapdoor, taking the steps two at a time. While most of the Flames hurry out, the Soulless are quickest to leave — running lost without the Masters' protection — and are eager to go into hiding.

Once I reach the bottom of the stairs, I look for Tuesday amongst the crowd, but I can't find her in the sea of random faces. My chest tightens at the thought of never seeing her again, but part of me warns it's better this way.

With how Tuesday and I ended things, I'm starting to think some friendships are only meant to get through a season instead of a lifetime, and if that's the case with us, we served each other well. I wish her and December the best life can offer, and if the universe is on our side, our paths will cross again.

Shouts, light and joyous, ring up ahead, disrupting my thoughts. Servants cheer and applaud as they run onto the train, escaping this wretched land to reunite with whatever friends and family the Masters haven't destroyed.

I understand their urgency, their need to get away.

I'm no different.

I squeeze onto the train with the rest of the pack, grateful for the Emperor's instructions back to the human lands. It takes us under an hour to return to my village, the air somehow thicker and harder to take in, but I manage. Grateful to be home.

As we reach Tempus' stop, my stomach knots in anticipation.

The moment the train doors open, I shove my way off the train with the few other servants who came from my village. The citizens of Tempus take off running, skipping up the stairs that'll take us back to ground level. Together, we push against the trapdoor and climb out. The sun blinds me as I take in my surroundings.

Tempus' forest. That's where we are.

After all these years, I don't know how I never found the trapdoor that led down to the Masters' train, but I don't care enough to think about that right now. Nobody does.

We take off running, the people dispersing this way and that, traveling down various streets and sidewalks once we're back on the main road.

I sprint as fast as I can, unable to delight in the confusion and relief passing over the villagers' faces as they are reunited with their loved ones. I do take quick note of the Market as I run by, smiling at how the Sacred Seven's flags have already been replaced with the Emperor's insignia — an eagle surrounded by seven stars to indicate the various virtues they represent.

By the time I reach the hill ascending to my house, I'm shaking and out of breath, overwhelmed with emotion. I made it. I'm finally here. I can't believe it.

Please, please, please don't let this be a dream.

I open my mouth to yell Elisha's name, praying he's somewhere inside, when the door to our home is flung open. Curious about the commotion coming from the streets, Elisha runs onto the front porch, nearly tripping over his feet when he sees me.

"Nadia?" He says my name like a question, unsure if this is real or some figment of his imagination.

I'm speechless. Too teary-eyed to respond. The reality of this moment far outlives any fantasy.

I run to him and he meets me halfway, embracing like this is the last one we'll ever share.

"Where were you?" he whispers, squeezing me so hard, my chest aches. It's a good pain though, one I don't dare pull away from. "It feels like ages since I've seen you. The last thing I remember is you leaving to get food and then . . . nothing."

He steps back to look at me, noticing the tears in my eyes, the exhaustion in my posture.

"What happened?" he asks, fear and realization dawning on him. "Where's Diana?"

My heart sinks at the sound of her name.

How am I going to tell Elisha that another one of our siblings has passed on? How am I going to explain everything that's happened these past few weeks? How am I going to tell him I died, but the Emperors somehow brought me back to life?

Just then, Elisha shakes his head, pulling me into another hug. "Never mind all that. We can talk about it later. I'm just so happy to see you."

The understatement of the century.

A part of me still can't believe I'm here, reunited with my twin brother.

It was worth it. Everything that happened in Airabeth was worth this moment.

I wish we could stay here forever, trapped in this bubble of happiness, but I know it can't last. Even though the Masters are gone and the Emperors are in rule, there is so much we need to figure out — so many moves we have to make, but haven't had time to plan.

When are the Emperors going to contact me again? What sort of power courses through my veins? Will I ever get the chance to see Cruelty again?

I hug Elisha tighter, Sasha's words echoing in my head.

We are all that matters now.

I delight in the steady rhythm of my brother's heartbeat, knowing this calm won't last. I don't know what tomorrow will bring, or what troubles lie ahead, but even though the Masters are gone, their strongholds still lurk in our lands, waiting to destroy every living thing without exception.

The Masters killed my parents. They killed Sasha. They killed Diana. They took Cruelty.

The battle is far from over.

Half free. That's what we are.

Freedom will never find us as long as the Sacred Seven are living, and their banishment is nothing but a temporary bandage to cover the wounds they've inflicted in our land.

I need to kill them. All of them. More than that, I need to get Cruelty back. There has to be a way to return him to earth. I refuse to accept that he'll live in the Underground Kingdom for the rest of time, tortured and suffering with no end in sight.

And with this strange, unknown power rising inside me, who says I can't be the one to save him? To save all of us?

All my life, I've had to be ready for the Masters.

The only question is, will they be ready for me?

Acknowledgements

Although one name is printed on the front of this book, it certainly isn't the only one you should know, as you hold *Airabeth* in your hands. It took numerous people to make this story possible, and I hope you read on so we can celebrate them together.

First off, I want to thank my Lord and Saviour Jesus Christ for giving me the strength, wisdom and authority to write this book. Anything is possible with You by my side. To You, I give all the glory.

Next, I want to thank my parents for their unending love and support.

Dad, thank you for believing in me more than I believe in myself. Thank you for keeping my path straight and for refusing to let me take on other people's opinions/ limits on what I should do with my life. It was a wild gamble to skip college and pursue authorhood, but you never once pushed me away from my dreams. Without you, I never would've committed to a career in writing because I didn't think I was capable of it, but you knew better. You always do. You're my greatest protector and I'm so blessed to have a father I can count on. I'm nothing without your love and guidance. I love you more than words can express.

Mom, thank you for being my biggest cheerleader and greatest champion. Whenever I start to let outside noise cloud my goals, you keep my vision clear. Thank you for encouraging me to travel the road less taken and for shutting down the haters whenever they had anything negative to say about it. Thank you for protecting my dream and for reminding me that it's not for sale. Thank you for giving me the freedom to create, and for pouring love into me every day. I love you double infinity.

My brother, Josh—aka, my very first editor—thank you for teaching me what it means to dream. Thank you for reading every word of my book and for helping me make it better after each revision. When life gets tough, you're always there to steady me, and that is a blessing I don't take for granted. Thank you for being the ultimate hype man, and for pushing me to be better every single day. I love you more than the moon and the stars combined.

To my extended family and friends (you know who you are), thank you for believing in me. Thank you for never telling me my ideas were crazy, or that I was living a pipe dream by wanting to be an author. You always had faith in me and that is a priceless gift. Thank you for loving me. You guys are my everything. I'm nothing without you. I love you with all my heart.

Thank you to my first professional editor, Kourtney Spak. I'm so incredibly grateful to have worked with you. Your guidance, honesty, and expertise took my book to the next level, and for that, I am eternally filled with gratitude. Thank you for championing authors and for caring about stories. We are so lucky to have you!

Kandace and Sarah, thank you both for your invaluable edits and for making me a better writer. I've loved working with you both, and the author community is so lucky to have such smart, kind, and dedicated editors like you. I I can't wait to collaborate with you both again soon!

Thank you to Torie and Cornelia, my graphic designers, for making my characters come to life with your incredible illustrations! You are both an absolute dream to work with, and I can't wait to create with you both again soon! You ladies are amazing!

Last, but certainly not least, I'd like to thank YOU, the wonderful reader of this book. I wrote this story with you in mind, and I hope you found Nadia's story helpful in some way. My biggest "why" to become an author was to tell stories that not only entertained, but inspired readers to overcome the obstacles in their own lives. Stories reflect life, and I write to prove that victory over our struggles is more than possible, but guaranteed, as long as we're brave enough to face them.

Life can be scary and uncertain at times, but don't let fear stop you from living yours to the fullest. Work hard. Be brave. Be bold. Don't let anyone put limits on what you can do, but most of all, don't put limits on yourself. Your dreams aren't an accident. You're meant to fulfill all the desires in your heart, so go and make it happen!

Alas, dear reader, in a world full of Soulless, be a Flame. Let your brilliance shine. Don't be afraid to step out of the ordinary. I'm rooting for you!

Thank you for joining me on Nadia's journey. I can't wait to continue it with you soon.

Until next time,

JoJo Bee

About the Author

JoJo Bee is a Canadian author whose fantasy novels blend emotional depth, vivid world-building, and empowering female characters. Her stories explore themes of resilience, love, and transformation, offering readers both escape and self-discovery. With each new release, JoJo Bee continues to inspire readers worldwide to find hope and heroism in their own journeys.

Read more at https://authorjojobee.com/.